Elise Title was a psychoth which time she worked prisons. Her first novel, *B* 1996. She lives in New England.

Also by Elise Title

BLEEDING HEARTS

CHAIN
REACTION

Elise Title

WARNER BOOKS

A *Warner* Book

First published in Great Britain in 1998
by Little, Brown and Company

This edition published by Warner Books in 1999

Copyright © 1998 by Elise Title

The moral right of the author has been asserted.

A CIP catalogue record for this book is
available from the British Library.

ISBN 0 7515 2276 7

Typeset in Adobe Garamond by M Rules
Printed and bound in Great Britain by
Clays Ltd, St Ives plc

Warner Books
A Division of
Little, Brown and Company (UK)
Brettenham House
Lancaster Place
London WC2E 7EN

Aphrodite and Ares shared a desperate longing. So they bed together only to be enmeshed in the chains which cunning Hephaistos had spread for them. The lovers could neither rise nor stir hand or foot. Thus did they learn they were hopelessly trapped.

The Odyssey
Homer

Prologue

'I'm getting ready for a delicious hot soak in my Jacuzzi,' Natalie says. 'Miles Davis is wailing on my CD. Sandalwood incense burning. I've got a sea of candles lit – I'm really getting into it. Only . . .'

'Only what?' Steve pushes her.

'He says – no.'

'He doesn't like candles?' Tina asks.

'It's not the candles.'

Greg prods, 'Then what?'

'He tells me he wants the truth. So I change it for him. Now I'm lying on my bed in a black lace teddy. I start to describe myself . . . well, I describe the kind of woman I think will turn him on.'

'Is he turned on?' Chris asks.

'No. So I say – I can give you anything you like. Just tell me what you want. But he's on this truth jag and no matter what I make up, he doesn't buy it.' Natalie scowls. 'He's confusing me.'

Steve says, 'I think he's scaring you.'

Natalie wraps her arms around herself. 'You're right.'

'Bullshit,' Meg jumps in. 'You're intrigued. Even more turned on.'

Natalie glares at her.

Chris puts a hand on Natalie's shoulder. 'Let it go, Nat. What happens next?'

Natalie visibly shivers. 'He asks me how long I've been at this. So now I'm feeling totally . . . inadequate.'

'And ticked off,' Meg adds, but Natalie pretends not to hear her.

'I say, look, obviously I'm not doing it for you. Maybe you want to speak to someone else. He says, I don't want someone else. I want you. I tell him he's got me.'

'And he says?' Greg asks eagerly.

Natalie hesitates. 'He says – I haven't really got you . . . yet. How long will it take you to get to the Parkcrest Hotel? I tell him he's crazy. I don't do that. It's the phone or nothing. He laughs and says room 1290, I'll be waiting.'

Chris sighs. 'You went, right Nat?'

Eyes downcast, Natalie nods. 'It's the first time I ever cheated on Brad.'

'What did it feel like having *real* sex with one of your phone clients?' Meg asks.

Natalie's eyes flick in Meg's direction. 'I know you're trying to needle me. But you know what? It was great. Totally romantic. He was wonderful. Handsome, gentle, adoring. He told me my skin felt like velvet. That I was beautiful. Desirable. He was so . . . attentive. I've never had sex like that. Not with Brad.'

Steve scowls. 'So, what are you saying? Brad isn't good in bed? You trying to blame it on your husband? Is that the way you're going to exonerate yourself?'

'No,' Meg says, 'she's telling herself, only this once. Never again . . .'

Natalie cuts her off. 'I haven't told you all of it.'

Tina leans forward. 'Did he get rough?'

'No. Not . . . that,' Natalie stammers.

'Come on. Give it to us straight,' Greg says.

Natalie's face is flushed. 'This woman burst into the room. She had a gun in her hand and was screaming – you fuck. You goddamn fucker!'

'Who was it? His wife?'

'I don't know, Greg. What difference does that make? She had a gun . . .'

'Don't tell me she shoots the creep?' Steve finishes excitedly.

'No. I wish . . . she had,' Natalie mutters.

'What was it, Nat? A set-up? Blackmail?' Chris asks.

Natalie shakes her head and starts to sob. 'Not a scam. A . . . game.'

Tina figures it out. 'Ménage a trois.'

Natalie nods, soundless tears washing down her face. She doesn't know what else to say. Neither do the others.

Seated on metal folding chairs, the six well-dressed, well-educated professional people look to the seventh person in their circle. The person who had been listening with great attention, but who hasn't spoken yet. They are waiting for her reaction. Her insight. Her understanding. Each group member craves her absolution.

In this room, Dr. Caroline Hoffman is God.

'Let's pause here,' Dr. Hoffman says as she uses her remote to stop the video. 'Are there any questions about the therapy session so far? Comments?' The psychiatrist eyes her colleagues. They are gathered around the conference table at Boston General Hospital's prestigious Institute for Special Problems.

'Natalie's certainly displaying a great deal of pain and shame over this episode at the hotel.' Dr. Alan Rogers, the chief psychiatrist at the Institute, removes his glasses, carefully placing them beside his note pad. 'But I'm also sensing continued denial. I'm sure she was terrified when she thought her life was in danger, but I think Meg was right. Natalie was turned on.'

'What I was picking up was the tension between Natalie and Meg,' Dr. Susan Steinberg remarks. 'True, Meg's only been in the group a few weeks, but she seems to be making a point of being antagonistic. Wanting to alienate not just Natalie, but all of the other members. I sense a lot of rage in her.'

Martin Bassett, a second-year psychiatric resident, raises his hand. 'Maybe Meg's still ambivalent.'

'About what?' Caroline Hoffman asks.

'About whether she really is a sex addict. Is it possible Meg's questioning where you draw the line between, let's say, a zealous interest in sex and . . . obsession? Isn't one man's – or woman's – perversion another's pleasure? I mean, if no crime's committed and you aren't putting your life or your partner's in jeopardy?'

'It sounds like it's a question *you're* asking, Dr. Bassett.'

The resident smiles disarmingly at Caroline. 'I suppose it is. Where exactly do you draw the line, Dr. Hoffman?'

'It's a matter of degree. Addicts – whether it's drugs, alcohol, or sex – feel hooked. Wanting – needing – it more and more. Feeling compelled to take even greater risks. Ultimately believing they're nothing without it.'

'Meaning that they only come alive when having sex?' Martin Bassett asks.

Caroline's finger moves to the *play* button on the remote control. 'Actually, Meg may provide the answer to your question in the group session, Dr. Bassett. Why don't we finish viewing the tape and take it from there?'

Tuesday

1

'Don't.' Her soft command.

Martin Bassett had been about to stroke Caroline's breast, but he dutifully spread his arms out over his head on the bed. 'Aye, aye, captain.'

Caroline pulled away abruptly. 'Are you making fun of me?'

The psychiatric resident sat up against the carved oak headboard, shifting the pillow so he could lean his head against it. 'No, I'm being playful.'

Caroline pulled the covers over her bare breasts. She felt foolish. Unsettled.

'I guess I was rushing it, huh?' Martin said. 'Sorry.'

'I'm just too wound-up tonight.'

'I think your problem is you feel like I'm abandoning you.'

'Martin, we both went into this relationship knowing it was going to be . . .'

'Dynamite,' he finished for her.

Caroline smiled. But only for a moment. 'And temporary.' Shortly after she and Martin had begun dating four months ago, he'd applied for and gotten a psychiatry post at a private hospital in Pittsburgh. 'We both accepted the limitations . . .'

'You've never pushed for the relationship to be anything more than it's been.'

'You're right,' she said. 'I never pushed.'

'You could've pushed a little.'

'Would it have made any difference?' Her voice held a bittersweet note.

'I guess we won't really know now, will we?' He glanced at her petulantly.

'Cheer up, Martin. You have only wonderful things to look forward to. In a few weeks you'll be out of here and immersed in your new psychiatry practice. Let's be honest. By the summer, you'll be involved with someone else and I'll be little more than a fond memory.'

'You really think all I've ever been interested in is the sex. Is that it?'

'You tell me.'

Martin laughed uncomfortably. 'Of course I'm crazy about having sex with you. But I adore your brilliant mind as much as I do your incredible body, Caroline. And if we had more time . . . Do you realize this is the first evening we've had together in close to two weeks? Your personal life – if you can even call it that – always has to be *squeezed in*. You're a workaholic, Caroline. If you're not seeing patients, you're doing reports, attending conferences, lecturing, writing . . .'

'Contending with endless piles of insurance claims,' she added. 'We all put in gruelling hours in this profession, Martin. It comes with the territory. You know that. You'll know it even better when you're on staff . . .'

'Yeah,' he said, 'but you're the only shrink I know who never bitches about it. You actually *relish* it.'

Caroline scowled. 'So I love my work. It's a good thing after all I've had to sacrifice to get here.'

'Fine. But now that you've made it, it's time to relax a little and enjoy the fruit of all your hard labour. Enjoy it with me.'

'So let's stop talking and get back to sex?' Caroline sounded peevish and she hated that. But she'd given Martin an opening as wide as the Grand Canyon. All he had to do was ask her, *what* sacrifices? Show some interest. But he hadn't. Then again, she could have pushed a little—

After an awkward moment, Martin toyed with a strand of her long, dark hair. 'Will you miss me when I'm gone?'

'Yes.' It was true. Caroline would miss him. And she would, she had to admit, miss the sex.

He seemed encouraged. 'Pittsburgh's not that far from Boston, Caroline. We could still . . .'

'Oh, Martin. We both know it really wouldn't work.'

'Wouldn't work for me? Or you?'

Caroline felt a gritty exhaustion settle in. 'Maybe we should call it a night.' She started to get up. But Martin's hands pressed down on her shoulders. Pinning her.

'Caroline—'

The pressure was like a high-voltage electric current that shot through her. She twisted away. 'Don't.'

Martin instantly released her. 'Caroline. Take it easy. I'm sorry . . .'

'I should never have started this affair,' she said.

'Hey, don't give yourself all the credit.'

She rewarded him with another smile.

'You need a good massage.' Gently, he eased her over onto her stomach and started kneading her knotted muscles.

Caroline began to let herself relax into the moment—

His sports jacket, a nubby grey tweed with charcoal grey leather elbow patches, is strewn on the black and white marble floor. His pale blue shirt is unbuttoned, hiked up tee shirt revealing a flat belly with a smattering of dark curly hairs. His white briefs and navy trousers are around his ankles.

She's on her knees. Drawing him deep into her mouth. He's never been this hard. This excited.

He gasps. 'Oh God oh God oh God.' Not wanting to explode. Not yet.

Her hand shoots up, presses against his mouth.

He understands. A museum guard might hear him. He grins even as he compresses his lips in compliance. Peter Korza doesn't want to screw it up. Miracles like this didn't happen every day.

Haydn's 'Farewell Sonata' is playing wildly in Peter Korza's head. This is crazy. This can't really be happening.

The thick strip of chain is draped loosely around his neck. Stark fear. The music continues, but it is punctuated now with desperation. God don't let this happen to me!

'Did you like it? Did it feel good? Did you want more?'

What should he do? Nod yes? Shake his head no? He pleads with his eyes. His body bathed in icy sweat.

'Are you sorry now, you greedy fuck?'

Greedy, yes. Hungry for his irresistible temptress. From the instant he saw her. That black jersey dress clung to her voluptuous body. And those mesmerizing green eyes. Wanting her. Wanting it all. Every which way. Couldn't get enough—

He wants to explain. But he can't with the gag in his mouth. Nor can he make a move with the metal choker tightening around his neck—

As Caroline was starting to get back into a romantic mood, a pager went off in her bedroom.

Martin groaned. 'Shit. Yours or mine?'

Caroline reached across him to her bedside table and switched on the lamp. 'Mine.'

Caroline tugged the blanket up over her as she gripped the phone. Martin sat cross-legged, still naked, at the foot of her bed.

'Can't it wait until tomorrow, Steve? I can give you an appointment at – Hold on a sec.' She placed her hand over the mouthpiece. 'Martin, could you get my appointment book?' she whispered, gesturing to the tote bag on her dresser.

Martin shook his head and grinned. Giving him the finger, Caroline flung the covers off and dashed naked across the room. Returning to the bed – Martin was stretched out on top of the covers now – she snatched up the receiver as she quickly flipped open her book to Wednesday. 'Ten o'clock.' It was very disconcerting – to say the least – to be sitting in her bedroom buck-naked booking a therapy appointment with a decompensating patient.

'Please, Caroline. I know it's late but if I could see you now. I'm at this place . . . Cuppa's. It's a coffee bar on Huntington. Not far from your apartment. If I could come over . . .'

'Why don't we talk on the phone for a few minutes?' Caroline suggested. Behind her, she heard Martin's exasperated sigh. She shrugged apologetically, but she wasn't really all that sorry for the interruption.

'I'm feeling so . . . disjointed.'

'Did something happen tonight, Steve?'

He laughed harshly. 'A brilliant deduction.'

'What was it?' Caroline asked, ignoring his sarcasm.

'I'm on a public phone. You want every latte drinker in the place to hear the sordid details? Aren't you confusing me with Natalie? I'm not the phone sex freak.'

'You've been drinking.'

'Will you see me?'

'Tomorrow. Ten o'clock.'

'Okay, I had a few.'

'Take a cab home, Steve . . .'

'I told you I'm not pissed.'

'But you are pissed off.'

'Better pissed off than pissed on, Caroline.'

'Wait,' she said. Another sigh from Martin. Out of the corner of her eye she saw him reach for his jeans.

'Forget it. I shouldn't have . . .'

'I'll see you at my office here in fifteen minutes.'

Martin groaned loudly. Caroline glowered at him as her hand shot to the mouthpiece. There was silence on the other end of the line.

'Steve?'

'No. Never mind. I'm sorry I called. It's late. I'm sure you've got better things to do.'

'Steve, you've got to make up your mind.'

'I have.' The phone went dead.

'Shit.' Caroline hung up. She threw on the grey jersey sheath she'd worn that day, snatched her white silk panties off the floor and hurriedly slipped them on before donning her shoes.

'Where's the fire?' Martin asked.

'Cuppa's,' Caroline said, grabbing her black blazer and snatching her car keys off the hall table on her way out. 'I hope I get there before it all goes up in smoke.'

2

'Hey you. It's about time.'

Startled, Meg Spaulding dropped her key ring as she stepped out of the elevator on the twenty-first floor of her harbourside high-rise and turned left towards her apartment. Ryan Gallagher, a draftsman at the architectural firm where she worked, was camped on the floor outside her door. He stood up and walked over to her.

'How'd you get the doorman to let you upstairs?' Meg asked curtly.

'He's seen me around enough times.' He paused. 'And I slipped him a twenty for good measure.' Gallagher bore a typically impish grin. He was close to six feet tall with wavy dirty blond hair, disarming cornflower blue eyes, a physique honed by regular workouts at the gym. And a face full of mischief, but eminently appealing. To most women.

Meg narrowed her eyes. 'What are you doing here at this hour?'

'Good question,' Ryan scolded lightly, bending to pick

up her keys. 'Considering it's after ten p.m. And we had a dinner date at eight.'

Meg frowned, heading for her door. 'No we didn't. You're dreaming.'

Gallagher kept pace with her. 'Okay, so it wasn't a date. A business dinner. Is that better?'

Meg tried to snatch her keys from his hand, but he tucked his arm playfully behind his back.

'Ryan, I don't know what you're talking about. Now please give me my keys and go home.'

Gallagher leaned against her door, arms behind his back, legs crossed. 'The Harbour Yachting Club project? Or did you forget you nabbed that golden plum? And that I'm your Boy Wonder on the renovation?'

The strap from her large tote bag slipped off Meg's shoulder. 'I thought we weren't meeting on that until tomorrow evening.'

'Tuesday, Meg. Today is Tuesday. What gives with you lately?'

A shadow crossed her brow. 'Nothing gives. I only missed a dumb meeting. It's not the end of the world. We can have it tomorrow.'

'You aren't going to New York tomorrow? What about the Jefferson Mall project?'

For a moment only Meg was confused. Right. New York. She was catching the eight a.m. shuttle. Staying over until Thursday. Possibly longer if there were problems.

'Friday. We'll meet on Friday,' she snapped. 'We've got plenty of time. Now, I'd like my keys, Ryan. I want to go inside, take a shower and go to sleep.' She held out her hand.

'How 'bout I turn down your bed?'

'Give it a rest, Ryan. It's getting tired. Really it is.' Her hand remained outstretched.

Gallagher dropped the keys into her open palm. He studied her thoughtfully as she fumbled with them before fitting the right key into the lock. 'You look different tonight, Meg.'

'No I don't,' she countered, turning the bolt and opening her door. 'Same as I looked all day. Same suit, same shoes, same pocketbook.'

Gallagher snapped his fingers. 'That's it. Now I know what's different.'

Meg stopped and shifted uncomfortably from one foot to the other. 'And what's that?'

'Your eyes.'

She turned to face Gallagher, but, as she glared at him, there were signs of strain at the edges of her mouth. 'What about them?'

'They're green.'

Meg Spaulding slammed her palms down hard on her bathroom basin as she stared at herself in the medicine cabinet. Stared into her emerald green eyes.

How could she have been so careless? It wasn't like her at all. She popped out the disposable green tinted lenses. Tossed them in the toilet. Flushed them away.

Again she rested her hands on the sink. This time to steady herself. *Get a grip. What does it matter? A little mistake. Everyone's entitled to a mistake. Even you.*

She blinked. Her reflection in the mirror was blurring.

But the contact lenses were purely *decorative*. She had 20/20 vision. It was the tears filling her eyes that were causing the distortion.

Irritated with herself, she turned away. Stripped off her clothes. Tossed her underwear into her laundry basket. Ran the shower hotter than usual. Lathered herself furiously with a fresh bar of exfoliating oatmeal soap.

Slough off the dead layer. Be refreshed, renewed. Cleansed. Yes, just what the doctor ordered.

Meg's psychiatrist instantly sprang to mind. No, exfoliation wasn't what her shrink would order. Dr. Caroline Hoffman would be on her case to examine every piece of dirt.

Her psychiatrist was the real problem, Meg decided. She'd been managing fine until she'd started therapy, and agreed, against her better judgment, to join that awful group. She blamed her boss, Sylvia Fields, who was in treatment with Hoffman and whose world seemed to begin and end with her. She'd noticed that Meg had seemed troubled and distracted lately and eventually, wore her down. Meg agreed to see this *amazing* Dr. Caroline Hoffman for an evaluation.

Shutting off the shower, Meg stepped onto the bath mat and hurriedly towelled off. She hated it when different thoughts crowded her mind. *Stay focused on the problem at hand. Dr. Caroline Hoffman.*

She padded naked into her bedroom, found a pen and paper next to the phone on her bedside table. She scribbled a note. *Quit therapy tomorrow.*

Meg felt better. Being in that group with those perverts

had only focused her on all the wrong things. Now that it was as good as over, she could get her life back in gear. She put on a pair of royal blue silk pajamas, swallowed down two over-the-counter sleeping pills and climbed into bed. Her hands slipped under her pajama top, palms trailing lightly over her full breasts, her concave stomach. Her skin did feel softer, smoother. Cleansed. She closed her eyes, her muscles relaxed, a faint smile on her lips.

He'd told her his name, but she couldn't remember it. Could hardly remember what he looked like. It was as if it hadn't really happened at all.

3

Caroline searched the neon-lit coffee bar on Huntington. She didn't see Steve Kramer.

Hoping he'd headed home rather than to a bar that served booze instead of espresso, Caroline asked one of the waitresses, a petite strawberry blonde with dayglo pink lipstick, where the phone was.

'We don't have a public phone.' The waitress tucked a loose pin back into her hair.

'But a man called from here less than fifteen minutes ago,' Caroline argued.

'No way.'

Caroline frowned. Had Kramer lied?

'Closest one's down the street,' the waitress said. 'Outside the Bullfinch Art Museum. The museum's open till nine on Tuesdays.'

Caroline checked her watch. Nine fifteen.

Halfway down the block, Caroline spotted the flashing blue light of a police cruiser in front of the museum. A second blue and white zoomed by her, lights flashing, siren blasting, brakes shrieking as it shuddered to a stop behind the first patrol car.

Caroline felt uneasy. The feeling got worse when the van from the Medical Examiner's Office shot past her.

The end of her conversation with Kramer played in Caroline's head. *Steve, you've got to make up your mind.* And his flat answer. *I have.*

She knew he'd tried to kill himself twice before he'd joined her therapy group. After his medical licence was revoked a year ago, he'd ODed on sleeping pills. Then, shortly before his arraignment two months later for lewd and lascivious behaviour, and solicitation, he'd locked himself in his office and held a gun to his head for nearly three hours while the police tried to talk him round. Before relenting he'd discharged one bullet. Into a diploma hanging on his mahogany panelled wall. His degree from Harvard Medical School.

A couple of cops held Caroline back as she ran towards the museum. She watched fearfully as the crime scene techs sprang out of the big white van and headed up the bank of stairs to the museum.

Had Kramer made it inside the building before closing time? Finished himself off there? Caroline knew she was probably overreacting. But there was something about the whole thing that felt wrong.

'What happened?' she asked the cops. 'Was there a robbery? Is someone hurt? Please, I—'

One of them, a short gaunt man with bags under his watery eyes, said gruffly, 'You have to move along, lady. Go home. You'll see it all on the eleven o'clock news.'

'Please. I'm a doctor. I'm concerned about one of my patients—'

He waved her away, turned, and headed for the sky blue van from channel eight that was pulling up.

His partner, a young, ruddy-faced cop with a crooked nose and broad enough shoulders to have been a college football linebacker, stayed put. He was assessing her carefully. 'Did you say something about a patient?'

'I'm a psychiatrist. About twenty minutes ago I got a call from a patient of mine who sounded very troubled. Possibly suicidal.'

'Male or female?' the athletic young cop asked.

'Male.'

'He told you he was at the museum?'

'No. At a place called Cuppa's.' Caroline pointed behind her as she spoke. 'It's a coffee bar down the street. They don't have a phone, though.'

'So?'

This time she pointed past the cop's shoulder. 'He might have used a phone over there. Or one inside the museum.'

'You say he was suicidal?'

Caroline swallowed. Her throat was raw. 'Yes.'

'Well then,' the uniform said to her, 'you probably got nothing to worry about.'

'What do you mean?'

'The guy we got didn't kill himself. He was offed.'

'Murdered?' Surely not Steven Kramer. Why would anyone kill him?

'Has he been identified?' she asked.

There was a brief silence. 'How old's your boy? What's he look like?'

Caroline frowned. 'He's not a boy.'

'Look, Doc . . .'

'Okay, he's in his late thirties.' Caroline tried to remember exactly. 'Thirty-eight, I think. No, thirty-nine,' she corrected, recalling some discussion in group a while back about Kramer's anxiety over his upcoming fortieth birthday.

'Yeah.' The cop was growing impatient. 'Thirty-nine. What else?'

'Average height and weight. Five nine, five ten. Probably around one hundred and seventy pounds or so. Brown hair, neatly trimmed. Nice looking. He dresses well. Suits and ties mostly. Expensive.'

'Any identifying marks? Scars? Birthmarks? Say, on his right thigh?'

'I'm his psychiatrist. I've never seen his thighs,' Caroline said tightly.

The cop rubbed the bridge of his nose with his index finger, then pointed at her. 'Maybe you better stick around, Doc. Let me go have a little chat with my lieutenant.'

Caroline pulled her wool blazer closed despite the relatively warm April night.

Jill Nugent, a trim, energetic newscaster from channel eight who'd spotted Caroline talking to the cop, had cornered her and was trying to pump her for information.

'I don't know anything. Really,' Caroline insisted. She started walking away when another woman came up behind her.

'You the shrink?'

Caroline spun around. This woman was small, dark-haired, and, despite the mannish blazer and navy skirt, very shapely.

'Yes,' Caroline said.

The newscaster perked up. 'Detective, be a pal and give me something. What's the story in there? Who's the victim . . . ?'

"No comment,' the detective snapped.

Nugent shifted back to Caroline. 'Where does a shrink fit in? How 'bout a last name, Doc? You have any idea who did this sex killing?'

Caroline blinked. 'Sex . . . killing?'

The plainclothes detective stepped close to the reporter, the top of her head barely clearing Nugent's pert nose. 'Get the hell out of here.'

'Shit.' Nugent reluctantly turned and walked over to one of the cops standing at the crime scene van. The detective rolled her eyes, then turned back on Caroline.

'I'm Lieutenant Amy DeSanto. Homicide. One of my boys tells me you're missing a guy with a screw loose and you think he might be our stiff.'

'Have you identified the victim?' Caroline asked.

The lieutenant shook her head. 'What do you say we go have a peek and see if it's your psycho.'

'He's not a psycho,' Caroline said acidly.

DeSanto shrugged. 'Guess you'd be the one to know.'

Caroline had not only viewed dead bodies before, she'd dissected her fair share in anatomy class back in medical school. She'd gotten sick to her stomach the first time, the smell almost worse than the sight – but she took it as one more challenge. She'd aced the class. Nothing new. A star pupil. Eager to learn. To prove herself. To be the best.

But this cadaver was different. The man was stark naked, his upper torso folded over his knees on the cold marble floor behind a curved partition wall of an empty museum gallery. His head was twisted to the right so that his protruding grey eyes appeared to be looking up at the domed gallery ceiling. Or was it the heavens? If he'd been besieging God for help, he would have had to do it silently. A pale blue dress shirt had been stuffed into his mouth.

Most gruesome of all was his face. It was a deep bluish purple, grotesquely swollen. The blood around the mouth and nose still looked wet. Caroline didn't need her medical degree to know that the damage was caused by the thick metal chain – the kind found wound around large reels in any hardware store – looped like a lasso around the corpse's neck. Pulled so tight it dug deeply into his flesh.

She looked away. She had never seen the man before, but she felt a shuddering wave of sorrow for him. It was evident he'd suffered terrible fear and humiliation before his final breath. Caroline knew all about fear and humiliation. She knew all about being at someone's mercy. The difference was – she'd survived. But survival was something you had to fight for on a daily basis. There were times Caroline almost forgot that. This was a gruesome and tragic reminder.

A short distance away, within the area marked off by the crime-scene yellow tape, Caroline saw two detectives dispassionately gathering up and searching through the victim's clothes that lay in a heap beside him. The crime-scene team was there along with a half dozen detectives, several uniformed cops, a videographer and a photographer. Two paramedics stood to one side with a wheeled stretcher, a third with a body bag slung over his arm waited to cart off the body. All in a day's work for the lot of them.

'This isn't my patient,' Caroline said at last. 'I never saw this poor man before in my life.' She felt sick to her stomach.

Amy DeSanto studied her closely. 'You sure of that?'

'Positive.' Caroline drew her shoulders back and looked DeSanto in the eye. Some of the nausea dissipated.

'Okay. Let's talk about your missing patient,' the detective said, undaunted. 'Your boy wouldn't happen to like dressing up in lady's clothes, would he? Into whips and chains? All that kinky stuff? Could it be he and the victim were getting it on until the poor schmuck realized the *she* was a *he* and freaked?'

'My patient isn't gay. And he's not a cross dresser,' Caroline said. Steve Kramer was, however, a voyeur. Could he have been at the museum and witnessed the pick-up? The murder? It would certainly explain why he'd phoned her, sounding so upset.

'Is there something on your mind, Doc?' DeSanto asked. Caroline hesitated. 'No.'

'I'd like his name,' DeSanto said. 'Your patient.'

'I'm sorry. It's privileged information.'

'Yeah? Well, I've got a real ugly murder on my hands . . .'

'Hey, Lieutenant, I found something.' One of the uniforms hurried over, carrying a clear plastic bag. As he approached, Caroline saw the bag contained a wallet-sized photograph.

DeSanto slipped on a latex glove and took hold of the find.

'It's the victim all right,' the uniform said. 'Looks a lot better in the photo. The gal's not bad either. Check the back. He's got her name scribbled . . .'

'Where'd you find this?' DeSanto asked abruptly.

'In the . . . uh . . . ladies' room right off the lobby, Lieutenant. On the floor in one of the stalls. We got a couple of boys in there dusting for prints. Maybe they were in there first.'

'That the ladies' room right next to those phone booths?'

'That's right, Lieutenant.'

Jerry Vargas from the D.A.'s office, a tall, rail-thin man with slicked-back grey hair, walked over. DeSanto passed the bagged photo to him. He nodded and took it away.

'I'm in the way here,' Caroline said, wanting to leave too.

The detective pulled out a small notepad. 'What about your name and address, Doc? Is that *privileged information*, too?'

Caroline's expression hardened. 'I'm Dr. Caroline Hoffman. Why do you need my address?'

'In case I have any more questions.' DeSanto looked equally resolved and her tone carried even more of an edge.

'All yours, Amy. We've got what we need here,' a CSU man with a video camera interrupted.

Caroline pulled a business card from her purse, dropped it on the lieutenant's notepad and walked away.

DeSanto checked out the card, tucked it in her jacket pocket, pensively watching Caroline stride off.

The lieutenant's partner, Detective Alfonse Green, came over. He followed DeSanto's gaze. 'Who's she?'

'A snooty bitch, that's who,' DeSanto muttered.

'You think she could be our perp?'

'Never know,' DeSanto said coolly. 'She was hanging around the scene.'

Green, with twenty years on the force, a good twelve more than DeSanto, gave her a look, but kept his mouth shut.

A half hour later, when Lt. DeSanto was on her way out of the museum, she spotted the TV anchorwoman who'd tried to hustle her earlier for a scoop. She gave her the nod. Nugent motioned to her cameraman and they came running.

'What can you tell me, Lieutenant?'

'You wanted to know the name of that shrink I was talking to?'

Jill Nugent flashed a toothpaste ad smile. 'I knew you'd come through with something for me, Lieutenant.'

'Her name's Dr. Caroline Hoffman.'

'What's she got to do with the murder?' Nugent asked, hurriedly scribbling down the information on her pad.

'Don't know yet, Jill. Could be she happened to be in the wrong place at the wrong time. Then again, our investigation is just getting started.'

4

Caroline's apartment felt too empty and silent. She wished Martin hadn't gone. She wanted nothing more than to crawl back into bed with him, feel his arms around her, have him hold her, comfort her.

She considered phoning him, asking him to come back, but remembered that he had to be up at the crack of dawn to catch his flight for Pittsburgh. Martin was going to scout out an apartment. He'd asked her to meet him there for the weekend, but she'd told him she had too much work to do – true, but also a convenient excuse. He hadn't pressed her. Had she wanted him to? Wanting to be wanted?

Caroline was in no mood for introspection. Instead, she focused on her missing patient, phoning him at home.

His machine picked up. *This is Dr. Steven Kramer. I can't come to the phone right now but if —*

Interesting that he still referred to himself as *doctor*, Caroline thought as the rest of the message played through.

After the beep, she left her name and asked him to please

call in to her service as soon as he returned so she could phone him back. She reiterated the importance of keeping the appointment she'd made for him at ten the next morning. There was nothing more she could do.

Sinking wearily into her sofa, Caroline kicked off her black leather pumps, put her bare feet up on her glass-topped coffee table and let her pounding head fall back on the soft grey velour cushion. She closed her eyes. An image of the dead man in the museum and then one of Steve Kramer rushed into her mind. Her eyes popped open.

Maybe she would fly down to Pittsburgh on Friday – surprise Martin.

'Slow down, baby. Give a gal a sec to catch her breath.'

Jesse Baush, a muscular, big-boned man with red hair cut military style, blue eyes, and freckles that dotted most of his naked body, had Amy DeSanto's still buttoned blouse bunched up to her armpits and was already nuzzling her breasts.

'Really, honey, take it nice and easy,' Amy murmured. 'I had one hell of a night. I wasn't even going to drop by, I'm so beat. But then I thought what a drag to go straight home to bed and have to listen to Vincent snoring away.'

Baush reluctantly drew his head back from Amy's large breasts and looked up at the pretty brunette. 'Bad night? Tell poppa all about it,' he cooed, lifting the blouse over her head.

'We got a real doozy. A stiff turned up over at the Bullfinch Art Museum. Wearing nothing but his birthday suit and a chain choker pulled real tight around his neck. Not a pretty sight.'

'You got anything?' Baush slipped his hands around DeSanto's back. Undid her bra clasp. He was not *that* distracted.

DeSanto gave his cheek a playful swat, but let him ease the blouse over her head, her bra straps slipping off her shoulders. 'A guard saw him, not too long before the museum closed, being approached by a curvaceous babe in a short, skin-tight black dress. Slutty but gorgeous. The guard's words. He figured her for a hooker.'

'Must be a highbrow one,' Baush mused as he tossed her bra to the carpet. 'Working art museums. You figure this hooker did him in?' Being that he worked Vice, he was starting to get more interested.

'I don't know. Could be there's some psycho involved.'

'What makes you say that?' Baush worked on the zipper of her wool skirt.

'A shrink showed up on the scene. Looking for one of her patients who phoned her from the museum or somewhere nearby. Seems he'd called her right around the time of the murder.'

'What you get on the psycho?' Baush frowned. The zipper was jammed.

'We got jack.' DeSanto paused to give him a helping hand. 'The shrink gave me the *privileged information* line. I'll do some more checking and see what we get on the prelims. Then I'll go pay her a visit. Get this. She works over at some clinic called the Institute For Special Problems. Dr. Caroline Hoffman.' Amy stepped out of her skirt and reached for his semi-erect penis. 'You wanna keep talking or you wanna little action?' she teased.

Baush wasn't listening. He was staring at her face as if it contained a hidden message.

'Baby?' When she got no response, she whispered, 'Jesse, what is it?'

'Did you say Caroline Hoffman?'

'You know her?'

'You could say that.' Baush was looking past DeSanto's bare shoulder now.

'Well. You gonna tell me?'

He didn't answer her.

Amy was quick to notice that her lover had completely lost his erection. 'Hey, baby. Cat got your prick as well as your tongue?'

When Jesse didn't so much as give her a dirty look for that jab at his precious virility, Amy DeSanto knew that she might as well head on home to her snoring husband.

Wednesday

5

Jesse Baush rapped the glass with the back of his knuckles. Then, without waiting for a response, he popped his head into Homicide Commander Louis Washburn's office. It was a little past five a.m. No surprise Washburn was working overtime.

The big man was swigging a Dr. Pepper. The tilt of the soda can obstructed the chief's view of his visitor. Continuing to drink, he lowered the can slightly, stared across at Baush, then made a beckoning motion.

'What the hell are you doing here, Jesse?' Washburn demanded.

'I heard about the poor shit that got it over at the Bullfinch last night,' Baush said. 'The talk is the doer was a woman. Maybe a hooker. I thought you might want to bring in Vice.'

'You got any hookers who're into choke chains?'

'None I can think of right off the bat. Got anything more, Chief?'

Washburn pressed a fleshy fist into his solar plexus and belched. Then he scooped up a report from the mess of papers on his desk. 'A prelim from the lab. Not only were there no prints at the scene, the doer wiped off the poor sucker's dick and balls with what the lab boys think is rubbing alcohol. What do you make of that?'

'Could mean your perp knows something about DNA.'

The chief lowered the soda can. 'Could be. But most hookers don't major in genetics.'

'If the broad really was a hooker,' Baush said idly.

'Or else the doer might have just been fastidious.' Washburn finished off the soda, crushed the can in his hand and tossed it across the room. It missed the waste paper basket by an arm's length, landing at Baush's feet.

Baush eyed the can, considering whether or not to dump it in the trash. He didn't move.

'They're still checking out hairs and fibres, but so far they've all been a match to the victim,' Washburn said, punctuating the remark with another loud, unapologetic belch.

'You got an ID on the stiff yet?' Baush asked.

'Yeah. His name's Peter Korza. Lived in Somerville. A violinist. So's Nora Oswain, the girlfriend who IDed him. Thought she might be our hooker. But a neighbour provided an alibi.' Washburn picked up his half-eaten pastrami, cheddar, and hot pepper sub. Took a large bite. A glob of deli mustard squirted out of the bottom of the roll and splatted on his tie.

Baush tried not to stare at the bright yellow stain. 'You heard about the shrink who showed at the scene looking for a missing patient? Thought maybe he was the stiff?'

'How the fuck do you know so much, Baush? As if I didn't know,' Washburn grumbled.

Baush smiled wolfishly.

Washburn stabbed a finger at him. 'DeSanto needs to spend less time on top of you and more time on top of her paperwork, or her ass is grass. You be sure to tell her I said that. Now what shrink are we talking about?'

'Take a guess.'

The chief glared at Baush. He didn't like guessing games.

Jesse knew it wasn't a smart move but he couldn't resist playing the mystery out a little more. 'An old friend of yours.'

'I got a lot of old friends, Baush.'

'Linny.'

'Shit.'

A smile crept on Baush's face until he realized the chief's expletive wasn't related to Linny, but to the discovery of the mustard stain on his prize tie.

'You remember my stepsister, Chief. Caroline Hoffman. You made the pinch fourteen years back. Then watched her walk. She's a shrink now. If that don't take the cake.'

Washburn took a couple of seconds. 'And she was at the scene?'

'Not long after the museum guard spotted that hooker cozying up to Korza.'

Washburn wiped his mouth with the back of his hand.

'Maybe she's the doer,' Baush said, the lightness of his tone at odds with the steely glint in his eyes.

'You really think your sister's that screwed up?'

'*Step*sister,' Baush quickly corrected.

Washburn eyed the detective sceptically. 'It's been a long time, but somehow I don't picture your *step*sister playing hooker with a perfect stranger . . .'

'I don't know about that,' Baush said.

'Then again,' Washburn went on, ignoring the interruption, 'there are a couple of other possibilities. Maybe Korza wasn't a stranger. And maybe Linny wasn't fucking him. Maybe she caught him fucking someone else.'

'Well, Chief, we both know Linny's got one hell of a temper.'

Caroline glanced at her watch as she sat at her kitchen table working her way through her third cup of coffee. 5:55 a.m. Her first appointment wasn't until 9 a.m. She considered going back to bed and trying to get some sleep, but she knew she'd have no better luck now than she'd had most of the night – much of which she'd spent tortured by visions of that brutally murdered man, worrying about her patient Steve Kramer, wishing she'd been more affectionate to Martin.

She eyed the small TV on her kitchen counter. Plenty of time to catch the early local news. Flicking to channel eight at six on the dot, Caroline immediately recognized the morning anchorwoman as the blond reporter who'd hassled her outside the museum.

She was stunned to hear the news begin with her name.

'Dr. Caroline Hoffman, a thirty-two-year-old psychiatrist who practises at the Boston General's Institute For Special Problems, was questioned by Homicide Detective Amy DeSanto at the scene last night after the naked body of

Peter Korza, a violinist with the Boston Players Ensemble, was found by a security guard behind a partition in an unused gallery at the rear of the Bullfinch Art Museum on Huntington Avenue. Korza was strangled to death with a metal chain. According to an unnamed source, the male victim may have been raped prior to strangulation. Interestingly, I have learned that Dr. Hoffman specializes in treating sexual deviants and runs a weekly group for men and women suffering from serious sexual addictions . . .'

Caroline angrily hit the off button. There was no question in her mind as to how the newscaster had gotten her name.

She glared at the phone, debating whether to call Homicide and give DeSanto a piece of her mind. Its abrupt ring startled her.

'Did I wake you?' Martin asked.

'No, I was already up.'

'I was rushing around, finishing packing and I had the TV on . . .'

'Let me guess. Jill Nugent and the Earlybird News?'

'What's it all about, Caroline? Is this dead guy the patient you went racing off to rescue last night?'

'No. I've never seen the poor man before.'

'So why'd she drag you into the story? This patient of yours—'

Caroline sighed. Interrogation all over again. No, that wasn't fair. Martin's questions came out of concern for her. 'He couldn't have anything to do with it. My patient has no history of homosexual activity.'

'Did you hear from him again?' Martin asked.

'No. I left a message on his machine.' A clap of thunder sent a riff of static down the line. 'Martin, are you there?'

'Shit. I hope this storm lets up by the time I get to Logan. Nothing I hate more than hanging around airports.'

'Yeah, it's a drag,' Caroline agreed. 'Listen, Martin . . .'

'I better get going. Traffic's going to be a bitch through the Callahan tunnel at this hour. Stay out of trouble while I'm gone,' he said affectionately.

'I was thinking . . .'

'Hold that thought till Monday. Gotta run.'

The phone line went dead.

Meg was wrenched from a deep sleep by her phone ringing. As she fumbled to pick it up, she squinted at her alarm clock. 6:10 in the morning.

Soft crying on the other end of the line.

'Mother? Is that you?' Who, but her mother, would call sobbing at this ungodly hour?

'I'm . . . in trouble. You've . . . got to . . . help me.'

Definitely not her mother. A man's tearful, unfamiliar voice.

'Who is this? Look, pal, you've got a wrong number.'

'Meg? Isn't this . . . Meg Spaulding?'

'Who is this?'

'They've got me . . . in jail, Meg. I can't . . . Oh God, I'm climbing . . . the walls. Please. Please . . . I've got . . . to get out of . . . here. You're the only one, Meg . . . who can . . . help me.'

'Who the hell is this?'

'It's me. Steve. Steve Kramer. You know. From . . . group.

I need five thousand dollars, Meg.'

'What?'

'To get out of here. Bail. And as a retainer for my lawyer . . .'

'Hey, I'm sorry you're in jail, but it's six a.m. And I'm leaving town in a couple of hours.'

'Tell me, Meg, do your colleagues know how much of an art lover you are? How about your family? Your brother owns a gallery, doesn't he? Maybe he'd like to know his sister shares his passion for art. Yes indeed, Meg, you're one passionate woman.'

'I don't know what you're talking about.'

'A regular *superwoman*. So you use a ladies' rest room instead of a phone booth to *get into costume*.'

'You son-of-a-bitch.'

'Only when I'm desperate. Meg, if I'm not out of here soon I don't know what I'll do . . .'

Meg stared down at her grey flannel duvet cover. It reminded her ominously of the colour of gathering storm clouds.

Shortly after 6.30 a.m. Meg showed up at her brother's smart Beacon Street townhouse apartment situated above the street-level Spaulding Art Gallery and facing the world-famous Boston Public Garden.

'You're kidding,' Ned said, groggily rubbing his eyes. Her younger brother was a lean, strong-looking man a couple of inches taller than his sister and with the same fine-boned features. He was strikingly handsome, despite his tousled dark hair.

Meg followed him into his trendy European-designed kitchen with its black and white tiled floor, stark white laminate cupboards, grey granite counters. She'd been in charge of the refit.

Ned filled the steel and bronze museum replica kettle. 'Tea?'

'Ned, I'm in a hurry. I've got to—' She almost said 'get down to the police station', but quickly changed it to – 'get to the airport for an eight a.m. flight to New York.'

He took the kettle over to the black six-burner stove. 'Why in God's name do you need that kind of money at this ungodly hour?'

'It's a long story.'

Ned leaned against the counter. 'I've got time.'

'Well, I don't. It's a loan, Ned. For chrissakes, you know I'm good for it. I'll wire the money back to you from New York later today. Okay?'

His expression became more serious. 'Of course I'll give you the money. I've got it in the safe downstairs in the gallery. It'll just take me a couple of minutes.'

Meg smiled weakly. 'Thanks, Ned.'

He came up to her, put his hands gently on her shoulders. 'Meg, are you in trouble?'

'No. It's nothing like that.'

'Then what is it like? You know you can tell me. We tell each other everything, don't we?'

'It's for a . . . friend.' She couldn't look him in the eye.

'A friend? A friend who needs five thousand bucks before the bank opens?'

'Please, Ned . . .'

'You look wiped, Meg.'

She tried to smile. 'It's work, that's all. I need some time off. Right now, I'm swamped.'

'Come down to Martha's Vineyard with me this weekend. I'm going out to help Mom clean out a bunch of crap in the attic. Maybe we'll find some buried treasure.'

'I'll be back in town on Friday. If I can clear the boards, I'll go with you. How's that?'

Ned brushed her cheek affectionately. 'If I believed you for even one minute, that would be ducky, Sis.'

6

Blackmail. Discovery. Disgrace. Humiliation.

As she rode in the cab from the police station, Meg imagined a wave rushing over her, sucking her into its mighty undertow. She was spinning helplessly, gasping for air, fluid filling her lungs. She couldn't breathe. She was drowning.

Salvation began the moment she slipped into a cubicle in the ladies' room at Logan airport, and began stripping off her business suit. Then she pulled out of her carry-on case the black silk bikini panties, the slinky patent pumps with the three-inch heels, the skimpy black jersey dress.

The entire transformation – clothes, wig, a fresh pair of contact lenses, make-up – was complete in a matter of minutes. But Meg was unaware of time. She was utterly absorbed in the orderly ritual of her transformation – almost an end in itself.

Martin Bassett rifled through the magazines at one of the

airport kiosks, trying to settle on something to read until the damn storm passed and the planes started flying again. At the moment, his flight to Pittsburgh had been postponed until 8:25. But, without a break in the weather, there was no telling when the plane would really get off the ground.

A model on the cover of ELLE caught his eye. She reminded him of Caroline. Not so much her actual features – although both women had shoulder-length dark brown hair and similar olive colouring – as the haunting glimmer in the grey eyes, the determined set of the full mouth, the defiant, dare-you, dare-me angle of the head.

From the first moment he met her, Martin had found Caroline Hoffman seductively enticing yet daunting. It was nothing to do with her being five years older than him. Men twice his age – he could name several of them at the Institute – were equally awed by her.

Martin felt the heat rise up his neck. He loved the contrast between Caroline's cool professionalism at the Institute and the hunger of her love-making. He resolved to make up for their ruined last night when he got back on Monday. He'd bring her flowers. Take her out to dinner. Wine her and dine her. Show her that sex wasn't the only thing on his mind when he was with her.

Martin could feel his erection growing as his thoughts ran on.

Standing a few feet away from him, he noticed an incredibly sexy young woman in a short skin-tight black jersey dress staring unabashedly at the bulge in his trousers. Slowly, she lifted her gaze to his face.

Martin was immediately riveted by her eyes. They were the most extraordinary shade of green.

The faintest of smiles shimmered across her lips. Martin experienced a vague sense of recognition. Maybe it was only that the raven-haired woman looked a bit like the model on the cover of the magazine he was still holding. Or a bit like Caroline.

The eye contact couldn't have lasted more than a few seconds. Then the woman turned. Slowly, she walked off.

Martin's hesitation was brief.

What the hell, he thought, shoving the magazine back on the shelf. He had time to kill.

The throbbing begins in his groin, travels up to his heart, climbs inside his brain. She's climbed inside, too. Taking full possession of his body and his mind.

Is he even breathing? At first, the acrid smell in the claustrophobic janitor's closet was overwhelming. Overriding the scent of her fruity perfume. Now, his sense of smell abandons him altogether.

There is only the sense of touch. Her touch. She's like a drug. He's high with desire. In another universe. Her moist tongue flutters like a hummingbird's wings over his skin. Her sculptress fingers explore, stroke, knead his body.

His head bangs into the rim of the metal slop bucket. But he is feeling no pain . . .

Too dark in the rancid cubicle to see anything. Only a crushing pressure behind his eyes. And now he does feel pain. An aching pain in his jaw caused by his mouth having been forced open, then stuffed with his balled up shirt. *If only he could swallow. If only—*

If only he could get the hell out of there.

He's twisted over. The painful contortions of his limbs bring on excruciating cramps. Goose bumps of terror chill his perspiration-drenched body.

Martin has come hurtling down to earth with a vengeance.

He feels the cold metal chain tighten around his throat. Over the roar of his pulse pounding in his ears, he recalls fragments of the newscast he heard earlier that morning . . . *the victim is believed to have died of asphyxiation, the result of a noose made of a metal chain . . .*

No air. Lungs burning. Body on fire. The metal noose cutting deeper and deeper. Martin knows precisely what is happening to his body. What horrors lie ahead. How many agonizing minutes more it will take for death to release him.

Tears flood his cheeks; that death should be his only hope.

Before he loses consciousness, he silently whispers, *I'm sorry, Caroline . . .*

7

Caroline buzzed her secretary. 'My ten o'clock hasn't shown up yet, has he?'

'No. Sorry, Dr. Hoffman. You did get another call about twenty minutes ago, though. From Jill Nugent. That makes three so far this morning.'

'Do me a favour, Renée. If she calls again, tell her I'm gone for the day.'

'Will do.'

Caroline turned to her dictating machine and started recording her observations on her previous session with the wife of the cross-dressing ex-judge from her group, when Renée buzzed her again. 'Mr. Kramer's here, Dr. Hoffman.'

Caroline felt a weight, if not lifting, shifting to a more tolerable position. 'Send him in, Renée.'

The door opened. Steven Kramer walked in and hurriedly shut it behind him.

He looked dreadful. Day-old growth of beard, hair uncombed, crumpled suit damp from the rain, tie askew.

And he had a lit cigarette dangling from the corner of his mouth even though he knew smoking wasn't allowed anywhere in the building.

Caroline waited, sensing that anything she might say could trip the charge.

'I've been drinking,' Kramer admitted finally, tapping his finger against his lips. 'There's this bar over on Washington Street. They serve a delectable breakfast cocktail. Filled with all the vitamins and minerals a body needs.'

Caroline was thinking that Washington Street – what was left of Boston's *red light* district – was an unlikely neighbourhood for her troubled patient.

Kramer took a long drag of his cigarette. 'I'm finished.' His eyes teared.

'Sit down, Steve. Let's talk about it,' she invited.

He squinted through the smoke at her. 'Talk?' He shook his head, wagging his finger back and forth. 'No. No. No. I don't want to talk.' He took a couple of shaky steps into the room. 'Talk's cheap, Caroline.' This seemed to amuse him. His laugh turned into a cough. Finally, he removed the cigarette from his mouth. 'Ah, physician heal thyself.'

Picking up a small bowl containing some paper clips, Caroline dumped the clips in a drawer and pushed the bowl across her desk towards Kramer.

He stared blankly at her.

Caroline rose and walked over to three comfortable armchairs in a corner of the room. She motioned to one of them.

'Sit down, Steve.'

He collapsed into it, his head sagging to his knees. The cigarette fell from his hand to the tan carpet. Caroline snatched it up, snuffed it out in the dish. She sat down across from him.

'I've really done it this time,' he mumbled. 'God, I stink.' He lifted his head. 'Can you smell it on me?'

'Smell what?'

'The piss. The shit. The vermin. Have you ever been in jail, Caroline?'

He chuckled as if it was some big joke.

Caroline wasn't laughing. Jail, as she knew only too well, was no laughing matter.

'No,' he said sombrely. 'No, it's not funny. My probation officer didn't so much as crack a smile either. All he wanted to know was what was I doing there in the first place?'

'Where?' Caroline's throat was dry.

'You know how long it's been since I've gone to the pornos?' He paused, eliciting a faint shake of Caroline's head. 'Close to five months. That's how long. Sexual sobriety as we say in the business, right, Caroline?'

'The pornos?' she echoed. Not what she'd expected him to say. She was almost convinced he'd been at the museum. That he knew something about the murder.

Kramer squinted at her, rubbing his eyes as if struggling to bring her into focus. 'They may be calling you.'

'Who?'

'The police. My lawyer. I had a brief pow-wow with him. Will you testify for me, Caroline? You know how hard I've been trying. The progress I've been making.' Kramer's voice was clearer, more composed.

'I don't understand what you're talking about,' Caroline said. 'Tell me what happened last night.'

'What happened last night,' he echoed quietly. A thin smile stretched across his lips. 'It's pathetic, really. I tried to pick up a whore at a porno flick. Only it turned out she wasn't a whore. She was an undercover cop. When she and her pimp partner went to cuff me, I panicked and took a few swings at them.'

'What time was this?' Caroline pressed.

'Christ, I don't know. I wasn't checking my watch. Around ten, ten-thirty, I guess.'

'After you phoned me then.'

'Seven nightmarish hours in that vermin-infested hole before—' He stopped abruptly.

'Before what?' Caroline prompted.

'Before I put together bail.'

'Steve, we need to backtrack for a minute.'

He gave her a wary look, then smiled. 'You never let anything get by you, do you, Caroline?'

Was he warning her to let it go? Or did he want her to press him? Did he want to confess? *But confess to what?* 'Where were you when you called me last night?'

His eyes darkened. 'Why? What difference does it make?'

'It was around nine o'clock or so. You were extremely upset. Do you remember?'

'I wasn't that drunk. Of course I remember. I guess I had a . . . premonition I'd get myself in a jam. Maybe I called because I wanted you to stop me.'

Caroline shivered. 'Stop you from what?'

'A little late now,' he said caustically. 'I swore, after that first time I got arrested, I'd never walk into another porno joint as long as I lived. That's what we addicts do, right? Swear we'll stop. We're all liars.'

Kramer began to tap his foot nervously. He shut his eyes, shielding them with his hands.

'It's not about lying to yourself, Steve. It's about understanding what triggered your relapse.'

Kramer rubbed his face. 'I can't think straight. I've got to go home and shower. Change.'

He rose abruptly, straightened his tie, raking his fingers through his untidy hair as he started for the door.

'Steve, you called me from the Bullfinch Museum last night, didn't you?'

Her words stopped him halfway across the room.

'If we could talk about it, we'd be able to . . .'

He turned slowly to face her. 'What would *we* be able to do, Caroline?'

His tone made her more than a little uneasy. A reaction she was careful to mask.

'After you phoned me last night,' she said, 'I went looking for you.'

'You did what?'

'I ended up at the art museum . . .'

Kramer took a step back, his hands pressing against his temples.

'We need to talk about it, Steve.'

'Later.'

'In group tonight?'

'No. Not . . . in group. I can't make it tonight.'

'All right. I'll schedule an individual session for tomorrow.'

She flipped open her appointment book, ran a finger down Thursday's hours, knowing it was important to get him in again as soon as possible. She was booked solid with patients, meetings, and consultations. The only opening was her noon lunch break. Oh hell, she thought, staring down at the blocked-off hour.

'I can see you—' Before she finished her sentence Caroline heard the door shut. Her eyes flicked up from her book. Steven Kramer was gone.

Caroline sat there, frightened that she had only got a glimpse of what had happened to Kramer, knowing that the real damage went a lot deeper.

It was still raining when Steve Kramer left the Institute For Special Problems a little after 10:30 a.m., got in his car and began retracing his route to the Peabody Bar. A liquid brunch was definitely in order.

As he drove down the rain-soaked streets, his face contorted in regret. How could he have screwed up his life so royally? A year ago, he was a respected physician, had a wife, friends, a Georgian brick colonial in Brookline, a sleek, white Lexus. A year ago he had it all. But he also had his *little secret.*

Shame swept over him, filling him with self-loathing. He thought of heading straight for a gun shop. Do it right this time. End it once and for all. Wasn't that preferable to jail? His lawyer hadn't sounded particularly optimistic about getting him off with probation this time.

One little slip-up. And it wasn't his fault. Not really.

How much had that lawyer said it would cost to

represent him? Three grand up front as a retainer. And it could go as high as ten before it was done.

Considering Kramer didn't have ten cents to his name, much less ten grand, getting his hands on the money posed a serious problem. As if he didn't have enough.

Twenty minutes later, sitting on a stool in the far corner of the seedy, amber-tinted Washington Street bar, Kramer was downing a double JB straight up when a man's face flashed on the TV overhead, catching his attention.

The photo only ran for a few seconds before the camera cut to the newscaster, natty, silver-haired, in a well-tailored dark suit, seated behind his anchor desk. The sound was turned too low to hear but it didn't matter. Sometimes a picture could speak a thousand words. *And,* Kramer mused, *be worth its weight in gold.*

The phone was out of order. But they did have a phone book behind the bar. Slapping a five dollar bill on the worn copper counter, Kramer hurried to the public phone across the street. Pressing his head against the cool metal phone stand, he took a few deep breaths of air, tried to clear his thoughts.

A sharp tap on his shoulder made him jump.

'Hey! Buddy! You using that phone or what?'

Kramer gave the guy the finger. Then punched in the number.

The receptionist at the architectural firm of Ferrara, Brown & Fields informed him that Meg Spaulding was out of town. Kramer explained that he was Ms. Spaulding's gynaecologist and that she was waiting for some test results.

The receptionist immediately gave him the number of the Fitzgerald Hotel in New York City.

He dialled the hotel, using his calling card. Meg hadn't arrived yet. He left her a message.

Meg Spaulding landed in New York at close to 11 a.m. A couple of hours later than anticipated. Half the delay was due to the storm. No shuttles had departed from Logan until the weather cleared at 8:30 a.m. But she'd missed that flight by a matter of minutes, being otherwise occupied.

It was only after she was checking in at her hotel that Meg realized she'd forgotten all about calling Dr. Hoffman's office to quit therapy. She made a mental note to take care of the matter as soon as she got to her room. Then she'd take her second shower of the morning – she could still smell the faint tang of ammonia from that janitor's closet – and hop in a cab over to 57th and Madison for her noon meeting.

'You have a couple of messages, Miss Spaulding,' the desk clerk said, handing her two folded slips of paper along with a room key. Assuming they were from her office, Meg merely slipped the notes into her jacket pocket.

When the bellhop went to gather up her luggage, Meg held on to her overnight case. He took her oxblood leather portfolio in hand, slung her wardrobe bag over one shoulder, and led the way across the hotel's tranquil, elegant lobby to the elevator. As the doors opened, he ushered her in and pressed 17.

'It was raining here all morning. The pits. And now it's clearing up. You must have brought the sunshine with you,' he remarked flirtatiously as the doors slid closed.

Meg glanced at the bellhop. A handsome, ash-blond hunk. Early twenties. He reminded her of a poster boy for men's briefs. Too young. Too eager. Too transparent. She wasn't interested. To emphasize this, she reached in her pocket for her messages, unfolding the first one and glancing at it. It was from her brother.

Mother's here. She doesn't look good. Call ASAP. Ned.

She doesn't look good. Ned's discreet way of saying that her mother's gone off the deep end. Again.

The doors slid open. Meg automatically started to exit. The bellhop caught hold of her arm. 'This is only twelve,' he said.

She nodded absently, staring back at the message from her brother. The words blurred. But she could hear Ned's old, familiar refrain in her head. *You can't blame her, Meg. She's sick. Don't worry. She's going to get the help she needs—*

'Your floor,' the bellhop said, holding open the doors.

Numbed, she followed him out of the elevator and down the corridor to her room.

'You got one of the nicest rooms in the hotel,' the bellhop said as he ushered Meg inside. He set her bags on the luggage stand near the closet.

Meg shoved a five dollar bill in his hand. 'Thanks,' she said dismissively.

'Sure,' he answered brightly. 'If there's anything else—'

She'd already turned her back to him. After a moment, the door closed softly behind her.

The message from Ned was crumpled in her hand. She let it drop to the rose-coloured carpet, then set her bag on the bed.

A high-pitched whine of police sirens filtered up from the street below. Without warning, Meg's eyes brimmed with tears. She clutched herself, rocking back and forth on her heels. 'Oh Momma. Momma. Momma—'

But Meg had no patience with her own weakness. She wiped away the tears and snatched the crumpled message off the floor, glanced at the phone, debating whether to call Ned now or after her meeting.

She dropped the note into a wicker trash basket beside the highly polished Queen Anne desk.

After.

Crossing to the bathroom, Meg turned on the shower, returning to the bedroom to undress. Only as she was laying her clothes out for housekeeping to have dry-cleaned, did she spot the other folded paper on the floor. It must have fallen out of her jacket pocket. The second message.

Carelessly, Meg picked up the note. She dropped it on the bedside table when her phone rang—

Meg gripped the receiver tightly as she sat at the edge of her bed. 'You're out of your mind.' Her jaw clenched, her voice constricted.

'I don't think the police will think so, Meg.'

Her hands shook. 'The . . . police?'

'The Homicide Division, to be precise. There's probably a reward. For information.'

She wouldn't give an inch. 'I don't know what you're talking about, Steve.'

'Don't you, Meg?'

'No, I . . .'

'If you're going to play, you've got to pay. I'm not judging you, Meg. Maybe things got out of hand. . .'

'I'm hanging up, Steve. I've had a long day and . . .'

'See, I didn't have the whole picture at first. I caught the beginning and the middle so to speak, but the climax – I missed that. I got nervous. Thought I heard a guard coming. You're lucky you didn't get caught in the act . . .'

'Good-bye . . .'

'Twenty thousand, Meg. It's not all that much to ask. I'm on your side, but I'm desperate. I can't handle going to prison. And something tells me, neither can you.'

He hung up. As Meg put the phone down, she was more than a little rattled by the conversation. She knew she had to get ready for her meeting, but she curled up on the bed, bringing an arm across her eyes to block out the glare.

But she could do nothing about the howling void that reverberated through her brain.

8

'Take a look at this, Lieutenant.'

Baush looked up from his desk. Darlene Lowell, a young undercover cop who'd been with Vice for five months, handed over a neatly typed crime report.

Baush scanned the paper quickly. Then he turned to the sultry, dark-haired detective. They'd messed around quite a bit, until she found out about Amy. No hard feelings, she'd told him, but she was big on monogamy. That didn't stop him from making a pitch when the mood struck. Once in a while, Darlene relented. Persistence and charm were two of Baush's prized assets.

'I picked the perp up at 10:52 last night at a triple Xer on Washington while I was undercover,' Darlene said. 'He followed me in there. Was on my tail for a good twenty minutes on the street first. Just watching.'

'And panting,' Baush said, inhaling Darlene's perfume. Not the crap she doused herself in when she was undercover.

Darlene accepted the compliment with a friendly wink. 'When he finally got down to business, guess what he wanted? To watch me going at it with another john. Slipped me a C note to seal the deal.'

'Too bad I wasn't available.'

'Don't you want to know why I'm telling you all this, Lieutenant?'

He raised an eyebrow. 'Okay, Detective. Tell me.'

'You see the perp's name? Steven Kramer.'

Baush shrugged. 'Never heard of him.'

'Kramer's on probation. He told me he's been in treatment with a psychiatrist for nearly six months. Said she'd vouch for the fact that he's made a lot of progress. Claimed this was his first slip-up since he started in her group.'

Lowell produced another piece of paper. A medical release form. 'Check out the name of Kramer's doctor.' Her tapered red nail marked the spot on the form. 'Dr. Caroline Hoffman. That's the shrink from the museum murder last night. The case Amy DeSanto's investigating. The story was all over the news this morning. I thought it was curious. I figured you might want to let your girlfriend know.'

'You feel that men take advantage of you. Make you do things you don't want to do.'

Natalie Deutch's lips quivered, tears welling up in her eyes as she nodded at Caroline during their individual therapy session.

'Phone sex gave you the feeling that you had the upper hand. And you thought it was safe.'

'Yeah, the ultimate safe sex. I actually convinced myself,'

Natalie said in a strained voice, 'that I wasn't really cheating on Brad. But I feel so guilty. And yet I'm scared I might . . . do it again.'

'Recovery doesn't come easily, Natalie. Or fast. And sometimes a person has to hit rock bottom before really believing that something's got to be done.'

'Do you think I hit bottom?'

'Do you think so?'

'I . . . hope so. Talking about it in group made me see how out of control I really was. Not that it was easy, going through it again. One thing about group, though. We're all in the same boat so I don't feel like a . . . freak.' Natalie hesitated.

'What is it?' Caroline asked.

Natalie threaded her fingers through her short, wavy ash-blond hair. 'I have something I need to tell you about Steve Kramer.'

Caroline felt her heart beat faster. 'Yes?'

'We've talked a few times. After group.' Natalie looked apologetic. 'I feel a little like I'm telling tales out of school . . .'

Natalie looked at her psychiatrist for approval. But Caroline made no response.

'Steve confessed that one night he followed me to my house, parked across the street and saw me and Brad in our bedroom . . .'

A frisson of alarm stiffened Caroline's spine.

'. . . It's on the second floor and faces right out onto Chestnut Street. With the curtains open and the lights on, he'd have had a pretty good view. Especially because he was using binoculars. I told Steve how sick that was.'

Natalie stopped for a moment, struggling with herself. 'What's really sick is, I was turned on when Steve told me. The idea that this guy was outside my house, watching me through a window. That Brad and I might have been making love—' Her face was flushed.

Caroline's mind was racing. Had Steve spied on any of the other women in the group? What about her? Had he ever focused his binoculars on *her* bedroom window?

Could it have been a group member whom Steve had followed to the museum the night before? If so, it wasn't hard for Caroline to guess which one.

The soft beep of the intercom line jolted her back to the present. Her secretary would never break in during a session unless there was an emergency.

Natalie glanced at her watch and exclaimed, 'Wow, we've gone over. You must be slipping, Doc. You're usually so fanatic about ending our sessions right on the button.'

Caroline picked up the receiver and punched the blinking button. 'Yes, Renée?'

'I'm sorry to interrupt you . . .'

'What is it?' Caroline asked with an uncharacteristic brusqueness.

'Someone's here to see you,' Renée said, her voice conspiratorial. 'I told him this was your lunch hour, but . . .'

'Who is it?' Caroline's first guess had been that annoying reporter, Jill Nugent, but Renée had said *him*.

'A police detective.'

Lieutenant Jesse Baush stood inside Caroline's closed door, giving her modest office a long, intense survey.

'Nice digs, Linny.'

Caroline didn't say a word, her gaze fixed on Jesse's familiar face. His appearance had hardly changed in years. He still had the incongruously innocent look of a choir boy. Looks, as Caroline had learned long before becoming a psychiatrist, could be oh so deceiving.

He still dressed the same, too. Blue jeans, scuffed black cowboy boots and a worn-out USAF brown bomber jacket. A Vietnam relic that still had its original name tag. Porter Baush. A hand-me-down from father to son.

He observed her, slightly smirking, arms folded across his broad chest. 'It's been a long time. You look good.'

Caroline eyed him right back. 'What are you doing here, Jesse? Last I heard, you were a private investigator in New York.'

Baush cocked his head. 'Who told you that? Your momma?'

Caroline looked away. 'No. We don't talk much.' As if that was anything new.

'Yeah, we don't talk much either. She's usually too drunk these days to engage in scintillating conversation. She sure did start hitting that bottle hard after losing my dad,' he added derisively.

Caroline had almost forgotten how easily Jesse could get to her.

Baush sauntered across the room. For a moment, Caroline was reminded of the way he'd looked the time he'd crossed the high school gym floor to ask her for a dance – setting her adolescent heart aflutter. But this time, the smile on his freckled, still boyish face was demonic rather than appealing.

Caroline chided herself. Jesse Baush wasn't a devil. He was merely an inadequate man with an obsessional grudge. Against her.

He strolled over to one of the chairs in front of her desk and casually lowered himself into it, stretching out his long legs and crossing them at the ankles. 'Made a career move. I'm with the Boston P.D. now. Would have dropped by sooner, but . . .' He shrugged.

'I'm busy, Jesse. And I have no interest in . . .'

'This isn't a social call, Linny.'

'What is it then? Did I forget to pay a parking ticket?'

'No, I didn't come about parking tickets.' He laughed coldly before straightening up in his chair and leaning forward, his blue eyes square on her face. 'I'm here about that poor guy who bought it at the museum last night.'

Caroline's mouth tightened.

'You look surprised, Linny. Or are you nervous?'

'I thought that policewoman – DeSanto – was in charge.'

He rose, pressing his large hands flat on top of her desk. Then he bent forward slightly. She was less than an arm's length from him.

'Yeah,' he drawled. 'I'm working on it, too. We've got a guard who saw Korza near closing time cozying up to some hot-looking babe in a skintight black dress. Long, dark hair, tall, stacked. Really stacked. Looked like a hooker.' He briefly snatched a lock of Caroline's dark brown hair, his eyes cruising audaciously down to her breasts and then up again.

Caroline glared at him. He made her sick. No big surprise, given his dad. The apple rarely fell far from the tree. *Psychiatry 101.*

'Look, Jesse, don't think I don't know what you're doing.'

'I'm investigating a murder, Linny. That's what I'm doing.'

'That's not all you're doing. And we both know it.'

A derisive smile twisted his lips. 'Is that right?'

'Don't mess with me, Jesse. I'm not eighteen . . .'

'So tell me about your buddy, Steven Kramer.'

'What?'

'The guy you were out chasing after last night. Your wacko patient?'

'I'm not at liberty to discuss who is or isn't my patient,' she said stiffly.

Baush dipped his hand in his jacket pocket and produced the medical release form with a flourish. He slapped it on her desk.

Caroline studied it carefully. 'What exactly do you want to know?' Her tone was formal.

'This guy, Kramer. He's a peeper, right?'

'He suffers from voyeurism.'

Baush chuckled. 'You always did get off on those big words, Linny.'

'What else do you want to know, Jesse?' she asked impatiently.

'Well now, I'm not a big-shot shrink or anything, but I'd say if your peeper *was* at the museum last night, it could mean one of two things.'

'Only two?' Caroline commented airily.

'Just out of curiosity, Linny. Why was it you picked sex

problems as your area of interest?' Before she could respond, he shrugged. 'Never mind. I think I can figure that out for myself.'

Caroline let his dig pass.

'Let's get back to your *voyeur*,' he said. 'Like I said, I see *two* main possibilities. Either he was peeping at Korza and this mystery lady. Or he got bored and decided to get in on the act.'

'Steven Kramer has never, to my knowledge, exhibited any sado-masochistic or violent tendencies.' Caroline could feel the pressure building in her head.

'Yeah? Tell that to the detective with the black eye who went to cuff him outside that porn house late last night.'

'I'm sure it was a panic response. He'd had too much to drink . . .'

'How'd you know that, Linny?'

'He has problems with alcohol.'

'Sounds like this wacko's got problems up the wazoo. Didn't you tell one of my boys at the museum that he was suicidal?'

'I thought it was a possibility.'

Baush grinned. 'So Kramer *was* the one you were hunting down last night.'

'I wasn't *hunting him down*.'

'Weren't you? But you were real worried about him? Now what would make you all that worried?'

'I told you . . .'

'You haven't told me anything,' Baush interrupted icily. 'But I'll tell you something, Linny. I don't think your peeper was the doer. I think the doer was the hot little number that fucked Korza every which way. So, that takes us back to what your peeper saw at the museum last night. Or more to the point – *who* he saw.'

Caroline's stomach lurched. 'If he saw anything. If he was even there.'

Baush looked long and hard at her. 'Oh, he was there, Linny.'

'You have proof?'

'We'll get it.'

'Have you talked with him?' Caroline was growing increasingly concerned about how Steven Kramer would fare under Jesse's interrogation.

'Not yet. I dropped in on the medical lab where he works, but he hadn't come in yet. What about you?'

Caroline hesitated. 'Yes. He showed for his scheduled appointment this morning at ten. But he didn't say anything about being at the museum.'

'What did he say?'

'Nothing that would help you.'

'Don't jerk me around, Linny.'

'I'm not.'

'Is that right?' Baush knew she was holding back. 'I hear this peeper used to be a doctor. Must be a bummer going from a successful physician to a lowly lab tech. Losing everything. Your whole life fucked because you had a *fucking* problem.'

Caroline frowned.

'Did I offend you with my foul language or did I touch a nerve there, Linny?' He managed to infuse the question with both contempt and menace.

The pressure in Caroline's head was escalating. 'There's nothing more I can tell you about my patient, Jesse. And since that's why you're here—'

He stabbed his finger at her. 'You know I've got a mind to bring you in for a lineup. 'Cause I was talking some more with that museum guard and I'll tell ya something, Linny. You come real close to fitting the description of that hooker. Same height. Same sort of curves. Put you in a tight little black dress, a black wig . . .'

'There are laws against harassment,' Caroline said sharply.

'Maybe you got to the museum way before you went rushing up with your story about a suicidal wacko,' Baush went on. 'Smart shrink like you are now, you'd figure that for a good alibi. Maybe you're into whips and chains. Is that how you like to get it on these days, Linny? Could be you were just playing rough. Trying to show that fiddler a good time. I hear choking is the supremo way for some guys to get their rocks off. Maybe you didn't really mean to choke the poor fellow to death. We both know how you can lose control when you're turned on.'

'You really do have some serious problems, Jesse.' Caroline's voice shook despite her efforts to control it.

'Don't you try to mind-fuck me, Linny. I'm not one of your sexual perverts. I don't have the foggiest notion what makes them tick. But you do. What's that old saying? Takes one to know one.'

Caroline was at the end of her tether. She also felt badly scared, not putting it past Jesse Baush to trump up some charges, drag her down to police headquarters, and put her through the mill. 'Look, Jesse. I was home until I got a call around 9:00 from Steve Kramer. He didn't say he was calling me from the museum. Just that he was in that vicinity.'

'So you were home until 9:00.'

'Yes. I left my apartment at around 9:10 and went looking for Kramer because I was concerned about his welfare. He has some suicidal ideation . . .'

'You got any way of proving that you were home until then?'

The last thing Caroline wanted to do was give Jesse any information about her personal life. She knew how motivated he was to use it to hurt her or at the very least embarrass her. Embarrass Martin, too. They'd taken pains to be discreet about their affair.

'One of my colleagues was with me when Kramer called,' she said finally.

Baush idly pushed aside some papers on her desk, then perched there, nailing her with his eyes. 'A colleague.'

'Yes.' Caroline forced herself to meet his taunting gaze.

Baush pulled out a Bic pen and a small note pad, flipping it open. 'And what's this *colleague's* name?'

'Jesse, this is ridiculous. You don't really think . . .'

'I'd enjoy questioning the rest of your colleagues, Linny. If that's what you want . . .'

It wasn't. As he well knew. 'Martin Bassett. Dr. Martin Bassett.'

Baush's mouth twitched in a *gotcha* smile. 'He work here?'

'For the next couple of weeks. He's completing his residency.'

'What say we ask this Martin Bassett to come on over to your office so I can get a statement?'

'He's not here. He's out of town. He'll be back on Monday.'

Baush leaned closer to her. Caroline could smell the coffee on his breath. She could see the muscles in his jaw clenching and relaxing. But he didn't say a word. Not until he straightened and started across her office.

'You know, Linny,' he drawled as he reached the door. 'You might not have everything go your way this time. Might be the first go-round was beginner's luck.'

'You hold everything against me, don't you, Jesse?' At last Caroline's temper got the best of her. 'I bust my butt working my way through college and med school and you resent me for succeeding. Your father tries to molest me and it's my fault for—'

The door slammed.

9

'She was very upset by my remarks on her paper. And by the grade I gave her,' Greg Pomeroy was telling the therapy group. 'I offered to discuss it further with her after class.'

'In your office,' Tina said pointedly.

The muscles in Greg's face were working. He'd told the group about several of his *escapades* with his students, but this was one he'd avoided until this evening. He wondered if he'd chosen tonight because two of the members were missing – Steve Kramer and Meg Spaulding. Each of them tended to make him feel particularly uneasy.

'We met that evening.' Greg's eyes flicked in Tina's direction. 'In my office.'

'What was it about her?' Chris asked. 'Did she have a certain look? Can you always tell which ones . . . ?'

Greg's mouth tightened into a grim line. 'Not always.'

'Go on,' Natalie encouraged. 'What happened when she arrived?'

'She told me she only took the course because she heard

I was a super professor. Actually she made the set-up very obvious. If I hadn't been so . . . horny,' he confessed, 'I might have gotten suspicious. She kept going on and on. Wasn't there some way she could improve her grade? Wasn't there anything she could do? I tested the waters. Gave her thigh a quick, friendly pat. She didn't seem to object, so I . . .'

'Kept it there,' Chris finished.

Greg gave a brittle laugh. 'I told her we could turn this D paper into a B+ or even an A- with a bit of effort on both our parts.'

'And you told her what would be required?' Tina smiled.

'Yeah, I told her all right. In X-rated detail. Which isn't normally my style. I like to show, not tell.' He flushed. 'But she wanted a blow by blow description of everything I planned for us to do. How I was going to slowly undress her, caress her whole body, take her places where she never dreamed anyone could ever take her.' His flush deepened. 'And the whole time she's looking so turned on.'

'And you're loving it. That feeling is everything, isn't it?' Natalie's eyes shone.

Greg was nodding. Tina and Chris nodded, too. They all knew that feeling. They'd all sold their self-respect – their souls – for it.

'Then, when I finished my spiel,' Greg went on, 'she asks if she's the first. And I tell her, no.'

Chris rolled his eyes. 'That was smart. Incriminate yourself.'

'I thought it would make her feel more comfortable. You know . . . to know other students did . . . this. That it was no big deal. No reason for her to worry, right?'

'Right,' Tina echoed drily.

Greg stared off across the room. 'I really believed I wasn't hurting anyone. That's what I told them.'

'Who did you tell?' Caroline asked.

'The chairman of my department. The dean. After they played the recording she'd secretly made while we were together.'

Greg Pomeroy's brown eyes glazed over. The self-assured expression was gone. All his charismatic appeal vanished with it. Emphasized now was the forty-seven-year-old professor's receding hairline, his prominent nose and slight overbite. He looked drained, slightly dissipated. 'I didn't know. I didn't know.' He gave his psychiatrist a wounded look.

'That she was taping your encounter?'

'That she was the roommate of another student I'd slept with that month. It was only after . . . after I made that inane remark about no one getting hurt, that the dean told me this other student . . . her name was Jennifer – was so traumatized by—' He stopped, choking on the words. 'She swallowed pills. Thank God, not enough to do any real damage.'

'Don't you mean,' Caroline asked softly, 'not enough to kill her? Because, intentionally or not, sex addicts can inflict all kinds of real damage.'

It was a little past 8 p.m. when Meg returned alone to her hotel room. Still strung out from her phone conversation with Steve Kramer that morning and exhausted from the business meeting that had stretched from lunch through dinner, she flopped down on her bed. No sooner had she closed her eyes than her phone rang.

What if it was Steve again?

She let five rings go before she angrily snatched up the receiver.

'Meg?'

'Ned. I was just about to dial your number,' she lied, sitting up and swinging her legs to the floor. 'My flight was late and then my meeting ran . . .'

'I had to have Mom admitted.'

'Where?'

'Boston General. The psych ward. The shrink who evaluated her felt she'd need to be an in-patient for a few days. Until he got her back on her meds regimen. Same old story.'

'What happened, Ned?' Meg demanded. 'What set her off?'

'Who knows? She showed up at the gallery a couple of minutes after I opened shop. Thank God, there were no customers. Meg, you should have seen her. She looked like a wild woman. Her hair flying every which way. Wet. Dishevelled. And talking crazy.'

'What did she say?'

'She started with sin and devils and burning in hell. In the middle, she dropped to her knees and began singing a hymn at the top of her voice. I tried to lift her back to her feet and suddenly she threw her arms around me, clutching me for dear life, sobbing that they were after her.'

'Who's *they*?'

'She wouldn't tell me. Or couldn't. I checked her purse to see if she had any medication on her. No pills. And then I came across this receipt for some sleazy hotel on Essex Street here in Boston.'

'I thought you took her to Logan Sunday night to catch a flight for the Vineyard.'

'I dropped her off at the terminal. Apparently, she made her way back into the city. God only knows what she's been doing here.'

Meg felt short of breath. 'Did she say anything else?'

There was a long pause. 'She talked about . . . the painting.'

Meg leaned forward, lightheaded. But she was listening with all her attention.

'Meg, did you hear what . . . ?'

'Yes.'

'This is the first time, Meg. Since – since the murder. Ten years, Meg.'

'I know.' She could barely speak.

'It was the best thing . . . Dad ever painted,' Ned murmured. 'I mean . . . artistically, technically. Of course that got completely forgotten because of the scandal. We could have made a fortune on it.' Another pause. 'But I'm not sorry she made me destroy it.'

'No,' Meg said in a pained whisper. 'Neither am I.'

A call came in to Homicide from airport security at a quarter to nine. The night janitor, Charles Turner, had discovered the body twenty minutes earlier when he'd gone into the closet to get his cleaning equipment.

Ninety-five minutes later, the medical examiner, Herb Filmore, an oversized man with a florid complexion, had to squeeze himself out of the narrow janitor's closet located down a desolate corridor in Terminal C at Logan Airport. The CSU team had already done their work. They were conferring with Vargas from the D.A.'s office further along the passageway.

Filmore pulled off his rubber gloves as he approached Amy DeSanto and Alfonse Green. 'Dead.'

'Yuk. Yuk. You're a regular stand-up comedian, Herb,' DeSanto said. 'How long?'

'Twelve hours, give or take. I'll know more when I get him downtown.' He gestured to the paramedics who were standing by with the stretcher and the body bag, then looked back on the two detectives. 'But I can tell you right now, kiddos, you've got yourself a real situation here.'

'Tell us something we don't know.' DeSanto glanced into the closet and eyed the naked body of the twenty-something male Caucasian, his contorted torso hunched against a slop bucket. Like last night's museum victim, a shirt – probably the victim's own – was stuffed in the dead man's mouth. And a metal chain was deeply embedded around the victim's neck.

A situation was what it was all right.

So far, there was nothing at the scene to identify the victim. His clothes, save for the shirt – blue jeans, tweed blazer, white socks, paisley silk boxers, and running shoes – all found in a heap near the body, had already been searched. As had the small overnight case located next to the garments. No wallet or other identifying information had been recovered. A half dozen cops were off searching rubbish bins in public rest rooms and elsewhere throughout the large airport terminal in hopes of turning something up. First thing the next day, they'd be questioning everyone who'd been on that morning's shift.

'Will it put a happy face on those sour mugs of yours if I ID your stiff?' Filmore questioned in his gravelly voice.

DeSanto and Green looked surprised.

'You knew him?' asked DeSanto.

The medical examiner waited while the paramedics hoisted up the body and slipped it into a body bag.

'Well?' DeSanto pressed irritably.

'He's a doc,' Filmore said.

'Shit,' Alfonse Green muttered. 'I was hoping for another musician. So we could narrow the field a little.'

DeSanto, on the other hand, looked like her antennae had shot right out of her skull. 'What kind of doctor?'

Filmore pulled out a rumpled white handkerchief from his jacket pocket. He blotted the sweat from his brow. 'A psychiatrist.'

'A name? You got a name, Herbie?' DeSanto asked impatiently.

Filmore raised his hands, palms up. 'Whaddah ya want from me? I'm giving you plenty here.'

'How do you know he's a shrink?'

'I've seen him at a few forensic psychiatry rounds at Boston General. He's one of the ones that's always popping up asking smart-ass questions.' Filmore rolled his eyes.

DeSanto frowned. 'But you don't have a name?'

'Hey, you can't expect me to do all the work, honey.'

'And that whale Filmore says to me, "Hey, you can't expect me to do all the work." And he called me *honey*, the little prick.'

Jesse Baush draped his arm over Amy DeSanto's shoulder as they snuggled on his living room couch. 'They're all trying to hit on you, baby. But you're m-i-n-e.'

'Yeah, yours and Vincent's. I swear, Jesse. If I really believed you'd settle down, I'd divorce that no-good husband of mine in the blink of an eye.'

Baush's hand trailed over Amy's shoulder and slid inside the vee of her sweater. 'You get a name?'

She gave him a provocative smile as he cupped her breast. 'Yeah, I got a name, honey. Took a little legwork, but I got it. What do I get if I give it to you?'

There was a sparkle in Baush's blue eyes. 'How 'bout I give it to you?'

'Huh?'

'How 'bout Bassett? Dr. Martin Bassett?'

Amy's dark eyes widened. 'You never do fail to impress, Jesse. How'd you do that?'

'Just a wild guess, baby. That's all,' he said. Thinking – *pay dirt.*

10

Caroline was in her kitchen having a midnight snack when her downstairs buzzer rang. The instant Jesse Baush identified himself, Caroline's stomach clenched. She wasn't surprised he'd turned up again. She just hadn't expected him so soon.

'What do you want, Jesse? It's late. I've had a long day.'

'This isn't a social call, Linny. Buzz me in. Or come downstairs.'

He was leaning against his red Jeep Cherokee when Caroline stepped outside her building onto St. Botolph Street. He wasn't alone.

'You remember Detective DeSanto, Linny.'

Caroline gave the female officer a terse nod. 'What's this about?'

'You might want to run up and get a coat, Linny.'

'I don't plan to stand out here with you for very long.'

'We're not going to stand here,' Baush said. 'We're going for a drive. The three of us.'

'I'm not going anywhere.'

'If you don't want to cooperate—' He let the rest of his sentence hang, but his eyes never wavered from her face.

'Cooperate how?' Caroline asked guardedly.

DeSanto spoke up for the first time. 'We need you to identify a body.'

Caroline could feel a rush of pulse in her ears. Her stomach turned. Kramer sprang instantly to mind. Had her patient killed himself?

'Who is it?'

'That's for you to say, Linny,' Baush replied grimly. 'You want to get that coat?'

Caroline numbly shook her head.

He shrugged, opening the back door for her. With both reluctance and trepidation, Caroline got into the car.

The three of them sat in oppressive silence as Jesse Baush drove down St. Botolph, cut over to Huntington and then headed southeast on Massachusetts Avenue. The neighbourhoods got progressively more seedy. Rundown old row houses, vacant lots, boarded up storefronts, abandoned warehouses.

When they reached the new Commonwealth of Massachusetts Medical Examiner's Office on Albany Street, Jesse pulled over.

Caroline sat rigidly in her seat, making no move. Her mind was racing through frightening possibilities.

Baush glanced back at her. 'You know, Linny. I *almost* feel sorry for you.' He and DeSanto led her inside the building and guided her across the lobby to the viewing room where less than twenty-four hours earlier Nora

Oswain had IDed Peter Korza.

Caroline stood firmly in the middle of the newly carpeted, den-like room. She concentrated on taking long, even breaths, but they did nothing to counteract her mounting anxiety.

DeSanto stood silently off to the side while Baush strode over to the large picture window. He rapped on it. A bored looking attendant with a scraggly goatee was already waiting to wheel over the corpse. Getting the nod from the lieutenant, he perfunctorily unzipped the top half of the body bag, spreading it open to expose the victim's upper torso.

'Do you recognize this guy, Linny?' Baush asked officiously.

Slowly, resolutely, Caroline looked over at the window, telling herself she could handle this, whatever – whoever – it was. But when her eyes fell on Martin Bassett's ash-white face, his mutilated neck, she gasped audibly, her knees buckling under her.

She would have collapsed had Jesse not grabbed her around the waist, holding her up.

Even in shock, she angrily pulled away from him, reaching over to the arm of the nearby couch for support. 'You bastard. You could have at least prepared me.'

'Tell me, Linny. You think the doc here was *prepared*? It is Martin Bassett, right?'

The room was spinning. Sinking into the couch, Caroline let her head fall to her knees in an effort to quell the dizziness. The shock. The horror.

'Why Martin?' A wave of pure sorrow swept over

Caroline as she thought about their phone conversation that morning. *'I was thinking . . .'* she'd said. But he'd cut her off. *'Hold that thought till Monday.'* Now she'd be holding it forever.

'You tell us why, Linny,' DeSanto said from her post at the side of the room.

Caroline gave the woman detective an icy look. It was bad enough putting up with Jesse calling her *Linny*. 'I wish to God I knew.'

Baush was uncomfortably close. 'Where were you this morning between six and ten?'

Caroline, caught up in her grief, gave him a dazed look.

'Is that a tough question, Linny?'

She'd heard her stepbrother's voice, but she was still trying to absorb that Martin Bassett was the corpse lying there on that cold metal gurney.

'Between six a.m. and ten a.m., Linny.' Baush's voice was laced with impatience.

'Why are you asking?'

He leaned closer, his expression ominous. 'We've collected two stiffs – same MO – in less than twenty-four hours. We can place you at the scene of the first murder not even a half hour after the fiddler bought it. And your boyfriend turns up less than twelve hours later, naked, stuffed in a janitor's closet, with a chain choker around his neck. That leaves you without an alibi for the first murder. And maybe a motive for the second. So that's why I'm asking, Linny.'

Caroline could smell the mustiness coming off her stepbrother's leather jacket as he loomed over her. The smell made her sick. His expression frightened her.

'Jesse, you can't really think I had anything to do with . . . Martin's murder.'

'Why not? It makes sense to me.'

'And what about Peter Korza? You said it was the same . . . MO. Are you telling me I choked a perfect stranger to death as well as a man I happened to care a great deal about?'

'This is real serious business, Linny. Now answer my question. Where were you this morning before ten a.m.?'

Caroline struggled to her feet. 'I was in my apartment until eight forty-five. And then I was at the Institute. I had patients all morning starting at nine. Now, I'm going home, Jesse.'

She turned, but he caught her by her sleeve. 'What happened, Linny? Did Dr. Marty know you were two-timing him with the fiddler? Maybe your boyfriend heard about Korza's murder on the news this morning. Put two and two together. Rushed over to your place and confronted you. What did you do, Linny? Drive with him to Logan? Get him all hot and bothered on the way? Suggest a little quickie to appease the horny schmuck when you got there? Duck into a nice, secluded closet for some action? Dr. Marty got some action all right, didn't he, Linny?'

'You have a serious emotional disorder, Jesse. You really need to get help.' Caroline's response was almost automatic.

'Talk about the pot calling the kettle black,' Amy DeSanto remarked drily.

Caroline was reeling. She had to get out of there. Before she came unglued. She turned to the door. 'I'm going home,' she repeated, resolutely.

'I don't think so. I think you better come down to headquarters. We've got a lot more questions for you,' Baush said threateningly.

Caroline spun around. Her panicked eyes rested on his face. 'Are you arresting me?'

'No. Not yet. Like I said, we have more questions. You remember the routine.'

Caroline shut her eyes. She remembered, all right. Eighteen years old. A freshman at Boston State. Sitting in a grey cubicle at police headquarters, hearing the hum of the fluorescent lights overhead, thinking that surely this was some terrible nightmare—

'Tell me exactly what happened, Caroline. In your own words.' The detective's voice was softly coaxing. His name was Louis Washburn. He told her she could call him Lou.

'He was touching me. I begged him to stop. He wouldn't. I don't even remember picking up the scissors—' She was shivering. He offered her a mug of hot coffee. She took it gratefully.

'I understand. You were scared.'

'Yes. I was scared.' Her hands were trembling, spilling the hot liquid.

'Have you ever been assaulted before?'

'Please. I'm not feeling well . . .'

'Linny – Can I call you Linny? That's what your family calls you, isn't it?'

She nodded. Only meaning yes to the latter question. She hated being called Linny.

'Okay, Linny,' the detective said softly. 'Now I'm going to tell you my problem. Your stepdaddy, Sheriff Baush, swears he never laid a hand on you. That you were the one that made the advances. And that it wasn't the first time. Not the first time with him, nor with other men back home. Wasn't there an incident a couple of years ago? A little skirmish with one of your momma's boyfriends? Not long before your momma married the sheriff . . .?'

'Yes . . . but . . .'

'Couldn't it be there was just a misunderstanding between you and your stepdaddy? Lots of teens get crushes, Linny. We could straighten this all out if you just tell me how it really was—'

Caroline felt a hand at her elbow. The contact jolted her back to the present. But the frightening memory did not fully dissolve.

'Are you ready?' Baush asked gruffly.

Caroline shoved his hand away. Fourteen years back she'd been a naive kid. Well she wasn't a kid anymore. And she sure as hell was no longer naive. 'I'm not answering any more questions, Jesse. Not now. And not at any time without an attorney.' Her voice registered cool control, disguising the fear inside.

Baush shrugged nonchalantly. 'That's fine, Linny. You get yourself an *attorney*. Because you're damned well gonna need one.'

Thursday

11

'Well, you haven't lost your killer instinct.' Phil Mason towelled off as he headed across the squash court. 'I really thought I had you pinned to the wall for a minute there.'

Ben Tabor got to the door first and made a big show of holding it open for his friend. But he couldn't resist one little gibe. 'Is that right? Which minute was that?'

Phil grinned. 'I see you haven't lost your dry wit either.'

The two attorneys had been playing squash together regularly for close to twenty years, starting back in law school when they'd met as adversaries in mock court. The pudgy, poor white scholarship boy from the backwaters of northern Vermont and the sleek, cocky African-American aristocrat from Chicago whose daddy was a superior court judge and whose momma'd recently been sworn in for her fourth term in the state congress. She was to die of breast cancer a month later, a month after her only child had received his acceptance letter to Harvard Law School.

Until the mock trial, Ben Tabor had been ambivalent

about law school. Ambivalent about following in his jurist father's very large footsteps. If it hadn't been his mother's wish, as much as his father's, he might have turned down the prestigious place at Harvard Law.

But during that mock trial at Harvard, Ben Tabor fell in love. He fell in love with the thrill of combat. And with the power and the majesty of the law. In large part, he had Phil Mason to thank for that. Phil was so unambivalent about becoming a lawyer. It was all he'd ever wanted to be. His enthusiasm, earnestness and idealism – however ingenuous, as Ben was forever quick to rib him about – rubbed off on Ben.

Soon after the mock trial ended, Ben bought Phil his first squash racket. A birthday present. Ben had only half-jokingly written on the card – Now you can try beating me on a real court!

Phil did try to beat him at the game – tried damn hard. But he rarely succeeded. The truth was Ben Tabor was a guy who hated to lose. He always gave it that extra something. Phil called it Ben's *killer instinct*. Ben never tried to define it. It was just a part of him. Like his dry wit. Like his black skin.

As they stepped into the locker room of the elite harbourside Bostonia Health Club, Ben peeled off his soaking wet maroon T-shirt. His dark, bony chest glistened with sweat.

Phil gave him the once-over and frowned. 'Jesus, you still losing weight, Ben?'

'You're just jealous that I'm a lean, mean fighting machine.'

'Lean? You're the incredible shrinking man. You don't start building yourself back up, I really will start whipping your sorry ass on the court again.' Phil, who'd long ago turned that baby fat of his into muscle, gave Ben a friendly nudge.

They headed over to their lockers. Spun the dials on their combination locks in casual unison. Phil opened his metal door and pulled out a fluffy white towel, a fresh bar of deodorant soap and a travel-sized dandruff-fighting shampoo.

Ben stared inside his open locker without removing a thing. As if he was looking for something that wasn't there. 'You know what I think, Phil?'

'If I knew even a fraction of what went on inside that overactive brain of yours, Ben, I'd quit law and join the clairvoyants at the *Psychic Network*.' Mason set his stuff on the bench in front of the locker, put his left foot up on it and unlaced his sneaker.

Ben turned to watch him, his arms folded across his chest. 'I think you handed me that win this morning. Not on a silver platter or anything, but you didn't really make me work all that hard. Not as hard as I should have had to. Like I used to.'

Phil yanked off his sneaker. Switched feet. Worked on the laces of the right shoe. 'Yeah, right. You not only have to beat me, you have to make me feel inadequate as well.' His tone was teasing. He didn't even glance up.

'Last week, too. And the week before that.' Ben's tone was as light as Phil's, but there was a faint undercurrent of irritation. He didn't like getting anything handed to him.

When he won, he wanted it on his own merit. On his own terms. *His father's son. Like it or not.*

'You trying to show me I'm as good as ever, Phil? Is that what it's about?'

Mason craned his neck and looked over at his friend. 'You ever think maybe I'm just not as good as I used to be?'

Tabor appeared to be giving his friend's question thoughtful consideration. But then a sly smile cut into his reflective expression. 'Nah.'

Mason laughed, snatching up his towel. Giving it a good snap in the direction of Ben's butt. 'Nah.'

The tension lifted. They finished stripping down and headed for the showers. As Ben led the way, Phil took a surreptitious glance at the scar zigzagging down his friend's right hip. The wound had healed nicely. As had the others. But Phil knew how deep those wounds ran.

It was almost 7 a.m. by the time they were dressed, Phil in his Brooks Brothers' blue silk and worsted pinstriped suit, Ben in a faded grey sweatshirt and frayed jeans. After tossing his gym clothes into his duffel bag, Ben pulled out a pack of Lucky Strikes. He wedged one in the corner of his mouth.

'You have time for a quick breakfast?'

'I don't have time for a piss.' Phil snatched the cigarette from his friend's lips. 'Good friends don't let their friends smoke.'

'Good friends don't let their friends drive drunk. Get your TV campaigns straight, man.'

'Seriously, Ben. It's time you got your act together. No one knows better than me what a rough stretch you've been through, but . . .'

'Save the sermon for Sunday, Pastor Phil.' Ben zipped up his duffel.

'It's not church you need, Ben. It's work. You keep this up much longer and your brain as well as your body's gonna go to shit.'

Ben squinted at him. 'So you did throw the match, you bum—'

Ben Tabor's usual breakfast consisted of several cups of black coffee, and a few bites of toast lightly coated with peanut butter – his one concession to protein intake. Today, thanks to his best buddy Phil's snide remark in the locker room about his *skin and bones* physique, Ben had ordered himself up a morning feast – a sky-high pile of blueberry pancakes swimming, make that drowning, in butter and real Vermont maple syrup, a matching set of four link sausages lined up atop three well-scrambled eggs, and an extra-large glass of milk thrown in for good measure.

'You gonna eat that, Bennie, or just commit it to memory?'

Ben's desultory gaze shifted from his gargantuan breakfast to the full-breasted, tawny-skinned waitress on the service side of the coffee shop counter. 'How many times over the past fifteen years have I begged you not to call me Bennie, Viv?'

'Fourteen years, but who's counting?' the robust, fifty-three-year-old waitress replied sassily, glass coffee pot in one hand, empty white mug dangling from the index finger of her other. 'You wanna cup?'

'No.' Before Viv could finish her shrug, he'd changed his mind. 'Yes. And ditch this mess, and get me some . . .'

'Toast?'

He nodded, shoving his loaded plate away, some of the goopy syrup spilling over onto the counter. 'I hate pancakes. I hate eggs. And those sausages look like dog . . .'

'Don't you say it, Bennie, or this coffee's gonna wind up in your lap.'

'And I hate the goddamn name, *Bennie*.'

Viv gave him a big smile. 'You really gotta work on that rotten disposition of yours, boy.'

'And *boy* is no improvement over *Bennie*,' he groused as she poured coffee into the mug.

She plunked a sugar bowl in front of him. 'Put a little of this in that brew. Might sweeten you up some. I remember back fourteen years when you were as sweet as they came.' She reached out and gave him an affectionate chin chuck – a liberty few would even consider – before blithely sashaying off with his untouched *He-man* breakfast special.

Ben pushed the sugar bowl aside, reaching for a *Boston Chronicle* left behind by the customer who'd been sitting on the stood next to him. He was about to head straight for the sports section – lately, he'd had no stomach for the tragedy and misery that passed for *news* – when a name sprang up at him from the front page.

Suddenly his attention was riveted on that morning's grisly lead story.

Ben Tabor drove home from the coffee shop on automatic pilot, memories passing like fog across his windshield—

His first impression of his eighteen-year-old client is

that she's very beautiful and very tense.

'We'll need character witnesses,' he's telling her as they sit across from each other at the police station. 'Anyone from your town . . .'

'Do you know what it's like growing up in a small town?' she demands.

The question throws him. She throws him. 'I grew up in Chicago.'

Frustration mixes with the angry look on her face. 'Shit. You don't know.'

'Tell me.'

'I've already been judged. Found guilty. By the whole town. My own mother won't even speak to me.'

'I know you're feeling real bad, Caroline. You've got plenty of reason. Your stepfather tried to rape you.'

He notices her lip begin to tremble.

For the first time, he sees beyond her anger to the deep hurt. In her sad eyes, he glimpses the pain of betrayal she's feeling. He senses how fragile Caroline Hoffman really is. But he's got to prepare her for the next assault she's going to suffer – when the D.A. takes her apart on the stand.

'I'll need to know every single detail of what happened between you and the sheriff that night, Caroline. Even if there are some things that you'd rather not talk about. If I'm going to represent you . . .'

'You have to represent me. The court assigned you.

You don't really have a choice. Neither do I. We're stuck with each other. Like it or not.'

'Like it or not, I don't want any surprises when we walk into court.'

'Are you sure you're really a lawyer? You don't look old enough or—'

He gives her a hard, defiant look. 'White enough?'

'I was going to say "tough enough".' A faint smile curves Caroline Hoffman's lips.

He can't help smiling back.

Ben found himself pulled up at a red light on the corner of Beacon and Berkeley. He had no clear recollection of any part of the drive up to that moment. It gave him a start. He might have gone right through that red light. Caused a smash. Run someone down. He felt damn grateful that, even when his mind wasn't on the job, he could still trust his instincts. Up to a point.

12

Caroline's service was flooded with frantic phone calls from patients. Several stunned colleagues had called her at home. As had a string of reporters who'd somehow managed to get her unlisted number. Caroline let her machine pick up the messages. She felt besieged. Couldn't they even give her a chance to catch her breath, much less a little time and space to grieve?

Martin was dead. Two nights ago they'd made pasta for dinner, almost made love—

Caroline hugged herself tightly as she sat on the edge of her bed, still wearing her clothes from the previous night. She hadn't had the strength to get undressed when she got back from the morgue. Besides, it had seemed pointless. Pointless trying to sleep. Pointless to do much of anything.

The room was dark. She'd deliberately kept the curtains drawn. There were reporters camped out on her street. Curiosity seekers, too. *Peepers?* Caroline wished she could figure out some way to keep out the nightmare image of Martin on that metal slab.

Some time in the night, she had forced herself to turn on the radio and listen to a report of Martin's murder, the graphic detail of how he'd been found naked, a chain wrapped around his neck, in a janitor's closet at Logan. The theory was that the killer had picked him up in the terminal in much the same way as she'd seduced her first victim at the art museum on Tuesday evening. Caroline heard her name come up several times in the broadcast. She was referred to as 'the latest victim's colleague and *personal friend*'. There was also a 'disclosure, from an unnamed source, that Dr. Caroline Hoffman, accompanied by two detectives, was taken to the morgue to view the body of Dr. Martin Bassett—' The newscaster, a man, ended the report with a nervous chuckle and a warning to 'all you guys out there looking for a cheap thrill'.

Caroline went to the bathroom and threw up.

Dr. Alan Rogers's call came in at a little past seven. She wanted to leave him to the answering machine as she had the others. But it wouldn't be smart to ignore her boss. *You're not as smart as you think, Linny.* Her stepbrother's old refrain ambushed her as she picked up.

After a minute or two of the requisite expressions of shock and sorrow over Martin's murder, Rogers cleared his throat and abruptly got down to business. Caroline had expected – and dreaded – as much.

'I know this isn't a good time . . . but we've got a real . . . management problem on our hands.' Rogers paused.

Caroline heard him clear his throat again. 'You can't imagine the number of calls that have come in already from the media. The clinic's answering service has been swamped. We're inundated.'

'Yes. Same here.' Caroline had to be careful not to give the head of the Institute any hint of her distraught state of mind. Rogers might seize on it as an excuse to suggest a temporary leave of absence. Maybe even a permanent one. When he'd hired her three years ago, despite the prominence she'd already achieved in her field, he'd made it eminently clear that, given her history, he was going out on a limb for her—

Caroline panicked at the thought that she might not have her job to go back to. Her work was her life. It was what grounded her, gave her a sense of purpose.

No, it was even more than that. Who she was now – who she'd become – had been her way of showing them all. Her mother. Jesse Baush. The kids at school. Her whole damn town. Ironically, her stepfather Porter had been the one who'd encouraged her to *make the break*. Now she wondered if she ever really had. There was the saying – you can't go home again. But Caroline thought – you can never really get away, either.

'. . . media constantly dragging not only your name but that of the Institute into this investigation,' Rogers was saying.

'Martin worked at the Institute, Alan. It would be rather difficult . . .'

Rogers cut her off. 'It's not only the press. We've got many very upset patients to deal with. We treat so many high-profile people and naturally they're quite concerned about possible . . .'

'Exposure?'

'If that was meant as a double-entendre, it's not funny.'

'It never is,' Caroline said soberly.

'Let me speak frankly, Caroline. It's being implied on the news that you and Martin were . . . well, I know you were . . . friends, saw each other occasionally, but—'

Caroline felt a hot flush suffuse her face. 'Dating a colleague isn't a crime, Alan.' Even if her stepbrother tried to make it into one.

'Please, there's absolutely no reason to be defensive,' Rogers said, affronted. 'I'm not criticizing you.'

'I didn't think I was being defensive. What reason would you have for criticizing me?' One thing about having suffered adversity. You either gave in to it or you fought back. Caroline had long ago learned to be a fighter. 'I know what you're trying to say, Alan.' And she quoted him. 'We have a management problem on our hands. I realize that.'

Rogers exhaled heavily. 'And it's getting more complicated by the minute. I received an especially disturbing call this morning. From one of your patients.'

Caroline scowled. 'One of *my* patients?'

'And Martin's. He was seeing her for individual therapy and she was in one of your groups.'

'Tina King?' Tina was the only patient she and Martin currently shared in common. *Currently.* Sorrow chased across Caroline's face.

'Yes.'

'I can see that she'd be particularly upset.' What Caroline

was having trouble seeing was why Tina had called the head of the Institute, instead of phoning her.

'Then she's told you?' Rogers asked.

'Told me what?'

'That she was having an affair with Martin.'

Caroline was dumbfounded. 'What? Oh Alan, I'm sure that's not true. Martin would never . . .'

'I'm not saying it's true, Caroline. But I am saying that Miss King *believes* it's true. Has she been delusional in the past?'

'Suicidal but not delusional. I would think it's an intense transference reaction brought on by the trauma of . . . Martin's death.'

Caroline choked up. It was unbearable even to say the words, *Martin's death*, much less absorb the reality of his brutal murder. A part of her kept thinking that the phone would ring later that day. It would be Martin. Calling from Pittsburgh. Begging her to join him there for the week-end—

'Not that I'm suggesting that Miss King might have any-thing to do with these murders,' Rogers continued in a strained voice. 'But you can imagine how things can spin wildly out of control here.' After a disquieting pause, he asked, 'Are you planning to see patients today?'

'Yes. Absolutely,' Caroline replied quickly, not giving Rogers a chance to suggest otherwise.

'I read about those terrible murders,' Sylvia Fields said. 'About that violinist. And Dr. Bassett. I remember passing him in the hall here a couple of times. Dr. Bassett, that is.

He was so young and attractive. I remember what a nice smile he had—'

A great smile, Caroline couldn't help thinking. A caustic sadness spread through her. *Did you smile for the killer, too, Martin?*

'You must be very upset.'

Caroline shifted uncomfortably in her seat as her patient gave her a disturbingly searching look. 'Naturally, everyone here at the clinic—' *God, she was starting to sound like Rogers.* 'If you're concerned that I might be too upset to concentrate on what you want to talk about, Sylvia . . .'

'Well . . . really, I'm not sure what I want to talk about today. I usually try to have an . . . agenda for our sessions, but for some reason, this morning I seem to be having trouble focusing.'

Caroline knew what that felt like. 'When we left off last week, you mentioned you wanted to talk some more about Meg.'

Sylvia Fields sat straighter in her chair. She was a trim, attractive woman in her mid-forties. Her make-up was understated, skilfully applied. She wore her light brown hair short and her style of dress exuded both taste and sophistication. Today she was wearing a chic and snugly tailored pale grey merino wool suit with a softly feminine peach silk shirt. Sylvia Fields did not wear her sexual preference on her sleeve.

'You know how I feel about Meg,' Sylvia said. 'I've talked about her ad nauseam. I don't really know what good it does.'

'You mentioned last week that you were going to talk to her about your personal feelings. Did you?'

Sylvia vigorously shook her head. 'I lost my nerve. Anyway, I'm sure she knows. I'm also sure it makes her uncomfortable.'

'How do you think Meg feels towards you?'

'Nervous,' Sylvia said. 'I really do feel Meg has some serious problems with her sexual identity. In the five years I've known her I don't think she's gone out on more than a handful of dates. Ryan Gallagher, that's the draftsman I've spoken to you about, well, he's crazy about her.'

'How do you know?'

'Oh, it's obvious. Besides, he told me. I think he sees me as a kind of . . . maternal figure.' Sylvia's cheeks reddened. 'I don't really mind. I suppose I get some vicarious pleasure, hearing Ryan talk about her.'

'Do you ever feel jealous?' Caroline asked gently. *What about her own feelings of jealousy? Was she jealous of some crazed killer who'd seduced her lover?*

'I suppose I would be if Meg showed any serious interest in him. Ryan's a very nice-looking fellow. Bright. Comes from a good family. I could easily count a dozen women at work who'd give their right arm to date him.'

'Not including Meg.'

Sylvia nodded. 'Of course Meg may not want to date someone from the firm. I could certainly understand that. Mixing business with pleasure. It can get very . . . messy.'

Tell me about it.

'But I've seen Meg in social situations,' Sylvia went on. 'Parties and such for clients. Men are always hitting on her.

But I've never seen her so much as flirt back. If anything, she gives them the cold shoulder.'

Caroline kept her expression blank. Apparently, Sylvia Fields knew nothing about Meg Spaulding's secret life.

Seducing strangers in public places.

Like museums? Airports?

Ever since her sessions with Natalie Deutch and Steven Kramer, Caroline had been greatly disturbed about the possibility that Meg Spaulding was the woman at the museum and at the airport. She kept trying to rationalize that Meg was only one of any number of women who might have picked up Peter Korza and Martin; knowing as Caroline did, how surprisingly common that sort of sexual misbehaviour was. Beyond that, it was difficult for Caroline to picture Meg as a serial killer. And Steve Kramer? Wasn't it equally hard to picture him?

'I'm sure you're concerned that Meg's quit therapy. As am I,' Sylvia was saying. 'I was thinking of giving her brother a call. See if he'd talk her into coming back in to see you. Ned seems to be the only one with any real influence on her.'

Caroline had to use all her willpower to concentrate on Sylvia. 'Meg told you she quit therapy?'

'Yes. This morning. When I called her at her hotel in New York . . .'

'Meg's in New York? When did she—?'

'I think I know what triggered Meg's decision to stop treatment,' Sylvia carried on her own train of thought. 'Her mother's been committed again. I'm sure it's brought the whole trauma back – only seventeen, and practically witnessing her mother killing her father. Then the trial. Seeing her mother get carted off to a locked ward at a state psychiatric hospital. Better than a jail cell, but still . . . The minute she told me about her mother's relapse, I knew Meg was in trouble.'

Caroline nodded slowly. She, too, knew in her gut that Meg was in trouble.

13

Chief Washburn bit into his second donut of the morning, then absently brushed the cinnamon dust off the report sitting open on his desk. He didn't, however, glance back down at the document. 'You've got zilch here, DeSanto.'

'It's not zilch that Dr. Hoffman can be linked to both murder victims.'

'I don't see much in the way of a link with Korza.'

'She was there. At the scene.'

'Looking for a suicidal patient who phoned her. Don't you think that patient's the one you should be getting a fix on?'

DeSanto dug her hands into the pockets of her blazer. 'We're trying to track him down, Chief. He hasn't been home. I'm going down to the lab where he works later this morning. But, to get back to the shrink for a second . . .'

'You get anything more from that museum guard? You show him a photo of Dr. Hoffman?'

DeSanto scowled. 'Yeah, I showed him a photo of her.

He says the build's similar, but the woman he saw wore dark glasses, was heavily made up and had long black hair – according to the lab's report, the black hair came from a wig. No way for him to make an ID. Unless we doll the doc up.'

Washburn popped another piece of his donut into his mouth, chewing slowly, taking time to digest both the food and DeSanto's suggestion.

'What's with you two?' he remarked after he finally swallowed.

'Me and Hoffman?'

'You and Jesse Baush. I know he doesn't have a particularly warm spot in his heart for his sister . . .'

'Stepsister.'

Washburn arched a brow as he continued. 'But it wouldn't be smart for you to let that influence your investigation, DeSanto.'

'That's not what I'm doing.'

'I hear Hoffman IDed Bassett last night down at the morgue.'

DeSanto shifted her weight. 'That's right.'

'Where was Green? What was Baush doing there with you?'

'Green's kid was sick.'

Washburn gave her a look that said it all. DeSanto knew she better watch her ass.

The chief brushed donut crumbs off his grey jacket. 'Two fine, upstanding men have been brutally murdered and that's making everybody in this city right up to the mayor real anxious. Nobody likes having a serial killer around town. And the fact that the killer may be some hot-looking broad doing these upstanding guys . . . well, that makes it all the more sensational. I don't want to be left with shit floating in the pot with this. Get me something I can flush down. That will stay down.'

DeSanto nodded.

'We sure as hell don't want to be accused by the press and the public of making a *rush to judgement* now, do we? Nor do we want to turn this investigation into a personal vendetta. Hoffman's a respected psychiatrist in this city. And right now you've got diddly squat . . .'

'Jesse told me that wound in his father's gut took four hours of surgery to repair. Hoffman didn't just poke him with those scissors, Chief. You made the collar. You heard plenty of the testimony in court. Including Jesse's. You tell me the jury didn't bring in the wrong verdict,' she challenged.

Washburn finished off his donut before answering her. 'Don't you think I'd like to solve this mess pronto? But we're not exactly sitting on a mountain of evidence here. All I'm saying is, if and when you bring me in one, that mountain better not be resting on a fucking toothpick.'

14

'I'm sorry, but Ben Tabor's on a leave of absence from the firm.' The Bostonian receptionist sounded uncannily like JFK.

'When is he due back?' Caroline could hear the panic surface in her voice.

There was an overlong pause. 'Would you like to speak to one of Mr. Tabor's associates?'

'No. I'd like to speak to Mr. Tabor.'

'I'm sorry . . .'

'Yes, I know. He's on a leave of absence. Could you give me a number where I could reach him?' Caroline had already found out Tabor's home number was unlisted.

'I'm not permitted to give out that information,' the receptionist said brusquely.

'I'm a former client of his. And something has come up that I really need to discuss with him . . .'

'I'll connect you to Philip Mason. He's handling Mr. Tabor's clients at this time.'

Before Caroline could object, her call was transferred to
Mr. Mason's personal secretary.

'Can I help you?'

'Yes, I hope so. This is Miss Simmons at L.L. Bean's catalogue department. We have a package for a Mr. Benjamin
Tabor, but the sender didn't know the street number for his
office . . .'

'Oh, Mr. Tabor isn't with us at this time. It would probably be better to mail the package directly to his home
address. Just a sec.'

Caroline held her breath.

'It's 1532 Memorial Drive, Cambridge. The zip is – hold
on—'

'That's all right,' Caroline said. 'I've got the zip code on
my computer here.'

Caroline was warned by her secretary that there were a slew
of reporters and cameramen hanging around outside the
Institute. Ducking out her private office exit after her last
appointment of the day, Caroline stealthily made her way
down to the basement and out a rarely used fire door to her
car. She drove straight to Cambridge. If she put it off, she
might lose her nerve.

1532 Memorial Drive formed the centre of a U-shaped
complex of three seven-storey brick buildings wedged
between two modern glass and concrete structures housing
married students from Harvard. While the small post-
World War II development was architecturally
unremarkable and even slightly rundown, its situation over-
looking the Charles River and its proximity to the

prestigious Ivy League college made it a definite high-rent proposition.

Caroline hesitated outside Ben Tabor's building. She was more anxious about this reunion than she'd anticipated. Fourteen years was a long time. Time she'd used to resolutely distance herself from a horrendous nightmare. Time she'd used to *reconstruct* herself. Everyone in her current life had bought the new, improved Caroline Hoffman. Everyone but her. Caroline couldn't escape her past. It didn't take much to make it come flooding back. Jesse Baush had the power to do that and so, in his own way, had Ben Tabor.

Caroline checked her watch. Nearly 6 p.m. Dinnertime. Not the ideal moment to intrude on Ben and his wife – what was her name? Kimberly? Kim? They'd met only once. At the celebratory dinner Ben Tabor had treated her to at the sumptuous dining room of the Ritz Carleton Hotel. A dual celebration. Her *not guilty* verdict, and his new job as a criminal attorney at the prestigious law form of Lambert and Doyle Associates. Only the third African-American to come on board and, at twenty-eight, the youngest.

Ben Tabor was so full of himself that evening, acknowledging and making a joke of it. As far as Caroline was concerned, that just made him endearing rather than self-centred.

As for Ben's wife, while Caroline remembered she was present at the dinner, that was really all she did remember about the woman.

She'd hardly got her name out over the intercom before Ben Tabor buzzed Caroline into his building.

His apartment was on the fifth floor. The hallway was narrow and dimly lit. A strong but not altogether unpleasant smell of onions and roasting meat hung in the air. When she got to his door, she heard the dead bolt turn even before she'd lifted her hand to knock. As the door opened, she nervously stepped back.

The tall, lean man standing in the doorway was in shadow, the apartment even more murkily lit than the corridor. Those cooking aromas definitely weren't wafting from here. It smelled of stale air and cigarette smoke.

For a moment, Caroline almost thought she'd come to the wrong apartment. 'Ben?'

He stepped aside, his movements uncharacteristically slow. Had he been drinking? The man she remembered was agile, quick. She vividly recalled how she'd had to practically run to keep pace with him – her long legs notwithstanding – when they'd be walking through the corridors of the courthouse.

Cautiously, Caroline stepped over the threshold into the apartment.

'How'd you track me down?' Ben asked.

She was taken aback by the surly greeting. 'I used the old mail-order ploy.'

He gave a distracted shrug, then gestured towards the living room. 'Wanna drink? I can probably dig up a dusty bottle of Scotch.'

Well, at least he wasn't an alcoholic. Unless he was on the wagon.

'I remember you used to drink martinis,' Caroline said. Really, she'd only deduced that from their one celebration dinner at the Ritz. Ben had had a couple of martinis that evening, a rare T-bone steak, baked potato with butter, no sour cream. Funny the things she remembered about that night. About Ben.

Caroline turned to face the man in whom she was about to put her trust. Hell. Her one-time lawyer looked in worse shape than she was. He had a permanent scowl line across his brow, giving him an angry *don't mess with me* look. He was badly in need of a shave, and a haircut. Then there were his clothes. Hardly the GQ look Caroline had expected. Grubby sweatshirt, battered jeans, and old green high-top sneakers *sans* laces. Taken as a whole, Ben Tabor looked wrecked.

When she first knew him, he'd been the kind of handsome that would stop women dead in their tracks with his movie-star chiselled features and sexual charisma. He'd still stop them. But they'd be a little wary. She certainly was.

Ben gestured again towards the living room. 'You want that drink?'

Caroline shook her head.

'You want to leave?'

'No.'

'Then go inside and sit down. And stop staring at me like I'm some sort of genetic aberration.'

She flushed. 'Sorry.'

She walked into the lawyer's beautifully proportioned but starkly appointed living room. Putty-coloured walls and carpeting seemed to meld together. A textured off-white-on-white modular sofa flanked one wall. The opposite wall was

given over to a massive built-in storage unit faced entirely in
a pearl-grey plastic laminate.

'I gather from your grim expression you don't approve of
the decorating,' Ben said drily.

'Maybe this is a bad time . . .'

'I assume that's precisely why you're here.'

One thing about Ben hadn't changed. He was still blunt
and still adept at manoeuvring you into the hot seat.

Caroline had improved at that manoeuvre herself.
'What's wrong, Ben? Are you sick?'

He hesitated, then tapped the right side of his skull with
his index finger. 'It's all in my head.' His full lips curled up
in a wry smile, but his enormous dark eyes remained una-
mused. It was, however, the intractable sadness she saw in his
eyes that disturbed Caroline. Professionally. And personally.

'Are you getting treatment, Ben?'

'Ambulance chasing, Doctor?'

'Very funny.'

Ben reached in his jeans pocket for a squashed pack of
Lucky Strikes. He tapped one out, stuck it in his mouth,
picked up a matchbook off the coffee table. No more
matches in it. He felt around his pockets, cursed softly after
coming up empty-handed. 'You wouldn't have a light?'

'Sorry.'

He kept the unlit cigarette in his mouth as he walked
over to the storage unit and rifled around until he retrieved
a matchbook from one of the drawers. The flame lit his
jagged features.

She watched him take a deep drag and exhale slowly.
'You want to talk about it, Ben?'

'You've got your own problems, Caroline.'

As if she needed reminding.

'Can I have a cigarette?' she asked.

He passed his to her and lit another one for himself.

Caroline took an equally long drag and shuddered. 'I quit three years ago.'

'You think this is a good time to resurrect bad habits?'

It was only at that moment that Caroline admitted to herself how much she'd foolishly romanticized this man who'd once saved her neck. Ben Tabor, Public Defender. Her knight in shining armour. Well, he'd sure as hell rusted over the years.

A silence hung between them.

'So, you want to talk about it?' Ben threw her own line back at her. Maybe that was why he hadn't immediately blown her off. Misery loves company, right? And maybe Caroline's company, in particular. Even with the drawn look on her face, the dark circles under her eyes, the nervous tension radiating from her, she still had that special something.

Caroline was infuriated with herself and with him. But for all her upset, the psychiatrist in her couldn't help wondering why Ben Tabor was trying so hard to provoke her. It curbed some of her anger. 'I assume you've read about the two recent . . . murders. The violinist and . . . Dr. Martin Bassett. The psychiatric resident who . . .'

'Was your lover.' He spoke matter-of-factly, taking direct aim.

She wanted nothing more than to return the shot, but found herself speechless.

Ben felt guilty. 'Sit down, Caroline. Please.'

Hearing the tenderness surface finally in his voice was Caroline's undoing. She covered her face with her hands as tears sprang to her eyes. She said something inane about the cigarette smoke.

Ben took the cigarette out from between her fingers, stubbing it with his in a nearby ashtray. Then he placed his palm flat on her back and guided her to the sofa.

'I'll get you that drink,' he said, thinking to himself she wasn't the only one backsliding emotionally. Until she'd arrived, he was forty-two going on sixty. Now, suddenly, he was feeling more like twenty-eight. More like he felt when he first knew her. And he most definitely did not want to resuscitate those feelings.

He went off to the kitchen where he found the booze and then took a few minutes to pull himself together.

Caroline did the same in his absence.

When Ben returned to the living room carrying an unopened bottle of Scotch and a single lowball tumbler half filled with ice cubes, Caroline was sitting stiffly on the edge of her seat.

'Aren't you having one?' she asked as he sat down beside her, handing over the glass.

He fumbled with the bottle cap. 'Booze doesn't agree with me these days.' That was putting it mildly. One shot and his head felt like a goddamn gorilla was trying to wrench it right off of his neck.

He started to fill her glass.

She said, 'Stop,' when he'd barely covered the ice, but he kept pouring until the tumbler was almost filled.

'I'm not in that bad shape.' But Caroline took a good, long swallow nonetheless, then held on to the glass. 'I need some legal advice, Ben. And I may need representation. The police are . . .'

'Are you being charged?'

Caroline gasped, not so much at his question but at the almost off-handed way it was spoken. 'No. God, no. It's just that the police – Jesse – you remember my stepbrother Jesse Baush.'

'Yeah, I remember,' Ben said. How could he have forgotten? At Caroline's trial, he'd shoved Jesse into the hot seat and kept him there, burning up, for hours.

'He's a cop here in Boston now. A lieutenant. In Vice.'

Ben smirked. 'Doesn't surprise me.'

'Only he's been butting his nose into the murder investigation.'

'That doesn't surprise me either.'

Caroline was depressed to hear the note of detachment return.

'Jesse's been harassing me, threatening me. He actually thinks I could have done it. It's crazy. He's crazy.'

'Why crazy? The cops have every good reason to suspect you might have committed the murders. According to what I've read in the papers, you showed at the museum the night the musician was killed, you were *involved* with the second victim, a colleague of yours—'

Caroline jumped up, the Scotch spilling down her moss green wool skirt, onto the carpet. 'I made a mistake coming here,' she said tightly. 'I thought you, of all people would—' She spluttered to a stop.

Ben rose. He took the glass from her trembling hand. His own hand wasn't all that steady.

'I'm just giving it to you from their perspective. Don't kid yourself, Caroline. If all that was going on was that your step-brother had it in for you, that could be dealt with pretty easily. But that's not all it is. If Jesse Baush didn't know you from Adam, you'd still be under investigation.'

His frank take on her situation hung between them as his dark eyes fixed on her face. Caroline felt horribly exposed while, by contrast, Ben looked remote, untouchable.

'I can't believe this is happening to me again. It's only a matter of time before . . . before my whole past gets raked over by the tabloids.' Her reputation was already taking blows thanks to Nugent's television broadcast. What if she was arrested . . . ? Even that slight possibility generated so much fear she could hardly breathe.

Ben knew Caroline didn't deserve the hand she was being dealt. But he was out of the lawyer business. Maybe for good. It wasn't that he didn't want to help Caroline. He just didn't have it in him any longer. And Caroline needed a lawyer who could give a full hundred percent.

Caroline saw a flicker in Ben's eyes and pressed on. If she couldn't win *him* over, who would she be able to get to believe her? Believe in her? If Ben turned his back on her, she was lost. 'Do I actually have to tell you I'm innocent? No, I forgot. Lawyers don't want to hear protestations of innocence or admissions of guilt from their clients. It only complicates matters. Your job is simply to come up with a slam-dunk defence. Not to judge . . .'

'Caroline, you're . . .'

'Right, I know,' she interrupted. 'I'm not your client now.'

'I'm not taking any clients. I'm on leave.'

'Why?'

He refused to be drawn. 'Look, I can make a referral . . .'

'I think I may know the murderer, Ben.'

That got his attention. She hastily capitalized on it, telling him about the phone call from Steve Kramer the night of the first murder, about Kramer's voyeurist addiction and his predilection for following women. Then, she told him about Meg Spaulding and her addiction to picking up men in public places.

She gave Ben a bleak look. 'I may be all wrong. I hope to God I am, but . . .'

'What about your voyeur?' Ben interrupted. 'Could be he's the guilty one.'

'I know that.'

'Have you told anyone else about your suspicions?'

'These people are patients of mine, Ben. I'm bound by confidentiality.'

'Unless you're sure one of them's a killer. A killer who's as likely to strike again as not.'

'I'm not sure of anything. What I need to do – have to do – is further evaluate these patients clinically. But the truth is, I'm worried Jesse's going to have me behind bars before I can manage either. Jesse hates me. He really believes I'm some kind of a monster.'

Caroline could feel tears threatening again. 'I'm scared, Ben.' A confession she had a hard enough time making to herself, much less to anyone else. But she'd revealed things to Ben Tabor before. He'd been one of the few people in her life with whom she'd ever risked sharing secrets.

Caroline despaired when all he did was nod distractedly. Obviously he didn't give a shit about her now. Probably never did. Humiliation quickly dried her tears.

'I shouldn't have come,' she said coolly. 'I'm sorry I disturbed you, Ben.'

Ben smiled faintly. 'Hell, I was disturbed long before you got here, Caroline.'

Caroline lifted a brow. 'Did you start to get disturbed before or after your wife left you?'

The corners of Ben's mouth lifted even as he told himself he deserved that jab as payback. 'Curiosity killed the cat, Caroline.'

'Curiosity keeps us searching for answers, Ben.'

'I'm not looking for answers. You are.' He reached into the back pocket of his jeans, dug out his wallet, flipped it open and removed a business card. 'Here. This is the guy you want. I'll give him a ring and let him know what's what.'

'You don't give a goddamn fuck what's what,' Caroline said acidly, her anger and frustration at the boiling point.

Ben stuck the card in her jacket pocket. 'They don't come any smarter. Or tougher.' He looked to see if his remark brought back a flash from the past, but Caroline looked merely pissed off. 'And I'll even pass on a piece of free advice,' Ben added. 'For starters, don't talk to anyone – cops, reporters, colleagues, friends, lovers – until you have Phil Mason on board.'

Caroline shot him a chilly look. 'For starters, Ben, I'm really sorry I talked to *you*.'

Alone again in his apartment, Ben dragged deeply on a cigarette as he snatched up Caroline's tumbler. He glared at it. Switched the glare to the bottle of Scotch on his coffee table. Seconds later, he was downing a healthy – make that unhealthy – double.

So maybe he wanted his head to erupt. At least it would drive out all his censurable thoughts about Caroline.

Caroline sat behind the wheel of her car, the engine running. She couldn't get herself to shift into gear. How symbolic of her life at the moment.

She needed a jump-start. Had counted on Ben Tabor, even more than she'd realized, to provide it for her. That would teach her to depend on someone else for *breakdown assistance*. Hadn't she learned that lesson a long time ago?

Caroline could still call up that vision of herself as an eighteen-year-old freshman at Boston State. Just another bright, pretty co-ed with no visible baggage. She'd even managed to make a few friends. She was more studious than most of them, more determined to succeed. For the first time in her life, she could walk down corridors without people whispering behind her back, pointing at her. *Did you know—? Have you heard the latest—? Can you believe she actually—?*

That first year at college marked the birth of her reinvention. Caroline Hoffman, the daughter of a happy homemaker and a revered small-town sheriff. She omitted telling her college pals about her belligerent, vindictive step-brother. Omitted mentioning that the comparatively blissful domestic scene she painted had been in existence for all of two years. Omitted any mention of the miserable years that had preceded them. Guilelessly believed the bad times were over.

It was a snowy winter night when Caroline got her rude awakening. She was studying for a sociology mid-term. Her friend Rick popped his head into her room and invited her to join a bunch of kids who were heading over to a popular bar down on Kenmore Square. She tried to beg off, saying she didn't have an ID to get admitted, but Rick said he knew the guy at the door and there'd be no problem.

There was no problem. Until she practically ran smack into a guy blocking her passage as she headed for the ladies' room. The back of the bar was so dimly lit, she couldn't make out the man's features. Just that he was broad, muscular and smelled of a mix of whisky and Old Spice cologne. That should have been a tip off.

'It's been a long time, Linny. I sure as hell never expected to see you again. Small world, huh?'

She froze, instantly recognizing the voice. She started to wheel around towards the exit, but he snatched hold of her arm.

Caroline tried to wrench free, but he only tightened his grip, pulling her closer to him.

'Let go of me . . .'

'How's your momma? She still mad at me? How 'bout you, Lin? You still mad at me for taking off?' He breathed the words into her ear so there was no chance she'd miss hearing them over the din.

'I *said* let go of me, Walter. I'm warning you—'

If he heard her, he gave no sign of it. 'You look terrific, Linny. Really terrific. All grown up. Why don't we cut out of here, go have a drink some place quiet? Catch up on old times?'

She shoved her hands hard against his chest. 'I mean it—'

Walter Jackson chuckled, his hands clasping hers. 'Okay, okay, I see you're with some other guy. Actually I was having a nice little chat with him over at the bar a few minutes ago. Hear you're a college girl now. What say I stop by your dorm room one of these nights real soon.' It wasn't a question.

The second Jackson released her, Caroline fled through the bar and out the door. Rick chased after her. She let him drive her back to school, but she wouldn't say a word to him.

As soon as she got up to her dorm, she locked and bolted her door. Shaking, she frantically called up the one person she could count on to come to her aid. One of the only people in the world she could trust.

Caroline began to feel better as soon as she heard her step-father's soothing voice on the phone – *Don't worry about a thing, Linny. I'll drive right down. I'll take care of everything.*

Porter Baush took care of everything, all right. He showed up at her dorm in the middle of the night and put his arms around her. But his warped notion of comforting her ended in attempted rape.

15

A flight attendant on the late afternoon shuttle to Boston handed Meg Spaulding a current edition of the *Boston Express*. It was the first Boston paper she'd seen since Tuesday morning: CHAIN-WIELDING KILLER SOUGHT IN TWO SEX SLAYINGS: MS. ALBERT DESALVO AKA THE BOSTON STRANGLER, ON THE LOOSE?

Meg's whole body wrenched taut as she began reading the article. When she got to the part about the second victim, Dr. Martin Bassett, being not only a psychiatrist at the Institute, but someone who may have had a *'personal relationship with his colleague, Dr. Caroline Hoffman'* Meg gasped audibly. How ironic that they'd be attracted to the same type of man. Meg continued reading until she got to the paragraph describing the striking woman with long, dark hair – possibly a wig – wearing a short black, tight-fitting dress, spiked heels, and sunglasses, who'd approached Peter Korza at the museum on Tuesday night, shortly before the time of his murder.

Her heartbeat pounded in her ears. The air from the vent above her seemed to stink. The old man sitting next to her was taking up all of the space, pushing her off. At the same time, the airplane was growing smaller, closing in around her as she found herself gasping for air.

Meg listened to Caroline's message on her machine when she got home to her apartment around 6 p.m. Her psychiatrist's entreaty for her to return to the therapy group or, at least, for an individual session to discuss termination was wedged between five other messages: two from Ryan Gallagher reminding her about the Friday meeting and suggesting dinner afterwards; one from the ever-solicitous Sylvia hoping she was feeling better; and one from her brother Ned asking her to meet him for dinner that evening at *Il Notte* if she got back early enough. The last message was from Steve Kramer. *Hope you had a safe and pleasant flight back, Meg. I'll be in all night. Let's make plans.*

Meg pressed the *Don't Save* button, deleting all the messages. If only it was as easy to delete some of the messengers.

Ned Spaulding was halfway through his *antipasto* when he spotted his sister enter the restaurant. So did almost all the other male customers in the bustling Charles Street trattoria.

Oblivious to the stir she caused, Meg made a beeline for her brother's table by the window. She slid stiffly into the seat across from him.

Meg filled her glass from the bottle of Chianti. 'You go over to the hospital yet?'

She lifted the wine to her lips. Took a sip. Set the goblet back down on the red-and-white checkered cloth. 'No.'

'I ran by after I closed the gallery. She was sleeping. The nurse asked me not to wake her,' he said.

'I can't believe she's been wandering around for days,' Meg said.

He stared at her intently.

'What? What is it?' she asked testily. Good as she generally was at concealment, Ned had a knack for making her feel uncomfortably transparent.

'You look even worse than you did yesterday morning.'

A young waiter with a winning smile approached the table. 'He doesn't think I look so bad,' she murmured provocatively.

Ned scowled.

The waiter presented her menu with a flourish. Meg waved it away. 'I'm not eating.'

'Of course you are. Tony, bring her a bowl of minestrone. And then some of your . . .'

'Just the soup,' Meg told Tony. She looked across at her brother insistently. 'Ned . . .'

He gave the waiter a nod.

She smiled gratefully. 'I'm planning to go see Mom tomorrow. I've got a meeting on a new project in the afternoon, but as soon as I'm done I'll head right for the hospital.'

'I wish you'd talk to me, Meg. I know something's wrong.'

She didn't want to talk or even think about it. She wanted all the terrible things that had been happening to go away.

Ned took a piece of crusty Italian bread from the wicker basket and buttered it for her. 'Did everything work out okay? With that five grand?'

Meg flushed. 'Oh Ned, I know I was supposed to wire that money back to you from New York . . .'

'Hey, that's not why I asked. You know that.'

She broke off a pebble-sized piece of the bread, rolled it absently between her thumb and index finger. If she liquidated all her assets – including savings, stocks, CDs – she had a little over twenty thousand dollars holed away for a rainy day. Returning five grand to her brother left her five grand shy of the twenty thousand Kramer was now demanding.

'If it's not too big a problem for you, Ned, could I put off paying you back for . . . ?'

Ned's hand shot out, snatching hold of hers. 'You don't have to pay it back, period, for chrissakes.'

Meg smiled gratefully.

'Not if you tell me what it's all about.'

She angrily wrenched her hand free. 'If there are conditions . . .'

'I'm sorry. I didn't mean that. I was only trying to be the big brother, I guess.'

'But you're not my big brother. I'm your big sister.'

'I know, Meg.' He sounded hurt.

Before she could apologize, the waiter arrived with her steaming bowl of minestrone soup and Ned's plate of veal piccata.

She managed a couple of spoonfuls of soup before she nudged the bowl away.

Ned noticed but let it go. 'Your boss, Sylvia, called me this afternoon. She was worried about you. Said you'd just quit therapy. I thought you were going to quit weeks ago. That you only went in the first place because Sylvia kept badgering you.'

'What difference does it make? What did Sylvia want?'

'She wanted me to talk you into going back to your shrink.' Ned rolled his eyes before turning more serious. 'Something's wrong, isn't it? That's the real reason you went into therapy. You never do anything you don't want to do.'

Meg looked at her brother sharply.

'I always thought you'd turn to me if you were having emotional problems, Meg.'

'It was no big deal, Ned. I was just sorting some stuff out. Stuff to do with work.'

'How come you told her about Mom?'

'My therapist?'

'No. Sylvia. You told her Mom was back in the hospital.'

Meg flushed. 'She . . . she caught me off-guard.'

They shared a look. Both siblings had made a pact long ago – long before their father's murder and their mother's hospitalization – to keep family business just that. Family business.

Steve Kramer slammed the phone down in disgust. No answer from Meg. This time the machine didn't pick up either. He glanced around his small, dingy galley kitchen. A plate of take-out sweet and sour chicken congealed on the narrow counter. There were a couple of swallows left in his beer glass. He scowled, thinking back to a time not so long ago when dinner had consisted of a delicious home-cooked roast, a good glass or two – or three – of a fine red Bordeaux or a fruity white Chardonnay. Had Marge sold off his wine cellar along with everything else he'd cared about?

He opened the fridge, pulled out another Rolling Rock.

He walked over to the counter, beer bottle in hand, snatched a piece of chicken and popped it in his mouth. Next to the plate was one of his XXX-rated porno flicks. He chuckled. At least now he could watch TV while he ate.

He stuck the cassette in the VCR, set his plate on the coffee table and settled down on his sofa.

A sharp rap on his front door brought Kramer up short. He was doubly shaken by the interruption. It wasn't like he was used to having people stop by his crummy apartment in Watertown. His so-called friends had dropped him like a hot potato. And he hadn't exactly been spending much of his time cultivating new ones.

Another rap. This one accompanied by a male voice calling out his name.

'Who's there?' Kramer called back nervously, hitting the *mute* button on his remote.

'Police.'

Kramer froze in panic. *Cops. Shit. Oh shit shit shit.*

'We'd like to talk to you, Mr. Kramer.'

Mr. Kramer. When he was *Dr.* Kramer he'd felt a lot less vulnerable. A third and sharper rap made him lurch up. He was halfway to the door when he remembered the video-tape still playing silently. He hurried back, ejected the tape and shoved it in a cabinet with the rest of his voluminous porn stash. Thousands of dollars' worth. He locked the cabinet and pocketed the key.

'Kramer.'

'Coming,' he shouted with a dry laugh at the double entendre. But even that flash of dark humour was extinguished as he opened the door.

'What do you want?'

'Take it easy, Kramer. We're not here to hassle you.' Alfonse Green held up his badge. 'Me and my partner just want to talk to you.'

Lieutenant Amy DeSanto flashed Kramer a friendly smile.

'About what?' Kramer asked warily, standing firmly in the doorway, keeping the cops at bay in the hall.

'We don't need to make this everybody else's business,' DeSanto said, glancing up and down the corridor.

Reluctantly, Kramer stepped back. DeSanto and Green walked past him into the small, sparsely furnished living room.

'I was about to go out.'

'You're out a lot,' DeSanto said. 'Where do you go, Steve? You haven't shown for work since Tuesday. You haven't been hanging around the house. We've come by a couple of times.'

'I've been extremely upset . . . about getting arrested at that movie theatre.'

'Where were you before you decided to go watch a porno flick?' DeSanto asked laconically.

'Nowhere.'

DeSanto smiled. 'You had to be somewhere.'

'I was at home.'

The smile on the lieutenant's face vanished. 'All evening?'

Kramer's eyes narrowed, but he could feel the sweat beading on his brow. 'What's this about? If you're trying to harass me . . .'

'No one's harassing you, Kramer,' DeSanto said coolly. 'It was a simple question.'

'And I gave you a simple answer. I was here. Home.'

'You didn't go out at all?'

'I went out around eleven. I wish to God I'd stayed in *all* night, believe me.'

'But you were feeling horny, or rather hornier, and went cruising at a jerk-off joint,' DeSanto elaborated, glancing around the room. She sauntered over to the window, pulling back the café curtain. A pricey pair of 70mm zoom binoculars were resting on the sill.

Kramer cursed silently. And his heart started working overtime as he watched the detective idly lift up the binoculars to her eyes and gaze out at the windows of the apartment building directly across the street.

'What else do you want?' Kramer demanded uneasily.

DeSanto, looking like she was enjoying the little drama, pivoted slowly around, binoculars still held to her eyes as she zeroed in on Kramer. 'Interesting, your psychiatrist working in the same place as that head-shrinker that bought it yesterday. Did you know Dr. Martin Bassett?'

'No.'

DeSanto lowered the binoculars. 'Did you ever see them together?'

'Who?'

'Caroline Hoffman and Martin Bassett.'

'No.'

'How about Hoffman and Peter Korza?'

'Who?'

'The violinist who ended up with a chain wrapped around his throat at the Bullfinch Art Museum,' Green contributed.

'No,' Kramer muttered. But his eyes skidded off the detective's face.

'You see Hoffman at the museum?' DeSanto pressed.

'No. I mean . . . I wasn't at the museum, so I couldn't—'

DeSanto lifted the binoculars, examined them like she might be in the market for a pair, then shifted her gaze to Kramer. 'Hoffman was there. Supposedly looking for you, Steve. She claims you called her. That you were at the museum.'

'Were you at the museum Tuesday night?' Green asked.

'No.'

'Did you phone Dr. Hoffman that night?'

'No.'

'Why would she lie?'

'Maybe she was . . . confused. Maybe someone else called.'

Kramer cringed as DeSanto's gaze fixed on him. It was as though she could see clear through to the back of his brain.

'Maybe you didn't call her because you knew she wasn't home,' DeSanto said.

Kramer looked confused. 'What do you mean?'

'Because you saw her, Steve. Maybe you just didn't recognize her. At first.'

'What are you talking about?' Kramer was truly baffled.

But DeSanto looked very sure of herself. 'In that wig and all. When she was hitting on Korza. Then you followed them. Wanted to watch the action. That's your passion, isn't it, Steve? Watching?'

'Do you have any luggage?'

'No . . . I . . . My apartment's being painted and the fumes . . . I live just . . . down the street.'

'I understand completely.' He gave her a rakish smile. He was young, mid-twenties. Angular features. Hawkish nose. Dark brown hair cut short. Electric blue eyes.

'Would you like a queen-size or king-size? We've got doubles too, but most folks like the extra elbow room.'

'It . . . doesn't matter.'

He retrieved a card-key from a drawer, slipped it into a small folder and held it out to her. 'Room 1202. King-sized bed. You should be very comfortable.'

'Thanks.' She took the key packet, but the clerk held on to it for an extra couple of moments.

'Are you okay? You look kinda pale. Those paint fumes can really do a number on a person. Tell you what. I'm off duty in – like twenty minutes. I could get you something for your stomach. Bring it up . . .'

'No thanks.'

'It wouldn't be any trouble. I know just what you need.'

Caroline stared at him dubiously. 'Do you?' Without waiting for a reply, she turned and headed for the elevator.

Twenty minutes later, Caroline lay naked on her king-sized bed in room 1202. The room was in darkness and she was just drifting off when there was a soft rap on her door. Caroline didn't move.

'I got that bromo for you like I promised.'

She didn't respond.

Another rap. 'Look, I can use my passkey. Let myself in. Unless you have an objection. Just say the word.'

She said nothing.

Her eyes closed as she heard the card key slip into the slot. When she heard the click of the lock, Caroline opened her eyes, slowly turning her head towards the door as it opened.

The door got no further than an inch or two before it jammed. 'Hey, you got the safety latch on?'

Caroline stared silently at the crack of light seeping into the room from the hallway.

A sliver of light in the darkness.

Rolling onto her side, Caroline heard the door close.

She hugged herself tightly, shut her eyes. A wave of relief carried her over the edge into sleep.

Friday

⊗

16

People sombrely – many tearful – filed inside St. Luke's Chapel, a small Episcopal church on Boylston Street in the Back Bay, for Martin Bassett's memorial service. Family, colleagues, friends going all the way back to grammar school. Martin had been very well liked. Very popular.

Outside the church, swarms of reporters and photographers, cordoned off by the police behind wooden barriers, were shouting questions and photographing the mourners. Caroline, wearing dark glasses, a black suit, her hair tucked under a wide-brimmed black hat, almost sneaked inside without attention. But just as she was starting up the church steps, she felt a hand on her shoulder.

'You always did look good in black, Linny.'

The instant Caroline made the mistake of turning towards her stepbrother, flashlights fired off in her face. No question the media thought anyone a police detective approached at this tabloid-worthy event might be of interest to their readers.

'This isn't the time, Jesse.' Caroline spoke between clenched teeth. She saw that her stepbrother had forgone his bomber jacket for a plain blue suit, white shirt, striped tie. The last time she'd seen him in a suit was at their parents' wedding. No. That wasn't the last time, she remembered with a start. The last time was at his father's funeral—

'We wondered if you'd show,' Jesse said as Lieutenant Amy DeSanto came up beside him. The female cop was also dressed in a blue suit.

'I stopped by your place last night – must've been close to midnight – you know, to catch up on old family news and stuff. Only no one was home. I hung around for quite a while, but you never showed. Lieutenant DeSanto and I thought maybe you'd decided to take some *vacation* time. Or maybe you were just spending the night at a *friend's* place.'

'It's none of your goddamn business where . . .'

'Okay. That's enough. Go on inside.' Despite a stretch of fourteen years and a weight gain of a good thirty pounds, Caroline instantly recognized the man who'd spoken. Detective Louis Washburn.

The muscles along Jesse's jaw line twitched at Washburn's order, but he kept his mouth shut. DeSanto gave him a nudge and they headed up the steps into the church.

Washburn offered Caroline a bare nod.

Was there a hint of sympathy in the gesture? Pity? Too distraught to analyze its meaning, Caroline merely nodded back, then quickly averted her gaze. Only to have it land on Tina King, who was stepping out of a cab.

Caroline was immediately struck by her patient's altered appearance. Tina's fashion model face was devoid of make-up, her light brown hair with bleached blond streaks was pulled into a severe knot at the nape of her neck. When the two women made eye contact, Tina gave her psychiatrist a pained grimace, then silently passed by her, dabbing at her doe eyes.

'A terrible business,' Washburn said.

Not a comment Caroline could argue with.

'If you want to talk – chat – whatever – wherever.' Washburn cleared his throat as he pulled a business card out of his jacket pocket. 'It's got my home number on it as well. Take it. You never know.'

She took Washburn's card, glanced at it before stowing it in her pocketbook. Detective Louis Washburn was now Commander of the Homicide Division.

Washburn headed up the church steps. He held open the door for her. Caroline hesitated. Attending the memorial service for Martin was going to be difficult enough without this cadre of detectives scrutinizing her. If she broke down, they could choose to interpret it as a sure sign of her guilt. If she sat there stoically, she'd no doubt be labelled a cold-hearted, cold-blooded murderer.

Of course, her absence would have raised a red flag as well. But more than anything, she felt acutely saddened by Martin's death and needed the communal comfort of the memorial service. She stepped into the church.

Washburn followed behind, discreetly taking a seat at the back next to Jesse and Amy DeSanto. In an effort to put as much distance as possible between herself and the police contingent, Caroline started down the aisle towards the front of the crowded chapel. Several colleagues had their faces buried in their service sheets as she passed. Caroline had no doubt it was deliberate. Not that being shunned was anything new to her. You didn't grow up the illegitimate child of a mother who had the reputation of being the town slut without suffering almost daily snubs.

'Caroline. Over here,' said a hushed female voice.

Caroline was greatly relieved to see her friend and colleague, Dr. Susan Steinberg, pointing to an empty space beside her. Caroline gratefully hurried over to fill it.

Susan, short, plump, with close-cropped, curly dark brown hair and a round, pretty face, was, like Caroline, in her early thirties. She'd been working at the Institute for the past six months, ever since she'd moved to Boston from Manhattan following a messy divorce from 'Brucethebastard'. Despite being Caroline's polar opposite, the outspoken, loquacious New Yorker had targeted Caroline for a friend right from her first day at the clinic. By the end of Susan's first week, Caroline knew her new friend's whole life story – especially all about Susan's rotten marriage to 'Brucethebastard'. Susan, on the other hand, would tease Caroline endlessly about being anal retentive because she never gossiped – especially about herself.

At the podium, one of Martin's closest pals since junior high school days back in Decatur was beginning his heartfelt eulogy. As Caroline settled into her seat, Susan rummaged in her black leather purse for a packet of tissues. She pulled one out for herself, and extracted one for Caroline.

'You coping?' Susan whispered, dabbing her wet eyes.

Caroline nodded, guiltily taking the tissue. Her own tears were bottled up. It wasn't that she didn't feel a terrible sadness. The problem was, she couldn't separate her grief from the angry and hurt thoughts that Martin's death was directly connected to his indiscriminate lust. That her patient Meg Spaulding might well have been Martin's femme fatale. And that a man she was treating for voyeurism might have a far more *deadly* sickness.

'I was afraid Jesse'd accost me again when I left the service. It would have been perfect timing. I was so upset. I still can't really believe . . . Martin's dead. He was twenty-seven years old. He had his . . . whole future in front of him. And he was such a sweet guy.' Caroline bit back the tears that hadn't come at the service. This certainly wasn't the place to break down.

Philip Mason slid a box of tissues across his shiny mahogany desk. Caroline gave her head a little shake to let the lawyer know she was okay. 'As it turned out Jesse didn't so much as look my way . . . afterwards. Probably because of Washburn. Not that I'd trust the head of homicide any farther than I could throw the whole lot of them. Washburn's more dangerous than my stepbrother, Jesse. Because he's more wily.' Caroline laughed harshly. 'He's like an expert fisherman. Uses grade A bait. You can't resist the lure. Then, as soon as you take so much as a little nibble, he reels you in ever so gently until . . .' Caroline stopped abruptly. 'Sorry. Sounds like I'm talking to my shrink.'

'Are you seeing one?'

'No. That's not what I need. I need a lawyer. That's why I'm here.'

Caroline gave Mason a resolute once-over as she sat across the polished mahogany desk from him. The seasoned criminal attorney had a coveted corner office at Lambert and Doyle, the renowned law firm that occupied an entire floor of a skyscraper by the commuter ferry slip a few blocks from Faneuil Hall Marketplace.

Mason's dark brown hair was combed straight back from his forehead. He had shrewd grey eyes. His finely tailored silk and worsted wool navy suit hung perfectly on his stocky but firm frame. For some reason, he looked vaguely familiar, but she couldn't place him. Mason gave no indication that he recognized her.

'I know they're not through with me. Washburn, DeSanto, and especially Jesse. And the problem is—' Again, Caroline stopped. She glanced at a brass-framed photograph on the desk. Mason and a lovely looking blond-haired woman and two young children. All smiling happily. A family photo, Caroline assumed. She felt a flash of envy.

'Sometimes it's difficult putting problems into words.'

Caroline smiled wryly. 'I'm trained to do just that.'

'So am I,' Mason said. 'But I can do it for others a lot easier than I can for myself.'

'Can you do it for Ben Tabor?'

For the first time, Mason looked uneasy. 'I don't think it's my place . . .'

'It doesn't take being a psychiatrist to notice that he's in bad shape.'

'Actually, his shape is much improved.' Mason frowned, realizing that he'd just bitten *her* lure.

'When Ben was my lawyer, he helped me through a very bad stretch . . .'

'Yes, I know.'

'He told you?' Before Mason could respond, it struck Caroline why the lawyer looked familiar. 'You were there a few times, weren't you? In the court room. During my trial. Ben used to talk with you after . . .'

'Ben and I go way back.'

'Then you knew his wife?'

'I was best man at Ben's wedding.' Mason's eyes shifted to the photo on his desk. 'And he at mine.' Mason smiled, but there was a bittersweet cast to it.

Trouble in Mason's paradise. Things, as Caroline reminded herself, were rarely as they first seemed.

'When was the split?' she asked.

Mason looked sharply over at her. 'Ben and Kim? It's been . . . a while.'

'Is that what triggered his depression?'

He tapped his thumb against his lip, giving her a con-templative look. 'Ben didn't say anything to you?'

'When I asked him what was wrong he said it was all in his head.'

Mason smiled grimly. 'I think he was referring, at least in part, to a gunshot wound he suffered about seven months ago.'

'Ben was shot? What happened?'

Mason hesitated. He was telling tales out of school. But he could see that Caroline was genuinely concerned about

Ben. 'It happened back in Chicago.'

'What was he doing . . .?'

'Ben had this cousin, Mitch – they were like brothers growing up. Lived right next door to each other. Anyway, Mitch had a kid – eighteen years old – who was into drugs and ended up getting himself into some serious trouble with the law. The boy, Jimmy, was Ben's godson.' Mason shook his head, but didn't continue.

'What kind of trouble?'

Mason sighed. 'He was accused of gunning down a clerk in a drug store during a hold-up. The boy swore every which way that he was being set up by the cops.' The corner of the lawyer's mouth curved. 'Hey, we all know the cops aren't always the good guys, right?'

Caroline flinched. Mason appeared not to notice. 'Ben managed to get the kid out on bail, then started nosing around. Only thing was, when Ben finished gathering up enough of the pieces it turned out it wasn't a frame-up.'

Caroline sat forward in her seat. 'His godson did kill the clerk?'

'Sure as hell looked that way to Ben. He tried to get the boy to cop to a manslaughter plea. Instead, the boy took off. Ben and his cousin managed to track him down at a crack house. Kid was high as a kite. He had a gun. And he opened fire.' Mason's face looked pinched. 'Killed his father.'

Caroline shivered. 'And . . . Ben?'

'One bullet hit his hip. Luckily did only minor damage. A second one grazed his skull right here.' Mason made the same gesture Ben had made the day before, his index finger marking a spot at the right side of his head, a couple of inches above and behind his ear. 'The impact caused a subdural haematoma. Even though they operated right away, it was weeks before his doctors could rule out residual brain damage. Let me tell you, I breathed a big sigh of relief when Ben was finally out of the woods. He's okay now – physically – except for the headaches he gets every so often.'

'What happened to the boy? Jimmy?' Caroline asked.

'He blew his brains out after gunning down his dad. Ben was unconscious when the paramedics showed up. I hope to God he was out when the kid . . .' Mason let the sentence trail off.

They sat quietly, contemplating the awful tragedy.

'Ben really went through hell,' Mason said after a few silent moments. 'Didn't say it – neither one of us is big on talking about our feelings – but I know he's been tormented by the belief that he did it all wrong. You tell me, Doctor, how do you really know what's the right way?'

Caroline wished she had an answer for that question. She was poignantly reminded of the last conference at the Institute when Martin had asked her where she drew the line between a healthy interest in sex and sexual obsession. She'd said it was a matter of degree, but couldn't actually pinpoint where exactly that line was drawn.

'Anyway,' Mason reflected, 'somehow we've got to live with the consequences of our actions. Ben hasn't figured out how to do that yet.'

'When did he go on leave?' Caroline asked.

'End of December. He'd only been back at work a little over a month. Claimed he wanted time to do some writing.

I don't think he's written one word. Or ever intended to. I think he's been sitting around in that mausoleum of an apartment of his for the past three and a half months contemplating his navel.'

'Did he get any help? Psychiatric help?' Caroline emphasized.

'No. I tried to talk him into seeing someone, but he insisted he'd sort it all out on his own.' Mason gave the family photo on his desk another brief glance. 'And, not to knock psychiatry, but I think what Ben needs is to get back to work. Get his mind on something new.'

'What about Kim?'

Mason hesitated. 'What about her?'

'Where is she?'

'Ben doesn't keep me posted on his ex-wife. I doubt they're in touch these days.'

'Because he doesn't care any more?'

Philip Mason's gaze returned to the happy family photo, lingering there now. 'Some people work hard as they can at not caring. The rest of us struggle not to care so much.'

17

Meg was seated on a high stool in front of her drafting table, making some sketches, when Ryan Gallagher popped into her office. She looked up, clearly unhappy with the interruption.

Ryan merely smiled. 'Thought we could go over these, before our meeting with the boys at the Harbour Yachting Club this afternoon.' He gestured to the rolled-up blueprints he was carrying. Before she could object, he quickly crossed the room and set the prints down over her sketch pad.

'How'd everything go in New York?' he asked, leaning across the table to unroll the prints, brushing against her shoulder in the process.

Meg automatically shifted away. 'Fine. Please don't hover over me, Ryan,' she said tightly.

'The other night you told me to give it a rest, Meg. Why don't you?'

She glanced up at him warily. 'What's that supposed to mean?'

'It's supposed to mean that I'm not your enemy. You always act like I'm out to get you.'

'No. I always act like you're out to get me into bed,' she said drily.

Ryan shook his head. 'No. That's not what really scares you. You like to pretend you're an ice maiden, but that's completely bogus and we both know it.'

A tremor shot right down Meg's spine. Her ears started to ring. 'What exactly do you know?'

'Have dinner with me tonight and I'll tell you.' His tone was playful as always. And he flashed her one of his winning boyish smiles.

Meg told herself this was merely another of Ryan's come-ons. She'd go completely psycho if she didn't stop thinking that everyone she knew was spying on her; knew about her secret life. Having to contend with Steve Kramer was bad enough.

Ryan sighed. 'Come on, Meg. I'm trying my best here. It's only dinner. You have to eat, I have to eat, so we'll eat together. You can handle that.'

'I can't.' She was flustered. 'I mean I can't have dinner with you. Not tonight.'

'I'm not taking no for an answer this time, Meg.' Before she could argue, Ryan began discussing the blueprints, pointing out how he'd incorporated the changes she'd wanted from his earlier set. Meg let him drone on for several minutes.

'So? Does everything meet with your approval?' he asked when he finished his brief presentation.

She nodded absently. 'Fine. Yes.'

'Good. Then we're all set. For now and for this evening.' As he rolled up the blueprints, he gave her a lingering look. 'The green contacts were cool, Meg. But you really don't need them. You're perfect just the way you are.'

After work, Meg headed straight to the hospital. She stood at the nurses' station on the seventh floor waiting impatiently for a hefty psychiatric nurse stuffed into a pale blue uniform to get off the phone and tell her where she could find her mother.

'Meg?'

Meg was startled to see her grandfather approaching the nurses' station. What struck her most – after her initial surprise at his being there – was how much Winston Spaulding had aged since their last meeting.

'What are you doing here?' she asked bluntly.

'Your mother asked me to come.'

Meg found that astonishing, since as far as she knew the two hadn't spoken in almost three years. Meg had not spoken to her grandfather in all that time either. She and her mother each had their own reasons.

'How are you, Meg? You look pale. Tense. When are you going to find yourself a nice young man?' Her grandfather reached out his hand to her.

Meg quickly took a step back. A pained expression crossed Winston Spaulding's face and his arm dropped. 'Ned's tied up with some estate sale and she knows how busy you are. So she asked if I could pick her up.'

'Pick her up?'

'They're releasing her,' her grandfather said.

But Ned had said she wouldn't be leaving until Sunday. 'Tonight?'

'Now. I'm waiting for her to get dressed. I'm going to bring her over to Ned's. He wants her to stay with him for a few days, maybe longer. And then, if Faith wants, she can come spend some time with me.'

Meg listened to the plans being made for her mother, feeling like a third wheel. Just like the old days. Ned and Grandy in charge, on top of the situation, doing what needed doing. She was present but superfluous. As always.

'Are you ready, Mother?' Meg asked. 'Grandy's waiting out in the lounge.'

Faith Spaulding sat on the edge of her hospital bed, an open overnight case beside her. She didn't answer her daughter. Less than a week ago at Ned's latest gallery opening, Faith had looked so young and vivacious. Positively glowing. Now her complexion had a distinctly greyish tinge to it; her grey-green eyes were glassy; stress lines punctuated the corners of her mouth. While her auburn hair was combed, it hung limply about her shoulders. Normally – that is when she was feeling normal – Faith would twist it into an elegant French knot. The way she'd worn it the night of the gallery opening.

'Mother?'

'In a minute.'

'Is there something—'

Faith held up her hand.

Meg felt uneasy. How often, as a child, had she yearned to talk to her mother, share things with her, confide in her?

But, most of the time, Faith was either too depressed or too manic. And even when she was in remission between one extreme and the other Meg hesitated, afraid she'd be responsible for setting her mother off.

Not that communication had been much better between herself and her father. Daniel Spaulding had been a man obsessed by only two things. His wife. And his art. With his children, he had been critical and often volatile. Coping with her parents had been like walking through mine fields. Step on a mine and you got blown to smithereens.

'Grandy's going to wonder what's wrong,' Meg ventured. She was anxious to get away from the bad memories aroused by the hospital.

Her mother nodded but made no move to leave.

'He's not well,' Faith said. 'I knew that, but still I was surprised when I saw him.'

'What's wrong with him?' Meg asked unfeelingly.

Faith looked over at her daughter. 'He has cancer. Pancreatic cancer. He's had treatment. He assured me he was going to be fine. But I don't believe him.'

That explained the rapprochement, Meg thought. Would Grandy want to make peace with her, too, now that he was dying?

Faith smiled faintly. 'He's equally confident about my recovery. He always was unrealistic.' She tucked her hair behind her ears. Her hands trembled.

'You'll be fine, Mother. As long as you take your lithium.'

'I couldn't find them.'

'Your pills?'

'I must have lost them.'

Faith turned back to the window, her hand fluttering up to her eyes as if she were blocking out a bright sun. Only the sun was already setting.

'Your father would have been furious. Dan hated it when I lost things.'

There was a dead silence.

And then her mother said, 'Your father could be so cruel.' She looked bleakly across the room at her daughter. 'But then, cruelty does seem to run in our family, doesn't it, Meggie?'

18

'At first,' Steve Kramer said, 'I thought I could solve this with the help of a top-notch lawyer. But I'm smart enough to know there's a chance I'd lose. There's no way I can afford to take that risk. It would kill me to go to prison.'

Caroline studied her patient closely. He'd been talking nonstop since he'd arrived at her office at 6:10 p.m., urgently requesting an immediate session. It was now nearly 6:30 p.m. and he'd barely drawn breath.

'You were only picked up for soliciting, Steve,' she finally broke in. 'I think your panic's got more to do with . . .'

'I broke probation. Even if I don't do time it goes down as a second strike. Third strike and that's it. They throw the book at you. It's like you're walking around with a time bomb. You think you've defused it only to discover it's still ticking away.'

Caroline had no trouble identifying with that. She'd been hearing a *tick, tick, tick* in her head for days now. It was getting louder and louder.

'. . . Besides, the police – they're not going to stop harassing me. Unless I play hardball with them. Which is where you come in.'

Kramer's words broke into Caroline's thoughts. 'What police?'

He shrugged off her question, intent on what he was saying. 'Look, we've both got troubles, Caroline. If you help me out now, I can solve yours as well as mine.' He smoothed back his hair nervously. Unlike last time, Kramer was looking like his old self – all spiffed up – charcoal grey wool suit, pale blue shirt and silk rep tie, buffed cordovan loafers, hair neatly combed, clean-shaven. And sober. The only giveaways to his hypertense state were his dilated pupils and the nervous tic at the corner of his mouth.

'I'm trying to help you, Steve. But I don't think you're telling me . . .'

'What I'm telling you is that I need fifty thousand dollars. I want out, Caroline. I've got this friend in Costa Rica. He says you can live like a king down there on next to nothing. Maybe I can even practise again.'

'You want to run away,' she said quietly.

'Call it a mid-life change. Look Caroline, what I need from you isn't psychiatric help. I need you to give me the money. Fifty thousand dollars. You make that twice over in a single year.'

'You know I'm not going to give you money.' Her voice was calm enough, but her mind was racing. Why did Steve want to run away? Because he'd witnessed a vicious murder? Or because he'd committed one? Two? 'Let's talk about . . .'

'For fifty thousand dollars,' Kramer cut her off, 'I'll tell the police in no uncertain terms that I didn't see you at the museum on Tuesday night.'

Caroline kept her composure. As if she didn't have enough to contend with, she was actually being blackmailed by her own patient. 'But you didn't see me at the museum, Steve.'

'Those detectives from Homicide think I did. Worse than that, Caroline – much worse – they think I saw you and that violinist. They think you're the one who seduced him. The one who killed him.'

Caroline went cold. 'But you know that's not true, Steve. Because you were there. You saw the woman . . .'

'How do you know *what* I saw?'

'Steve,' she said firmly, 'you've got to tell the police the truth. I'll go with you. I'll help you . . .'

'The truth? The truth is, Caroline, the police think you strangled your boyfriend to death as well. They kept pressing me. Especially that woman detective, DeSanto. She told me to be sure and get in touch with her if I remembered anything else. Funny thing is, I *am* starting to remember some things.' He looked thoughtful. 'When was it? Oh yes, it was a Wednesday night, a week before Bassett was murdered. After group let out. Remember, Caroline? We all walked out together. The others took off, but I was waiting around for a ride. And Martin Bassett pulled up, beeped you. I saw you get into his car. He didn't pull away right off. He was saying something. I don't know what it was, naturally, but my oh my, you really blew up. I saw you hit him, Caroline.'

'No one's going to believe those lies, Steve,' she said

flatly. But she knew DeSanto and her stepbrother would be only too happy to believe Steve Kramer's fabrications. With her own patient as a witness, they might well be able to press charges against her. Murder charges, this time.

Caroline felt trapped. She stared into Kramer's disquietingly impassive face. But Caroline had no trouble discerning the telltale signs of psychopathy – deceit, aggression, and particularly, his utter lack of remorse. Whoever had killed Peter Korza and Martin could certainly fit that profile.

A smile played on Kramer's lips. He held all the cards now. 'Don't be a fool, Caroline. You've got more reason to fear prison than I do. My career's already up in smoke. Yours is still on the line.'

Caroline could picture all too well her career, her entire life, going up in smoke. Now she was the one who wanted escape.

'I'm glad you're giving this such careful thought, Caroline.'

She *was* thinking carefully. If she let a patient demoralize or scare her, she really was done for. And so was her patient.

Controlling her panic, Caroline tried a new tack. 'We have almost fifteen minutes left, Steve. I think it would be helpful to use that time to examine your feelings of rage and panic.'

Kramer stared at her in disbelief. 'You really don't get it.'

'You're obviously feeling very angry at me,' she went on evenly. 'Possibly thinking to yourself – not so long ago I was in her position. I was a doctor. I had respect, money . . .'

'I can live without respect. I've been doing it for quite a while now. What I need is money. Fifty grand, Caroline. That's what it's going to take to cure what ails me. And you.'

'Your father was a physician, too. Isn't that right, Steve? A neurosurgeon. You mentioned in group that he was a strict taskmaster; that he was always badgering you.'

'You're wasting your breath, Caroline.'

'I think you're afraid, Steve. Remember when you talked in group about your father beating you for wetting the bed? And how, after those beatings, you'd feel compelled to masturbate?'

Steve's eyes darkened with anger, but he said nothing.

'When your father beat you, sometimes he touched you, didn't he? Sometimes you felt aroused. And confused. And frightened.'

'You're crazy. He never – he was a tyrant, not a sexual pervert.'

'That was when you first began to make the link between pain and pleasure. When the fear itself began to spark excitement. That fear both terrified you and turned you on.' She knew she might be pushing this too far. What if Steve Kramer *was* the killer? What if he watched Meg having sex and then – ?

Kramer leaned forward adopting a leering smile. 'It's you who's afraid right now. I can see it in your eyes. Tell me, Caroline, does it turn *you* on?'

She forced herself to meet his gaze levelly. 'Why don't you tell me why you're really running away, Steve?'

'I told you, I'm not . . .'

'Two innocent men are already dead. There could be more. Please, Steve, what did you see at the museum Tuesday night? *Who* did you see? What really happened there?'

Kramer leaped to his feet and pounded his hand down hard on the desk. 'You don't want to know, okay? I'll be back Monday morning. You have the fifty grand here in cash. Or you're fucked, *Dr. Hoffman*!'

Kramer stormed out. Caroline closed her eyes, palming her face. She felt utterly depleted.

'That was one furious patient.'

Caroline dropped her hands as Jill Nugent sauntered into her office. 'So tell me, Dr. Hoffman. Do all your sex addicts blow up like that?'

Jill Nugent slowly and deliberately spread the old news clippings across Caroline's desk. Caroline didn't so much as glance at them. She didn't need to. She knew them by heart. COLLEGE STUDENT ASSAULTS SHERIFF STEPFATHER. BOSTON STATE DEALS WITH STUDENT'S ARREST FOR ATTEMPTED MURDER. A YOUNG WOMAN'S LUST OR ATTEMPTED RAPE. And on ad infinitum.

Caroline gave the trim reporter a hostile glare. 'What is it you want?'

Jill Nugent slid gracefully into the upholstered chair vacated by Steve Kramer moments ago. 'Your stepbrother's mentioned in several of those articles. Jesse Baush. He testified against you at your trial fourteen years ago.'

'I know. I was there,' Caroline said curtly.

Nugent continued. 'At one point when Baush was on

the stand, he called you a "nymphomaniac".'

'I really don't need a recap.'

'It must have been pretty rough. Cards stacked against you. Your stepbrother wasn't the only relative who testified against you . . .'

'That's enough.' Caroline's voice came out a harsh whisper.

The reporter looked at her for a long moment. 'Try to believe me, Dr. Hoffman, I'm one of the nice guys.'

'What do you want?'

Nugent smiled. 'An exclusive.'

'There's absolutely nothing I can tell you.'

'Tell me about your relationship with your stepbrother.'

The question took Caroline offguard. She'd expected to be grilled on her relationship with Martin Bassett. 'Jesse and I don't have a relationship.'

The reporter leaned forward. Any pretence of being one of the *nice guys* vanished. 'Jesse Baush testified that a couple of years before the incident with your stepfather, you had a thing going with one of your mom's boyfriends.' Nugent flipped the news story over. She had a note stuck to the back. 'Walter Jackson. That was his name, right?'

'I'd like you to leave my office. Now.'

Nugent sighed. 'Okay, let's try a different approach. What about that patient you were looking for at the museum on Tuesday night? Is he one of the sex addicts you treat? I know you can't name names. Doctor-patient confidentiality and all. But, it seems to me, if this patient were to verify your story, it would certainly let you off the hook. I mean, it would keep them from assuming *you* were the hooker.'

'Get out of here,' Caroline said tightly.

Nugent ignored her repeated command. 'Listen, Dr. Hoffman, depending on how you look at it, I can be your worst nightmare or your best hope. I know, right at this moment, you're thinking I'm the former. But, I'm giving you the opportunity to put a positive spin on your situation.'

But Caroline knew it was too late. The die was cast.

Ben Tabor woke from an early evening catnap with a splitting headache and the bitter after-taste from a bad dream.

Over the past few months, his dreams had centred almost exclusively around his cousin, Mitch. A theme that Ben knew would haunt him for the rest of his life. He held himself responsible for what had happened.

But this nightmare had taken Ben by surprise. It hadn't been about Mitch. Or even about Kim, who invariably crept in to his tortured dreams. This time, he'd dreamed about Caroline. She was chasing him through a crazy mirror maze in a carnival fun house. He could see their distorted reflections in the mirrors. He was dressed in a business suit, carrying an attaché case. Caroline was naked, bloodied, her empty hands outstretched. She was crying out to him. He kept running faster and faster, not knowing why he was so afraid to let her catch up with him, just that the terror he felt was overpowering.

Then Ben saw in the mirrors that there was someone chasing Caroline. At first, all he could make out was the reflection of a shadowy figure. A man dressed in black. Wielding a butcher knife. At last, he got a better look at the man. He wasn't dressed in black. He had dark brown skin.

It was him. Naked. Chasing Caroline as well as being chased by her. The pursued and the *pursuer*.

Despite the pounding in his head, Ben smiled crookedly. A shrink would have a field-day interpreting that dream. Especially a shrink by the name of Caroline Hoffman.

'I spoke to Washburn at Homicide and Vargas over at the D.A.'s office late this afternoon. They're a long ways from making an arrest, but Caroline was right. They *are* keeping an eye on her.' Philip Mason scooped shrimp with spicy tea sauce onto his plate, then slid the serving platter across the table to Ben Tabor. The pair were seated in a faded red plastic booth at the back of Chen Wa's, a store-front Chinese restaurant on Dunster. It had become one of Ben's frequent haunts over the past few months.

'Anyone else they're investigating?' Ben asked, helping himself to a small portion of the Schezuan dish. Placing the spicy shrimp in red sauce on top of a scoopful of pork lo mein. Pretending the glop didn't turn his stomach.

Phil frowned. 'That's the problem. They don't seem to have anyone else. Except Caroline.'

'Are you telling me Vargas really believes that Caroline Hoffman's a man-hating sex maniac serial killer? Give me a break.'

'You know that's not what they're thinking, Ben. The serial killer story sells papers, gets big ratings for TV news shows. The cops are betting your girl had a motive for killing her psychiatrist boyfriend and they're working overtime to link her to Korza. If they do, we've got our work cut out for us.'

'Hold on, Phil. First of all, Caroline's not *my girl*. And second of all, *we* don't have *our* work cut out for *us*. She's your client, not mine.' Who was he kidding? If he wasn't getting involved, why the hell was he grilling Caroline's lawyer? Why were his temples hammering?

'Fine.' Phil took a bite of shrimp.

Ben merely moved some of the food around his plate.

'Another bad headache?'

Ben didn't try to deny it. Phil knew him too well. 'Not all that bad.'

'Bullshit. You're not still taking those pain killers? The last thing you need is to get hooked . . .'

'I'm not taking anything. I'm not getting hooked on anything. Look, just drop it, okay?'

'Sure. No problem, Ben.'

'Now you're pissed off, right?'

Phil smiled faintly. 'A shrink would call that projection.'

Ben could feel himself losing it. 'I'm getting good and tired of everyone trying to analyze me.'

Phil eyeballed him. 'How about giving *me* a break? It's been a long day. A long week. A lot of long weeks.'

Ben stared at his friend. It wasn't as if he hadn't noticed the strain on Phil's face before. Hell, what lawyer's face didn't show the intense wear and tear of the job? What Ben noticed about Phil now was simply that there was more of it.

'Let's get back to *my* client,' Phil said gruffly.

Ben got the message. *I love you like a brother, but don't*

pry. It was a message the two friends had tossed back and forth over the last twenty years. A message they both heeded. Out of love. He was not about to change the pact. 'Did Caroline tell you about this patient of hers who's a voyeur?'

'The one who called her from the museum the night of Korza's murder? Yeah, she mentioned him but she didn't say much.'

'Did she tell you he might have seen the babe who picked Korza up? That it might have been another of her patients?'

Phil's eyes narrowed, emphasizing the worry lines on his face. 'No. We had to cut the meeting short because she had to get back to her clinic.'

Ben shared what little Caroline had told him about the woman, particularly her sexual addiction.

Phil grew quiet. Thoughtful.

'Interesting, huh?' Ben said.

'Do the police know about this woman?'

'No. Nor about the peeper. Caroline can't say anything. Doctor-patient confidentiality.'

'So, again, that leaves Caroline hanging out there.' Phil took a long swallow of Chinese beer. 'Especially considering her past.'

'Her past? Shit, Phil. Caroline was protecting herself against being raped by her stepfather. The jury acquitted her. Afterwards, despite the publicity, she had the moxie to go back to Boston State, get her degree, put herself through medical school. She's a respected psychiatrist now, for chris-sakes.'

'A psychiatrist who treats sex addicts.'

'Meaning?'

'In case you forgot, I sat in on Caroline's trial whenever I got the chance. Your young client wasn't presented by the prosecution in shall I say a particularly *virginal* light. Even her own mother testified . . .'

'Caroline's mother was a drunk and a slut,' Ben said acidly.

'She was dead sober on the stand,' Phil said quietly. 'And, according to other witnesses, Laura Hoffman had been on the wagon from the time she and Porter Baush started going together. Anyway, she was far from the only prosecution witness who had tales to tell about Caroline's promiscuity.'

'*Tales* is right,' Ben was quick to emphasize. Not that he could forget every salacious detail those witnesses recounted. Some of which Caroline had warned him he'd hear. Some which had caught him completely by surprise.

'I know she denied it on the stand,' Phil persisted, 'but privately, did Caroline ever cop to sleeping around?'

'I was her lawyer, not her father confessor,' Ben snapped.

'There isn't always that big a difference and you know it. Besides, Caroline thought you were God's gift to law. If she was going to open up to anyone . . .'

'She was a kid.'

'A kid with a lot of experience. As Homicide well knows,' Phil added pointedly.

'How many guys Caroline Hoffman fucked wasn't the point.' Ben could tell by the flash of a smile on his friend's face that he'd gotten nailed. It made him even angrier and made his migraine even worse. 'The point was, Phil, she didn't want to fuck her stepfather. And Porter Baush didn't exactly have a sterling reputation out there in Brookhaven. In case you forgot, or missed those court sessions, I had a couple of young girls on the witness stand telling about how good old Sheriff Baush fucked them both over – literally and figuratively.'

'One was a hooker. Multiple busts for soliciting. Not that I'm questioning her veracity, but . . .'

'The other gal was a waitress in a perfectly respectable pizza parlour and attended church every Sunday. What are you doing here, Phil? Retrying Caroline's case? The not guilty verdict came in a long time ago.'

The two lawyers ate in silence for a few minutes.

Finally, Ben asked, 'How does she seem to be . . . holding up?'

Phil lifted one eyebrow. 'Caroline? Why don't you give her a call and find out for yourself?'

19

'You're not eating,' Ryan Gallagher chided lightly.

Meg frowned. 'I told you I wasn't up for this.' She'd called Ryan from the hospital, cancelling their dinner date only to find him waiting outside her apartment door once again when she arrived back home a little after 7 p.m. 'If Mohammed won't come to the mountain . . .' he'd said with that fetching smile of his.

Meg rested her elbows on her dining-room table and stared at her barely touched plate. The rich, peppery Bernaise sauce had started to congeal on the *veau au poivre*. A perfectly good dinner gone to waste. She still couldn't eat. Her stomach seemed to be permanently tied in knots.

'Your mother?'

'I really don't want to talk about it, Ryan.'

'Sometimes talking about it helps . . .'

'Don't play shrink with me. I already have a real one.' Now why did she bring that up? Until now, only Sylvia and Ned knew she'd been seeing a psychiatrist. So much for that. By Monday, the whole office would know.

He must have read her mind. 'I'm really very good at keeping confidences, Meg. Maybe this will give you the chance to appreciate how trustworthy I am.' He reached for the bottle of Pouilly-Fusé he'd brought along with the take-out gourmet French dinner and moved to top up her glass.

Meg put her hand over it. 'I've had more than enough.' She blamed the two glasses of wine she'd already had for her loose tongue.

Ryan filled his own glass. 'I don't want to be your shrink, Meg. Your friend, yes.' He paused. 'Your lover, yes and then some.'

Meg stood up suddenly. 'You need to go home, Ryan. This little seduction scene isn't working. And it's never going to.'

He leisurely lifted his wine glass to his lips, took a sip. 'Why is that? Because I'm not a stranger?'

Meg recoiled as if she'd been punched. 'What?'

Ryan got up from the table, came around to her side. She was clutching the back of her chair for support.

'Let's go sit on the couch where we'll be more comfort-able,' he said softly. 'We need to talk.'

Meg felt dizzy and frail as Ryan guided her to the olive-damask down sofa in her living room.

'It's okay, Meg,' he said as he sat down beside her. He took hold of her hand. Normally, she would have pulled it away. Now she didn't have the strength.

'It's like ice,' he murmured, cupping her hand between his.

Meg grimaced. The hands of an ice maiden.

'Look, I was over at this toy store in Faneuil Hall a couple of weeks ago.'

The wine soured in Meg's stomach.

'And I saw you, in a hot little outfit, sauntering over to this guy, flirting with him.'

Ryan's words hung in the air. Meg sat there, frozen.

'I'm not going to tell anyone, Meg,' Ryan said soothingly. 'What you do is nobody's business.'

With a strange sense of detachment, she watched Ryan lift her hand and press her stone cold fingertips to his lips, which, by contrast, were so warm.

She wanted to look away, but couldn't. She was mesmerized. Like when she was in one of her trances, only with some big differences. She wasn't off in a hidden alcove or closet of some public place. She wasn't with a stranger. She wasn't calling all the shots. Hell, she wasn't calling any of the shots—

'Am I losing you?'

He'd unbuttoned her pale blue silk blouse, pulled it down past her shoulders. Unfastened her bra. Her short grey wool skirt had risen up of its own accord, revealing her long, shapely legs, her black satin bikini panties.

He was naked from the waist up, his crew neck sweater and shirt carelessly tossed on the floor by the sofa.

'Stay with me, Meg,' Ryan crooned into her ear, letting his fingers lightly trail down her thigh.

Meg didn't try to stop his seductive efforts. She half lay, half sat on the sofa, eyes closed, impassive, arms splayed out on the cushions. She might have been tolerating a physical exam from her doctor. Or putting up with a fitting for a dress.

'Don't be scared to let yourself go. Give me a chance here.' While he spoke, he stroked her – her legs, her belly, her breasts.

Meg remained unresponsive even as his caresses began to arouse her. She pulled in deeper until she was safe inside herself. Until he couldn't reach her.

Finally, Ryan drew away from her. 'Okay, I give,' he conceded. 'You win.'

As she opened her eyes, Meg saw him reach for his shirt. He didn't put it on immediately but held on to it as he sat on the edge of the sofa. He stared at her as if debating what to do next. She fought the urge to shut her eyes again.

'Are you angry?' she asked.

'Forcing yourself on someone is hardly a turn-on.' Something flickered in his eyes. Something Meg could relate to.

'You *are* angry.'

He shrugged.

As Meg tugged her skirt back down over her hips, she was trying to come up with some way to appease him. His anger could mean serious trouble for her.

'It's not that I don't find you attractive, Ryan.' Her sweaty palms belied her words. 'It's me. Please, can't we talk?'

He held up a hand, shook his head. 'Don't worry,' he said with a small smile. 'It'll be our little secret.'

Meg warily examined Ryan's face. With so many to choose from, which secret did he mean to keep?

*

After Ryan left her apartment, Meg showered and changed. She needed to get out, go some place where she could unwind, pull herself back together. She was furious with herself for having let Ryan's implied threats and seductions unnerve her. Control and detachment had always been her watchwords. They made up her survival kit. Without them, she was doomed.

Yet there was no denying the unexpected pull she'd felt towards Ryan that evening. Even though she'd done her best to mask it. A spring storm was raging as Meg drove across the Anderson Bridge that took her over the Charles River into the Harvard square section of Cambridge. She turned up J.F.K. Street, heading off the square to the upscale Blackstone Hotel, and parking in the hotel's underground garage.

She got off the elevator on the third floor, deposited her raincoat with the hat-check girl, and walked down the corridor to the hotel's popular jazz club.

She hung back at the entrance and surveyed the room. The club was bustling with a young, affluent, after-dinner crowd. Mostly couples and small mixed groups gathered around tiny tables.

Close to the stage, a man sat alone at a table for two. Meg was immediately drawn to him. Funny how that happened. There wasn't anything remarkable about his appearance. He looked like a carbon copy of most of the guys in the club. Late thirties, lean, nice looking, well dressed in a smart, dark suit. He hadn't even glanced her way. Oblivious to her presence. Self-absorbed. And yet there was this aura surrounding him. Meg could feel it.

Instinctively, her hand moved to her wig, making sure it was in place. She was wearing contact lenses as usual. But this time she'd opted for a vibrant violet shade. She'd chosen a different dress, too. A slim, supple sponge crêpe sheath in deep purple. With matching stacked heel pumps.

She moved towards the man as the combo struck the first notes of a jazzed-up rumba. The pulsating beat of the music, the hazy, romantic lighting, the fading din of voices, supported her euphoric trance.

She was feeling totally in control. In full command. Supremely confident.

'Are you waiting for someone?' she asked.

He smiled up at her. An instant before, she hadn't existed for the man. And now, she could see in his smile, she was all that did exist.

She slid into the empty chair across from his. Their eyes met. And locked. *This is just a test.*

'Would you like a drink?'

She automatically nodded yes. She would simply let him buy her a glass of white wine; they would sit there across from each other and make pleasant chit-chat. Hell, even play a little footsie under the table. No harm in that.

But she was already slipping into that special place – where her judgements were vague, at best.

'Are you staying at the hotel?'

She shook her head, trying to control herself. The thing to do was to simply get up and go home.

The stocky young waiter was standing by their table, eyeing Meg appreciatively as he waited for her to order.

'Chardonnay.'

'Another martini. Shaken not stirred,' the man said.

The waiter nodded and took off. The man smiled at her. Not a big talker. Good.

She moved in slightly, making a more solid physical contact between them.

His smile deepened.

They were on the same wavelength. He wanted her. She wanted him.

'My name's Don Russell.' He extended his hand.

She held hands with him across the table.

'Hello, Don Russell,' she murmured. His name flew out of her mind the instant she spoke it. She was picturing him naked. Naked and quivering with sexual desire, willing to do anything, take any risks.

She'd spotted several empty meeting rooms at the other end of the hall.

The waiter returned and set a glass of white wine down in front of her. Meg gave it a cursory sip. All she could taste was desire.

'How's the wine?' he asked.

She edged the goblet away from her and smiled seductively. Without a word, she rose from her chair.

Quick on the uptake, her conquest slapped some bills on the table. He was only a step behind when she started for the club's exit door.

Meg floated across the room. Revelling in her power. This time it was going to be so perfect.

'Don. Don Russell.'

Meg heard the deep male voice behind her.

'Hey, I thought that was you, Don.'

Meg swung around as she felt a large hand land heavily on her shoulder. Its owner was short. Wiry. Reminded her of a weasel.

The weasel crooned, 'Who's this lovely creature?'

A feeling of intense hatred shot through Meg as she stared at this intruder. She swallowed the emotion, concealing it. As she concealed so many others. Dislodging his unwelcome hand, she gave the weasel a bemused smile. 'Sorry to disappoint you,' she told him, 'but this gentleman and I aren't together.'

'Hey, I'm not the one who's disappointed, beautiful. But I bet my buddy Don sure as hell is.'

Without a word, Meg turned and made a beeline for the exit. In another second the little creep would have suggested a ménage à trois.

That was Tina King's scene. Maybe Natalie Deutch's. Not hers.

Meg ran out of the lobby doors of the Blackstone Hotel, completely forgetting she'd parked her car in the underground garage. She'd also forgotten her raincoat. And it was still pouring out. By the time she raced back to the garage, she was soaked to the skin. Shivering, she sat behind the wheel, eyes closed, her head dropped back against the leather headrest.

How long had she been sitting there? A minute? An hour? She'd disconnected from time. All Meg was aware of was an aching loneliness.

She blamed Ryan Gallagher. Ryan had made her feel vulnerable, weak, defective. But he'd also sparked something else in her. Something even more terrifying. In this rare unguarded moment, Meg could sense how incredible it would be to have a normal relationship with a man. Perversely, she knew she'd cruelly rejected Ryan for that very reason. Because he was decent, tender, caring. Because he offered a relationship that didn't have the usual predetermined ending.

20

'A couple of patients I saw this afternoon were really flipping out,' Susan Steinberg said to Caroline as they sat in a glass-fronted café on Arlington Street. Susan had caught Caroline as she was rushing out of the Institute and insisted they have a late dinner and unwind. It wasn't working for Caroline.

'How about you?' Susan asked, finishing up her grilled portobello mushroom sandwich. 'Did any of yours put you through the wringer?'

Caroline absently stirred her double espresso.

'I'm sure some of them must have reacted to all the press you're getting.' Susan dumped two packets of sugar into her drink. 'I mean, give me a break, so you and Martin were involved. I still don't get why the hell the cops dragged you down to the morgue to see his body. It's no wonder you've been green around the gills for days. Oh, I know, it's grief, too. What can I say? You know the whole grief process as well as I do. No way to get around it.

You've simply got to go through all the stages. It's like with my divorce. Right now I'm still in the angry stage – No, I don't even want to think about Brucethebastard. So, what's with the cops, Caroline? They obviously think you know something.' Susan paused, giving her friend close scrutiny. 'Do you?'

'No. Not really,' Caroline hedged.

'*Not really* means yes. But I don't have to tell you, another psychiatrist, that.'

Caroline sighed inwardly. She was truly fond of Susan, but she could be a little overbearing at times. This was definitely one of those times.

'Is it somebody from your sex addicts' group?' Susan persisted.

'You know I never discuss patients in public places,' Caroline said in a whisper.

'Just nod your head. Yes or no.'

Instead, Caroline rolled her eyes.

Susan pursed her lips in frustration. 'Okay. Fine. I'm not going to say another word.'

Caroline raised an eyebrow. 'You mean it?'

'Brucethebastard used to say things like that to me, you know. Come to think of it, so did my father. Men stink. Well, not all men. Not Martin. He was a terrific guy. You thought so, right?'

Caroline looked out of the window, thinking that if she appeared distracted, Susan might let up on the questioning. Her gaze fell on a woman in jeans and a dark jacket standing across Arlington Street in front of the Public Gardens. Looking intently over at the café. At her? Too dark outside to see who it was. Besides, the woman was already heading down the street towards Newbury.

Caroline told herself it was nothing, but it had unsettled her. She wouldn't put it past her stepbrother to have a tail put on her.

When she turned back to Susan, her friend was eyeing her thoughtfully. 'Were you in love with Martin? Oh, I know you told me that it wasn't serious, but I have a feeling you wouldn't admit it if it was. Even to yourself. I don't have to tell you you've got a problem with intimacy. You may not believe this, but so do I. I just talk a lot to cover it up. But I do not want to talk about me tonight. What about you and Martin?'

'Please, Susan . . .'

'I know what's torturing you, sweetie. It's that Martin picked up his killer. Or got picked up by her. Point being, he cheated on you. Brucethebastard would have cheated on me with hookers. But he was too cheap. Anyway, it's natural you're feeling betrayed, but you don't know what really happened—'

Caroline held up a hand. 'That's not what I'm thinking about.'

Susan took a sip of her cappuccino. 'So, what are you thinking about? What *is* on your mind?'

'What mind?' Caroline said dully.

Susan dabbed the milky foam off her lips. 'I guess I should tell you that a detective questioned me early this afternoon. About Martin. And the other guy.'

Caroline looked over sharply. 'Baush?'

'I thought his name was Korza. Peter Korza. You want to

know something crazy? When I saw Korza's photo in the paper, it really shook me. He bore an eerie resemblance to my ex. Brucethebastard even played the violin as a kid.'

'I mean the cop,' Caroline said impatiently. 'Was his name . . .?'

'Not *his*. It was a woman. Detective DeSanto.'

'Did you tell her about Martin and me?'

Susan sighed. 'I promise you I didn't say anything about you and Martin to the detective. But you should know that DeSanto seemed to already know you two were more than *friends*.'

Caroline's eyes darted to the window again. Was it DeSanto out there? Watching her? Spying on her? But the woman with the dark jacket was no longer in sight.

'Let's face it, sweetie. The cops have to ask questions, investigate anyone who knew Martin and the other murdered man.'

Caroline's head snapped back. 'I didn't know Peter Korza.'

'Of course you didn't. Take it easy, Caroline. I'm on your side.' Susan reached across the table and gave her hand a supportive squeeze.

Caroline put her hand over her friend's. 'I'm just so stressed out. I know you're on my side. And it means a lot to me. More than I can say.' She could feel tears start to well in her eyes.

'Of course it's more than you can say,' Susan teased affectionately. 'You hardly say anything.'

Caroline smiled. Maybe spending this time with Susan was just what she needed, after all.

'You should take a little vacation, Caroline. Give yourself a week or two. I know this lovely little bed and breakfast in Vermont. Okay, so Brucethebastard and I spent one whole weekend there. The only decent weekend in six years.'

'I can't go away now. I can't run out on my patients. Not that I may have them for very long. Rogers will probably ask me to resign,' Caroline said bitterly.

'Because the cops are questioning you? Because of you and Martin? Rogers can't can you for either one of those reasons,' Susan declared.

Caroline hesitated. 'There are other things that are going to come out about me. Rogers knows about them, but he certainly never expected they'd be made public—'

Susan's eyes widened. 'Let's go back to my place and talk,' she said after asking the waiter for the bill.

'Thanks, Susan. But the truth is, I'm drained. If you could just give me a lift back to the Institute to pick up my car?'

'Caroline, you're a shrink. You of all people should know the merits of spilling your guts to the right person. And I'm not only your friend. I happen to be a very fine therapist. Not that I'm tooting my own horn. Well, I am, but I'm a firm believer in self-promotion,' she added with a lopsided grin.

'We'll talk, I promise,' Caroline placated. 'Just not tonight.'

The waiter returned with the bill. Susan was adamant about paying. 'My treat. If ever a person needed a treat, it's you.'

It was drizzling when the two women left the restaurant.

Susan tried to hold her umbrella over them both. As they headed past the Ritz Hotel to the corner of Newbury and Arlington, Caroline looked nervously up and down the street. She couldn't shake the impression that the woman she'd spotted across from the café had been watching her.

Susan took a firmer hold of her arm, pulling her closer so the umbrella would better shield them. 'Look, I know it's going to be rough for you, Caroline. Certainly until the cops find this sex maniac. But you really have to guard against getting too worked up about the cops. Or,' she added pointedly, 'pulling away from your friends.'

But Caroline wasn't listening. She'd glanced back over her shoulder and saw the woman she'd seen earlier. This time the dark figure darted into a bookstore midway down the street before Caroline could get a close enough look to see who it was.

Susan pulled her Mercedes alongside Caroline's Saab at the Institute's parking lot, watched her get safely into her car and then drove off. Caroline sat behind the wheel, but didn't start the engine. She waited nervously to see if anyone else was going to pull into the lot. If someone did, it would confirm her suspicions that she was being followed, and she'd take off. Otherwise, she'd run back into the Institute and retrieve some papers from her office that she wanted to examine more thoroughly.

She gave it five minutes. One psychiatrist – Stanley Howe – exited the Institute's rear door. Several doctors held evening hours for patients, but they rarely scheduled appointments later than eight, especially on Friday nights.

Since the lights were out in all the offices facing the lot, Caroline guessed that Howe was the last to leave.

Howe's sleek, silver BMW was three spaces down from her. As he passed the rear of her Saab, she sunk down to avoid being seen. He might think it odd her hanging around the parking lot at that time of the night when she had no patients to see. Overnight, Caroline's reputation had been transformed from respected psychiatrist to suspicious individual.

As soon as Howe's BMW was out of sight, she dashed across the lot to the Institute's rear entrance. Fumbling for the right key, she unlocked the door and slipped inside. She used the back stairs, hurrying up the two flights to the narrow hallway that led directly to her consulting office. But as she slipped the key into the lock, the door gave way.

Caroline paused. What with everything that had happened at her office early that evening – the disturbing confrontation with Jill Nugent coming on the heels of that totally unexpected session with Steve Kramer – could she have been so rattled she'd left her door unlocked?

She was always so careful – fanatical in fact – about securing her office. There were confidential records—

Caroline's chest tightened. Clutching her key ring as though it were a weapon, she gingerly cracked the door open. The office was dark. She held her breath.

All she heard was the faint hum that came from the electric baseboard heater. She reached in and flicked on the lights, cautiously peered inside from the doorway.

Everything looked in order. Still—

She turned to her filing cabinets on the other side of the

room. The file drawers containing her case records were all closed as they should be.

But were they locked?

The thought that they might have been broken into made her rush across the room to check.

Heart pounding, she gripped the metal handle of the top left drawer where she kept her current patients' records. She squeezed her eyes shut.

Don't give way. Be locked.

The faintest tug and it slid effortlessly open on its gliders.

Oh shit!

Caroline's trembling fingers sped through the alphabetical progression of her patients' case folders. She began to breathe easier as she saw that everything seemed to be in order. Until she got to the Ss and discovered the exact file she'd come for was missing. Meg Spaulding's.

Had Meg broken in and stolen it? To destroy incriminating evidence?

There was a sudden clanging sound behind her. Caroline spun around. Expecting—

Expecting what? To see a maniacal Meg Spaulding leaping out of her supply closet, metal chain in hand?

The room was empty. A second *clang* drew Caroline's eye to the baseboard heater that ran along the wall to her right. Only the heat cycling on. That's all. Susan was right. She did need to take a little time off.

Turning back to the file cabinet, Caroline methodically rechecked the folders before and beyond the spot where the Spaulding folder should have been, hoping Renée, her secretary, had merely misfiled the record.

The instant Caroline considered that possibility, she remembered, with relief, why Meg's folder wasn't there.

She'd left the file and the videotape containing Meg's last session with her secretary. Renée was going to transcribe the tape to get Meg's recitation of her addiction episode accurately into her record. Chances were, Renée hadn't finished yet.

Caroline hurried out to the reception area. She found the Spaulding folder, the tape tucked inside it, in the locked bottom drawer of her secretary's desk. She slipped the bulky folder into her tote bag. But that still didn't explain the open office door or the file drawer. Meg could have broken into her office and failed to find her folder.

There was a new, louder squeaking sound. Coming from her office. Caroline froze, even as she told herself it was just the electric heat doing its thing.

But this sound was different. She turned around, gasping in shock. A woman wearing a black jacket and jeans stood across the room.

'Tina.'

'You spotted me back on Newbury, didn't you?'

Caroline nodded. She kept her expression as neutral as she could.

Tina King sighed, smoothing back her hair. 'I'm not very good at it.'

'Why?' Caroline asked.

'Lack of practice. Oh, *why* was I following you. That's what you meant.' Tina smiled ingenuously. 'Sorry. I guess I'm . . . nervous. I wanted to talk to you.'

'Why didn't you make an appointment? It's late.'

Tina fidgeted with the gold bracelet around her wrist. 'I came over here earlier this evening. But when I was pulling into the lot I saw you and this other woman get into a car and drive off.'

'Why did you follow us to the café?'

'I'm not sure. I guess I didn't want to lose the connection.'

'The connection?'

'We're sort of tied together. Don't you think?' Tina King smiled distantly, but after a few moments, her eyes grew intent. 'Oh I know. It's what I think that counts. Isn't that what you were going to say, Dr. Hoffman?' The anguish on the model's pale face was palpable. 'I loved him. I trusted him completely. I offered myself completely. But he . . . he . . . couldn't handle all that love. He was afraid. He kept telling me how I didn't understand. But he was the one who didn't understand. And . . . and now he'll never understand.'

Tina King turned away, abruptly letting out a cry of terrible despair. Caroline barely caught the flash of silver until Tina turned fully back to face her.

Caroline's gaze flicked from the bleak eyes of her patient to the extended silver blade of the hunting knife grasped in Tina's hand.

'Tina, please listen to me. What you're feeling . . .'

'Did Martin ever look at you the way he used to look at me, Caroline? With such desperate yearning? Every time I close my eyes I can picture that look. It hurts so much.'

As Tina's hand visibly trembled, Caroline could see her patient's knuckles whiten as she gripped the rubber handle of the knife even tighter.

'Let me help you, Tina. I understand your pain. It feels intolerable, but that's because it's so fresh. So raw.' It was taking a concerted effort for Caroline to articulate. What was Tina planning? Murder? Suicide? Both?

'I know Martin loved me. You tried to make him stop, didn't you?' Tina said accusingly. 'You told him I was perverted, disgusting . . .'

'No, Tina. I'd never say anything like that. I don't think those things about you. You know better than that.'

'You were jealous of what we had.'

'I was the one who referred you to Martin for therapy, Tina. I thought he could help you . . .'

'Martin could have saved me,' Tina cried.

'No, Tina. Only you can save yourself.' Caroline gasped as Tina lifted her arm. The blade glinted as it rose. The point of the knife was aimed at Caroline's heart.

Tina's mouth quivered. 'Martin was the only one—'

Caroline stared in horror as Tina suddenly turned the point of the shimmering blade towards her own chest.

'No!' Caroline yelled, lunging at Tina, trying desperately to grab her arm away before the woman killed herself.

They fell heavily to the floor, overturning a glass-topped side table.

Caroline landed half on top of Tina, her face pressed into her patient's collarbone. Beneath her, she heard a faint wheezing. Tears of relief stung her eyes. Thank God Tina was still alive.

Breathing heavily, Caroline lifted her head. 'Tina—'

Tina looked up at her, a startled expression in her eyes. Caroline gently eased herself off the woman.

Tina blinked. Her lips were still parted.

'You're going to be all right, Tina,' Caroline said. Then she saw the rubber handle of the knife protruding from just above her patient's hipbone, the blade having pierced through Tina's jeans and embedded itself deep into her flesh.

A gust of wind drove rain against the window of the hospital lounge. Caroline shivered. It was almost 11 p.m. Tina King had been wheeled into surgery nearly two hours earlier. At the same time, a fierce spring storm broke.

Caroline was staring out into the raging darkness when she heard footsteps behind her. She turned, expecting to see Tina's surgeon. Desperately hoping for a good report. At the very least, praying that Tina was still alive.

It wasn't the doctor. It was, instead, the last person on earth she wanted to see at that moment. Jesse Baush. His red hair was slick from the rain. Water dripped off his bomber jacket onto the institutional speckled tile floor.

Caroline stared at him.

'How did you—?' she began. The EMTs or someone at the hospital would have reported the incident. Routine procedure.

'You've sure as hell had yourself one busy week, Linny. The victims just keep piling up around you. This makes for a shitload of paperwork for the poor working stiffs down at Homicide.' Bausch smiled insidiously. 'Jeeze, I hope you're gonna take the weekend off so they can catch up.'

It took a couple of seconds for the implications of what he was saying to sink in. 'Tina King tried to commit suicide. I'm sure you read the report I gave to . . .'

'What was she doing at your office on a Friday night?'

'She needed an emergency appointment.'

'You've become quite the devoted do-gooder, Linny.' He sauntered past her, over to the complimentary pot of coffee, took a Styrofoam cup and filled it. As he slowly pivoted round to face her, he swallowed down a gulp of the black coffee, and grimaced. 'Only you didn't do Tina much good, did you? But then, maybe that wasn't your treatment plan.'

Caroline was exasperated. 'For God's sake, Jesse, she brought the knife with her. She pulled it out of her pocket without any warning. At first I thought she meant to kill me . . .'

'Now why would she want to kill you?'

Caroline stiffened. 'I can't discuss that with you. All I can say is that she tried to kill herself. I tried desperately to stop her. That's what happened, Jesse.'

'We'll see, Linny. Of course, if you've got yourself a witness – someone who can stay alive long enough to back you up.'

'Damn it, Jesse.' Caroline's voice cracked. The sheer cruelty of her stepbrother's remark cut right through her. If she'd been a few feet closer to that coffee pot she might have grabbed it and thrown it at him. But Jesse would love that. He could bring her in for assaulting an officer. *Again.*

Casually, Jesse smoothed his damp hair. 'Let's trot over to headquarters so you can make a full statement. I told DeSanto I'd escort you myself. She's waiting for you.'

'I'm not leaving the hospital until Tina gets out of surgery. Until I get a report from . . .'

'Surgery's finished.'

'What? Why didn't . . .'

'I spoke with the doctor. Told him I'd fill you in.'

Caroline's heart slammed.

'You're lucky this time 'round, Linny. The doc stitched that gash up good. Gonna be hurting real bad when she wakes up, though. Yeah, just like my old man hurt.' He flipped up the collar of his jacket. 'Let's go.'

Caroline balked at his order. Was there no way she could get through to him? 'You think your father didn't hurt me, Jesse? You think I'm not hurting?'

He rubbed his jaw, looking as though he was giving her remark careful consideration. 'You know what I think, Linny? I think – you better call your lawyer.'

21

'Are you up?'

'I am now.' As Ben Tabor lifted the phone, he sat up in bed, rubbed his face, glanced at his alarm clock. Just before midnight.

'She called.'

He didn't have to ask Phil who *she* was. Instead, he asked, 'What happened?'

'One of her patients tried to commit suicide.'

'Why phone you about that?'

'She was with the patient at the time. They were at her office.'

'At the Institute?'

'Yes.'

'Is she going to make it?'

'I presume,' Phil told him, 'you mean the patient. Yes. As for Caroline, that's another question altogether.'

'Get to the point, Phil.'

'Baush is bringing her down to headquarters to make a

statement. The patient pulled a knife and was going to commit hara-kiri. If Caroline's fingerprints show up on the knife, you can damn well bet they're gonna book her.'

'What does the patient say?'

'Nothing yet. She's still in recovery. They won't be able to get anything from her until later today.'

'Where are you now?'

'I'm home. The call just came in.'

'How did she sound?'

'Like a woman trying real hard not to sound scared,' Phil said. 'Listen, Ben. I'm way down here in Scituate. It's going to take me a good half hour or more to get up there. If you dragged your ass out of bed, you could be over at headquarters in ten minutes flat.'

'She's your client, Phil.'

'Who's saying otherwise? I'm leaving now. But like I said, it's going to take me a while. I just thought she could use seeing a friendly face.'

'My face isn't all that friendly,' Ben groused. But he was already swinging his legs over the side of his bed.

Caroline rose from the hard wooden chair and started pacing restlessly in the small interview cubicle. She was confused and very anxious.

'Sit down, Caroline. You don't want to let them think you're worried.'

Caroline gave an exasperated sigh. 'I am worried.' But she did sit down next to him. 'What's taking them so long? What are they doing?'

'Making you sweat. And doing a good job of it.'

'You're calm enough.' Caroline didn't mean it as a compliment. Although she had to concede she was glad to see Ben Tabor looking better than at their last encounter. His hair was combed and he'd shaved. He wore a decent pair of chinos, a long-sleeved maroon polo jersey, a pair of cordovan loafers. Even socks. Caroline would have been happier if his expression weren't so grim. Still, she was grateful and relieved that Ben had shown up to substitute until Phil Mason arrived.

'I thought you said Mason would be here by now.'

That's what Ben had thought. 'Maybe he got held up in traffic.'

'At one in the morning?'

Ben glanced at Caroline. Her mouth was tense. He knew she was distressed. But he was proud of her. She'd done fine during DeSanto's interrogation, giving the detective a clear, concise statement about her involvement in Tina King's attempted suicide. Whenever DeSanto'd pressed for information that Tabor considered off limits, he'd solemnly advised *his client* not to answer. Each time, Caroline took his advice.

Ben ran his fingers through his damp hair. A sign that the waiting was starting to get to him, too.

'Did you touch that knife at any time, Caroline?'

'You asked me that already,' she snapped. 'I told you, I don't think so. I'm a doctor. I knew that it might cause more damage if I pulled the knife out. But, during the struggle, I could have – I don't know. I don't know.'

'Okay, take it easy.'

'I should have called Tina yesterday morning. She's obviously going through post-traumatic stress. She's created this fantasy about Martin being her lover. If I'd gotten her in for an appointment right away, maybe this wouldn't have happened.'

'Still taking the weight.'

Caroline scowled. 'What does that mean?'

'You're the shrink. You tell me.'

'I'm not saying I'm to blame.'

'Aren't you?' Tabor countered. 'Don't you always end up finding some way to blame yourself?' Look who was talking. He could write a book on the subject.

'There's a difference between blaming yourself and taking responsibility for your own actions. Or – your own failings.'

'You can't always give people what they want, Caroline. Or save them. Hard enough trying to save your own ass.' He could write that book, too.

Caroline looked at the wall clock. DeSanto'd been gone for over ten minutes.

'What's going to happen if they find my prints on that knife, Ben?'

He didn't respond, but Caroline already knew the answer. It would mark the beginning of the end. No. The end began with Steve Kramer's frantic phone call Tuesday night. It began with her decision to chase him down. *Superpsychiatrist to the rescue. Some psychiatrist! Some rescue!*

DeSanto walked in. So did Jesse Baush. Caroline regarded the pair with nervous expectation. Tabor remained poker-faced.

'Let me tell you something, *Linny*,' DeSanto said

between clenched teeth. 'It's only a matter of time before you slip up. I've got your number. I know all about your fucked-up past. All about your extra-curricular activities . . .'

'Is that it?' Tabor cut her off brusquely.

'For now.' DeSanto made it sound like a temporary reprieve at best.

Caroline wondered how long it would last. From the hostile look on her stepbrother's face, she doubted she'd have much hang-time.

'What about Mason?' Caroline asked Ben as they stepped out of police headquarters onto rain-swept Berkeley Street. 'Shouldn't we wait?'

Ben snapped open his large black umbrella. 'He isn't coming. You need a lift home?'

'No. That's okay. I'll get a cab.'

He snatched hold of her arm. 'Come on,' he said impatiently.

Ben's car, a vintage racing green Porsche, was parked down the street. Once they were settled inside, Ben turned to her.

'You okay?' he asked.

She nodded.

'We could go have coffee or something,' he suggested as he turned on the ignition.

She was more than a little surprised by his offer. And oddly pleased.

'How about if I make us coffee back at my place? I'm just over on St. Botolph Street.'

He pulled out without responding. Instead, he said, 'Tell

me about Tina. You think she really meant to kill herself? Or did she mean for you to stop her?'

'Probably a little of both. She was very angry, but she was also in a lot of pain.'

'How did she know you and Martin were lovers?' he asked.

'Tina didn't know. It's a common enough fantasy for patients with dual therapists. It was clearly a mistake to try that approach with Tina, given her particular disorder. A monumental error, as it turned out.'

'What *is* Tina's particular disorder?'

'She has sexual encounters with multiple partners.' Caroline paused. 'And . . . she has an obsession with something called erotic asphyxiation. The choking reduces the oxygen flow to the brain and erotic sensations are greatly heightened.' She looked over at Ben. 'I know what you're thinking, but Tina isn't the giver, she's the receiver. She's the one wanting to be choked. It's become the only way she can reach orgasm. She also knows it could very likely kill her.'

'Maybe Tina decided to give her sex partner the same experience,' Ben said grimly.

'Martin was never Tina's sex partner. I won't believe it. He wouldn't . . . not with one of his own patients.' Her voice lacked conviction. She now realized she hadn't known Martin Bassett any better than he'd known her.

Ben wasn't so quick to write Tina King off. 'How do we know Tina didn't pursue Bassett to the airport and finish him off there? A jilted lover's a prime candidate. Maybe she forced him into having sex with her first. Threatened him with that knife . . .'

'Tina's suicidal, Ben. Not homicidal. Neither is . . .'

'Your patient who likes to go cruising for pick-ups? Yeah, I've got Meg Spaulding on my list, too.'

Caroline looked over at him. 'I didn't realize you were keeping a list.'

'Yeah – well – a figure of speech,' he mumbled. Cursing himself for walking right into that one.

But Caroline had more pressing concerns than catching out Ben Tabor. 'You have the voyeur I told you about the other night on your list? If not, definitely add him. You might want to put him right on the top. He's desperate for money to flee the country. I'm supposed to provide it.'

'You? Why would you give him money?'

She gave Ben a rundown of Kramer's extortion scheme. 'He's coming to my office Monday morning expecting me to hand over fifty thousand dollars.'

Ben almost ran the red light at Huntington and Cumberland. He slammed on the brakes, his tyres squealing to an abrupt stop. 'Don't even think about it.'

'If Kramer carries out his threat, it'll be precisely the smoking gun Jesse and DeSanto are begging for. Especially Jesse. He's obsessed with pinning these terrible murders on me, Ben. It's a personal vendetta.'

Ben pulled into a parking space near Caroline's building. He switched off his windscreen wipers, cut the ignition and was about to open his door when Caroline asked, 'Why did Mason stand me up, Ben?'

'The jerk thinks he's playing matchmaker.'

She was startled. 'Matchmaker?'

Ben smiled wryly. 'Professionally speaking. He thinks I should be the one representing you.'

'And what do you think?'

'I think maybe it's late and we should skip the coffee. It'll keep us up.' It was a pathetically weak comeback and Ben knew it. But it was the best he could do on such short notice.

Caroline wasn't going to let him off the hook that easily. 'I'll make decaf.'

'No, really. Another time.'

Caroline's gaze fell on her tote bag. The video cassette she'd taken from her office earlier that night was tucked down at the bottom. Along with Meg Spaulding's case file.

'Okay, we'll skip the coffee,' she said. 'But I'd still like you to come up. There's something I want you to see.'

Ben had to admire Caroline's persistence. 'Your etchings?'

'Close.'

'. . . I was at a morning meeting when it came over me,' Meg is saying on the videotape. 'I can't really describe the feeling. Only that it's so intense my mind reels. I can hardly breathe.

'I had to get out of there. That's all I knew. I have no idea what excuse I offered.

'I started walking. No specific destination. The need leads me. I ended up at Faneuil Hall Marketplace. Late morning. Lots of shoppers, tourists milling around the outside on the malls. In the shops. I felt a little like a vampire. So many delicious possibilities.

'I saw him first on the North mall. He was suave, very well dressed, handsome, sure of himself. I followed him into a toy store. Saw the wedding band. Imagined he was shopping for a present for one of his kids.

'A saleswoman came over to me. The interruption pulled me out of myself. I almost left. But then the saleswoman walked off and I caught his eye.

'That's one thing. I can always tell. Always spot them. The ones who will respond. They look at me and they know I'm the one with the key. They can feel my power. They crave it.

'He followed me down and around the aisles to the back of the store. Through the storage area to the employee rest room. We slipped inside. I locked the door. When I turned to face him, I slapped him. Once. Across the face. To let him know.'

'Let him know what, Meg?'

'Who's in charge.

'At first it's a struggle for him to concentrate. He's all keyed up. Wanting to lose himself, but hyper-alert to the danger of being discovered. He begs to go some place more private. Some place *safe*. But I know he's already losing it. His breathing's changed. Rapid little pants. His face is flushed. Oh, he's not forgetting about the risk of getting caught and all the consequences – the humiliation, the shame, the possibility even of arrest – but he's wanting me so much he can't stop himself.'

'Any more than you can stop yourself?'

'I don't see it that way. It's not a matter of what I can or can't do. It's only a matter of what I *want*. That's the thing.

Doing what I *want*. Getting what I want. I'm on such a high.'

'And the risk to you? The danger of you getting caught? Are you thinking about that?'

'That's the key. That's what really excites me. Take that vital element away and I'm bored.'

'Bored?'

'It's not really the sex. That's what's so strange. It's everything that precedes it. Coming – having an orgasm – is the least of it. In fact, there's a part of me that dreads that moment. Not only because it marks the end, but . . .'

'It takes you out of the trance.'

'Yes. All I want the instant it's over is to get the hell away. That guy in the toy store. Afterwards, he revolted me. I couldn't run out of that bathroom fast enough. He wasn't even dressed. I left him naked, begging for more, as I took off. It's the same way with all of them.

'Each time it's over, I always tell myself it wasn't worth it. I feel so miserable. I feel like I'm unravelling.' Meg stops abruptly, giving the group a hostile look. 'There. Are you all happy now that I've given you one of my juicy stories?'

'How does it feel to share your feelings with us?'

'It doesn't help, if that's the answer you're digging for. If anything it makes it worse.'

'In what way?'

'Because . . . because now you all know me. The secret me. I feel exposed. Ugly. Repellent.'

'Don't you also feel . . . ?'

'No more. NO MORE!'

*

Caroline pressed the stop button on the videocassette player. The television went blank. She and Ben Tabor continued staring at the screen for a few moments, lost in thought.

'It was after Meg told the group about this encounter that the first man . . . was killed. I think Steve Kramer might have started following Meg from that point.'

'Kramer or anyone else from your group. I wonder where that guy from the toy store is today,' Ben said.

Caroline shivered. 'You don't think . . .'

'I suppose his body would have turned up by now if one of them had finished him off. If he is alive and kicking, I'd sure like to hear this guy's version of what went down in that bathroom. Especially like to find out if Meg was into getting him off by erotic asphyxiation.' Ben looked over at the closed folder on Caroline's lap. 'Is there more?'

Caroline nodded grimly as she opened Meg Spaulding's case record, pulling out the transcription of their initial evaluation session, and began reading it aloud to Ben—

' . . . My father was extremely jealous. Obsessive. He was always sure my mother was sneaking around, cheating on him.'

'Was she?'

'My mother would go off, sometimes for days on end. We'd never know where.'

'Who'd look after you and your brother when she was gone?'

'We pretty much looked after each other. My father was always in his studio.'

'That must have been hard for both of you.'

'Sometimes. Sometimes it was harder when my mother was around. My mother was diagnosed with schizoaffective disorder. She had these episodes. Maybe there were other men. Sometimes I'd hear them argue. My parents.'

'Were they arguing the night your father died?'

'It was one of her bad days. And then, that night, he came home with this painting. And I think she totally freaked over it.'

'What was the painting?'

'I don't remember.'

'It sounds like the painting disturbed you, too.'

'It's not something I think about.'

'You mean it still disturbs you.'

'No. Not really. I told you – it's not like it's on my mind.'

'Where were you when you heard the shot?'

'Upstairs in my room. It was late. I was in bed. Practically asleep. When I first heard the shot, I thought it was a car backfiring. Or fireworks. You certainly don't think, oh shit my mother's just shot my father to death. Sure she had emotional problems, but I just didn't think . . .'

'That she would be violent?'

'I went running downstairs to their bedroom. I saw my father sprawled on the floor near their bed. There was a lot of blood. He wasn't moving.'

'And your mother?'

'She was on her knees beside him. Holding the gun.'

'No one else was there?'

'No.'

'Your brother? Where was he?'

'At my grandfather's house. Ned slept over there that night.'

'And where was your father's painting?'

'What?'

'Wasn't the painting still there?'

'No. Yes. I don't remember the fucking painting. It's gone now. Ned took care of it years ago . . .'

Caroline set down her case notes and looked at Ben. 'Meg was extremely agitated at this point. She terminated the meeting. I saw her for one more evaluation session a week later, but she refused to regress any further into her past or her family.'

'Can you think of anything that happened recently that might have set her off?'

'Meg's mother was just hospitalized again. Sylvia, Meg's boss, told me at our last session. She thought that was why Meg quit therapy. Because she was so upset about her mother having a relapse and she didn't want to talk about it. If Meg is overidentifying with her mother, especially on a primal level . . .'

'Hold on. Exactly how does Sylvia fit in here?'

'She was the one who referred Meg to me. When Meg told her she'd quit therapy, Sylvia was quite upset.'

'Because Meg's work was suffering?'

'No. It's more personal. Sylvia's emotionally and physically attracted to Meg. When I saw Sylvia for her session on

Thursday, she also mentioned having phoned Meg in New York that day,' Caroline said.

'When did Meg get to New York?'

'I didn't get the opportunity to find out. But, if Meg was in New York on Tuesday night, she couldn't have been the one Steve Kramer saw at the museum. Or at the airport. That would provide Meg with an alibi, but there's still Steve.' Caroline had to face it. Steve Kramer could be a killer. Her patient. Her *ultimate failure*!

'Don't write Meg off so fast, Caroline. What if she left for New York on Wednesday morning? Then she could have been at the museum the night before. And she and Martin Bassett could have both been at Logan at the same time.'

Caroline flashed on her own unconsummated liaison with Martin, the night before the murder. In sharp contrast to their interrupted encounter, her mind involuntarily formed an image of Martin and Meg together at the airport that next morning. In a janitor's closet. The sex – urgent, intense. Wanting, needing. Boundaries shot. Driving blindly, with complete abandon. No thought of consequences on Meg's mind. Or Martin's.

'Easy enough to check,' Ben was saying.

It took Caroline a moment to block out the painful vision and connect with his remark. 'Yes. Easy enough,' she echoed.

'Caroline?'

'I'm okay,' she mumbled.

'No, you're not,' he said.

Caroline didn't bother to argue. She was even slightly relieved to drop the pretense.

Ben glanced at his watch. 'You better get some sleep,' he said, rising from the couch. 'I'll give you a buzz later. Don't talk to anyone . . .'

'I have to talk to Meg.'

'No way,' he said sharply.

Caroline wasn't listening. 'I should have seen it. I should have . . .'

'Don't start looking at this as a test of your clinical skills, Caroline. Being a doctor doesn't make you infallible.'

Caroline stared past Ben. 'Less than a week ago, I actually thought I was a half-decent psychiatrist. Making progress with my very troubled patients. Today, one's trying to blackmail me, another tried to commit suicide in my presence, a third may have had sex with my lover. And one of them could very well be a killer. Now, not only do I feel totally inadequate to help them, I feel like a complete . . . fraud.' Her voice broke.

Ben placed his hands on her shoulders, instantly recalling the times he'd touched her like that in the past, telling himself now, as then, that he was merely giving comfort; trying to inspire confidence. 'Stop being so rough on yourself, Caroline. You're a terrific shrink, doing the best you can with a bunch of seriously screwed-up people. You're also only human. Just like the rest of us poor saps.' He talked fast, as if the speed of his words would dispel the feelings he was experiencing.

Caroline smiled faintly.

Ben dropped his hands to his sides. 'What is it?' he asked anxiously, afraid she'd seen through his act. Again.

'It's always been one of my hang-ups. Trying to be

superhuman.' She paused. 'Maybe because I've often felt so lousy about myself.' She smiled wryly. 'It's called compensation.'

'As in warding off *decompensation*?'

'Exactly.'

Caroline's candour brought them to another one of those awkward silences.

Ben made a big show of checking his watch again. 'Yeah. Well, it's late. I better . . .'

'Ben?'

He wore an edgy look. 'Yeah?'

'I'm glad it was you. At my police interrogation tonight.'

Ben scowled. 'I'm not making any promises here, Caroline. I still think you'd be better off with Phil Mason.'

'He told me about your cousin in Chicago. And his son, Jimmy. Your godson,' she said quietly.

'What else did Phil tell you?'

'Is there more to tell?'

'No.'

Caroline didn't believe that for one instant, but she sensed that if she pushed for the rest of the story – a story she knew had to include Ben's wife – she would really scare him off. And that was the last thing she wanted to do. So all she said was, 'I'm sorry, Ben. It must have been awful for you.'

She was giving him an out. He could say, 'yeah', and leave it at that. But Ben couldn't leave it. He'd never be able to leave it. 'I got too caught up in the whole sad mess. Lost my perspective. Lost my grip.' Lost everything that had ever mattered to him.

'Same struggle therapists have,' Caroline sympathized. 'We're forever trying to keep from getting emotionally caught up in our clients' problems. Maintaining that precious professional distance. But it's not always possible.'

'No. It's not always possible,' he repeated.

They fell silent again. A lot was being said here after all.

'Are you awake?'

'I am now,' Phil Mason grumbled. 'What time is – ? Holy shit, Ben. It's three a.m.'

'Aren't you going to ask what happened?'

'I know what happened. You're doing just fine, Ben. She needs you. And, whine about it all you want, you need her.'

'I need her like I need another hole in my head. And I don't *whine*. I have never *whined* a fucking day in my life.'

'Now you're sounding like the Ben Tabor I used to know and love.'

'Fuck you, Phil.'

'More like your old self by the minute.'

Ben grunted and hung up. What really got him was Phil was right. He was firing on all cylinders again. The wheels in his head that had come to a grinding halt back in Chicago were once more spinning like gangbusters. He was back in the game. Caroline was stuck with him again. *Like it or not.*

He stretched out on his bed, blowing smoke rings up at the ceiling. More than his mind had suddenly snapped back into operating order.

Saturday

22

'Washburn wants to see you, Jesse,' DeSanto told Baush when he dropped into the homicide squad room to say 'hi' early on Saturday morning.

'As in N-O-W,' Green said gruffly from the desk facing his partner's.

Baush eyed DeSanto, gesturing at Green. 'What's his beef?'

'If I were you I'd be worrying about Washburn's beef, not mine,' Green said caustically.

'Lou and I go back a long way, Alfonse. So, let's just say I'm not quaking in my boots.' Baush lifted Amy's mug of coffee off her desk, taking a few quick swallows before he headed for Washburn's private cubicle.

Washburn was hanging up the phone when Baush knocked and walked in. The homicide commander regarded him for a moment before speaking. 'You know who that was?'

'I could make an educated guess,' Baush said, trying to sound breezy.

'That was Vargas over at the D.A.'s office.'

'That was gonna be my guess.'

Again Washburn eyeballed him in stony silence.

'Look, Chief . . .'

'Vargas called me after he got an earful from Ben Tabor.'

'What'd that ni—?'

Washburn pointed a finger at the detective. 'You stepped way over the line here, Baush. I've got to take some of the blame. I should have spelled it out to you right after her boyfriend bought it. Truth is, I thought she'd be a minor player in this mess. That you'd spin your wheels for a while and get it out of your system. But now it's all over town that you hauled Hoffman's ass in here last night and grilled her for over an hour . . .'

'I didn't grill her. DeSanto did.'

Washburn grunted.

'If it were anyone else but Linny, you wouldn't be on my case,' Baush argued, trying to keep his anger and frustration in check.

'She isn't anyone else. She's your sister. Okay, okay, your stepsister,' Washburn snarled before Baush could correct him. 'Any way you cut it, you've got a serious conflict of interests here. As my pal Vargas put it to me. And as, no doubt, Tabor put it to him.'

'I don't see it that way.'

'Frankly, Baush, I don't give a flying fuck how you see it. I'm concerned with how it's playing in the D.A.'s office. In the news.' Washburn added, eyeing the stack of morning papers on his desk. 'Vice detective pursuing stepsister as siren suspect in two sordid and brutal murders and . . .'

'Look, Lou, you're just pissed because Homicide isn't getting all the press . . .'

'Christ!' Washburn threw up his hands. 'If this ever gets to court how do you think your stupid vendetta's gonna come off? Tabor made a complete jackass out of you once on the stand. You want to give him a second shot?'

Despite the insult, Baush smiled. 'So you're thinking we do have a case against her.'

'What did Washburn want? I'll tell ya, babe. That ass-kisser wants me to butt out!' Jesse Baush fumed, slamming his fist against his steering wheel. He was sitting in his unmarked black Chevy Nova in the police headquarters parking lot with Amy DeSanto riding shotgun.

Amy shifted in her seat, smiled a little, tilted her head at what she hoped was a provocative angle. Finally, she said gently, almost in a whisper, 'Washburn's got a point, Jesse. You don't want to mess up the investigation.'

He let the remark hang for several seconds, an unnerving blankness in his expression. 'You know what I think, Amy?'

'What's that, Jesse?'

'I think you don't like me horning in on your act. I think you're worried I'm gonna steal your glory.'

Amy bristled. 'Watch it, Jesse. Or you'll get me started thinking,' she warned.

He grasped the wheel, studying his knuckles like they held some kind of a clue. Then he shifted his gaze, challenging her. 'Go ahead and start.'

'Screw you.'

'No. Really. I wanna know.'

They eyed each other in dead silence. Amy knew she'd be wise to keep her trap shut, but if she were all that wise she wouldn't have gotten herself in this dicey situation in the first place. 'Okay, I'll tell you what I'm thinking,' she said, aware how thin the ground she was treading. 'I'm thinking maybe you're hung up on your stepsister. That you've got a real thing going for her.' She braced herself for Jesse's explosion.

Only this time Jesse Baush defied her expectations. Far from snapping, the clenched muscles in his face slackened. His boyish face suddenly assumed an incongruously tragic air.

'There was a time when I was hung up on Linny, I'll admit that. Way before my dad and her mom got hitched, of course. And before I knew what she was really like.'

There was so much pain in Jesse's voice, Amy immediately forgot how furious he could make her. She even ignored the stab of jealousy she felt. Reaching over, she rested her hand lightly on his arm. 'Did you really walk in on her while she was making it with her mother's boyfriend?'

Baush stared out the windscreen at the rows of cruisers and unmarked cars in the lot. 'Ready for a laugh? I was picking her up for our first date. Got there a little early. No one answered the door, but it was unlocked so I walked on in. Thought maybe Linny didn't hear me ring the bell. I started to call upstairs to her when I heard this moaning. Shit, I thought Linny was sick or something. I rushed upstairs to see if she's okay and what do I find? Linny and her momma's boyfriend Walter fucking their brains out on

Linny's bed.' Jesse said all this in a ghastly monotone.

'But she claimed at her trial a couple of years later that the guy raped her.'

Jesse sneered. 'Oh, yeah? So, how come Linny never pressed charges? Because she knew I saw how much fun she was having – until she spotted me standing there in the doorway, stunned out of my gourd. And then her mom shows up, too. Oh yeah, once Linny realized she had a goddamn audience, she put on quite an act for the two of us, wailing, screaming how Walter forced her. But her mom and me knew the real score. Just like we knew the real score with her and my old man. Linny didn't get to screw him like she wanted, but she sure as hell got to screw him over. And got clean away with it. Well, Linny's screwing days are numbered. If it's the last thing I do, I'm gonna see to that.'

Amy DeSanto moved to stroke Jesse's cheek, but he jerked away.

'Hey, Jesse, I'm just trying to make up.'

'You want to make up, huh?'

She eyed him warily. 'I don't like that look, Jesse.'

'Are you going over to the hospital to get a statement from King?'

'Jesus, Jesse. You know what Washburn's gonna do to me.'

'Come on, Amy. Who's gonna tell him?' Jesse coaxed.

DeSanto wavered. No question but if word got back to her chief, she could lose this plum assignment, which meant she could say good-bye to her hopes of that promotion she wanted so bad she could taste it.

But she wanted Jesse Baush, too. Wanted him just as bad. The taste of him was just as sweet.

Maybe sweeter.

Tina King stared up at the white plaster ceiling as she lay in her hospital bed. Her Kabuki-like pallor matched the stark white bedding pulled up to her chin.

Lieutenant Amy DeSanto sat in a green moulded plastic chair beside the bed, her notepad open on her lap. 'I'm sure you remember some of what happened last night, Tina.' She was doing her best to keep the frustration out of her voice. Twenty minutes sitting there and she had squat. Even though Jesse Baush stood quietly way over by the door, it still felt like he was breathing down her neck.

'Did you bring the knife with you to Dr. Hoffman's office, Tina?'

'What difference does it make?' There was no inflection in Tina's voice. Hardly any sign of life.

'It makes a *big* difference,' DeSanto said.

'I wanted to die. She should have—'

DeSanto leaned in a little. 'She should have what? Aimed the blade better?'

Tina slowly shifted her gaze to the detective. Her wide-set blue eyes cruised DeSanto's face.

'Did Caroline Hoffman threaten you?'

Tina blinked several times, but made no response. DeSanto heard footsteps behind her. She shot Baush a warning look. He ignored it and headed over to the side of the bed.

'Your psychiatrist claims you're a very unstable woman,

Tina,' Baush said. 'She told me you were delusional.'

Tina's face came alive. Her eyes flashed with anger. 'Caroline's the one with the delusions. Martin loved me and she couldn't stand it. She was so possessive. He wanted to end it with her.' Her voice cracked, tears spilling down her cheeks. 'That's why Martin's dead.'

'You willing to say all that in a court of law, Tina?'

'Yes.'

Baush nodded solemnly at her. But when he turned and glanced over at his girlfriend, his lips were curved in a savage grin.

23

The muscles in her jaw tensed and relaxed in rage and frustration. But it was the shame and despair that Caroline's body language radiated the most powerfully to Ben. He felt helpless as he looked across the room at her. She was doubled over on her sofa, her shoulders sagging under an invisible weight. She made a heartbreaking picture of a woman under siege.

Caroline's heart *was* breaking. As she stared bleakly at the front page of the morning's paper, she could see the safe, secure world she'd so carefully constructed over the past fourteen years collapsing around her.

The headline screamed – PSYCHIATRIST QUESTIONED IN SEX SLAYINGS – HISTORY OF PROMISCUITY AND VIOLENCE REVEALED. Beneath the banner was an old photograph of a grim, very frightened eighteen-year-old Caroline with a booking number plaque hanging from her neck. She had little doubt who'd passed that gem along to the media.

'You knew all this crap was going to come out, Caroline,' Ben said softly.

Yes, she knew. She had even thought she was prepared for it. But she was wrong. How do you prepare for your entire life being utterly ruined? And as awful as it was, Caroline knew there was worse to come. The police would now hound her as a suspect in these hideous murders. They'd hound her colleagues, friends, patients, family. People who once knew her in even the vaguest capacity would come out of the woodwork with tales to tell. Every indiscretion, real and fabricated, past and present, would be splashed across papers and television screens. And even if the killer was ultimately caught, it could never undo the terrible harm she was being forced to suffer now.

Once again, Caroline felt her life taking on the texture of a nightmare. As in nightmares, there was no logic, and some higher force pulled the strings.

Ben came and sat beside her. 'I know how painful this is, but you're going to have to . . .'

'Have to what, Ben? Be tough? Fight back?'

'Yes. Exactly. Fight back,' he said gruffly. He wouldn't let Caroline fall apart if he could help it.

But all he got out of her was a hoarse laugh. 'What am I supposed to be fighting for? My reputation? Tell me, Ben, how do you think my colleagues and patients are going to feel about a therapist for sex addicts who's allegedly got her *own* history of promiscuity? A therapist who stood trial for assaulting her own stepfather? A therapist the police believe seduced and strangled to death her own boyfriend and a perfect stranger? I don't think it's going to fill any of them with confidence, do you? Of course all that will be beside the point if I'm found guilty.'

Her breath caught at the awful possibility . . .

Ben drew her into his arms. Screw professional distance. Besides, he was feeling he needed to hold her as he believed she needed to be held.

Ben was right, but Caroline quickly pulled away, nonetheless. There was too much warmth and caring in his embrace. She was afraid to trust it. Trust anyone. Especially now, when she was feeling so needy. Mistakes in judgement were all too easy to make when you felt that way, when you weren't thinking straight. Caroline told that to patients all the time.

'We've got to get you past this,' Ben said awkwardly, trying not to show how rebuffed he felt.

'There is no getting past it. It's over, Ben. I'm finished.'

'Look, Caroline. I'm a first-class champ when it comes to cutting myself off when I'm in pain. I've been doing it for months. Problem is, it doesn't work. It starts to spread and fester like a cancer. The pain just keeps on getting worse.'

Any other time, Caroline would have used the opening Ben was giving her to get him to tell her about *his* cancer. At the moment, however, she simply felt too sick herself.

'We can't undo what the media's done,' Ben doggedly went on. 'But you can't let them do a number like this on you.'

'And just what am I going to do?' A purely rhetorical question.

But he answered firmly. 'You're going to go outside with

me and make a statement to those reporters in front of your building.'

'I know,' Caroline said witheringly. 'Maybe we can replay that fantastic opening statement you made to my jury fourteen years ago. How I'm a young, innocent victim – only I'm not so young any more. And the prosecution didn't exactly present me as all that innocent even back then. Hey, if you've forgotten any of the salacious details of the life and *loves* of Caroline Hoffman, I'm sure you remember Officer Del Lewis's lurid testimony. I can still picture that look on your face when he was up there on the witness stand tearing my innocence to shreds.'

'Yeah, well, if you recall, Lewis was one of the little surprises you didn't prepare me for.'

'Del's testimony was a bald-faced lie,' Caroline said, still as angry now as she was at the time. 'I didn't proposition him. I certainly didn't ask him for money. He came on to me at the mall. And the only reason he made up that cock and bull story that I was soliciting was because his girlfriend spotted him and he wasn't about to let her know he was planning to cheat on her.'

'The trial's over, Caroline.'

But it wasn't over. The trial, her whole excruciating past, was all being dredged up again. And Caroline still felt a desperate need for Ben's understanding. 'I was so messed up at the time. It was just a couple of months after my mother's boyfriend Walter molested me. After which, I was ostracized by the whole damn town. Thanks to Jesse spreading the story that I'd been the one who seduced Walter. I even started believing maybe he was right. That somehow I'd led

Walter on. Anyway . . . I was so lonely. And so desperate for someone to care about me. To want me. I stupidly thought Del did. Instead, he hoists me off to jail and charges me with prostitution. If it hadn't been for Porter getting him to drop the charges—' A stone suddenly hit the living room window, cracking the glass.

Ben sprang up from the sofa, telling himself he was stirred by what was happening outside in the street. Not with what was happening inside the room. 'I'm calling the cops!'

She caught his arm. 'The cops will cheer them on. Maybe throw some stones themselves.'

'Yeah, well they're all throwing stones at the wrong window. Meg Spaulding's the one who should be worrying about splattered glass. She should be worried about a lot worse.'

'Ben, we have absolutely no proof that Meg . . .'

He sat back down on the sofa. 'I have proof.'

Caroline's breath caught. 'What?'

'Proof that Meg flew out to New York on Wednesday morning at 9:35 on United, Caroline. And proof that Martin Bassett's 7:50 a.m. flight on USAir didn't get off the ground until 9:05 because of the storm and the jam-up of planes that morning. Both airlines fly out of Terminal C, Caroline. That places Meg and Bassett in the same terminal at the same time.'

He paused for a moment to let the full impact of what he was saying sink in. 'I'm still checking on Meg's whereabouts Tuesday evening. Your patient Kramer could be our key. If he followed Meg to the museum, why not to the airport the next day? If Kramer witnessed her and Bassett go off—'

Caroline winced. Ben put his hand over hers. She didn't draw her hand away.

'Look, I don't think it's safe for you to see Kramer at your office on Monday . . .'

'You think he's the killer?'

Ben shook his head. 'No. It's far more likely that it's Meg, but I do think that Kramer's running scared . . .'

'It doesn't make sense. Meg's had this sexual addiction for a long time. Why would she suddenly start killing the men she has sex with? You heard what she said in the tape. She has absolutely no interest in her pick-ups afterwards. So why strangle them to death all of a sudden? And why use a chain?'

'Why not a chain?' Ben countered. 'It's a popular enough S&M sex toy. Maybe Meg didn't mean to strangle them to death. If Tina talked in your group about the highs of erotic asphyxiation, why couldn't it have given Meg the idea . . . ?'

Caroline shook her head. 'It's so hard for me to believe it's Meg.'

'I'll put in a call to Washburn now,' Ben said, squeezing her hand. 'We'll go in together and have a private talk with him. You can tell him about Kramer's blackmail scheme and maybe he'll be able to get the truth out of him. Kramer could be the eyewitness the cops need. If he saw Meg . . .'

Caroline gazed at Ben with dark, tired eyes, her face drawn and pale. But her appearance did not reflect any tempering of her resolve. 'Try to understand, Ben. I'm being stripped of practically everything I hold dear. All I've really got left is my integrity. I turn over confidential information about my patients to the police and I've lost it all. I don't just mean my professional licence. I mean . . . everything. And I could be throwing one of my most seriously disturbed patients, a woman who may very likely be innocent, to the wolves.'

Ben gave Caroline a hard, uncompromising stare. 'You willing to be thrown to the wolves instead?'

It was a question Caroline didn't want to have to answer. 'If Meg Spaulding is guilty, I think I can get through to her – convince her that she needs to turn herself in.'

Ben's austere expression remained fixed on his face. 'And if you can't? If she turns against you instead?'

Shortly after Ben left, Caroline played back her long collection of telephone messages. As she'd suspected – and dreaded – there was one from her boss, Alan Rogers.

I'm at the Institute. I'll be here until noon. Please call me as soon as possible. I'm afraid this situation calls for immediate measures.

Immediate measures. Code, as Caroline easily decrypted, for her dismissal. Yes, she thought, just call and get it over with. It would be easier to let Rogers can her over the phone. Better than enduring the humiliation in person.

She got as far as dialling half the number before she slammed the receiver back down. No, she wasn't prepared to let Rogers do that. She'd done nothing wrong. If patients didn't want to continue with her, it was their decision. But she had to fight for the right to treat the patients who not only wanted but needed to see her. She prayed that Meg Spaulding would be one of them.

The phone's sudden ring so startled her, Caroline found herself automatically lifting the receiver again.

'Linny? Is that you?'

Her mother. Caroline's throat dried. She hadn't spoken with her mother in several months. Their last conversation had been an awkward duty call that had lasted all of two minutes.

'Are you there, Linny?'

'Yes. I'm here. How . . . are you?'

'That's a fine question. How would I be with reporters and detectives chasing me, asking me all sorts of questions about my wayward daughter? I always told you one of these days you'd pay for your sins, Linny.'

Caroline felt the familiar nausea overwhelm her. 'I haven't committed any sins . . .'

'Haven't you hurt and humiliated me enough? You know what everyone's going to say now? That it was my fault. My fault you turned out the way you did.'

'I didn't do anything.' How many times over the years had she uttered just those words in response to her mother's endless litany of accusations?

'First Walter. Then Porter. Every time someone loved me, you stole them away. Porter was like a father to you, Linny. They didn't come any better. But you couldn't leave me one shred of happiness . . .'

'That's not true, Mom . . .'

'I told you, way back when you had the nerve to show your face at Porter's funeral I told you, I never want to hear you call me *Mom* again so long as I live. And don't go telling people how I'm some stinkin' drunk who doesn't know what's what. 'Cause no amount of booze is gonna change what I know about you, Linny. What I've seen with my own eyes. I only wish to God it could.'

'Please listen . . .'

'No. You listen to me. Like I told those reporters today, and Jesse last night . . .'

'You saw Jesse last night?'

'He called me. But he promised to come visit me soon. Poor boy. He's still grieving over his dear dead father. Just like me.'

Caroline knew her mother would never understand that she grieved for Porter, too. For all that he'd meant to her before his terrible betrayal.

'I made it clear to all of them, even Jesse, that I don't want to get involved, Linny. I'm not going to let you drag me through the mud again. If I had gone and gotten an abortion like my momma wanted me to, I could have finished high school and gone to college. Hell, maybe I'd have been the psychiatrist. I was smart as a whip. You got your brains from me, you know . . .'

'I do know that.' Caroline's eyes watered. 'Teachers who'd had you in their classes were always telling me how smart you were. How they thought it was such a shame you . . . dropped out.'

'Right. What was I supposed to do? Who was going to look after you while I was back in high school? My momma? She wouldn't so much as change your diaper. And you weren't even crawling yet when she took off with her new husband and moved down to Virginia. Leaving me to fend for myself. I should've given you up—'

Caroline could only choke out, 'Why didn't you?'

There was a long pause. 'Because you were all I had, that's why.' Laura Hoffman's voice exuded a rare note of poignancy.

Although she shielded the mouthpiece, Caroline suspected her mother could hear her crying because Laura's tone instantly sharpened. 'But you have brought me nothing but problems my whole life. Well, no more. You hear me, Linny. You're not my problem any more!'

'Yes, I hear you.' But the phone had already gone dead.

Caroline clutched the receiver against her breast, the anguish burning in her heart.

24

After leaving Caroline's apartment, Ben had decided he needed to get more information about Meg Spaulding. Her brother's art gallery seemed a good place to start. Ned Spaulding would certainly have a different take on his sister than Caroline had.

Ben gave the large, airy gallery a sweeping once-over, taking in the young man's butter soft brown leather slacks, blue silk shirt and cream silk jacket, his dark brown hair pulled straight back in a ponytail. 'You one of the owners here?'

'Don't I wish? I just work here part-time. Ned Spaulding's the owner.'

'He's got a lot of terrific paintings. Is he around?'

'No. But if you're interested in making a purchase or want to know more about any of them I'd be happy . . .'

'I was hoping to touch base with Spaulding.'

'Are you selling something? Because . . .'

'No, no. I'm not a salesman. Actually, I think I might

have met Spaulding's sister a while back and I was curious . . .'

'Meg?'

'Yeah. You know her? She a friend of yours?' Ben asked, careful not to sound too interested and make the guy nervous.

'I wouldn't say Meg and I were ever bosom buddies, but her brother and I go back a long way. We used to hang out together summers on the Vineyard when we were kids. Meg tagged along with Ned a lot so I saw plenty of her. But I wouldn't call us friends.'

Tabor gave him a thoughtful study. 'Were you on the Vineyard the summer Daniel Spaulding was killed?'

Sean Cowen was fingering his lapel, suspicion showing in his eyes. But Tabor had quickly realized that he was a guy who enjoyed dishing the dirt, so he steamrollered on. 'A friend of mine who knows Meg a lot better than I do told me about the tragedy. Christ, I can't imagine . . .'

'You and me both. Ned never talks about it. I mean never.'

'And Meg?'

Cowen shook his head. 'No way. But of course there were rumours galore.'

'What kind of rumours?'

'Not that I'm saying Faith didn't do it – hey, she confessed, not to mention them having her fingerprints all over the weapon – but word around was she wasn't alone that night when her husband walked in on her. A lot of people said her psycho behaviour was an act.'

'You saying she was covering for her lover?'

'I'm not saying anything. Except I did happen to see Faith Spaulding that very day. And she wasn't acting crazy then.'

'Where was this?'

'On the beach, flirting with a few of the local boys.' Cowen shrugged. 'Faith was always playing up to them. Anyway, she came over to chat with us – well, mainly to Ned and Meg – and she didn't seem nuts to me. When she left, Meg made some sort of cutting comment which angered Ned. Not that he said anything, but he threw her one of his looks and Meg clammed right up.'

'Was she scared of her brother?'

'Scared? Good God, no. Meg adored Ned. Still does. And believe me, the feeling's mutual.'

From the way Sean Cowen said it, Ben most definitely did believe him.

There were a series of penetrating rings. Meg suddenly realized the sound wasn't part of her dream.

Eyes still closed, she fumbled for the phone.

'Meg?'

This time she had no trouble recognizing the caller's voice. 'What do you want now, Steve?'

'Have you seen the news yet this morning?'

'No.' She peered blearily over at the clock. It was almost 11 a.m. She never slept that late.

'Seems the cops think our lovely shrink may be moonlighting as a crazed serial killer.'

Meg stiffened. 'Dr. Hoffman?'

'Yes. Poor Caroline. Of course, I could set the police

straight, but then where would that leave you, Meg?'

Meg knew exactly. Where Caroline was now. 'I don't have the money – yet. A person doesn't keep twenty thousand bucks lying around . . .'

'You forgot a zero there, Meg.'

'What?'

'It's five zeros, not four.'

'I don't understand.'

'An architect who's weak in maths? Come now, Meg. How much is a two followed by five zeroes?'

Meg took in a sharp breath.

'Why don't I drop by and add it up for you?' Kramer said.

Meg shivered, pulling the blanket up to her neck. 'No. You can't. Really. I was about to go out.'

'I'm heading over right now. It'll only take me ten, fifteen minutes. I think you'd better wait for me. Oh, and I've got a little something for you, Meg. Something you left behind while you were out last night.' There was the briefest pause, before Kramer added in a seductive whisper, 'Your raincoat.'

Kramer heard the police siren bearing down on him when he was driving past the train and bus terminal at South Station. Beads of cold sweat broke out across his brow as he checked his rear view mirror and saw the cop behind the wheel of the B.P.D. cruiser motion for him to pull over. What the hell did they have on him now?

He felt nothing but relief when it turned out all he'd done was run a red light. A routine traffic violation. He politely took the pricey ticket from the cop. Not that he had any intention of paying it. He'd be lounging on a sunny beach in Costa Rica long before the due date.

Kramer remained stationary until the cruiser took off and was way down the block. He wasn't taking any chances.

Once the cruiser turned the corner, he continued along Atlantic Avenue. No hope of making up for lost time with all the road work going on. Construction crews were in the midst of a monumental project to tear down the heavily trafficked I-93 overpass that cut right through the city's historic district and bury it underground. Kramer passed the time fantasizing about traffic-free Costa Rican beaches.

Instinctively, he reached for his car phone to ring Meg again to make sure she'd stayed put. But then he remembered – he'd let the contract on his cell phone expire. Ex-doctors couldn't afford such luxuries. That really hurt.

As he turned down the narrow access road to Meg's apartment complex – still worrying that she might have bolted before he had the chance to impress her with the seriousness of his *need* face-to-face – he caught a glimpse of a woman darting from the last building on the street into a waiting cab.

He smiled at his good luck.

The cab pulled out and drove right past him.

Kramer did a U-turn and followed.

Of all the possible destinations, The Institute For Special Problems would have been the last on Steve Kramer's list. But there was Meg, springing from the taxi and hurrying through the double glass doors into the main reception area.

Questions were flying through his mind as he drove around back to the Institute's parking lot. Had Meg called Caroline after their phone conversation and spilled the beans? If they joined forces, his plans would be ruined. He couldn't very well threaten to finger the two of them for the same crime.

There were only a few cars in the lot since most of the therapists took Saturdays off. He pulled into a corner parking spot near the wire mesh fence that separated the property from a mansard-roofed townhouse facing onto Beacon Street.

He let the car idle for a couple of minutes before switching off the ignition. He continued to sit there, not sure what to do next. What if Caroline talked Meg into going to the cops? That would be the end of his hopes of profiting from all of this. And what if they charged him with blackmail? Shit.

He slammed his palm against the steering wheel. Or what if the police decided to charge him as an accessory to murder? Jesus, they'd throw the goddamn book at him. Lock him away for—

A sharp rap on his window made Steve Kramer almost jump out of his skin.

25

Knowing that the reporters would have their eyes out for her car, Caroline deliberately bypassed the Institute's private lot, parking her Saab down an alley a couple of streets away.

As soon as she stepped into the Institute's lobby with its grey-green walls, and traditional English-style furnishings, Caroline felt an unfamiliar unfriendliness about the place. Maybe, one of these days, she'd write a treatise on *The Fugitive Complex*. No question she was going to have plenty of time on her hands to work out the details.

Caroline's footsteps echoed across the highly buffed black and grey marble floor as she headed for the walnut panelled elevator. She came to an abrupt stop when she saw Meg Spaulding stepping out of the ladies' rest room.

Meg started towards Caroline, but paused mid-stride, nervously smoothing a loose strand of hair back into her untidy French knot. 'I found myself at a loose end.'

Caroline thought it an apt description. Meg, usually so

meticulous, looked unsettlingly unkempt. Not just her hair, her entire appearance – no make-up, creased cranberry silk blouse, shirt-tails hanging out over a pair of rumpled jeans. She was jockeying her tote bag and denim jacket between her hands.

'I was here earlier . . . I went up to your office, but you weren't there. I know you sometimes work on Saturdays, so I went and got some coffee, came back, hung around – just in case.'

Caroline looked quickly past Meg. With sickening clarity, she recalled that policeman coming over to DeSanto at the art museum on Tuesday night carrying that snapshot of the victim and his girlfriend that he'd found in the museum's ladies' room. The killer must have been in there. Changed her clothes in there?

Meg pressed a hand against her chest. 'My heart's racing. I feel like I've just run the Boston Marathon.' A lopsided smile crossed her face. 'I saw the papers. I'm so sorry about what's happened, Caroline.'

Caroline was assessing Meg's appearance, her exaggerated mannerisms, the pitch of her voice, her rapid-fire delivery. At the same time, she was monitoring her own responses – a quickened heart rate, cold, sweaty palms, dry mouth, muscular tension. She was panicking.

Meg began walking towards her again. 'Can we talk, Caroline? In your office? Please?'

Caroline felt cornered. But wasn't this precisely the opportunity she had wished for? To meet with Meg? Evaluate her mental status? Find out the truth? And if, even though she was desperate to believe otherwise, Meg was the killer, help her patient to come to terms with it and turn herself in?

Still, Ben's admonition reverberated in her head. *What if she turns against you, instead?*

Meg stopped a few feet from Caroline. 'If you're seeing someone else, I could wait. I wouldn't mind waiting. I have no plans.'

Caroline knew it was likely, after she met with Alan Rogers, that she, too, would have no plans. Of course, if Rogers fired her, she couldn't legitimately conduct any further therapy sessions at the Institute – with Meg or any of her other patients. This might be her last chance to offer help. Not to mention Meg's last chance to ask for it.

Meg nervously crossed then uncrossed her legs. Her eyes darted around the office. She reminded Caroline of a caged animal.

'I read the morning papers. What they're saying about you.'

'How did you feel, reading about me?' Caroline asked, striving to conceal her own feelings.

Meg frowned, snagged a loose tendril of her auburn hair, winding it tightly around her finger. 'I don't know. Confused. Frightened. Repulsed.'

'What repulsed you?' Caroline managed to keep her voice steady.

Meg leaned forward, draping her arms around her crossed legs, eyes cast on Caroline's carpet. 'The way people are always twisting things. Making you think something's your fault when it isn't.'

Caroline saw a glimmer of an opening. 'Does that happen to you? People blaming you for something you don't think is your fault?'

Meg tensed, her head jerking up. 'Has he been talking to you?'

'Who?'

'Kramer.'

The opening widened. Now Caroline had to be careful. 'About what, Meg?' she coaxed.

Meg gave her a long, hard stare. 'You know, don't you?'

'What do you think I know, Meg?'

Meg continued assessing her. 'That he's been following me. That he saw me. At the museum. Don't you think that's truly sick, Caroline? Steve spying on me like that? Watching? Talk about disgusting.'

There it was. Meg openly admitted she was the woman with Peter Korza. Little doubt then that Meg was also the woman who'd been with Martin at the airport on Wednesday morning. Unless Steve Kramer—

'You're disgusted, too,' Meg observed, displaying no emotion herself. 'I can see it in your eyes.'

Caroline's impulse was to look away. As much to keep Meg from seeing her too clearly as to keep herself from completely losing it. But to break eye contact might provoke Meg. Her only hope was to concentrate on being the therapist – not the grieving lover, nor a terrified potential victim.

'Tell me about being with Peter Korza at the museum, Meg. Do you remember – everything that happened?' A memory of the dead musician crumpled obscenely on the gallery floor flashed through Caroline's mind, followed by a devastating image of Martin's corpse laid out on that metal slab.

Meg's expression became coolly calculating. 'Don't think I don't know what you're trying to do. I'm not stupid, Caroline. And *I'm* not the one who's in serious trouble here. Everything I've ever told you is confidential, as if I'd confessed my sins to a priest. You can't say one word to the police.'

'That's not strictly true,' Caroline said, struggling to keep her voice under control. 'If you were to tell me you planned to harm yourself – or someone else, I would have to report it.'

Meg eyed her defiantly. 'I'm not suicidal. I want very much to live. I may be a sex addict, but I'm *not* a killer. So there's nothing for you to report.'

'Then you can tell the police the truth—'

Meg cut her off with a harsh laugh. 'Granted, that would help your situation, but it certainly won't help mine. You think they'll buy the truth? You obviously don't.'

'What is the truth, Meg?'

'The truth? I didn't kill either one of those men. I swear, Caroline.'

'Why did you come to see me today, Meg? You seemed frantic in the lobby. Afraid.'

'I am afraid. Don't you see? Somebody who hates me is responsible for what's been happening. Maybe Kramer—' There was a touch of desperation in Meg's voice now.

'You think Kramer watched you with those men and then killed them after you left? Why would he . . . ?'

'Why else would he be following me around? Blackmailing me? He's twisted. Perverted. All I know for certain is that I had no reason or desire to hurt those men. Why would I? I didn't give a damn about either of them. It was just something I needed. Something,' she added with a cruel smile, 'they needed just as badly.'

Caroline could feel her insides roil. 'What is it that you need? Deep down? It isn't just the high. The escape. What else is it you need?'

The frantic edge vanished from Meg's features. She gazed into Caroline's eyes dispassionately. 'I think you know exactly what it is.'

'Darlene. Come on, Darlene. All you had to do was a little baby-sitting. What do ya mean, you lost her.' Baush switched the car phone from his right hand to his left as he shifted into drive and started out of the hospital parking lot.

DeSanto had her arms clamped across her chest, her full lips drawn into a thin line. She was totally pissed at Baush. Not only had he butted into the King interrogation, now he'd put one of his vice cops on Caroline Hoffman's tail.

'. . . I'm sorry, Lieutenant. The street was packed with reporters and cameramen. It was gridlock. I do have something for you, though.'

'Yeah? What's that, Darlene?'

'I chatted up this anchorwoman, Jill Nugent. She was hanging around that sex clinic yesterday bird-dogging Hoffman, when this patient comes storming out of the shrink's office, cursing a blue streak. From the description she gave me of this guy, I'll lay you odds it's our peeper, Steve Kramer. Sounded to her like Kramer was threatening Hoffman.'

'I'll check it out. I'm heading over to Kramer's place now.'

'Forget it. When I drove over to the clinic looking for Hoffman, I spotted Kramer's car in the lot behind the building.'

'What about Hoffman's car? You didn't happen to look to see if a white Saab . . .'

'Cut the sarcasm, Jesse. Her car's not there.'

'You go inside, Darlene?'

'No. I thought I'd wait until I checked in with you.'

'Where are you now?'

'I'm watching the lot. What do you want me to do?'

'Sit tight. We're on our way.'

Caroline was growing concerned by Meg's mood swings and matching transitions in body language. As soon as Meg's anger surfaced, she sat rigidly upright, her jaw jutting out aggressively. But down, Meg's shoulders drooped, she stared at the ground, bending forward as if trying to fold herself in half.

'Do you hate me now that I've told you I was with your boyfriend?'

Never had it been so hard for Caroline to keep her personal feelings out of a therapy session. Never had it been so vital. 'No, Meg. I want to help you. But I feel you're holding back. It's possible you don't remember everything that happened. You could have blocked it out. A form of amnesia . . .'

'You still think I'm guilty.' Meg glared at Caroline.

'I'm not here to accuse you or to judge you, Meg. All I want to do is help you.' Caroline knew she was saying this partly out of her fear that Meg was responsible for the murders of Peter Korza and Martin, and partly it was her own guilt talking. She may not have single-handedly turned Meg into a deranged killer, but she certainly hadn't done much to prevent her from becoming one.

Despite her inner turmoil, Caroline was doing reasonably well maintaining her professional demeanour. But when Meg abruptly leaned forward, and snatched hold of her hand, Caroline felt another rush of panic. Although she was quick to conceal it. Meg smiled slyly and released her. 'You don't like to be touched.'

'There are all kinds of ways to be touched, Meg. I think I touched you when I offered you my help. But that kind of touch made you uneasy. Because it's hard for you to feel you deserve help.'

'I honestly do feel sorry for you, Caroline. That the police suspect you. But I can't get involved. If I admit I was with those men, the police will pin the murders on me, no matter what.'

Caroline was afraid Meg was right.

'I watched my mother stand trial for murder, Caroline. It was unbearable. I couldn't live through a trial, being sent to prison, or even worse an insane asylum.'

'Meg, I have to assume you came to see me today because, as scared as you are, you do want my help. You must want this to stop, but you can't do it on your own. What if Steve Kramer or someone else is responsible for the murders, then we need to figure out together how to find out. Do you have any idea at all . . . ?'

'I know you're humouring me,' Meg sneered. 'And I'm warning you, Caroline. Don't even think about turning me in. If you betray me, you'll be very, very sorry.'

Caroline leaned back. *What if she turns against you instead?*

Caroline's anxiety was abruptly diffused by a loud rap on her office door. But her relief was short-lived when the door flew open and, to her astonishment, her stepbrother burst into the room with Detective Amy DeSanto right on his heels.

Meg leaped up in alarm. But Jesse gave her only a cursory glance, zeroing in on Caroline, who was staring back at him, aghast.

'Who are . . . these people, Caroline?' Meg stammered as she edged warily towards the open door.

Amy DeSanto, only a few feet from Meg, flashed her badge. Meg paled.

'For God's sake, get a hold of her,' Caroline called out to DeSanto, seeing that Meg was about to pass out.

'No, no!' Meg screamed, misinterpreting Caroline's command.

'Take it easy, Miss,' DeSanto said. 'It's okay. No one here's gonna hurt you.'

Meg looked at Caroline with sheer loathing. 'How could you . . . do this?'

'Meg, I didn't. It's not what you're thinking.'

Baush had little interest in this exchange. 'Where's Steve Kramer, Linny?'

Meg gasped.

Suddenly, Baush extended his interest to her. He pivoted round and squinted at Meg. 'You know Kramer? He have a session with the doc before you . . . ?'

'Stop it, Jesse!' Caroline shouted. 'What you're doing is totally reprehensible.'

Baush looked back at her. 'We know Kramer's here, Linny,' he said, his voice thick with accusation. 'His car's parked out back. It's been there for at least forty-five minutes. Maybe longer.'

'I am in the middle of a psychotherapy session.' Caroline spat out each word. 'You have no idea the irreparable damage . . .'

'What's going on here?' a deep voice boomed over them all.

Everyone's eyes turned in the direction of Dr. Alan Rogers as he strode into Caroline's office. Before the director of the Institute got an answer, undercover vice cop Darlene Lowell burst in on the gathering. She was wearing a tight powder blue angora sweater, a black mini-skirt and a smirk that went from ear to ear.

'I found Steve Kramer. Wearing the same M.O. as the other boys,' she announced with macabre good cheer.

26

Caroline squeezed her eyes shut, blotting out the painfully bright overhead light that glared off the puke-green tiled walls of the stinking holding cell. Hell revisited. Caroline felt herself losing touch with her new self – the self-assured healer, the woman who, for the past fourteen years, had been the object of admiration and respect.

Her eyes reflexively opened to the crack of the uniform's nightstick as she strode past the pen. Like every time before, the guard singled her out from the rag-tag collection of hookers, bleary-eyed, bone-thin druggies, drunks and vagrants all around her. She turned away and stared blindly at the back wall.

Is this my reward for clinging to my ethical principles? How far am I willing to take this? What if I'm charged with murder? Tried and found guilty? Locked up for life . . . ?

'Who the fuck do you think you're looking at?'

Caroline snapped out of her trance. She saw a rhinestone

nose-stud inches from her face. And then took in its wild-eyed owner.

Instinctively, she drew back. She tried to look away. But the eel-thin woman ruthlessly grabbed her chin. 'You dissing Monique, girl?' Monique's pupils were pinpoints. 'You fucking blowing me off, you high-priced piece of shit?'

'I'm trying to mind my own business.' Caroline twisted her head to the side, breaking her cell mate's grasp. But when she tried to stand up, the wired-up blonde caught hold of her ivory cashmere blazer and yanked her violently down onto the metal bench.

The back of Caroline's head smacked against the tiles, her skull exploding with pain. She froze as Monique smiled licentiously down at her, and a small group of menacing faces crowded around. Her heart thudded against her rib cage. *So much for fearing a lifetime in jail. She might not live through the first day.*

'Stuck up little bitch, ain't ya? But you do got style, girlfriend. Take that classy jacket . . .'

'Yeah, Monique, why dontcha take it, girl?' a huge woman with glitter in her black hair goaded.

A kid, the left side of her face swollen, both eyes black and blue, sprang forward and snatched hold of Caroline's foot. 'These heels are bitchin'.' She looked up for approval from Monique. 'I gotta look good for . . .'

'Yer comin' out party, honey?' Monique cracked as she ran her hand down the front lapels of Caroline's jacket, her fingers deliberately, provocatively gliding over Caroline's breast.

Caroline tried to shrink against the wall, but Monique

gripped the collar of her beige silk blouse, just about cutting her airway off.

'Please—' Caroline rasped, envisaging herself being raped, beaten, killed . . .

'Hey, our scared little pussy's saying *please*. Now, that's what I call manners. *Please* what, pussy?' Monique taunted.

'What's going on in there, ladies?'

It was the guard. Tears of relief welled in Caroline's eyes.

'We're having ourselves a cozy little coffee klotch,' Monique called out glibly. Caroline felt her tormentor's red fingernails digging into her skin. ''Course it'd help if there was some coffee.'

That got a big laugh from the other women. Much to Caroline's horror, the guard laughed, too.

No help there. How could she have thought there would be?

'Well, just as long as you girls don't go leaving any telltale marks on our celebrity,' the guard said airily as she passed.

Monique raised a pencil-thin eyebrow. 'Celebrity?' she murmured against Caroline's ear.

Caroline yanked Monique's hand from her mouth. 'I'm no celebrity. Trust me, I'm nobody.'

The fat woman with the glitter in her hair came in for a closer look. 'Wait. Wait. Shit, I know who she is, Monique. She's the shrink that strangled those johns with a chain. You know. That serial sex killer that's all over the news.'

'No shit,' Monique mused, letting go of Caroline and stepping back.

Caroline was quick to pick up the note of awe in her abusive cell mate's voice. She felt the lessening of the tension all around. *From fallen healer to terrified victim to admired killer, all in a matter of minutes. What a sad commentary on how fast and how deep she'd sunk.*

'Can you state your name and address for the record?'

'Gary Whalen. That's W-H-A-L-E-N.' The young man smiled nervously. 'I've never done this before. Made a statement. That's what this is, right?'

'Address?'

'Right. Thirty-four Cherry Street, Braintree.' He lifted the paper cup of water off the table in the interview room. He took a sip, then held on to the cup. 'I swear to God I almost passed out when I saw her picture in the paper this morning and realized – shit. Sorry, it's just when I think how close I came . . .'

'Don't get ahead of me, Gary.'

'Sorry.'

'And you say you work at the Regency Hotel at Copley Centre here in Boston.'

'Night clerk. Since last November. I go on duty tonight in a couple of hours. You think there'll be reporters wanting interviews? I mean, I don't know what I should say . . .'

'For now, we'd rather you said nothing to anyone but us, okay, Gary?' DeSanto flashed him one of her winning smiles.

'Yeah, sure. No problem, Detective. I mean if you're worried I'm gonna sell my story to one of those tabloid shows or something, I'm cool. Really.'

DeSanto's smile vanished. 'Don't mess up on me, Gary. We might need you to testify. There'll be plenty of time after this ugly business is wrapped for you to – tell the world your story.'

'Right. Gotcha.'

'Good. Now let's start with Thursday night. What time?'

'Around twelve minutes past eleven. The check-in time's on the card.'

'You have the card, Gary?'

'Yeah. I mean I didn't think to bring it. She got her signature on it and everything.'

'We'll send someone over for it. No problem. What name did she register under?'

'Uh . . . Not Hoffman, but believe me, it was her. I don't have a single doubt . . .'

'What name did she use?' DeSanto repeated patiently. Hoffman using an alias might well work in their favour. If the writing sample and the line-up came out the right way.

'Brown. Carol Brown. No luggage but she did have this tote bag, though. Coulda had a few feet of chain in there.'

'Go on, Gary.'

'Yeah, right. She told me she lived down the street, but that her place was being painted. She made a big thing about wanting a king-sized bed. She went on and on about having this wicked headache. The whole time, she's batting those doe eyes at me. I told her I had some aspirin in the office and if she wanted to hold on a sec, I'd get 'em for her. This is the clincher. She says to me – "Give me a few minutes and then bring 'em up to my room." I'm not a jerk. I get the message, believe you me. And – okay, I gotta admit I'm tempted. She's got the looks, the style. But, I don't know. There was something *off* about the broad. I was pick-

ing up these vibes – this baby was not someone to be mess-
ing with . . .'

'So, you didn't go up to her room?'

'Well, no. No, I . . . uh . . . chickened out.'

'You're sure now.'

'Yeah, I'm sure. Good thing, huh?' He did a mock choke
hold on his neck for visual emphasis.

'Yeah. Good thing.'

Washburn's sardine can of an office was wall-to-wall people.
Besides the chief there was Washburn's secretary, the assis-
tant D.A. Jerry Vargas, Ben Tabor, Detective Amy DeSanto
and her *rightful* and less than gleeful crime fighting partner,
Alfonse Green. Green was still steaming because his so-
called partner had been consistently cutting him out of the
loop. DeSanto wasn't feeling all that great herself. That
statement from the hotel desk clerk had fallen way short of
her expectations.

Ben slapped his hand down on Washburn's desk. 'You've
got absolutely nothing . . .'

The chief cut him off. 'We've got three stiffs, two of
whom your client happened to have been associated with.
Maybe all three. The jury's out on that one, but you never
know . . .'

'Okay.' Ben got back his cool. 'I'll amend that statement. You haven't got a stitch of physical evidence, you're
weak on opportunity, and utterly lacking for motive. You
book her now and you're just going to make a lot of work
for everyone. And come off looking like you don't know
your ass from your elbow.'

'And what should we make out about that blow-up between Kramer and Hoffman? We have a very reliable witness . . .'

'You should make the same out of it that any reasonable person would. Kramer was Dr. Hoffman's patient. Patients often get angry at their shrinks. Shrinks encourage it.'

'You got anything more illuminating to say, counsellor?' Washburn inquired.

'Yeah, I've got plenty more,' Ben snapped. 'Caroline wasn't the only person at the Institute this morning. In fact, she was with a patient when you people dropped in on her.'

'So?' Washburn derisively rolled his eyes.

'So, did anybody think to question the patient? Even bother to get her name?' Ben saw DeSanto shift uncomfortably.

'Well, DeSanto?' Washburn demanded.

The corners of DeSanto's mouth twitched. 'She was freaked, Chief. No reason to think – discovering another strangled guy was taking up pretty much all of our attention.'

'So you didn't get her name?' Washburn rubbed his thumb across the bridge of his nose.

'I did, Chief.'

All eyes turned to Detective Alfonse Green.

He pulled out his pocket-sized note pad and flipped it open. 'Her name's Meg Spaulding. She was heading out of the Institute when I got there. I figured she'd probably been questioned already, but just to play it safe, I had a few words with her. She told me she'd been meeting with Dr.

Hoffman when DeSanto – and Vice Lieutenant Baush – interrupted the therapy session.'

DeSanto clenched her fists at her sides. *Yeah, Alfonse, you getting a big high riding my ass?* 'Okay, so I missed one. I did get statements from everyone else on the scene. The janitor who discovered the body. Dr. Alan Rogers, who runs the place. Another shrink—' DeSanto flipped open her notepad. 'Susan Steinberg. Neither of the docs were seeing any patients that morning. Steinberg said she was there catching up on paperwork. And Rogers – he was upstairs in his office waiting for Hoffman. Only she never showed up.'

'They didn't have an appointment scheduled,' Ben said. 'Caroline made that perfectly clear in her statement.'

DeSanto snickered. 'Right. She was busy keeping another appointment. With Steve Kramer.'

Infuriated, Ben turned to the A.D.A. 'Vargas, these people here are so off-track, it's not funny.'

'Nobody's laughing,' DeSanto said.

Ben levelled a look at Vargas. 'What if I told you that Dr. Hoffman has some evidence that could put you on the right track?'

'If she knows more than she's told us – which doesn't add up to a hill of beans,' the A.D.A. said, 'I'd strongly suggest you encourage her to share it.'

'There's an issue here of patient-doctor privilege.'

'Well, if the patient is Steve Kramer, I don't think he's gonna put up much of a stink,' DeSanto said sarcastically.

'Yeah, well it's more complicated than that,' Ben said.

'Serial killings are always complicated.' Washburn

reached for the can of Dr. Pepper that was serving as a paperweight on his desk.

'I've had it with you clowns,' Ben said. 'I want to meet with my client.'

'No problem, counsellor,' Washburn said affably.

'Oh, when you do see your girlfriend, Tabor,' DeSanto paused for effect, 'be sure to ask her how she liked her king-sized bed at the Regency Hotel.'

27

Caroline looked dreadful. Ben could hold the fluorescent lighting in the windowless cubicle partly to blame. It certainly added an unhealthy yellow tinge to Caroline's skin. But the rest – the slackness around her mouth, the haunted look in her eyes, the dark circles under them, the brittle way she was holding herself in that beat-up wooden chair – they had nothing to do with the lousy lighting. It broke his heart to see her like that.

'What's going to happen now?' Caroline asked flatly.

Ben knew better than to suggest he could very likely walk her out of there *if* she broke confidentiality. Instead, he gave the alternative to her straight. 'They can detain you for questioning without pressing charges for up to forty-eight hours.'

'And will they be pressing charges?'

Ben hated hearing the note of resignation in her voice. He had to bring her around. 'Caroline, we've only got one option here and you know it. Meg admitted being with

Korza and Bassett. She was at the Institute when Kramer was killed . . .'

'She swore to me she didn't kill Peter Korza or Martin. That it was only about . . . sex. She thinks someone who hates her must have been following her.'

'Like Kramer? Yeah, he followed her, all right. And look what happened to him. Come on, Caroline. You know she's the one. Hey, she's got a good shot at going with an insanity plea. Like mother, like daughter.'

'I'm not fully convinced Meg's guilty. Or psychotic,' Caroline said stubbornly. 'There was a lot stronger case against me at my trial and I was innocent.'

'And you know what that says to me? That you're over-identifying here, Caroline. Your situation was altogether different. I know you. And you are not Meg Spaulding.' He smiled faintly, hoping she'd smile back.

She didn't.

He lit a couple of cigarettes, handed one to her. Caroline took it without hesitation, pulled in a long drag, grimaced, and stubbed it out in the metal ashtray.

'Maybe Meg and I are not as different as you think,' she said.

'Does this have anything to do with you and the Regency Hotel? Because we sure as hell can't afford a rug getting pulled out from under us this time. What aren't you telling me, Caroline?'

'How do you know about the Regency?'

'I don't know about it. But Amy DeSanto seems to.'

Caroline looked away.

Ben drew his chair closer to her. He wanted to shake her.

He wanted to take her in his arms. *Talk about conflicted emotions.* 'I want to help you, Caroline. We're in this together. Like it or not.' Ben stubbed out his cigarette.

'It's no big deal,' she said, slowly meeting his eyes. 'There were so many reporters hanging around my building. So I decided to spend Thursday night at the hotel. The desk clerk flirted with me and tried to get into my room with his passkey. Fortunately, I was smart enough to flip the safety bar on the door. He got the message I wasn't interested and left. And I went to sleep. End of story.'

'That's it?' Ben didn't sound convinced.

Caroline wished she hadn't put out that cigarette. She was still afraid to open up. Yet she knew Ben was probably the one man who could handle it. The one man she might dare to trust.

She wanted to tell Ben the whole sad, sordid story. Possibly more than she'd wanted anything in a very long time.

'The problem really isn't what happened at the Regency Hotel, Ben. It's . . . what *might* have happened. What *has* happened . . . in the past.'

'I'm listening.'

Caroline couldn't meet his steady, caring gaze. It only made her feel more uncomfortable. More ashamed.

Ben gently placed his hand over hers. His touch, the gentle expression on his face, the bond she'd felt between them all these years, gave her the guts to go on. 'I thought I had it licked. What a laugh. I make my living confronting patients so they'll face the fact that recovery from addiction is always conditional.'

Ben's throat went dust-dry. 'What are you trying to tell me, Caroline? That *you're* a sex addict?'

'What I'm saying is that I've had more than my share of sexual problems. You commented before that I over-identify with Meg. It was an astute observation. It's always dangerous for a psychiatrist to do that.' Caroline flicked imaginary ash off the table. 'Oh, I've never put on a disguise before I went out. Or deliberately picked particularly risky places to have sex. But I did go through a period of seeking liaisons with practical strangers. And just like Meg, I didn't really want to get to know them. And I certainly didn't want them to get to know me. Oh, I've been *on the wagon* so to speak for over six years,' Caroline went on. 'When I went to the Regency, I was setting myself up for a fall. This mess I'm in now rekindled all those old feelings of frustration, hopelessness, fear, anger. When I used to feel like I was coming unglued, I'd mend the cracks with sex.'

'Okay, so you used to be promiscuous. You had some one-night stands.' Ben had guessed as much. 'Hell, I've had my share of those. Maybe you were driven by all those bad feelings, but maybe, like me – like thousands of others – you were also just plain lonely.'

'I never felt more lonely than I did after those empty encounters,' Caroline said. 'Lonely. Ashamed. Disgusted. That was when I'd swear, never again. But the pressures would build up again and there I was, flirting with some guy, pretending I was interested in him, pretending he was interested in me. A brief – very brief – courtship ritual that began in a club, bar, whatever, and ended in a hotel room.' Caroline clenched her hands together so tight, her fingers went numb.

'I finally sought help after a very ugly encounter with a man who I totally misread.' Now that she'd started, Caroline couldn't stop. 'He . . . he beat me up pretty badly. It was when I was still in medical school. I took a six-month leave and went into therapy. I stayed in treatment for three years – and found my calling.'

She dropped her gaze. 'So, that's the long away around what happened at the Regency Hotel, Counsellor.'

In sharp contrast to Caroline, Ben was at a complete loss for words. He lit another cigarette for himself, cuffing the struck match between both his hands. The air in that claustrophobic interview room was as still and oppressive as the heavy silence that had settled between them.

This time, when the metal door to the holding pen clanked shut behind her, the sound was lost on Caroline. Why in God's name had she told Ben all about her sex addiction? Had she subconsciously wanted to disgust him? Drive him away? Or was she actually seeking forgiveness from him? Absolution? Unconditional love?

Caroline slumped onto a metal bench in the far corner of the large, crowded pen. Folding a stick of gum into her mouth, Monique sauntered over to her on spiked mules and offered a stick to Caroline.

Caroline shook her head. The cigarette had left a rancid taste in her mouth. She felt bad inside and out. Worse, she felt like she deserved it.

'Look,' Monique said, cracking her gum. 'I know a couple kick-ass lawyers. If you don't like the one you got . . .'

'No. I like him.' Caroline looked at Monique with a

pained smile. 'That's the problem. To name just one.'
Without warning, Caroline started to laugh hysterically.
She had the passing thought that if she was lucky, maybe
she'd die laughing!

Caroline hadn't been back in the holding pen an hour when
the guard returned. Once again, the cuffs were unceremo-
niously clamped on her wrists and she was led out of the
cell.

'Is it my lawyer again?' She was counting on Ben devis-
ing some brilliant move to get her out but maybe he was so
repulsed by her, he'd come back to ask her to release him as
her lawyer.

'Nope. You got a date with the head honcho, honey.'

Caroline tensed, but the guard merely smiled sourly,
giving Caroline's cashmere blazer and tailored blue slacks an
appraising once-over. 'You should be flattered. The chief
doesn't give every *perp* this kinda royal treatment.'

Perp. Not even charged and already she was permanently
marked. Hot-iron branded.

'Here we are,' the guard announced.

Unlike the cramped, airless interview room where she'd
met with Ben, the room into which the guard now showed
her looked more like a doctor's waiting room. There were
several tweed upholstered chairs, beige carpeting, even a window. Seams of sunlight – the last of the day – filtered past the
angled grey blinds into the room. Outside these walls,
Caroline thought morosely, people were heading home from
work. Dinners being made, kids doing their homework, all
the mundane activities of daily life going on as usual.

Louis Washburn lumbered to his feet as she entered the room. He ordered the guard to remove the cuffs, then waved her out.

'You want some coffee? Soda?' he asked.

Caroline shook her head.

'I'm gonna arrange for you to be moved to an individual cell.'

Caroline laughed harshly. '*Solitary confinement*?'

Washburn shrugged. 'I thought you'd appreciate a little breathing space. A cot to stretch out on . . .'

'And to what do I owe this incredible consideration?'

'Hey, if you'd rather stay where you are, fine. No sweat off my back.' He gestured to one of the chairs. 'Sit down, Caroline. Now that we've established that you're peeved . . .'

'Peeved? Is that what you think I am?' She stopped abruptly, this encounter bringing up in a rush all the bitter memories of her last interrogation by him when he played on her naiveté to set her up. Washburn and her stepbrother might have their own inimitable interrogation styles, but neither of them was going to have his desired effect on her this time around.

She gave the homicide commander an icy look. 'Let's not waste your time or mine, Chief Washburn. I have absolutely no intention of saying a word to you without my lawyer present.'

'Good enough. I'll do all the talking. Only thing you have to do is listen. And you can do it sitting or standing. Me, I'm gonna sit back down. I got these wicked bunions and the wife just bought me this pair of loafers. I swear they're aggravating the condition.' Washburn eased his ample butt back into his chair. 'You mind, Caroline?' he asked as he slipped off the shoes.

'I mind a lot of things, Louis.'

He smiled. 'Here's the way it is, Caroline. The circumstantial evidence against you is piling up fast. Do we have enough to make a case stick against you? We're working on the first two murders, but as for Kramer . . .' Washburn paused, the thick vertical ridges along his brow furrowing. 'Let's say we're off to a real good start. We've got a statement from a reporter who saw you and Kramer having a row. And we've got one from this young fellow, a night clerk at the Regency Hotel. On its own, I grant you it's not going to win any prizes, but it'll have its impact. And, who knows what other witnesses will come forward? What they'll have to say? Not to mention that stepbrother of yours who's hell-bent on getting something solid on you. Naturally, I've given him fair warning to leave this to Homicide, but you know Jesse. He's a hard man to derail.'

As if Caroline didn't know. She wouldn't put it past Jesse to get something solid on her even if he had to *create* it.

'I gotta tell you, Caroline. You're going to think your last trial was a picnic compared to what you'll face this time round. We're talking murder in the first degree. With Special Circumstances. You're looking at a life sentence with no parole, kid.'

Panic rose up in Caroline's throat. She had to sit down.

Washburn's gaze probed her face once they were at eye level. 'See, I'm putting my cards right on the table for you.'

'But you always manage to hide your ace.' Caroline's voice was raw with emotion.

The Homicide chief leaned forward, resting his elbows on his knees, cupping his double chin. 'I'm not holding the ace. But for your sake, I hope you are. And, trust me on this one, Caroline, if ever there was a time to pull it out of your sleeve, this is it.'

28

Ben headed from the jail straight to his old law firm, hoping his pal Phil Mason was still putting in long Saturday hours, and could contribute some bright ideas about how to spring *their* client. The rest of what Caroline had told him – well, he just wasn't going to deal with the rest. Not now.

Phil Mason wasn't in his office, but Ben was relieved to see his jacket draped over the high back of his black leather desk chair. Phil's antique mahogany desk was clear of papers except for one folder with SPAULDING written on its tab. Ben reached for the folder as Phil entered the room.

'Ben! Hey, make yourself at home, buddy,' he said drily.

'What have you got here?' Ben glanced over his shoulder at Phil, pointing to the folder.

Mason crossed the big office and took his seat behind his desk. 'My clerk's been busy collecting some very interesting items for your perusal, counsellor.' He flipped open the folder. Inside was a sheaf of photocopies. He slid them across to Ben.

Ben pulled up a chair. Studying Phil, he reached for the papers and turned them around to face him. 'You feeling okay?'

'What? Sure. Why?'

'You look beat. And tense,' Ben said.

'Ditto, buddy. Must be we're twins.'

They shared tired smiles.

Mason nudged the papers a few inches closer to Ben. 'Go ahead,' he said. 'Take a look.'

Ben eyed Phil for a few more beats, then started flipping through what turned out to be a collection of newspaper articles – all of which dated back ten years and concerned the murder of Daniel Spaulding and Faith Spaulding's subsequent trial for the murder of her husband. The clippings ran from July 15th, the day following the shooting of Daniel Spaulding in his cottage on Martha's Vineyard, straight through to December 22nd, the day Faith was acquitted of his murder on the grounds of temporary insanity and remanded for an indeterminate period of time to a locked ward at Neponset State Psychiatric Hospital.

Ben was scanning through the top articles when Phil pulled a sheet out from near the bottom of the pile that he'd tabbed earlier. 'Take a look at this one,' he said, placing it on top of the other clippings. It was a colour copy of a *Bostonian Magazine* article whose headline read – SPAULDING PAINTING CAUSES STIR.

Ben glanced at the headline, but his eye was quickly drawn to the photo of a painting that took up the whole bottom half of the page. He let out a low whistle.

'Yeah,' Mason said. 'Thought that would catch your interest.'

'This is it.' Ben lifted the photocopy up to examine it closer. 'The painting Meg Spaulding's father brought home the night he was murdered.' Staring at it, he felt an involuntary shiver streak down his spine.

Daniel Spaulding had painted a nude couple lying on a Persian carpet, passionately entwined in a lovers' embrace. Two slender, elongated figures, both with smooth, tawny skin. The man's face wasn't visible. It was buried in the crevice of the woman's full breasts. But the woman's face, even in the photocopy, was not only clearly discernible but startling. Startling in that the woman looked so much like Meg Spaulding. And also that the artist had captured a plethora of emotions on her face all at once – lust, vulnerability, guile, violence. And above all else, horror. Because, entwined around the lovers, was a metal chain – part of which was coiled like a lethal snake around the woman's neck.

Scrawled in red paint across the bottom of the painting were the words – *The Goddess Aphrodite.*

At least that's what it appeared to say at first glance.

When Ben examined it more closely, thanks to the magnifying glass Phil handed over to him, he saw what had actually been written.

*The God*less *Aphrodite.*

'What do you mean, it doesn't mean shit?' Jesse Baush snarled. 'If this hotel clerk picks Linny out of a line-up—'

Amy DeSanto gave a cautious look around Checkers, a

50s-style diner down the street from police headquarters. The only cops around were a couple of detectives way down at the other end of the room, but she was still uneasy about being overheard. 'Keep your voice down, Jesse. Washburn won't authorize the line-up. He says since the hotel clerk says he didn't go up to Hoffman's room at the Regency, much less escape a chain noose, the *alleged* fact that she came on to him is diddly squat.'

Baush slapped his hand down on the pink Formica table. 'It's another peg . . .'

'For fuck's sake, it's a *toothpick*. I gotta go with Washburn on this one, Jesse. And you gotta get a grip.'

'Linny did those guys, Amy. You know it. And I know it. Fuck, Washburn knows it, too.'

'Washburn's working on her personally, Jesse. We need a strong case here. She's not your average moronic perp with some shit-for-brains lawyer. The chief is not about to risk losing her a second time. We need real solid proof.'

'I'll find the proof all right.'

'Uh, uh. By *we*, I mean Homicide, not Vice. And most emphatically not you, Jesse Baush. You've gotta stay outta this. My ass is on the line here.'

'Yeah, right,' he said off-handedly.

DeSanto's face went crimson with anger. 'You're not even fucking paying attention, Jesse. Seems like the only ass you can think about lately is your stepsister's.'

He heard his girlfriend's snide remark. Fuck Amy. Yeah, he was thinking about Linny's ass, all right. About how he was gonna keep that hot little ass of hers in jail.

*

Susan Steinberg gave the detective an impatient look. 'I don't see any reason for you showing up at my home at seven o'clock at night when I already told your partner, Detective DeSanto, everything I know this afternoon at the Institute. Which is that you've made a dreadful mistake—'

Jesse Baush had his pad flipped open as he sat on Steinberg's blue-and-white striped sofa. 'Sometimes when a person gives a statement in the midst of a . . . commotion . . . they forget things. Or overlook them. I'm sure you understand, Doctor, that we have to be very thorough.'

Steinberg sat in a navy corduroy club chair close to her sofa. 'I don't think you understand, Detective, the bad effect this is having on Dr. Hoffman's patients. Or, for that matter, on all of the patients we see at the Institute. Not to mention the entire staff, myself included.'

'You must love to read,' Baush interrupted, looking around the room, which had a cozy private library feel with floor to ceiling built-in bookcases lining three of its four walls.

'I'm sure you're not interested in my reading habits, Detective.'

'Lieutenant,' he corrected as he unzipped his bomber jacket.

'You're wasting your time, *Lieutenant*. To repeat myself, I was in my office the whole morning with my door closed. Until I heard all the uproar when you and your people got there.'

Baush lazily draped an arm across the back of the couch. His jacket fell open, revealing a black tee shirt. 'I noticed you at the memorial service yesterday. You were sitting with Dr. Hoffman. I could see you were real upset.'

'Implying that Caroline wasn't? I'm sure you know from your professional experiences as well as I know from mine, that people show their feelings – or don't show them – in different ways, Lieutenant. I assure you Caroline was extremely upset about Martin's murder.'

'She talk to you about it?'

Susan started to speak, then stopped abruptly, aware she'd almost walked into the detective's little trap. The *ready* tone went off on her microwave.

He smiled. 'Saved by the bell.'

'It's my dinner. If that's all, Lieutenant . . . I'd like you to leave. I'm certainly not going to let you use me to hurt my friend.'

'How could I do that, Susan?'

'Doctor,' she corrected tartly. 'And you could do that by twisting my remarks around, reading into something I might say. Using it against Caroline. She's already going through hell. And from what I read in the paper, this isn't the first time the cops have wrongly accused her of a crime.'

Baush lifted an eyebrow. 'She's your good friend, but she never told you about standing trial for attempted murder?'

'There was no reason why she should,' Susan faltered. 'We're friends, but we haven't known each other very long. And Caroline's not much of a talker.'

'She's not talking to us either. And that puts the police in a really bad bind, Doctor. Believe me, if we've got the wrong gal, we want to straighten it out pronto and get back out there and nab the real killer. Now if you truly are Caroline's friend, there may be things you can tell me that can help her . . .'

'I can tell you, as a psychiatrist, if Caroline was that troubled – that sick – I'm sure I would have detected some signs of psychopathology.'

Baush kept his impatience in check. He needed to get her into talking specifics. 'Did you see Caroline with Steve Kramer this morning?'

'No.'

'Did you see Kramer at all? In the parking lot? In the building?'

'No.' She was stony-faced now.

'So you knew him. Or else how would you know you didn't see him?'

She arched an eyebrow. 'You would have made a good shrink.'

He grinned. 'I presume you mean that as a compliment.'

'Take it any way you like. The point is, I didn't see him.'

'But you've had dealings with Kramer in the past. Otherwise, how do you know what he looks like?'

Susan didn't respond immediately. 'I saw him on tape,' she conceded finally. 'I'm sure you'll find out anyway, if you don't already know. Caroline tapes her group sessions. Occasionally, she presents them at staffings.'

He ran his hand idly through his hair. 'Is that right? What's your take on Caroline and her patients?'

'I gave that at the office, Lieutenant,' she said tartly. 'I'm off-duty now.'

Baush dug up a look of contrition. 'I'm sorry, Doc. You

have to understand, this case is driving me crazy. I'm just trying to do my job.'

'And does that job include harassing psychiatrists?'

'Meaning Caroline or you?'

'Take your pick.'

His eyes never left hers. 'Last thing I want to do is harass anyone. Especially you. Look, Caroline Hoffman wasn't detained on a whim, believe me.'

Susan's steadfast expression wavered ever so slightly.

'You never saw her with that violinist by any chance? Or maybe she mentioned him and you forgot . . .'

'No,' Susan said sharply. 'She had no connections . . .'

'You sound like you know that for a fact.'

'Well, no, but . . .'

'Would she have confided in you?'

Susan scowled. 'Caroline was seeing Martin. It seemed to me to be an exclusive relationship.'

'And you had no idea Martin was going to dump her?'

Susan gave him an incredulous look. 'Who told you that?'

'Caroline didn't say anything to you about that either?'

'I suppose next you'll ask me if I'm certain Caroline wasn't dating any of her patients.'

'No. I don't think Caroline and Steve Kramer were dating. He's not her type. What I think is, he was threatening her.' Baush kept his baby blues fixed on Susan. 'And maybe she killed him because he knew too much. Because he was already starting to open up to us.'

'I don't want to talk about this any more.' Susan looked stricken. But Baush saw something more in her attractive face. A flicker of uncertainty.

'You're not as sure about Caroline as you wish you were.' He reached over and slipped his hand over hers. Leaving it there. 'You know that people can have a dark side, Susan. Even shrinks.'

Jesse's pager went off.

'Shit,' he muttered, annoyed at the interruption. 'I gotta call in.'

Susan reached over to the cordless phone that sat on a nearby oak pedestal table, picked up the receiver and handed it to him.

He punched in the number for the Vice office.

'Baush here – yeah, I'll hold.'

Susan Steinberg stared at him, stunned. 'Baush? Jesse *Baush*? Caroline's stepbrother? You never told me—'

'Hey, you never asked. Anyway it's not what—'

She yanked the base cord out of the wall.

'You shit!' She shrieked. 'You were setting me up. To help you nail your stepsister. God, and I thought my ex-husband was the king of bastards. You could give him lessons.'

'What are you saying, Doc? That you *could* help me nail her?' A smile crept over Baush's face.

29

'Why do you keep on shutting me out? If you can't trust me, who can you trust?'

'I do trust you.'

'Then tell me what's really going on here. Level with me.'

'Where've you been all day? I called and called. You only picked up an hour ago.'

Ned Spaulding snagged his sister's hand as they sat on his sofa. 'I told you, Meg. I went to an estate auction out in Wayland, chasing after a set of pretty decent German Expressionist drawings, but they weren't even worth the opening bid.'

'You took Mom with you?'

'No. She made plans with Grandy. He was going to take her shopping this morning.' Ned frowned. 'Turned out, he didn't show up until the afternoon. But she was okay about it. Grandy took her to a matinee and then he's going to take her out for dinner. He invited us to join them.'

Meg squinted at him. 'Mom shouldn't have been left alone all morning.'

'She was fine, Meg. She did a double-crostic, puttered around the apartment. She looks much better. If the hospital was concerned they wouldn't have released her. It isn't like I've got to watch her every minute. I know she took her meds. I gave them to her. Last night and this morning.'

'You don't know that she stayed here in the apartment all morning. You don't know anything, Ned.'

'Meg,' Ned said gently. 'Mom's not the one I'm worried about. Will you please tell me what's going on?'

Meg had been sitting with her shoes off, her feet tucked under her, but now she put them flat on the floor. 'My psychiatrist was arrested for murdering those men.'

'Those men? You mean the sex killings?'

'Yes.'

'That's unbelievable. Horrible.'

Meg looked at her brother's shocked expression and, unexpectedly, burst into tears.

'I'm scared. I'm so scared of her, Ned,' she sobbed, clutching his hand to her breast.

He wrapped his arm around her shoulder and drew her to him. Meg didn't resist her brother's tender embrace. Ned was the only man who'd ever made her feel safe. Protected. The only person in the world who truly loved her.

He was rubbing her back, pressing his cheek against her hair, holding her close. 'It's going to be okay. If that madwoman is under arrest, she can't hurt you, Meggie,' he soothed.

Meg clung to him. 'Oh yes she can, Ned. Because . . . because . . .'

He drew back to arm's length, his expression sombre but concerned. 'Because what?'

Tears continued streaming down her cheeks. 'Because she can tell them things. Terrible things.'

'Terrible things about you.'

Meg nodded.

'You mean things you told her when you were in therapy?'

'Yes.'

'No she can't. There are rules about that. She can't betray any confidences you shared with her, Meggie. It's privileged information.' He was trying to sound authoritative but his voice lacked assurance.

Meg buried her face in the crook of his shoulder. 'What if she breaks the rules? I think she might, Ned. What if she turns over her file on me? If she does, then . . .'

'Then, what?'

She lifted her head, placing her trembling lips next to her brother's ear. Whispering. 'I don't want you to hate me, Ned.'

'Meg. Oh Meg, you know I could never hate you. There's nothing you could ever do – nothing that could make me stop loving you.'

They held on to each other in silence for several moments.

'Remember that night, Meg? After they carted Dad's body off in that beat-up old ambulance? Mom was sitting there on the rocker in the living room, practically frozen.

Grandy was beside himself, running around the house like a chicken without its head. And there you were, huddled in a ball on the floor, crying so hard I thought your heart would burst. And I was holding you, Meg. Holding you so tight. Promising you everything would be okay. Promising that I wouldn't let anything bad happen to you. No matter what. Do you remember that, Meg?'

'Yes. Yes, I remember.'

'Well, I'll never break that promise. I'm never going to let anything bad happen to you, Meggie. Do you believe me?'

She nestled in his arms, closed her eyes, began to feel more secure. 'Yes, Ned. I believe you.'

Meg was having trouble focusing. She'd been aimlessly walking through the Public Gardens and then along the picturesque streets in the Back Bay ever since she'd left her brother's apartment. Now she realized with a start that she'd ended up only a few blocks away from the Institute for Special Problems. She'd come full-circle.

Tears filled her eyes. In a haze, she walked into the Ritz Hotel and made her way to an ornate mahogany-lined phone booth off the elegant main lobby. Her fingers trembled as she rifled through the phone book on the polished wood shelf.

She was so wound up, she misdialled the number. Then she panicked when she couldn't find another coin in her purse. Frantic, she dumped the entire contents of her tote bag onto the open phone book. She was practically ecstatic when she unearthed a quarter in the resulting jumble.

He answered on the second ring.

'Hello, Ryan. It's me. Meg. I was wondering if I could come over.'

He watched Meg hurry across the lobby and leave the hotel. Saw her step into a waiting cab out front. As soon as the cab pulled away, he slipped out of the narrow alcove where he'd hidden while she was making her call. Passing by the phone booth, he saw that, in her haste, she'd left the receiver off the hook.

And then something else caught his eye. Lying on the floor in the corner of the booth. At first glance it looked like a small, dark animal.

On closer inspection he made out what it really was. A wig. A black wig.

He stepped inside the booth, stooped down, gathered up the soft, silky hairpiece. Pressed it to his chest.

'Meg. Oh, Meggie,' Ned Spaulding cried out in a voice he hardly recognized as his own.

'You didn't sound surprised that I called you,' Meg said.

Ryan beamed. 'I was too happy to be surprised.'

'I thought you might have plans. After all, it's a Saturday night . . .'

'My plan was to get up the courage to call you and see if you'd spend the evening with me. Things got a little intense last night. You thought I was angry. I was afraid you were angry. Now we've got a chance to sort it all out.'

'Ryan, I'm not sure what I'm doing here.'

'Why can't it be something simple like you wanted to be with me?'

Meg sighed. 'Because nothing in my life has ever been that simple.'

He took her arm and led her into his spacious living room. 'I've been racing around trying to clean the place up,' he said apologetically as she hung back at the threshold.

Meg surveyed the cluttered and yet decidedly artistic space. The walls were painted a deep shade of toffee, but covered with so many prints, drawings, and architectural drawings that very little of the rich brown showed. The furnishings, a half dozen tables of different shapes, sizes and periods, several overstuffed chairs and a pair of brocade Victorian sofas seemed to have been placed around the room with little regard for traditional groupings. Yet, exemplifying Ryan's considerable design skills, all of the parts added up to an exciting whole.

'This isn't what I expected,' she said, reacting with more than a little surprise at the presence of several beautifully framed architectural sketches of hers.

'You already know I'm a great fan of your work.'

She walked over to her sketch for a lavish North Shore library addition. 'I thought I'd tossed that.'

He came up behind her. 'You did.'

She glanced over her shoulder at him. Saw his sheepish but appealing smile. 'I'm flattered.'

'Really? Because I feel like I just got caught with my hand in the cookie jar.'

She gave him a long, lingering look. 'I guess that sort of makes us even. Each of us catching the other off-guard.'

'I should never have mentioned seeing you . . .'

'There was another murder today.' Meg cut him off abruptly, eyeing him with a calculating look.

'Yeah, I heard it on the news.'

'What did you think?'

He frowned. 'I'm not sure what you're asking, Meg.'

'Yes you are. You're just not sure what to answer.'

He looked puzzled.

'I knew the man,' she said. 'He was in my therapy group.'

'God, that's awful.'

'You look nervous, Ryan. Are you nervous? Are you still so happy that I'm here?'

'Yes, I'm still happy. It's figuring out how to make you happy that's got me stumped, Meg.'

'Tell me the truth. Do you think I killed those men?'

'Why the hell would I think that?'

'Because *the woman* you saw at the toy store fits the description of the woman who picked up the first murder victim in the museum.'

'The police have already arrested the killer. Your psychiatrist. Is that why you're freaking out? Because I can certainly understand . . .'

'How did you know *she* was my psychiatrist? I didn't tell you her name.'

'No. Sylvia did.'

'Ah, Sylvia again. I never realized how tight you two are.'

'If we are, it's because we both care about you.'

'What else has Sylvia told you? Did she tell you about

my tragic past? Did she tell you that my mother killed my father?'

Ryan gave her an uneasy look. 'I knew about the murder before I started working at the firm, Meg.'

'What?'

'I had a job on the Vineyard – shucking clams at a seafood joint right by the ferry. The summer after it happened.'

She was horrified. Stunned. 'You never said anything.'

'Why would I? Rehashing that painful time can't be any good for you. None of what happened was your fault.'

'How do you know that?' she challenged. 'You weren't there when it happened. You don't know what was or wasn't my fault. I was the only other person there. It was just my mom, my dad, and me.'

Ryan's gaze skidded off her face.

'What is it?' she demanded.

'Nothing.'

Meg gripped his forearm. 'Tell me, damn it.'

Ryan looked back at her in silence for several uncomfortable moments. 'Some people were saying there might have been someone else there that night. With your mom.'

'Who?'

Ryan took hold of her hand. 'It was dumb gossip—'

She yanked her hand away, furious. 'Who?' she shrieked. 'Who did they say was there, Ryan?'

'They said that your dad walked in on your mom and her boyfriend. And she went berserk over getting caught.'

Her face was red with rage. 'Her *boyfriend*? Did they have someone in particular in mind?'

'People talk trash.'

Meg thumped him hard in the chest, her fury growing with each evasive remark. 'Who was she supposed to be fucking, Ryan? Who?'

He caught her wrists, pressing them against his chest. 'Some of them said . . . your brother. Okay? Are you satisfied? Are you happy now?'

'It's a goddamn lie. Let me go!' she shouted, struggling to free her hands. 'I have to go.' Memories crowding her mind, Meg looked distractedly around for her tote bag. Avoiding eye contact.

'But you don't want to go,' he said with such confidence that Meg was taken aback.

'How do you know what I want? You don't know me at all, Ryan.'

'I know you're attracted to me. Just like I'm attracted to you.'

She felt suddenly nervous. 'Ryan, aren't you even a little afraid of me?'

'I wish you'd stop asking me that. We've been all over that territory. Your psychiatrist has been arrested.'

'She hasn't been charged. They're just . . . questioning her. She told me she thinks *I* did it. She thinks *I* killed those men. I think she thinks I'm psychotic. Like my mother.'

'Wouldn't that be convenient? It'd certainly get her off the hook,' Ryan said contemptuously. But then his features softened. 'So, tell me. What do I have to do to convince you I would never for an instant think you could hurt a fly, much less be a killer?'

They looked at each other. Their faces almost touching. Meg felt an unexpected and surprising warmth spreading through her body.

'Maybe you are what I need, Ryan,' she whispered, overcome by his ingenuous belief in her innocence. She pressed her cheek against his. Slipped her arms around his neck. Startled at how aroused she felt.

He undressed her slowly, planting tender kisses along her body. Then he took her hand. He led her to his bedroom. She let him take charge.

If only those sex perverts from her group could see her now. Dr. Caroline Hoffman, too. She'd show them all. What better proof than this, that she didn't have a sexual addiction?

'Ned, is that you?'

Ned Spaulding dropped his keys in his pocket, smoothed back his auburn hair in a nervous gesture. 'Yes, Mom.'

Faith Spaulding, dressed in a simple but elegant champagne-coloured pants suit, her hair swept up in a French knot, was standing by the window in his living room. Hard to imagine, seeing his mother now, that she'd been in a psychiatric ward for the past two days. The progression from raving lunacy when she'd first burst into his gallery Wednesday morning, to the worn, melancholy disorientation she'd displayed at the hospital, to her current lucid manner and refined appearance was amazing.

'Where've you been, sweetheart?'

'Out walking. Is Grandy here?'

She shook her head. 'He dropped me off a while ago so that I could change. He's meeting us at the restaurant on Charles Street. Armando's. He says you know it.'

'Do I have time for a quick shower?'

Faith walked over to her son. 'What's wrong, baby? You don't look well.'

'Just feeling a little clammy. Maybe I'm coming down with the flu or something.'

'I don't think you have a fever,' she murmured, her hand on his brow, then his cheek. Holding it pressed there.

Ned backed away from her cool touch. 'I'm going to hop in the shower.'

Faith caught hold of his sleeve. 'Are you still angry at me, baby?'

'I wasn't angry to begin with. I've told you that over and over.'

'You've been acting so distant, Ned. I know I slipped up.'

'You didn't slip up. You had a relapse. Because you weren't careful with your pills.'

'It wasn't my fault.'

'It never is,' he said sharply before he could stop himself.

'That's a very unkind thing to say, Ned.'

'I'm sorry. I didn't mean it. I'm really not feeling well. Maybe I should skip dinner with you and Grandy tonight. Will you be okay taking a cab over to the restaurant by yourself?'

Faith ignored her son's question. 'Is it Grandy? Is that what's bothering you? That we've mended our fences?'

The corner of Ned's mouth twitched. 'Is that what you've done?'

'Oh, Ned,' Faith said sadly.

Ned held up a hand. 'Sorry. I'm sorry. It's just that it's been so upsetting.'

'Meg's upset, too,' Faith said. 'I could tell when she came to the hospital. Even when I told her Grandy was dying, she hardly batted an eye.'

'He's not dying. He told you he's in remission. He could outlive us all.'

Faith smiled faintly. 'You always were a bit of a dreamer, baby. Not Meg, though. She's been a realist from day one. Taking such a harsh view of life. And of her grandfather. She and Grandy have been like oil and water since as far back as I can remember. Yet, I know he adores her.'

'We all love Meg, Mother.'

'Meg has made a practice of rejecting those who love her. Her whole life could be different if she would just stop—'

'Stop what?'

Faith patted his cheek, much as if he were still a child. 'I think it will work out in the end. For all of us. I really do. We have to stick together. Look after one another. Protect one another. We've always done that. And we always will.'

Ned managed a quick nod as he brushed by his mother, desperate to escape. He hurried upstairs, stepped inside his large, cool, aquamarine tiled bathroom. He leaned his back heavily against the door, then turned to lock it.

From the deep inside pocket of his windbreaker, he pulled out the black wig he'd found in that phone booth a couple of hours earlier. Why hadn't he thrown it away in some dumpster? Or dropped it off one of the wharves into Boston Harbour? Why couldn't he let it go?

He stared at the wig with an almost ghoulish fascination. Then, grimacing in agony, he pressed the soft, silky, flowing wig to his face. He picked up the faint fruity scent of his sister's perfume. Breathed it in deeply. Felt as if it were seeping through his pores.

Faith knocked on the door. 'Ned? Baby, are you sure you're all right?'

He was staring at himself in the mirror above his sink. Staring at himself in his sister's wig. 'I'm fine, Mom.'

30

Amy DeSanto was filing away the last of her reports when Green ambled into the squad room with a clear plastic garment bag draped over his arm.

'What's that?'

'What's it look like?' Green said snidely.

'Will you give me a break here, Al? It's almost six o'clock on a Saturday night. I'm already up to my neck in shit. You gonna rub my face in it?'

Alfonse Green sighed. Precisely his plan. But he relented. That hangdog look of Amy's always got to him. 'It's a raincoat.'

'I can see it's a raincoat.'

'Then again, it might be Cinderella's glass slipper.'

DeSanto arched a brow. 'Run that by me again.'

'This *glass slipper* was lying on the passenger seat of Kramer's '93 Lincoln Continental. It's made by Burberry. Lady's size eight. Way too tight a fit for Kramer even if he was into drag.'

'You're loving this, aren't you, Alfonse?'

He grinned. 'Gotta admit it's the most fun I've had all day. Then again, this hasn't been a particularly fun-filled day so it doesn't take much.'

'You really can be obnoxious, Alfonse.'

Green laughed, but only for a split second. Then he pulled out a small plastic bag from his jacket pocket and held it out to her.

DeSanto took hold of it. Inside was a circular red plastic disc about the size of a half dollar. There was a number on it. 36. And some smaller writing on top. DeSanto squinted rather than pull out the reading glasses she hated to wear. 'The Blackstone Hotel.'

'It's a coat-check tag.'

'I can see that, Al. I don't suppose you found the owner's name tag on the coat?'

'Not quite. I did, however, find an old crumpled up credit card receipt in the left front pocket. Real faded and blurry.'

'You got a name or the number off the slip?'

'The boys are still working on it.' Green paused. 'You ever see the coat before?'

She shook her head.

'So, that means you never saw Hoffman wearing it.'

'So what? What's the big deal about whether I saw her in the coat?'

Green gave her a sly look. 'I guess the big deal is that our Cinderella shrink would not be wearing this *glass slipper*. We examined the jacket Hoffman wore over here. It's a size six. The sleeves are a good two inches shorter than the coat sleeves on this here raincoat. Also measured the length. Hoffman's five foot five and a half inches. This coat would come down to her ankles.'

'So, this isn't Hoffman's coat. Couldn't be Hoffman's coat. I still say, what's the big deal?'

'Now don't be so impatient, girl. Me and the lab boys, we're estimating this coat belongs to a woman around five eight or even five nine,' Green went on laconically. 'We're guessing, from the crease lines in the tie belt, that she's svelte. Expensive but not flashy taste. The coat runs for about two fifty, three hundred bucks. Of course, our killer could've picked it up on sale—'

DeSanto's eyes narrowed. And her voice cracked as she echoed, 'Our *killer*?'

'Okay,' Green said, 'now ask me what else the lab boys found.'

DeSanto glared at him, but she could feel her ulcer kicking into action. 'What did they find?'

'Some real interesting fibres. Especially around the collar of the raincoat. Black fibres that are a match to the ones we found at our first two crime scenes.'

DeSanto slumped into her chair, tilting it back, staring up at the cracked white ceiling.

'You wanna go tell Washburn?' Green asked with a modicum of sympathy. 'Or you want me to give him the cheery news?'

Caroline's hands were shaking as she punched in Ben's home number at a little past nine that night.

'Oh God, Ben, how can I ever thank you for getting me

out of that hellhole?' Her voice was thick with gratitude and relief. 'How did you manage it?'

Ben was so stunned, he took the receiver from his ear and stared at it for a second. 'Where are you, Caroline?'

'I'm home. I still can't believe it. I'm in a daze. One minute Washburn's trying to intimidate me. Next thing, he's providing me with a police escort to my apartment. Ben, you didn't say anything to him or the D.A. about Meg?'

'I haven't said anything, period, to any of them.'

Caroline was on her couch huddled under two blankets. Her body temperature had to be over a hundred yet she was still freezing. 'I don't understand.'

'That makes two of us.'

'Do you think it's a set up? They figure to make the case stick, they'll need to catch me in the act? Please tell me I'm just being paranoid.'

But he didn't. 'Nobody there said anything to you?'

'A female guard came and got me out of my cell twenty minutes ago. All she said was – you're free to go.' Caroline shivered. 'So how come I don't feel particularly free? And what do I do now?'

'Sit tight. I'm coming straight over. I've got a real compelling magazine clipping I want to show you. By the way, how much do you know about Aphrodite?'

Caroline blinked at this apparent non sequitur. 'What in the world does the goddess of love have to do with any of this?'

'You'd be surprised.'

*

'You sure you don't want some milk? Coffee? I could put on a pot . . .'

Ben removed the milk carton from her hand, steering her over to her kitchen chair. 'Sit down and eat. I don't need anything. You're the one who's been through hell, not me.'

'I'm fine. Well, not fine . . . but better.' She sat down. He poured her a glass of milk and brought it to the table. He sat across from her, eyeing her critically.

'Really,' she insisted. 'I'm much better now that I've showered and put on some clean clothes. And this sandwich you made looks great. You didn't have to . . .'

'I had to,' he said quietly. 'I wanted to do something for you. Okay?'

It was more than okay. She was truly touched. She took a bite of the cheddar cheese sandwich, chewed, washed it down with a swallow of milk, forcing a second bite after the first.

Ben watched her as she ate. Her damp hair curled at the ends, framing her freshly scrubbed face. She'd changed into a snow-white blouse and crisp, spotless tan linen trousers. A definite improvement. The gruelling emotions that had played across her face earlier had faded. A testament, he knew, to Caroline's steel-will in coping with the horror she'd gone through. But he recognized that inwardly she was still in turmoil.

Caroline finished her sandwich and took a few sips of milk. Ben noticed her hand was steadier.

'Okay,' she said. 'No more delay tactics. I've showered, changed, eaten. So, where's this magazine clipping you were so anxious to show me? Something about Aphrodite?'

Ben nodded, reaching for his briefcase near his chair. 'That's right,' he said. 'I guess you could see it as looking into the tortured soul of Meg Spaulding.'

'I don't get it.'

'You will.' He opened the briefcase and pulled out a blow-up he'd made of the Aphrodite painting from the magazine article. He laid it on the kitchen table in front of Caroline.

Caroline stared amazed at the tableau that had been the catalyst for so much tragedy in the Spaulding family.

'It looks just like Meg,' Caroline whispered.

'Yeah, but according to the news clippings Phil dug up, the woman in the painting is Meg's mother, Faith,' Ben said. 'The press called her the Aphrodite *Killer*.'

Caroline stared at the painting that had so greatly upset Meg, she'd refused to discuss it in her therapy sessions. Seeing it for herself, Caroline certainly could understand why Meg was trying so hard to forget – not only the eroticism depicted in the painting, but the violence implicit in that chain coiled around Meg's mother's neck.

'I have to think that's where the idea of choking victims with a chain comes from,' Ben said.

'But it doesn't necessarily point the finger at Meg. This painting had to have had a traumatic impact on the entire Spaulding family. Any one of them . . .'

'Just answer me this,' Ben cut Caroline off. 'Could whatever traumatic events Meg witnessed or participated in the night of her father's murder have caused her to slip into some form of temporary insanity? Couldn't a flashback like that trigger a psychotic killing spree?'

'It's conceivable,' Caroline granted. 'But it would be quite difficult to establish Meg – or whoever – was actively psychotic during each and every murder. Unless we consider Faith Spaulding as the prime suspect . . .'

Ben was lost in his own train of thought. 'The chain's the problem. Suggests premeditation. You can be sure a temporary insanity plea isn't going to cut it. And you can bet Vargas is going to jump all over this painting when the media and his people get their hands on their own copies. If they haven't dug them up already. I promise you, Vargas will milk the Aphrodite painting to explain why *goddess* Meg used strangling with a chain as her MO. It provides him with the missing link.' Ben gave a brief, dry laugh. 'No pun intended.'

Amy DeSanto frowned. 'I'd go a little easy on that poison.'

Baush glowered at her and poured himself another whisky. His third. 'Tell me more about that coat.'

'There's nothing more to say.' DeSanto was beat. And furious at herself for being too weak to stay away from Jesse Baush. 'I told you everything I know.'

'Yeah, well, it isn't much, Amy.' Baush took a hefty swallow of the booze. It was hitting him hard. Not as hard, though, as the news that they'd let Linny walk.

'So anyway, where were you tonight, Jesse?' DeSanto got up from his sofa and walked over to him.

'I do have to work Vice occasionally, Amy. You want me to start checking in with you before I go out on calls, so you can keep better tabs on me?'

'You know, I could have kept the news about the raincoat to myself. I didn't have to come over here ten o'clock at night. I could have gone straight home.'

'Why don't you do just that, Amy? Go on home to that dipshit husband of yours.' Baush sidestepped DeSanto and headed over to the window. He tugged up the blinds. The pane was streaked and didn't look out on much – a row of double- and triple-deckers just like his own, running up and down the narrow side street.

Anger and hurt played on her face. 'I wasn't planning on going home, Jesse. My *dipshit* husband went to visit his mother in New Jersey. You've been asking me for months to spend the whole night.'

He turned back to her. 'What is this? A pity sleep-over?'

DeSanto stormed over to him and slammed the whisky glass right out of his hand. It sailed halfway across the room before it crashed on the floor next to his brown vinyl recliner, the liquor splashing all over the place.

'Jesus, you get me so goddamn mad sometimes.'

Baush actually laughed. 'I can see that.'

'When are you gonna let this thing go? Think whatever evil thoughts you want about her, but your stepsister didn't do those guys, Jesse. No way she could have worn that coat. And if the coat don't fit . . .'

'Fuck the coat.'

'Fuck you. You're so goddamn blind with hate for Caroline, you got everything out of whack.'

Baush looked right past Amy like she didn't exist. 'Shit, this place smells like a fucking saloon now.' He walked over to the recliner, kneeled down by the broken glass and started picking it up.

DeSanto stayed put. 'You know what they say, Jesse. There's a thin line between hate and love.'

He laughed sourly. 'Yeah? Who's they?'

DeSanto saw her chance to get in a jab. 'I bet your shrink stepsister, for one.'

The phone rang at a little past 10 p.m. Amy was about to step into a nice, hot bubble bath. Fitting a towel around her, she dashed out of her bathroom and picked up in her adjoining bedroom. Hoping it was Jesse. Hoping he was calling to apologize. Hoping he was dying for her to come back to his place—

It was Green on the other end of the line.

'What do ya want, Alfonse?' she barked.

'I just thought you'd like to know who belongs to that raincoat we found in our dead peeper's car.'

The towel slipped off DeSanto's body. 'Who?'

'Wanna make a guess?'

'No,' DeSanto replied economically.

'For a little while there, I thought it might be Tina King. That lovely young model lying in that hospital bed over at Boston General. The one I *didn't* get to interrogate with you this morning.'

'You're really getting on my nerves, Alfonse.'

'Of course, if the coat did belong to King,' Green went blithely on, 'we'd have ourselves a mighty frustrating dilemma. Since she's got a pretty airtight alibi – at least for this morning's murder. Seeing as how you and your boyfriend were getting her statement around the same time as Kramer was getting his comeuppance.'

DeSanto stooped down for her towel, throwing it over her legs as she sat on the edge of her bed. 'Okay, so it isn't King's raincoat,' she said with more than an edge of irritation.

Green, however, was in the best of moods. 'Right you are, girl. But when I showed it to her this afternoon, King did recognize it. She told me she'd seen someone wearing a coat that looked awfully like the one I was holding. Seen someone wearing it on three, four occasions.'

DeSanto held her breath. 'Who is it?'

'First I'd like to take a moment to point out to you how beneficial it is when partners who are assigned to work together on a case do, indeed, work together.'

'Stop fucking with me, Alfonse.'

'Only if you say please.'

'I swear . . .'

'Okay, I guess I've made my point. Her name's Spaulding. Meg Spaulding. Ring a bell?'

'Shit. The wacko who was with Hoffman this morning.'

'You mean the woman you and Jesse let slip right by. The woman whose name I happened to get on her way out of the Institute.'

'I'm still not hearing anything like proof.'

'Listen harder. Remember that blurry credit card slip I found in the raincoat pocket?' Without waiting for a response, he said, 'Yup. Meg Spaulding. Lab says that's the signature on the slip all right. Oh, yeah,' he added, 'also got me a nice, clear search warrant with Ms. Spaulding's name on it, too.'

DeSanto got off the bed, receiver cramped between her shoulder and the side of her jaw as she pulled on a pair of panties. 'Where are you now?'

'Where do you think I am?' Green quipped.

'Where's Spaulding?'

'Not home yet. But I imagine she'll show up sooner or later. Let's hope it's sooner. And that this morning's romp used up her quota of chain for the day.'

As the lights came up in the movie theatre, Ryan Gallagher helped Meg on with her denim jacket.

They stepped into the aisle. There was a bit of a gridlock as the rows emptied out all at once.

'I hope you're not sorry we came.' Ryan slipped his arm lightly around Meg's shoulder. It had been his idea, after they'd made love, that they go out to dinner and a movie – have a real date. He didn't want Meg to think his feelings for her were predicated only on a sexual attraction.

'No, I'm not sorry. It was a good movie,' she lied.

He grinned. 'It stunk.'

Meg laughed. A girlish, carefree laugh. 'You're right. But I still enjoyed it.'

Ryan gave her an affectionate hug. 'And I enjoyed watching you enjoy it.'

'I'm not thrilled about being watched,' she snapped.

'I only mean that I like seeing you happy. I'm going to keep on making you happy.'

As Ryan breathed the words in her ear, Meg could almost believe it was possible.

*

Amy was growing increasingly impatient by the minute. She and Alfonse, along with several techies from the police lab, had spent over an hour combing through Meg Spaulding's twenty-first floor apartment at Harbourside Plaza. They'd turned up zip. At least they had enough back at the lab to justify bringing her in. And the best bet for that, they figured, was simply to hang around the glitzy marble and burled wood two-storey lobby, until their prime suspect returned home.

The doorman, George Madison, a friendly, barrel-chested man with smooth chestnut-coloured skin, removed his peaked cap and scratched his balding skull. 'You gotta give it to that relief staff. Three ninth-inning saves in a row and the Sox are in first place.'

Alfonse smirked. 'Yeah, like that means anything. We're talking our beloved Red Sox here. Talk to me in September.'

'You planning on hanging out here that long?' Madison asked wryly.

Amy was already feeling like this wait was taking months. 'How about a seventh-inning stretch here,' she said. 'Talk to me, George, about something you don't have to guess about. You ever see Spaulding all dolled up? Like for a real hot date? Recently?'

'Not really. I was out sick last night, but I was here the rest of the week. Fact is, I never see her go out much. Not that she couldn't have every single guy in Boston eating out of her hand. She's a beauty.'

'How about visitors?'

'Well, there's her brother. Comes by every so often. Last

time was a few weeks ago. They went clubbing. She told me about it when he brought her home.'

'She usually chat about her dates with you?' DeSanto asked.

'Hardly a date. I mean, it was just her brother. And no, she usually doesn't stop to shoot the breeze. But she was kinda mellow that night. Like she'd had a couple of drinks.'

'Mellow,' DeSanto echoed. 'Shit, I got a brother and he's never put me into a particularly mellow mood. Never took me out on a date, for that matter.'

'You sure it was her brother?' Green asked.

George nodded. 'Two peas in a pod. Could have been twins, except she did call him her *kid* brother.'

'He take her out a lot?'

'No. I told you already. Miss Spaulding doesn't go out much, period.'

'She's out tonight,' DeSanto cracked. 'Any idea where she might be?'

The doorman shook his head. 'Could be she's working late.'

DeSanto and Green shared disgusted looks. Thinking the same thing. That Meg might be out there working on victim number four.

'Any other guys ever come by besides her brother?' DeSanto persisted.

'There is one. I think the poor fellow's really gone on her.'

'Who's that?'

'A young man from her architecture firm. Something-or-other Gallagher. Nice boy. Actually, he came by on

Monday . . . no, Tuesday night . . .' The doorman paused; his gaze shifted from the detectives to the glass doors behind them. 'Speak of the devil.'

DeSanto and Green both turned in time to see a buoyant couple walking arm in arm into the lobby.

Ryan greeted the doorman with a warm smile, hardly noticing the two cops who'd turned around to face them.

But Meg wasn't smiling. She recognized DeSanto as the homicide cop she'd encountered that morning at Caroline's office. Her tote bag slipped from her shoulder and dropped to the floor.

Ryan automatically stooped down to retrieve it. Still not catching on.

'Don't touch that,' DeSanto said sharply.

Ryan frowned. 'What's this all about?' he demanded, straightening.

DeSanto wasn't listening to his question. Her eyes, like Green's – and Meg's – were riveted on one of the items that had spilled from Meg's bag when it fell.

On the floor, in brilliant contrast to the shiny white marble, lay a black jersey dress.

Alfonse Green reached for a glove from his jacket pocket so he could pick the item up for tagging.

Not Amy DeSanto. She was reaching for her gun. Because there was no question in her mind that Meg Spaulding was about to bolt.

Caroline and Ryan sat at either end of a long wooden bench in the drab pea-green hallway outside the homicide division at police headquarters. Every so often detectives and uniforms passed by, never giving them a glance. Caroline had tried several times to engage Ryan in conversation, but each attempt was greeted with stony silence.

Stiff, weary, and upset, Caroline got up from the bench. She walked down the hallway to the ladies' room. Went over to the sink, turned on the tap and began splashing cold water on her face.

'You get off scot-free and Meg gets arrested for murder. Now, why doesn't that feel like a fair exchange to me?'

Caroline's hands dropped from her wet face. She saw, in the mirror, Ryan Gallagher come up behind her, his eyes dark with rage and disgust. Surely he wouldn't be stupid enough to assault her right in the police station. But people do plenty of stupid things when they are emotionally overwrought.

She turned, strategizing how to defuse the situation. 'This isn't very smart, Mr. Gallagher . . .'

'And you're the expert on smarts, aren't you, Dr. Hoffman? You used your smarts to get yourself out of some serious shit. All it took was selling out an innocent patient.'

'I did not – will not – ever say anything to the police that Meg told me in confidence.'

'What are you doing here, anyway? I can see why Meg called your lawyer, Tabor, to represent her. He got you off, so he must be damn good. But I didn't know you and Tabor were attached at the hip.'

'I'm here because Meg is my patient . . .'

'You don't know the real Meg. You'll never begin to know her. Meg's no psychopathic murderer. The way she was tonight – the way it was for us both – it was a real breakthrough. She was relaxed and tender. She was terrific.'

Her own fear of being attacked by Ryan abated as Caroline saw her chance to turn this around. 'Meg must trust you very much. And she needs you more than ever. But you won't be much help to her if you get yourself arrested in a precinct ladies' room.'

It was as if it had first dawned on Ryan that that's where they were. 'Jesus.' He looked disorientated. 'Jesus,' he repeated, stepping away from Caroline, shaking his head.

She gave him a sympathetic look. 'What do you say we go get a cup of coffee, Ryan? I'll go first and make sure the coast's clear.' She put a touch of lightness in her voice. And she was careful to wait until she got the okay nod from Ryan before making a move.

They walked out of the ladies' room undetected. Caroline left a message for Ben with the desk sergeant and steered Ryan out of the building.

A few minutes later, they were sitting with mugs of black coffee in a far booth in the diner down the street. Much to Caroline's relief, Ryan's belligerence remained in check. Not, however, his anguish.

'I can't believe this is happening to Meg. It's so unjust. She's not going to hold up under this. You must know that much about her. And God knows what she said to the cops when they carted her off in that cruiser. I told her not to say a word – but she was so out of it. She looked totally freaked.'

Caroline was equally worried. 'I'm going to see her as

soon as I can and if she's suicidal or showing signs of an acute breakdown, I can have her moved to a hospital for observation and treatment.'

Ryan watched the steam rise from his coffee for several moments, then looked across at Caroline. 'What if I provide Meg with an alibi for that first murder?'

Caroline eyed Ryan dubiously. 'Can you?'

'It was Tuesday night, right?'

Caroline nodded.

'Well, I was with Meg that night . . .'

'Ryan . . .'

'The doorman from her building. He'll confirm it. So she's got an alibi. How could she have been at the museum if she was with me?'

'Are you saying you were with Meg the *entire* evening?'

Ryan carefully straightened the silverware in front of him so his knife and spoon were perfectly aligned. 'Not . . . the whole evening.'

Caroline saw a flicker of something in his eyes. Doubt?

'Ryan, if you're going to provide Meg with an alibi, you better be certain it's air-tight. Or you'll end up hurting her case even more.'

Ryan slammed his fist down on the Formica table. 'It's not fair. She's already been through so much heartache. None of it her fault. If you had a mother like hers – Christ, you don't know.'

But Ryan was wrong. Caroline knew all about how deeply troubled mothers could wreak pain and havoc on their children.

*

It wasn't easy for Caroline, walking into the very same interview room she'd been in as a prisoner barely twelve hours earlier. The turn-around of events felt surreal. Until her eyes fell on Meg. Caroline was jolted into the harsh reality of her patient's situation as well as Meg's wretched physical and psychological condition.

Meg sat in a straight-backed wooden chair turned slightly away from the deeply gouged wooden table. She was staring expressionlessly at a blank wall, her legs apart, her arms hanging limply at her sides. Much of her hair had fallen loose of her French knot.

'You must be very frightened,' Caroline said softly. She'd come in the role of therapist, but having suffered so much herself, Caroline was acutely aware of what Meg was going through.

Meg seemed not to hear her at first, but then her head snapped abruptly in Caroline's direction. 'How the tides turn. Is that how you were feeling when you were in jail this afternoon, Caroline? Frightened?'

'Yes.'

Meg looked surprised by her candid response. 'They're watching me like a hawk. I hate to be watched.'

'They're afraid that you might try to harm yourself.'

'Of course I'm going to. Only problem is, I can't think how. They've pretty much stripped me. I don't even have a sheet on my bed. Got any bright ideas? You could get me pills.'

'What I can do is have you put in a hospital.'

'You think I'd rather be carted off to a psycho bin like my mother was? Think again.' Meg was constantly moving.

'You know what I learned from my mother's trial? If I claim I was nuts and didn't know what I was doing, I lose all my confidentiality rights. You could tell them anything. That's what my mother's shrink did. He even made up things about that hideous painting.'

'The one your father painted of your mother and a man wrapped together in chains? I saw it.'

Meg became even more agitated. She shook her head violently. 'No. You couldn't . . . you couldn't. Ned destroyed that painting. He swore . . .'

'I only saw a print of it,' Caroline said quietly. 'That's all.'

Meg's whole body stilled. In a voice that was barely audible, she whispered, 'The Godless Aphrodite.' She began rocking slowly back and forth in her chair. And then, her voice even lower, she muttered, 'But Daddy didn't write that.'

Stunned, Caroline breathed in sharply. 'Who wrote those words then, Meg?'

Meg's mouth remained tightly shut.

31

At 11.40 that night, a channel eight local late night talk show was interrupted with a *Breaking Story* news flash.

Jill Nugent, looking fresh and bright in a tailored coffee-brown suit and buttercream silk blouse, not a blond hair out of place, appeared behind her anchor desk. Immediately above her left shoulder, in a square that covered the top corner of the television screen, was a grainy blow-up of Daniel Spaulding's erotic painting.

'. . . titled *The Godless Aphrodite*. Ten years back, this painting was a key piece of evidence in the notorious Spaulding murder trial. Faith Spaulding, the female subject in the painting, dubbed The Aphrodite Killer by the media, was ultimately found innocent by reason of insanity in the murder of her artist husband, Daniel Spaulding.

'Now this painting depicting lovers snared in chains may prove once again to be of critical importance – this time in the case against Faith Spaulding's daughter, Meg Spaulding, who was arrested this evening at her home in Boston's

Harbourside Plaza. Is Meg Spaulding a new and more terrifying Aphrodite Killer?

'What I can tell you for certain is that Ms. Spaulding is currently being held for questioning in the murders of violinist Peter Korza, psychiatrist Martin Bassett, and physician Steven Kramer – all three men sexually molested and brutally strangled to death. My sources tell me that the District Attorney is very close to an indictment. The suspect has been remanded to Neponset State Hospital where she is currently on suicide watch . . .'

The remote control fell from Ned's trembling hand. Fear numbed him for a few seconds, before he hastily pulled himself together. Switching off the TV, he dashed upstairs. Cautiously, he opened his bedroom door and peered inside.

It was all right. She was in bed, asleep. Sometimes she watched TV late into the night. Thank God, not tonight. He closed the door carefully and went back down the stairs. Silently. Grateful that he would be able to keep the secret at least until the morning.

Secrets were as much a part of his life as the air he breathed.

He made himself a stiff drink, swallowed it down in one long gulp, then stretched out on the living room sofa. He smiled, thinking he would have made a good CIA agent.

The smile instantly invoked shame. How could he, knowing the terrible trouble Meggie was in? He'd get her out of this mess. He wouldn't let her down. He just had to figure out how—

A sudden blinding light made him abruptly raise his arm across his eyes.

'Was that you at the bedroom door just now?'

'Please turn off the light.'

'Shouldn't you be getting ready for bed?' A disembodied voice, tender with concern. But the bright light remained on. The tenderness was, and always had been, based upon her needs, not his.

'I thought you were asleep,' Ned said.

There was no response.

He lifted his arm, squinting at her. She stood in front of him by the couch. In a sheer raspberry silk nightgown.

He rolled onto his side, turning away from her. 'Go back to bed. You need your beauty sleep.'

'You're still angry at me. But it isn't my fault, Ned. I try my best. I really do.'

'I know,' he said. 'We're all trying our best, Mother.'

Winston Spaulding couldn't sleep. The pain in his gut was so bad, he reached for the vial of Demerol on his bedside table and swallowed down an extra pill with the little bit of water that was left in his glass. He flicked on his TV, surfing the channels until he settled on the channel eight talk show, hoping that its combination with the extra painkiller would lull him into unconsciousness.

No sooner had he shut his eyes, than the show was interrupted with a news flash. He heard his grand-daughter's name.

Winston Spaulding's eyes opened wide. The pain in his gut replaced by a sharp new pain.

Ryan Gallagher saw the start of the Nugent broadcast in a

rundown bar on Stuart Street, not far from police headquarters. The guy watching from a few stools down
grinned drunkenly, grabbed his neck with one hand, his
balls with the other, and shouted, 'Hey boys, guess it's safe
to fuck our brains out again!' Gallagher punched him in the
jaw, and walked out.

Sylvia Fields was awakened from a deep sleep by a call from
her secretary, Louise.

'Turn on your television. Channel eight,' Louise told
her. 'And prepare yourself.'

Groggily, the architect reached for the remote.

Within seconds, Sylvia was wide awake. But nothing
could have prepared her.

A big-boned waitress with baby-blue sparkle eye-shadow,
and collagen-enhanced pink-frosted lips caught the news-
break on the TV in the kitchen. She started the buzz going
and it quickly spread through the club. Within minutes, it
made its way to a couple of lookers at a table in a far corner
of the main room. On hearing the news, one of the pair, a
raven-haired beauty wearing a skin-tight black jersey
minidress and black spiked heels, went ash white under
her expertly applied matte finish pancake base.

'What is it, darling?' her well-endowed flaxen-haired
companion asked solicitously.

'I know her. I know the woman they've arrested.'

'Oh my God. Is she the type to do it, Christina? Think
she really strangled those poor men?'

'That's not for me to say,' Chris Metcalf commented

sombrely, sounding as if he were in his judge's robe instead of all decked out in drag.

Tina King saw the newscast from her hospital bed. She watched intently, her head throbbing badly. Then she closed her eyes. Thinking about Martin. Picturing his handsome face in her mind. Smiling at her. Reaching out for her. Touching her.

She opened her eyes again. A picture of Meg Spaulding flashed on the television screen. Tina's features hardened as she stared at the face of the bitch responsible for destroying all her hopes and dreams.

Natalie Deutch spoke softly into the receiver of her cellular phone. The television was on just loud enough to cover the sound of her voice. In case Brad woke up, heard talking, and came padding downstairs to see what was up.

'. . . your lips have found their way to my ruby nipples. I've rouged them for you. Are you pleased?' Natalie spoke with a slight lisp.

'Mmm, yes,' a deep male voice murmured on the other end of the line. 'You're driving me wild, baby. I'm so hard. Oh man. Are you there, baby? Are you watching? Huh?'

Natalie was watching, all right. Not their make-believe scene in a make-believe mirror. Watching, instead, the cool, attractive blond anchorwoman on the very real television screen.

Greg Pomeroy was flirting with a pretty, dark-haired co-ed at a Cambridge coffee house. He knew all too well that, for him, scoring with a college student was no different from an alcoholic falling off the wagon.

But, oh man, he was on such a roll. The nubile brunette was hanging on his every word, her dark grey-green eyes laden with that familiar, delicious adoration.

He was imagining fucking her in a succession of Kama Sutra positions when he picked up a conversation at the next table that stopped his fantasies dead in their tracks.

Pomeroy missed most of what was said, but two words stuck in the classics professor's head.

Aphrodite Killer—

Sunday

32

Caroline couldn't sleep. Her mind was whirring about in overdrive. By two in the morning, she realized she was never going to drift off without a little pharmaceutical assistance. She pulled a vial of pills out of her bedside drawer, hesitated for a couple of seconds, then shook out one small powder-blue pill into the palm of her hand. She remembered with a jolt of sorrow the reason she'd first prescribed the sleeping pills for herself a few months back. She'd been experiencing a terrible bout of insomnia which, not surprisingly, coincided with the start of her torrid affair with Martin Bassett. Eventually, it reached the point where she'd automatically reach for that little blue pill as soon as he left for the night.

Caroline eyed it cautiously. She'd made a concerted effort over the past few weeks to wean herself off these little devils. Not that she was addicted. Yet, she well knew how easy it was to take that one extra step down the slippery slope.

Deciding on a compromise, she broke the pill along the scored centre, swallowed half a .25 milligram dose and crawled back into bed. But, when an hour passed and she still hadn't fallen off, she gave in and downed the other half.

That did the trick.

She was back in that holding cell. Monique taunting her. The hooker's bony, calloused hand clamping down hard – so hard – over her mouth. And then that battered little girl spying, not her shoes, but this shimmering gold – no, silver – necklace around her neck. She needed it for her coming-out party.

Caroline gasped as the girl grabbed for the necklace. But suddenly it wasn't the girl, but Meg Spaulding tugging at the necklace around Caroline's neck. Tugging, then twisting. Tighter and tighter.

Caroline was gagging. She couldn't cry out—

She was having a dream. She wasn't really in that horrible holding pen. No one was trying to strangle her. All she had to do was open her eyes and everything would be all right.

But her lids were so damn heavy.

She was hearing someone whispering in her ear – a sharp warning – *keep quiet or else.*

Martin. It sounded like Martin. What was he doing in jail with her?

No. Not jail now. The morgue. Just her and Martin. Zipped up together in that awful green plastic body bag. Martin on top of her. His hands around her neck.

Harsh rasps. Hers? His?

Inability to distinguish self from others. Dissociative Disorder. This is serious.

Help me! Ben, help me.

Someone was looming over her.

Not part of a dream. He was very real.

Panic flooded her body. Her arms swung out wildly.

'Jesus Christ, Linny. What the fuck are you on?'

Jesse Baush gripped her shoulders, lifting her and shaking her as he spoke.

'Please don't.' It was all she could get out.

Remarkably, it worked. Jesse released his grip on her shoulders.

Caroline fell back against her pillow, catching her breath. Things started to come into focus, particularly her stepbrother's leering freckled face.

A resurgence of panic. 'What are you doing here? How'd you get into my apartment?' Caroline squinted at her bedside clock radio. 7:55 a.m. 'What's going on . . . ?'

'Listen to me, Linny. I came here to have a little heart-to-heart with you. Only to find the lobby door ajar and your front door wide open. Looks like someone broke in while you were lying in bed zonked out of your mind.'

'What?' Caroline sat up, her head feeling like a hornet's nest had broken loose inside it – buzzing and stinging. Slowly, she gave her ransacked room a dazed, then horrified look. 'Oh my God. It wasn't a nightmare.' Her hand went up to her neck. The skin felt sore to the touch.

'For a second there, I thought he finished you off.'

Caroline looked back at Jesse. Was that real concern in her stepbrother's voice? Impossible. Her headache must be affecting her hearing.

'I'll file a report on the break-in. But don't hold your breath we'll ever find the sneaky fucker. Probably hunting for drugs. And from the look of you, he found them. What the hell are you on, anyway?'

'Nothing,' she snapped. 'I took a sleeping pill. And he wasn't looking for drugs.'

'What was he looking for?'

Without thinking that all she had on was a short cotton nightgown, Caroline flung off the covers, got out of bed and lurched her way across the room to her oak roll top desk. It was already rolled up, her papers, bills, correspondence all over the place.

Caroline dragged a shaky hand through her tangled hair as she looked down at the locked file drawer that had been pried open. Most of the papers and reports she kept in there had joined the mess on the carpet. She dropped to her knees and frantically rummaged through them.

'It's gone.'

Jesse walked over to her, taking a good long look at the scene. 'What's gone?'

Caroline got to her feet and grabbed her flannel robe from the back of her desk chair, quickly shrugging into it. 'Meg Spaulding's file.' She shot her stepbrother a suspicious look. 'How do I know you didn't take it?'

'You think records stolen by a cop would be worth shit in court?' He rolled his eyes. 'Why'd you bring the Spaulding file home in the first place, Linny?' Now he was the one with the accusatory look. 'Could it be you wanted to doctor it up, so to speak, before it got subpoenaed?'

'What in the world are you talking about, Jesse?'

'See, I started thinking about things, Linny. About how easy it would be for you to have set Spaulding up. You needed *someone* to take the fall for you. Who better than one of your sexually screwed-up wackos?'

Caroline flung up her hands in frustration. What was it going to take for her stepbrother to drop this obsession?

'First you needed to do a little planting. You know, sow the seeds. Bet it wasn't even that hard. You could have stuck that black dress in Spaulding's bag while she was up there in your office yesterday. When you had her sprawled on your couch with her eyes closed, pouring her heart out to you.'

Caroline knew she was probably wasting her breath, but she tried to reason it out with him. 'Meg isn't in psycho-analysis. She wasn't on the couch, Jesse. She was sitting in a chair. Her eyes were wide open. What you're saying couldn't have happened.'

'And then there's her raincoat we found in Kramer's car. I got that figured out, too. Spaulding could easily have left that coat behind in your office after one of her sessions. Maybe you stashed it in your closet, not realizing until yesterday morning how handy it could be. See, Linny. I'm pretty clever, aren't I?'

Caroline reached for the phone on her desk.

'Calling your lover-boy lawyer?'

She jabbed her stepbrother in his chest with the receiver. 'Why don't *you* go ahead and call Lou Washburn and tell him your brilliant deductions, Sherlock?'

He snatched her arm. The receiver dropped to the floor. 'Let go of me, Jesse.'

'What are you going to do, Linny? Cry rape? *Again?*'

Music suddenly filled the room – a melodic James Taylor ballad – startling them both. It took a few seconds before they realized it was Caroline's radio alarm going off. Even on weekends she liked to be up by eight. Hating to waste the morning in bed.

Jesse was still holding firmly on to her arm. The Taylor song still playing. 'Wanna dance, Linny?' His smile managed to be both seductive and malicious.

'Stop this, Jesse. She spoke sharply, trying to sound like she was scolding an incorrigible child. But her escalating anxiety kept her from pulling it off effectively.

'Remember our very first dance, Linny? In the high school gym? You were wearing that hot pink satin number and those high-heeled shoes—'

Caroline remembered vividly. She'd *borrowed* the too tight dress and those ridiculous spiked heels from her mother's closet. And got walloped real good by Momma for it when she got home that night. But at the time, Caroline thought it was worth it because that outfit had caught Jesse's eye. First time ever he'd asked her to dance. A teenage dream come true—

'You don't know how much it took for me to get up the courage to ask you out on a date that night, Linny. The whole time we danced I rehearsed it. Then blurted it out when the song ended. Kicking myself for asking you out for the very next night. 'Cause it was so uncool. Made me sound so desperate. But you said yes without hesitating one split second. I was like flying home on cloud nine that night. And then the next night came and I was so worked up, so goddamn excited about getting over to your place on time, that I read the clock wrong. Got there early. Remember, Linny? Remember how I caught both you and old Walter with your pants down? Saw him humping away on top of you like a jackhammer. And you loving every minute of it . . .'

'That's a complete and utter lie, Jesse. You've always twisted everything around when it comes to me. You did it then. And you're doing it now.' Despite her scolding tone, Caroline was good and scared. Her stepbrother was edging close to a precipice, dragging her with him.

'You still can cast that magic spell of yours, Lin. Even knowing everything I fucking know about you – you can still turn me on.' The tip of his tongue darted out, moistening his dry lips.

Caroline's mind reeled. If Jesse assaulted her, raped her, they'd never believe it. Not the police, not the media. Possibly not even Ben.

Overwhelmed by fury, Caroline understood how one might be driven to kill. But fortunately just the thought that she was capable of such violence brought her reason back. Eyeing her stepbrother squarely, Caroline said in a low, cold voice, 'If you force yourself on me, Jesse, then you're no better than Walter Jackson. No better than your father.'

Jesse stared back at her. The fury was still in his eyes, but he let go of her. 'My old man never had to force *anyone*. And neither do I,' he said contemptuously, blocking her as she started to side-step away.

Caroline couldn't make out from her stepbrother's expression what was going on inside his head. She could still hear Porter Baush's soft, seductive voice that night in her dorm room as she pulled away from what had begun as an innocent, comforting embrace— *You know you want me, honey girl. You know you've wanted me for a long, long time. That's the real reason you phoned me. Had me rush right down here. It'll be our little secret, baby. It's gonna feel so good—*

'You know the irony, Linny?'

Jesse's voice, low and insidious, was so like his father's, Caroline felt history repeating itself.

'The irony is, back there in high school you'd gone and fucked Walter and God knows who else by the time it was supposed to get around to be *my* turn. And, jerk that I was, I never even got to kiss you.'

Before Caroline could dodge away, Jesse grabbed her chin in the vice of his right hand, pulling her face to him. She gasped as he quickly pressed his mouth to hers, his tongue sliding across her lips and then into her mouth in an obscenely intimate gesture.

'So what do you think, Linny?' he drawled before she could react. 'Worth the wait?'

Caroline showered under steaming hot water, scrubbing herself extra hard, but she couldn't get clean enough. She finally got out, dried off, and put on a pair of jeans and a brown lamb's-wool sweater. Still feeling shaky – from the break-in and far more so, from her unhinging encounter with Jesse – she went into the kitchen and made herself a cup of coffee. Even contemplated but vetoed running down to the 7-Eleven for a pack of cigarettes.

What she really wanted was for the cops to show, so she could clean up the mess.

Sweep everything under the rug?

Sometimes being a shrink was far more a curse than a blessing.

She took her coffee into the living room. Trying not to overreact to what she knew were the normal everyday apartment sounds she always heard. Ridiculous to think the intruder would make a second appearance. The whispered warning echoed in her head – *Keep quiet or else.* Or else *what?*

And what about Jesse? Her stepbrother was a one-man demolition team. And she was the target he was hell-bent on demolishing.

Shivering, Caroline stepped through the chaos to the fireplace. She set her coffee mug on the mantel – one of the few places the intruder hadn't disrupted. The only items on the narrow marble shelf were a pair of brass candelabras she'd bought at a flea market in New Hampshire that past summer, and a lovely hand-painted blue-and-white Delft porcelain clock. A Christmas gift from Martin.

The clock read eight fifty-five, but it had been running ten minutes late for a couple of months. Caroline remembered how, whenever he was over the apartment, Martin kept saying that one of these days he had to find the time to get it fixed for her.

She ran her fingers lightly over its S-shaped curve. Then lifted the surprisingly weighty object, cradling it in her palms. Staring at it until the numbers on the face blurred. Her throat constricting. Thinking about time – lost and gained. The finality of time—

A couple of sharp raps on her front door so startled her that the clock slipped from her hands, crashing on the brick hearth. Caroline stared down at the shattered pieces of Martin's gift, tears suddenly flooding her eyes. Rolling soundlessly down her cheeks.

More insistent raps. 'Caroline? Caroline, are you in there? Are you okay? It's me. Susan.'

Wiping away her tears with her sleeve, Caroline took a couple of moments to collect herself and then went to the door and let Susan in.

'How'd you get into the building? You didn't buzz.'

Susan shrugged, plopping her large tapestry pocketbook on the hall table. 'I did. Or I hit somebody's button. I wasn't wearing my glasses. Anyway, I got buzzed in. You'd think in the city, people'd be a little more cautious. You can bet your bottom dollar it would never happen in New York. No one would buzz you into their building unless they eyeballed you on their screen if they had one, or if there was only a voice box, they'd make you recite your social security number and give them your mother's maiden name, so they'd be sure you really were who you said you were. All right, maybe I'm exaggerating. But only a little. By the way, I'm sorry I didn't call, but I was afraid you'd put me off. I decided I'd give you a chance to get a good night's rest and then come over here and take you out for a big, celebration breakfast. And find out the story about Meg Spaulding's arrest. I'm telling you, my head is positively spinning. But you – you look like you've gone into orbit. You look worse than I looked when I found Brucethebastard humping *my* secretary in *our* bed!'

Susan finally stopped for a breath, and noticed the mess. The shattered clock by the mantel, CDs, tapes and papers strewn across the carpet. Books and magazines, piled in front of the bookcase—

Susan squinted at Caroline. 'Don't tell me. Spring cleaning?'

Ben shook his head as he glanced around Caroline's bedroom. Caroline had called him and asked him to come right over while Susan Steinberg was still there. Although Susan's presence had been a welcome relief, Caroline found it exhausting fending off her friend's barrage of questions but she reluctantly took her leave as soon as Ben arrived. The police still hadn't shown up to carry out their investigation of the break-in.

'One thing this proves,' Caroline said, sounding remarkably cool and collected. 'Somebody, other than Meg, is involved in this mess.'

'Could be Ned,' Ben said.

Her face brightened. 'You took the words right out of my mouth.'

'Don't jump to any conclusions. All it probably means is that he's trying to protect his sister. Not because she's innocent. Because he's afraid she's guilty. Or knows for a fact she's guilty.'

'That's one theory. It would be nice if – when the cops finally get here – they come up with Ned's fingerprints. But he was probably smart enough to wear gloves.'

'He or whoever,' Ben felt it necessary to emphasize. 'Ned's the most likely candidate, but I'm keeping an open mind. And so should you.' Ben knew how big a mistake it could be to miscalculate the source of the real danger and never see it coming. Until it was too late.

Caroline was staring at Ben, something important having popped into her beleaguered mind. 'Wait a second. Ned may not have left his mark here, but he might have left it someplace even more significant.'

'Where's that?' Ben asked.

'On the *Godless Aphrodite* painting.'

'You've lost me. There is no *Godless Aphrodite* painting. It was destroyed.'

'That's not what's important. Last night, Meg told me her father wasn't the one who put the writing on that painting.' Caroline's voice rose and then fell when she added, 'Unfortunately, she won't say who did. If she even knows.'

Ben remained puzzled. 'And the significance is . . . ?'

'It's easy enough to understand why the aggrieved husband might have viewed his wife as a *godless* Aphrodite. And might have expressed his overwrought feelings of betrayal that way. But think about it, Ben. If it wasn't Daniel Spaulding, it had to have been written by someone who felt profoundly tortured and tormented by . . .'

Ben got Caroline's message. 'Ned.'

'Psychologically, it fits,' she said. 'Meg's the spitting image of her mother in that picture. Unconsciously, Ned may be replaying the primal scene over and over. Killing his sister's lovers just as he killed his father . . .'

'Faith killed her husband, Caroline. It was her prints on the gun. She confessed.'

'But I'm sure Ned believed he was partly to blame.'

'What about Faith? She could have written that epithet about herself – out of feelings of self-hatred,' Ben underscored. 'Or the grandfather. The old man had plenty of reason to hate the woman who murdered his own son. Or maybe he lusted after his daughter-in-law himself. Any one of them, Meg included, might still be replaying that *primal scene*, as you put it.'

'So you admit this could be an important clue. A place for us to start . . .'

'A place for me to start. Not you,' Ben said emphatically. 'This break-in was about more than ripping off Meg's case record and that videotape. It was a warning to you to keep your mouth shut. To stay out of it. And that's precisely what you're going to do.'

Caroline shook her head. 'I'm not going to *say* anything. Not if it violates confidentiality, certainly. But I'm not about to sit here *doing* nothing. I'm not the only one in danger now, Ben. I'm not the only one who could jeopardize Meg's case or point the finger in somebody else's direction. What about the other members of my sex addicts' group – whose identities have all been compromised because of that stolen videotape? What about Sylvia Fields? Ryan Gallagher? Anyone else who knows Meg intimately? They could all be perceived as possible threats. They could all be in danger. If something happened to any one of them, and I stood idly by, I couldn't live with myself . . .'

'If you don't stand idly by, you may not live at all, Caroline.'

A conversation stopper that left them both scared.

'Look, Caroline, you want to tell the police you think Ned was the intruder, fine. Let them investigate. And I'll pass your theory on to Marcia Kirshbaum. She'll conduct her own inquiry about the break-in and the handwriting on the painting . . .'

'Who's Marcia Kirshbaum?'

'One of the top private investigators around. She's already on the job.'

'Look, I'm not going to do anything stupid, Ben. But I could talk to Ned. I often bring in family members of a patient I'm treating—'

Caroline felt Ben notice her neck. Even though she knew the faint red marks from last night's attack had all but disappeared, his look was an acute reminder of the intruder's assault and of how helpless she'd been to defend herself.

'What do you want to do? Give him a second go at you?' Ben, exhausted from lack of sleep and worry, couldn't bear to think what might have happened to Caroline. What could still happen. And how devastated he'd feel if it did.

Caroline was touched by his concern. She couldn't help contrasting it to the expression she'd seen etched on her stepbrother's face earlier that morning. Her agitation resurfaced at the memory.

'When are the police going to get here? I wonder if Jesse even reported the break-in.'

Ben watched her pace back and forth in front of him.

On her second pass, he said, 'Tell me again exactly why he showed up?'

She stopped mid-stride. 'I already told you about Jesse's screwball theory about how I set Meg up to take the *rap* for me. Do we have to go over that again?'

Caroline could hear the testiness in her tone. She knew it wasn't because Ben continued to question what happened with her stepbrother. It had to do with her own niggling sense of responsibility for somehow having provoked Jesse's assaultive sexual behaviour. Yet, if she were counselling one of her own patients in that same situation, Caroline would be advising that self-recriminations were a normal but invariably self-defeating way of coping with feeling power-less.

'I get the distinct feeling,' Ben said, 'that you aren't telling me everything that went down between you and that stepbrother of yours.'

Caroline couldn't argue that point. And didn't.

33

'What time you got?' Green asked Jerry Vargas.

'Little before noon.' The A.D.A. popped the last of his antacids into his mouth. He crumpled up the empty foil wrap. 'Christ, my stomach's killing me. If my wife ever tries to get me to eat raw fish again – sushi, my ass.' He belched. 'And on top of a rotten case of indigestion, I'm missing my Sunday round of golf.'

'You know, Jerry, maybe it's not indigestion. You could have food poisoning or one of those real nasty parasites,' Green offered. 'Sushi can be a killer.'

Vargas looked worried. 'Maybe I should get checked.'

'For chrissakes, you guys are driving me nuts,' DeSanto snapped.

Green quirked an eyebrow. 'Not to worry, Amy. You're already in a mental hospital. Got the doc *you* need right here.'

'The only docs I want to see are Dr. Caroline Hoffman and Neponset's chief of service, Dr. Gilbert Fuller.'

Alfonse Green poured a third packet of sugar into his coffee. 'Relax, Amy. Our turn'll come.'

Too antsy to sit, DeSanto strode across the small room over to the barred dirt-streaked window. The sun was shining. A bright, breezy Sunday afternoon. Best weather Boston had seen in days. She glanced down at the street below. It was cluttered with media vans – reporters and photographers milling about the hospital like a swarm of hungry ants.

Vargas emitted another loud belch. 'I gotta fish up more antacids.'

Green got a laugh out of that.

DeSanto rolled her eyes and followed Vargas out. She headed over to the orderly posted outside Meg Spaulding's door.

'Hoffman still in there?' she asked.

The orderly nodded.

DeSanto eyed that closed door. What she wouldn't give to be a fly on the wall.

'. . . just want the agony over with. Why not end it all now?' Meg avoided making eye contact with Caroline.

'Suicide's not a very productive solution,' Caroline said. 'If you're innocent, Meg . . .'

'You're saying you think I could be guilty,' Meg challenged.

'Is that why you asked the question?'

'What do you think?' Meg smiled slyly.

'I think it is. You're testing the limits. Seeing how far you have to go before I'll reject you. Abandon you. But I'm not going to do either. And that presents another frustrating problem for you. Because you don't want me getting too close.'

Meg turned her head away as if to confirm Caroline's analysis. 'I suppose you'd prefer if I simply confessed. Mea culpa, mea culpa.' She gave her chest a couple of light thumps.

'Is this about what I'd prefer, or what you'd prefer?' Caroline kept her voice neutral.

'Confession's good for the soul, right?'

'I'm in the mind game. You'll have to ask a priest or minister . . .'

'I've done a lot of bad things, but I am not going to stand trial for crimes I didn't commit. I am not going to prison. And I most definitely do not want to spend the rest of my life locked up in this hospital for lunatics.'

'Tell me what you *do* want.'

'I want . . . I want to feel . . . worthwhile. I want to . . . lead a normal life. I thought for a minute with Ryan I had a chance at it.'

'You haven't used up all your chances, Meg.'

Meg gazed hopelessly up at the ceiling. 'Haven't I?'

Vargas belched.

'You might as well pack it up until Wednesday,' Ben told the A.D.A. 'The law's completely clear on this. You don't get to have a go at her until Fuller lets you have her back.'

'Let me get this straight,' Amy DeSanto said, angrily shifting her gaze back and forth between Doctors Hoffman and Fuller. 'You're putting our prime suspect in a series of brutal serial sex killings on ice for another forty-eight hours because she's down in the dumps.'

Caroline glared at the detective. 'Meg Spaulding is not *down in the dumps*. She's suffering from an Acute Reactive Depression with suicidal ideation and concomitant thought disturbance.'

'Yeah, well I'd be pretty depressed myself if I were in her shoes.' Green smirked.

Dr. Fuller, a tall, rangy man in his mid-sixties who wore a short-sleeved white shirt, a floral print bow tie, and olive green slacks – and who'd dealt with scenes like this many times – took this as his cue. 'Ms. Spaulding's shoes would not be a comfortable or happy fit for you, Detective Green. Let me emphasize that I've met with the patient and I fully concur with Dr. Hoffman's assessment. At this juncture you could not rely on anything Ms. Spaulding says.'

'Well, in my professional opinion,' DeSanto said, 'I don't concur. I say we're dealing with a cold-blooded psychopath who's manipulating the shit out of both of you.' She eyed Fuller. 'I'd have thought, with all your experience, Doc, you, at least, wouldn't fall for this crap.'

'Leave it, Amy,' Green said. 'We're over a barrel here till Wednesday.'

'At the earliest,' Caroline said. 'Meg's observation period could be extended, depending on her condition.'

DeSanto turned on Caroline. 'Spaulding's guilty as hell. And I think you're covering up for her. What's it like, Linny, to be the hand behind the hand that yanks the chain?'

*

'Don't let that jerk detective get to you.' Ben gave Caroline's shoulder an affectionate squeeze as they walked down the hospital corridor. 'This gives me a little more time. Who knows? Maybe something'll come up that'll establish Meg's innocence. See how optimistic I'm trying to be?'

'I'm glad to hear it,' Caroline said.

'What are you going to do now?'

'Stick around the hospital for a while. Meg might want to talk with me again.'

'Why don't you come back to my office? I'm going to put in a few hours . . .'

'What are you going to do? Baby-sit me?'

He glanced at his watch. It was close to two o'clock. 'All right. How about I pick you up here at . . . ?'

'I told you, I don't want to be baby-sat.'

'I'm talking about dinner. I'm talking about . . . a date.' He flashed a nervous smile.

Caroline eyeballed him. 'A date?'

He shifted awkwardly. 'Dinner. You know.'

'Not like at a diner? Or a coffee shop? A real restaurant?'

'Jesus. What do you want? Candles? A harp? Gold-leafed menus?'

'No.' She smiled. 'You can skip the harp. Violins might be nice.'

'You know I haven't been on a date like that in . . . a long time.'

'Me neither,' Caroline said.

'Might do us both good to unwind a little. Relax.'

'Right,' she quickly agreed.

He nodded. 'So, okay. I'll pick you up here at . . . say five. We can have a cocktail first.'

She grinned. 'It's a date.'

Smiling to herself after Ben took off, Caroline walked down the hospital corridor to the doctors' lounge to get a decent cup of coffee.

Caroline was settled into a comfortable armchair, sipping her coffee, skimming a *Health Today* magazine, and thinking about her dinner date with Ben when her pager went off. Caroline's brief romantic musings came to an abrupt halt. She used the phone in the doctors' lounge to call in to her service.

'Dr. Hoffman, I've got a very distraught woman on the line who says she desperately needs to speak to you. She sounds really shaky, Doctor. I can put her through.'

'Thanks. Go ahead.'

Seconds later, Caroline heard soft crying on the other end of the line. A woman's cry.

One of her patients? Tina? Natalie? Even the usually stoical Sylvia Fields passed through Caroline's mind.

'I need . . . to talk . . . to you,' the caller finally stammered.

Caroline didn't recognize the voice. Or did she? There was something vaguely familiar . . .

'Who is this?' Caroline asked.

'Faith Spaulding.'

'Faith, I know how upset you must be about Meg. We definitely should talk. Where are you?'

'Home. I'm home in Martha's Vineyard. Where else would I be?'

'I can see you at the Institute here in Boston tomorrow if you'd like.'

'No. I'm so confused. Why is this happening?'

'Faith, do you have a doctor on the Vineyard?'

'You want to have me locked up again. You're like the rest of the vulture shrinks. I should have known . . .'

'No. No, Faith. I assure you I don't want you to be locked up. I just thought you'd like someone to come over to your house and be with you. It doesn't have to be your doctor. It could be a friend, a neighbour . . .'

'There are things I could tell you. You do want to look after Meg, don't you? Help her?'

'Yes. Very much.'

'Then you'll come out here? You can fly from Logan. Be here in no time. And don't go calling any doctors on the Vineyard. Don't you call a single soul. What I've got to say is for your ears only. Do you understand?'

'Yes, Faith. I understand.'

The cabbie negotiated the ramp up to the departures level, jockeying his way around the madhouse traffic pattern to the Cape Air section of Terminal A. He jerked the cab sharply to the left and screeched to a stop at the only possible spot across the congested roadway from the sliding glass entrance.

Caroline looked over at the terminal. The last place in the world she wanted to be was Logan Airport. A place defined for her now by Martin's brutal murder. Fortunately, she wasn't going to be at the airport long. Her plane left in less than ten minutes.

The cab driver flipped off the meter. Caroline paid him, adding a substantial tip. She was about to open the door when a car parked itself right in line with the cab, inches from it, the driver letting out a teenager clutching a knapsack who dodged across the traffic to the terminal.

Caroline was in no small hurry, herself. As soon as the car drove off, she threw open her door.

'Hope you make your flight,' the cabbie said. 'What with all the obstructions from burying the expressway, it's a real nightmare getting here at all.'

Caroline hopped out, saw a break in the traffic and made a run for it.

The cab driver was just pulling out when he spotted a car come ripping down the road right in the path of his exiting passenger. He slammed his hand down on his horn to alert her.

Caroline was halfway across when she heard the loud blast. Instinctively, she glanced over her shoulder. She glimpsed the speeding dark blur and reeled backwards in sheer terror as the maniac shot past. She slammed into the side of the cab. The impact knocked the air right out of her. On the verge of blacking out, she doubled over, gasping for breath.

The cabbie jumped out and rushed around to her.

'Jesus, lady. Are you okay? You get hit? Need a doctor?'

Caroline looked at the cab driver, confused. Did she need a doctor? She started to take a mental inventory. Then realized if she could think to do that she must be okay.

'Shit, where's those stinking airport cops when you need 'em, huh? That's what I wanna know,' the cabbie said. 'It looked for all the world like that reckless son-of-a-bitch was aiming for you. Ain't got no enemies who drive black Mercedes, do ya, lady?'

'You promised you'd stay put at Neponset. Not to mention I thought we'd decided you weren't going to go off digging up family secrets. In Martha's Vineyard, no less—'

Caroline gripped the airport phone like it was her lifeline. 'Will you listen to me for a minute, Ben? I nearly got run down not two minutes ago.'

'What? Are you serious?'

'Believe me, I've never been more serious.'

'Are you hurt?'

'No. Just shaken.'

'Caroline, I don't want you going anywhere. Stay put. Find an airport cop and stick to him like glue. And call Washburn . . .'

'Right. Like Washburn's going to listen. He'll probably have me arrested for jaywalking. I can't prove the driver was deliberately gunning for me. Any more than Meg can prove . . .'

'You're going far beyond your duty to care for a patient here, Caroline.'

'This isn't just about Meg. It's about finding out who killed three men, one of whom I cared a good deal about. It's about getting that monster who has practically destroyed my career, caused me to be publicly humiliated and defamed, got me thrown in jail – and now nearly runs me over. . .'

'So you're talking revenge. What are you doing, Caroline? Following in your stepbrother's footsteps?'

Caroline bit back her response.

'Another thing you should seriously mull over, Caroline. What if the killer is Meg? What if *she* turns out to be the one you have to settle the score with?'

'I don't think that's the way it's going to turn out,' she said stubbornly. 'One thing we know, Meg didn't break into my apartment. And she didn't just run me down. And we can eliminate Faith as the attempted hit-and-run driver since she can't be in two places at the same time.'

'Caroline, you're only seeing half the picture.'

'Look, I've got to go or I'll miss my flight. Besides, I feel like a sitting duck in this terminal. But have that investigator of yours find out who on our list drives a black Mercedes. Have her start with Ned Spaulding, of course. And I'll need to take a rain check on our date.'

'Oh no you won't. I'll catch the next plane out . . .'

Ignoring the pain that was once again flaring up in his gut, Winston Spaulding glared at his grandson. 'Mr. Tabor was kind enough to meet with us in his office on a Sunday afternoon. You are not adding anything worthwhile to this discussion, Ned. Why don't you go out to the waiting room, while we finish strategizing?' It wasn't a request. It was an order.

'I think I'll stay put,' Ned said defiantly.

Ben wasn't interested in playing referee. But he knew if these two kept going, one or both of them might say something relevant. Besides he still had plenty of time before heading to the airport to catch his flight to the Vineyard. He tried again. 'It's only natural you're both upset about Meg being under suspicion of murder.'

Ned laughed drily. 'My grandfather would say you have a knack for understatement, Mr. Tabor. Wouldn't you, Grandy?'

'What I'd say, Ned,' Winston Spaulding replied icily, 'is that you're making a complete ass of yourself.'

'If anyone's acting like an ass here, it's you,' Ned spat.

Winston Spaulding's face twisted in pain. Ben thought it was because of Ned's insult. But then the older man pulled out a vial from his jacket pocket. With shaking hands, he uncapped it, shook out a pill and swallowed it down.

His eyes fell on Ben. 'I'll be fine. It comes in waves.'

Ned said nothing. Neither did Ben.

After a minute, Winston signalled with a nod that he was doing better. 'My daughter-in-law always believed that sex, and not money, was the root of all evil. If this family is any example, she was absolutely accurate.'

'Are you referring to Faith or Meg?' Ben asked the old man.

'Both. I've known about Faith's sexual promiscuity for many years. And discovered Meg's . . .'

'Shut up, Grandy!' Ned shouted.

'If you don't want to hear it, then leave,' Winston said tightly. 'If Mr. Tabor is going to defend your sister, he needs to have the whole picture.'

Ned scowled but stayed put. His grandfather continued. 'About three years ago, not long after her mother's release from Neponset, I saw Meg at a Celtics game.'

Winston's face once again looked pained, but this time Ben felt fairly certain it wasn't related to anything physical. 'I didn't recognize my granddaughter at first. I thought she was . . . a hooker. She was with a man—'

Winston's deep-set eyes narrowed. 'I confronted her. We ended up in a row. We didn't speak again until Friday at the hospital when Meg came to see her mother. It was the first time I'd seen Faith myself in as many years.'

'You had a row with Faith, too?' Ben asked.

'Not exactly a row. We simply saw things differently when she got out of Neponset. I was opposed to her returning to the Vineyard. I thought she should live . . . in Boston. I wanted to . . . look after her.'

'The woman who murdered your son?'

The old man recoiled. 'I never blamed Faith for Dan's death. She was mentally ill. She couldn't be held responsible for her actions. Even a jury believed that.' He wiped his damp brow with the back of his hand. 'And my son Dan was . . . a difficult man.'

'Difficult how?' Ben persisted.

Winston exhaled heavily. 'Dan was deeply troubled, frustrated with his art – with his life.' He pulled a white linen handkerchief from his jacket pocket and patted the line of sweat that had beaded across his forehead.

'So, you were on Faith's side, but the two of you haven't spoken pretty much since her release from Neponset until you saw her at the hospital on Friday,' Ben clarified.

'People do drift apart. But when Faith phoned me from Boston General, I was extremely happy to hear from her. Until . . .'

'Yeah?' Ben encouraged.

The old man fiddled with his paisley necktie. 'She told me she was worried about Meg. Said she'd heard Meg was doing . . . some terrible things . . .'

'Heard from who?' Ben cut in.

Winston shrugged. 'I asked her, but she said she didn't know who it was. That she didn't *recognize the voice*. I thought it was in her head. But now . . . I'm not so sure. Regardless, she was very upset and she told me she didn't know who else to turn to for help.'

'That's a goddamn lie and you know it. My mother always turns to me when she needs help. Always,' Ned charged. 'You just wanted to try to worm your way back in . . .'

'*How* did Faith know about Meg?' Ben cut Ned off. '*What* did she know?'

Winston Spaulding sighed. 'I'm afraid I can't answer those questions, Counsellor.'

Ben's eyes fastened on the old man. 'Can't? Or won't?'

34

The tiny prop plane made a smooth landing in Martha's Vineyard thirty-three minutes after take-off. Thirty-three minutes for Caroline to try to collect herself. As she stepped off the plane onto the tarmac, her legs wobbly, her heart rate still accelerated, she knew she could have used some more time.

There were two cabs parked at the kerb. A young couple who'd held hands across the aisle during the whole flight rushed over – still hand in hand – to the first cab. As Caroline buttoned up her mauve wool jacket against the brisk sea wind and headed for the second, she couldn't help thinking how nice it would be if she and Ben could be together here on the Vineyard for nothing more than a romantic get-away.

'No luggage?' the driver asked as Caroline settled into the back seat.

Caroline shook her head. 'Just a day trip.'

'Name's Bart,' the cab driver announced cheerily as he

slipped in behind the wheel. 'Where to?'

Caroline gave the driver Faith Spaulding's address.

The cabbie, an older man with white hair, a jowly face and inquisitive eyes, shifted around in his seat to scrutinize her. Nothing cheery about his demeanour now.

'You a reporter?'

'No, Bart, I'm not a reporter.' She looked at him directly. 'Do you know the Spauldings?'

He waved a finger at her. 'You're that shrink that was in the papers. Hoffman. I recognize you from your pictures. Especially the one of you coming out of that Institute handcuffed after that patient of yours was found strangled. Oh, I keep up with all the news. The papers, TV, radio. Guess you must be mighty relieved you're off the hook. You think she did it? Meg Spaulding?'

'She hasn't been charged . . .'

'The *Gazette* here's gotten into the act in a big way. Oh yessirree, the Spauldings are headline news on the island once again.'

'What are they saying in the local paper?'

Bart turned back around and started the engine. 'In a nutshell? Like mother, like daughter.'

He gave his side view mirror a check before pulling out. Caroline checked, too. Just to be on the safe side.

'Yup, them reporters'll be comin' 'round again. Raking up all the old dirt.'

The cab headed down West Tisbury Road which cut right through the main drag of Edgartown. 'You ever come here in the summer?'

'No. Never have. I bet it's great.'

'Great, my patootie. Summers, there's traffic jams from beginning of this road right to the end. Tourists flocking to all the fancy shops and pricey restaurants. Closed off-season, most of 'em. A few places stay open, though.'

'Any nice restaurants? I've got a . . . friend coming out to meet me later. Maybe you've got a recommendation.'

'There's L'Etoile. French. Fancy. Pricey. Supposed to be romantic.'

Caroline smiled. 'That'll do.' She looked out the window, enjoying the stillness, the salty smell of the ocean, the picturesque shops and cottages as they drove through the quaint seaside village.

'Sounds like you're combining some pleasure with business on this day trip of yours,' Bart observed, turning north onto a coastal road that hugged a beautiful stretch of pristine and almost empty sandy beach facing onto Vineyard Sound.

Caroline let his comment slide. Looked out at the calm blue sea.

'Suppose you know all about the Spaulding murder,' Bart said.

That got Caroline's attention. 'Were you here on the island back then?'

'I been here goin' on forty-three years.' He was silent for a bit like that was all he was planning to say. But then he added, 'People in these parts – well, they still got their opinions about that whole sad affair.'

'And you have yours?'

Bart glanced in his rearview mirror and gave Caroline a shrewd look. 'She expecting you? Mrs. Spaulding?'

'Yes. As a matter of fact, she asked me—' He'd almost reversed the tables on her. 'I really would like to know your opinion, Bart.'

'About then? Or now?' He chuckled. 'Aw hell, I'm feeling generous today. I'll give ya two for the price of one.' He smoothed down his fluffy white hair with the flat of his hand. 'The women in that family – Mrs. Spaulding and her daughter – they have their mental problems. No denying that. But they've got plenty of competition in that category from the Spaulding men. That goes for back then. And for now.'

'So you think . . .'

'I told you what I think.' Bart turned left onto a winding unpaved road. 'Well, here we are.'

The cab pulled around a U-shaped drive and stopped in front of Faith Spaulding's natural cedar-shingled saltbox. Caroline got out, pausing to take in the lovely old house, perched on a knoll, with a sweeping vista of Nantucket Sound behind it. Caroline couldn't help contrasting this exquisitely set *summer cottage* to the dilapidated mill house in Brookhaven that backed up on railroad tracks where she'd spent her first eighteen summers – and every other season.

Bart gave his horn a little toot as he drove off. The unexpected blast made Caroline nearly jump out of her skin.

Taking a few seconds to get a firmer grip on herself, she strode purposely up the slate path and knocked on the faded red four-panelled front door of the Spaulding house. She got no response. After knocking several more times,

Caroline walked around to the back of the house. There was a beautiful but empty deck and beyond that, a broad field of blue heather and wild flowers. But no one in sight. Her hair flying about her face from the brisk salty breeze, she looked up at the house, noticing a huge skylight in the sharply pitched roof. Facing north. A perfect spot for an artist's studio. She wondered if any of Dan Spaulding's paintings might still be up there. Maybe the *Godless Aphrodite* had been one of a series. Maybe there were other paintings in which Faith's lover was more clearly depicted.

Crossing the deck, Caroline knocked sharply on the back door. Again, she got no answer. Maybe Faith had gone for a walk or driven to the store for something. She knocked again, then tried the knob. It turned readily, the door swinging open into a small, tidy old-fashioned kitchen. No cooking smells or obvious signs of somebody being around. She stepped inside. No dishes in the soap-stone sink or on the draining board. Nothing on the stove or on the antique oak pedestal table in the centre of the room. Nor were any of the three windows facing out to sea even slightly open to let in some fresh sea air. And the only sound was the rumbling of the old refrigerator.

She nervously called out. Silence.

Quickly crossing the kitchen, Caroline entered a small rectangular dining room with faded floral wallpaper, a worn Persian carpet and a large oval walnut table surrounded by chairs that took up most of the rest of the space. Heavy beige brocade drapes were drawn and the room had a musty smell, as did the living room across the hall, cluttered with mismatched furniture. It looked deserted. But Faith had been in Boston for the past week. If she'd just come home that day, given her distraught state of mind—

There was one more room at the end of the hallway, past the stairs on the right. It would have to be the master bedroom if Caroline remembered Meg's words accurately—

. . . heard a shot and ran downstairs to my parents' bedroom . . .

Her hand was shaking as she touched the cool brass knob and slowly, warily inched the door open.

The room was empty. *Completely* empty. Not a stick of furniture. Not so much as a picture hook on the stark white walls. No curtains on the closed windows. The bare floor was stained a dark mahogany. Had it always been that shade? Or had the dark varnish been applied to the pine to cover up Dan Spaulding's blood stains?

Caroline could feel the horror of it. Letting herself imagine Meg's experience ten years back: the sound of a gunshot tearing her from her sleep, her breathless race down to her parents' bedroom; bursting in and seeing her father splayed on the floor gushing bright red blood, her deranged mother on her knees beside him, gun clutched in her hand.

A thumping sound brought her up short.

Faith?

She quickly went back into the hall, shutting the door behind her and calling out as she hurried to the front of the house. 'Mrs. Spaulding? Are you here? It's Caroline Hoffman.'

No reply. Caroline looked nervously up the stairs. Faith must be using a second-floor bedroom. That thump could have been her falling. Collapsing.

Filled with dread, Caroline raced from room to room, but Faith wasn't in any of the three second-floor bedrooms. Only one showed any semblance of being currently lived in, with an open book on the table beside the made-up four-poster double bed. Tolstoy's *Anna Karenina*. A novel whose tragic themes revolved around obsession and infidelity.

Caroline spotted a piece of white notepaper next to the book. Nothing more than a short grocery list. It was the penmanship, however, that interested her. If this list was in Faith's handwriting, it didn't at all resemble the script on the *Godless Aphrodite* painting.

Stepping back into the second-floor hallway, she started for the one other logical place left to check for Faith Spaulding.

All that saved the huge attic from total darkness was a narrow ribbon of daylight sneaking out of the edges of the huge boarded-up skylight. Caroline found a wall switch, but nothing happened when she flicked it on.

'Mrs. Spaulding?'

Again, silence.

Caroline was spooked, but her eyes were adjusting to the murkiness. Along with stacks of cartons, a steamer trunk and the odd piece of furniture, she spotted something irresistible. Over at the end of the attic. An artist's easel. With a canvas resting on it. Facing the wall, unfortunately.

Her heart raced with anticipation as she made her way across the pine planked floor. She wished there were more light. Or that she'd thought to look for a flashlight down in the kitchen.

'It's blank.'

Caroline saw the woman's ghostly form almost at the same moment as she heard her voice. She was sitting on a high wooden stool not ten feet away from the easel. Her long dark hair hung loosely about her face, obscuring her features. Her dark sweater and slacks helped her to meld into the dimness. She sat very still, her arms behind her back, her head tilted downward, one shoulder jutting forward. As if she were a model holding a position for an artist.

'A blank canvas. A blank screen. A blank mind. A blank life—' All spoken in a girlish singsong voice.

'Mrs. Spaulding? It's Caroline Hoffman. I've been looking all over the house—'

'Faith. My mother dreamed of having three girls. First came Faith. Then Hope. Then Charity. She died a day after my birth.'

'I didn't think you were here, Faith.'

'To be safe, it's wise to be neither seen nor heard.'

Caroline could feel her stomach knot. Precisely the motto a voyeur would live by.

'You, on the other hand, are very noisy. I hope you're satisfied. Now you've gone and put us both in danger.' Faith spoke with sharp irritation – not fear.

'Danger from whom?' Caroline asked softly, careful not to sound deprecating or demanding.

Faith held her frozen pose. 'Why not you? You could be the real danger. That's what I've been hearing.'

'Why don't we go downstairs, Faith? We could have a cup of tea in the kitchen. Or we could go outside for a walk.' Caroline thought it would do Faith good to get out of Daniel Spaulding's dark, airless studio attic. It would do her a world of good, too.

But Faith didn't budge. 'Oh yes, I've been hearing all about the trouble you're causing.'

'Someone told you I was causing trouble, Faith?'

'Wouldn't you like to know?'

'I would. Very much.'

A caustic laugh. 'You think it's voices in my head. Don't you? You think these voices are telling me bad things? Bad things about Meg? About what she's been doing? So tell me, Doctor Mind-Stealer, are you sure my little girl killed those men?'

'No. I'm only interested in helping Meg. I'm her psychiatrist . . .'

'My psychiatrist didn't help me. He said all kinds of terrible things about me.' Faith leaned forward on the stool, but otherwise maintained her position. 'Made Ned and Meggie cry. Right in the courtroom.'

'I'm not going to make them cry, Faith.'

'You think I don't remember what you said!' Faith shrieked at her. 'I remember everything, Doctor Mind-Fucker.'

Faith Spaulding was clearly in the throes of a psychotic episode – delusions, paranoia, hallucinations, rapidly surfacing rage – and it was all being directed at her.

Caroline was scared. That fear induced a valuable dose of caution. Psychiatrists who treated agitated psychotic patients and felt impregnable were invariably the ones who got hurt. A few of them got themselves killed.

In the past, she had turned around a number of precarious, potentially life-threatening situations like this, by acknowledging the danger, but not letting it cloud her judgement. A balancing act. Especially crucial now, because she had no back-up and because she had to accept that she could be tangling with the real Aphrodite killer.

'This must have been Dan's studio,' Caroline said, careful to maintain a tone of clinical detachment. 'Do you like to spend time here, Faith?'

'No.' A long pause. 'I used to be up here all the time.'

'Before Dan died you mean. Do you think about that night he died, Faith? Do you remember . . . ?'

'I remember plenty, Doctor Flesh-Sucker.' Faith's voice was taunting.

'When you called me up earlier today, you wanted to share some of your secrets with me, didn't you, Faith? Because you know in your heart, no matter what you've heard, that I can be trusted.'

Faith shook her head. 'You're not going to get under my skin.'

'I don't want to do that.'

In a flash, Faith leaped up from the stool and lunged towards her. 'And he's not going to get under my skirt again.' She laughed hysterically, arms waving wildly. All this accompanied by a jangling metallic sound.

Caroline's professional cool evaporated as she saw the flashes of silver. A good yard's length of metallic chain swung from Faith's right hand.

A coquettish smile played on her face as she stood no more than three feet from Caroline. She was no longer swinging the chain but held it taut in both hands. 'Should I tell you a secret?'

'Yes. Please tell me a secret.' Caroline nodded encouragingly as she willed her muscles to relax. If Faith did attempt to attack her with that chain she had to be ready to fight her off.

'Here's the secret, then.' Faith lowered her voice to a conspiratorial whisper. 'Dan didn't always paint from his imagination, you know, you know—'

Caroline was stunned.

'Oh Faith,' she said softly. Sadly.

'Now I've done it, now I've done it, now I've done it,' Faith shrieked, swinging the chain as if she were fending off demons swarming around her head. 'He had to see me naked. Wrapped in chains, wrapped in chains, wrapped in chains with my Ned—'

Ben flung open the glass doors of Vineyard Haven Hospital and raced over to the front desk. 'Where's Caroline Hoffman?' he demanded.

The young female candy-striper nervously gestured to a late middle-aged woman with short brown hair and a round, pleasant face who was camped in one of the waiting area chairs, reading the local paper.

The woman, dressed in a plaid flannel shirt and black corduroy slacks, took her time getting out of her seat and ambling over. 'Sheriff Marge Chapin. What can I do for you?'

'I'm Ben Tabor. Meg Spaulding's lawyer. A cab driver at the airport tells me there's been some kind of fracas out at the Spaulding place, and that I'd find Faith and her daughter's psychiatrist here.' He tried to sound crisp and professional, but he was quaking inside.

The sheriff gave him a slow once-over. 'So you want to see Faith Spaulding, is that it?'

Ben always bristled inwardly at those inspections. Always thinking being black had something to do with it. Most always right about that. 'No, I want to see the psychiatrist.'

'Hoffman?'

'Yes. Caroline Hoffman. Where is she, damn it?' So much for self-containment.

Sheriff Chapin didn't seem perturbed. 'Room 112, right down the hall there, last room on the right. But I don't think Dr. Elgar's gonna let you in right now.'

'Screw him.' Ben took off down the hall.

The door to room 112 was closed. A few short knocks brought a small, wiry man with a receding hairline and a pencil-thin moustache out the door. He was wearing a white lab coat that hung down below his knees.

'Dr. Elgar?'

The man nodded solemnly.

Ben's anger disintegrated in the wake of his panic. 'How is she?'

'Gave her some Ativan to calm her down.'

'Caroline needed drugs?'

'Caroline?'

'Dr. Hoffman.'

Elgar smiled. 'The doctor's doing fine. The Ativan was for Mrs. Spaulding.'

'I don't get it. The sheriff said you had Dr. Hoffman in there.'

'Mrs. Spaulding insisted Dr. Hoffman sit with her until she fell asleep.' The doctor started to walk off, but then turned back to Ben. 'You a friend of Dr. Hoffman's?'

'Yes.'

'I'm not one to admonish a fellow psychiatrist – everybody's got their own approaches – but she really wasn't wise to go out there by herself to deal with Mrs. Spaulding when she's in the throes of one of her psychotic episodes.'

'I couldn't agree with you more, Doctor.'

Caroline sat on the four-poster bed in the antique-filled guest room of the Menemsha, a bed and breakfast down the block from the hospital. It was after ten and there were no more commercial flights or ferries back to Boston that night. Besides, Caroline wanted to check in on Faith Spaulding again in the morning.

Ben couldn't keep still. The entire day's events – from the break-in at Caroline's apartment that morning to his frantic arrival at Vineyard Haven Hospital that evening – had him completely keyed up.

'I thought psychiatrists were supposed to cure crazy people, Caroline, not *drive them crazy*!'

'I had to come out here and see Faith. And it all worked out . . .'

'Christ, I can't tell you what went through my head when that cab driver said you were in the hospital.'

'I still don't feel so hot,' Caroline confessed.

Ben lifted a peach wool throw off a chintz chaise longue,

came over and draped it around her shoulders. Then he knelt down in front of her and took hold of her cold hands. 'I'm sorry for getting on your case. My timing's been lousy lately.'

'Apology accepted.'

'Want a cigarette?'

'No. I'm quitting all my – bad habits.'

'When did you decide that?'

Caroline smiled faintly. 'When I was staring at that chain in Faith Spaulding's hands and thinking it might *wind* up around my neck!'

Ben knew all about the horror of looking into the face of death. Hadn't he, too, made his vows to quit bad habits when Jimmy had pointed that pistol at him and his cousin Mitch seven months ago?

Ben didn't even realize he was stroking the side of Caroline's face until she tilted her head and pressed her cheek into his hand.

She smiled. 'I'm glad you're here, Ben.'

'I'm glad *you're* here.' He smiled back at her.

'Now what?' Caroline asked softly.

Ben sucked in his breath. 'I better let you get some sleep.'

But he couldn't pull either his hand or his eyes away from her.

There were nights Caroline had put herself to sleep imagining Ben doing exactly this. Wishing—

'I'm . . . just across the hall,' he mumbled. 'If you . . . need me . . . just . . .'

'I need you.'

Ben wasn't ready for this. He was scared. Not of the sex.

But of the tenderness he was feeling. Of where it might lead. Most likely, once this was over, she wouldn't need him any more. He drew his hand away from her face.

'Caroline—'

She stiffened. 'It's okay, Ben. I understand.'

'No, you don't. I know what you're thinking.'

'Forget it. I'm tired. You're tired. It was stupid. What I said – stupid.'

He took hold of her shoulders. 'Stop it, please. This is not about you. It's about me.'

'What about you?' she challenged.

He let go of her. Got to his feet. 'What about me? What's about me is I don't want to screw this relationship up, okay? Or I guess I should say I don't want to risk screwing it up before it gets to be a relationship!'

'Is it going to get to be a relationship?'

'I don't know. You know? Who the hell knows these things? You show up in my life again after fourteen years – out of the blue – and you're all grown up and look terrific. Only it's at a time when – let's just say – not a great time in my life.' He pressed his palms to his temples. Making a complete ass of himself was giving him a first-class migraine. 'I'm going to go, okay?'

'Would you do me a favour first?'

'What?' He spoke so sharply that he immediately held up his hand in a gesture of apology.

Caroline walked slowly over to him. 'Just hold me for a minute, Ben. Nothing more. A minute. You can time it.'

Without a word, Ben drew her into his arms. He felt the need as much as she did.

To Caroline's complete astonishment, no sooner did Ben wrap his arms around her than she found herself sobbing.

Ben's own eyes welled up, too. He wasn't even sure why. But pretty soon he was sobbing, too. They held on to each other until they were both cried out.

It was more than a minute. But neither of them was counting.

Monday

35

By early afternoon, Marcia Kirshbaum, Ben's private investigator on Meg's case, had a preliminary report ready. Ben and Caroline took the call in Dr. Elgar's office at Vineyard Haven Hospital. Caroline had not gotten to talk with Faith Spaulding so far that day. Faith currently believed that Caroline was the devil and that she'd come to the hospital to steal her babies from her womb. At this point, Faith was slipping into a catatonic phase.

After Ben briefly introduced Caroline and Kirshbaum over the speaker phone set-up, the investigator got down to business.

'Well, for starters, you can pretty much scratch Winston Spaulding off your list,' the investigator relayed. 'The old guy was at some holistic health centre up in Kennebunkport, Maine. "WellWood." Checked in on Tuesday afternoon around two and didn't check out till Thursday noon. His whereabouts can pretty much be accounted for almost all of that time. They keep 'em real busy. Yoga, meditation, breathing exercises, chanting . . .'

'What about Faith Spaulding?' Caroline asked.

'I'm getting to her. Had a chat with her son Ned this morning. He was practically beside himself. Not that I can blame him. Sister wigged out in one hospital, Mommy in another. He said he was heading for the Vineyard as soon as he could get away. He show up there yet?'

'Yeah,' Ben said impatiently. 'He's with his mother. I don't think she knows it, though. So?'

'So, Ned wasn't too co-operative when I asked him where his mother was during the week before he had her hospitalized at Boston General. But I did manage to finally track down where she had hung out . . . at least for part of the time. She booked herself a room at the MacKenzie for a week. A dump over on Essex in what's left of the Combat Zone. I showed the manager a picture of Faith and he recognized her right off the bat. Says she stayed there Tuesday through Friday morning even though she paid up front for a week. *Them's* the rules. The creep was worried I'd come for a refund. Can you beat that?'

'Marcia . . .'

'You never did learn the art of kibitzing, Ben. Pity.'

'What'd you learn, Marcia?'

'On Tuesday night around six p.m. the manager says he saw Faith go up to her room with some young stud who took off about an hour later. But according to the manager, Faith had several more *visitors* that night. A regular stud parade. Turns out she was ordering 'em up by phone. One of her boy toys stayed overnight. Goes by the name of Spunk. Real name's Harvey Pigott. Guess he imagines

Spunk is preferable to Piggy. Anyhow, I'm still trying to track him down for a statement. But I'd say Momma's alibis for Tuesday night and Wednesday morning are pretty solid. I'm still checking on Saturday. You want me to pass on what I got so far on Faith and Winston to Boston Homicide?'

'Just give them what you've got on Faith. If we clear the mother, it'll quiet things down out here at the Vineyard,' Ben said. 'She's in for a hard enough time as it is.'

'Anything yet on Ned Spaulding?' Caroline asked.

'Not yet. According to the statement he gave the police, he was home all Tuesday night and Wednesday morning. No visitors. No calls that he remembers making or getting. Leads a quiet life for a guy who looks that good. His gallery doesn't open till ten. His employee, a nifty dresser by the name of Cowen – who, I might add, *is* quite the kibitzer – told me Ned gets down there around nine Tuesdays through Friday mornings. Sometimes on Saturday. Gallery's closed Sunday and Monday.'

'He there this Saturday?' Ben asked.

'Nope. This Saturday was an exception. Cowen told me Ned was at an estate sale out in Wayland from around nine in the morning till two, two-thirty in the afternoon. Didn't buy anything. Cowen also said he was a bit surprised about that. Seems there were some paintings Spaulding claimed he'd been particularly interested in snaring. Cowen also heard they went for a song to one of their competitors. My buddy over at Homicide says Ned told the cops he doesn't remember talking to anyone at that sale. Doesn't know if anybody noticed he was even there.'

'You'll . . .'

'Yeah, yeah. I'm heading out to Wayland right now, Ben. But at the moment, I'd say Ned's got *bupkus* for alibis. Rough translation of *bupkus* – shit!'

'Anyone on our list drive a black Mercedes?' Ben asked Kirshbaum.

'As a matter of fact, we've got ourselves two Mercedes in the bunch. You hang with a rich crowd, Counsellor. Lexuses, Acuras, BMWs, Mercedes . . .'

'Tell me about the Mercedes.'

'Right. One's Winston Spaulding's. A '91 300E. It's a dark green. Could pass for black, though.'

'And the other one?' Caroline asked.

'Belongs to Meg Spaulding's boss, Sylvia Fields. She's got herself a real nice '95 Mercedes 320SE. Jet black.'

Caroline's heart sank. This was all she needed. Yet another one of her patients a potential suspect. And a personal threat.

'Nothing yet on whether either of those cars could have been at Logan yesterday afternoon at approximately 2:50 p.m. Hard checking folks' whereabouts for a nice springtime Sunday—'

'I had Winston and Ned in my office,' Ben said. 'But they didn't show up until around 3:30.'

'Ned could have borrowed his grandfather's car, followed me to Logan, and still made it to your office when he did,' Caroline pointed out.

'I'm checking on Fields for the pertinent times. Nothing solid yet. What about the daughter? Meg?' Kirshbaum asked. 'You don't want me to check on where she was when the murders took place?'

Ben glanced at Caroline. 'No, Marcia. Unfortunately, we know exactly where Meg was when.'

'Wrong places at the wrong times?'

'You put it so well.'

'Well, it's nice to know you're back in the thick of it, Ben,' Kirshbaum said warmly. 'I'll be in touch.'

'Okay,' Ben said, having no idea how soon that was going to be.

Meg sat in an orange vinyl upholstered chair. She'd put on a hospital-issue blue-and-white striped seersucker robe over her white nightgown. She was still pale, but the late afternoon sun streaming in through the grimy barred window framed her in a nimbus of light, making her appear almost luminescent. Not for the first time in his client's presence, Ben was ashamed to find himself experiencing a disturbing flash of arousal. He had no trouble seeing how this alluring *goddess* came by her men.

'He thinks I'm psychotic, doesn't he?' Meg's question was directed at Caroline.

Caroline gave Ben a sidelong glance as they both sat down in a couple of grey plastic chairs.

'Not him. That hospital shrink. Fuller. Dr. Fuller-Shit, my mother would call him. She probably did. He told me he'd treated her for a couple of months when she was locked up here.' Meg laughed. But she stopped abruptly, shifting her gaze to Ben. 'So, counsel. Do you think I'm crazy, too?'

'Are you speaking in the legal or psychiatric sense, Miss Spaulding?'

'Is that a joke? They've got me so doped up I'm afraid my sense of humour isn't what it usually is. You'll have to forgive me. Do you forgive me, Ben?' Meg smiled seductively.

Ben could feel Caroline's eyes on him. He fought the urge to clear his throat. 'If you'd be more comfortable with another lawyer, Miss Spaulding, I'm sure someone in your family will be more than happy to find you . . .'

'Why should I want another lawyer?' Meg cut him off. 'You got a jury to acquit Caroline. I'm banking on you doing the same for me.'

Caroline felt the sting of that remark. And knew Meg had meant it.

'But let's get something clear,' Meg continued, her gaze fixed on Ben. 'I won't permit you to resort to an insanity defence. If I *didn't* kill anyone, how could I have been crazy when I did it? Do you see what I'm saying? I'm innocent. Of murder, anyway. Somebody else killed those men. But there's probably not a jury in this country who's going to believe that. Isn't that right, Counsellor?'

'It would help if you had any ideas as to whom that somebody else might be. I'm not going to pull any punches with you, Meg. This is going to be a tough rap for us to beat. So if you have any thoughts about this *somebody else*, you need to tell me. Now.'

Meg squinted as if the sunlight was suddenly too bright. Rising abruptly from her chair, she walked to the right of the window and leaned back against the drab green wall. She stared straight past them, lost in her thoughts.

'What's happening, Meg?' Caroline asked gently.

Meg gave her a distracted glance, then slowly scanned the

dreary hospital room. 'I positively hated visiting my mother in this revolting place. Hardly ever came. Ned and Grandy were here all the time. They loved visiting Mother. Did you know Grandy actually asked my mother to marry him? She hadn't been out of the hospital a week before he proposed to her. Her dead husband's father. How's that for sick?'

'Did your mother think it was sick?' Caroline asked.

Meg scowled. 'I did. Ned certainly did. He was fit to be tied.'

'Ned was upset with your grandfather?' Ben asked.

'Ned was upset with both of them. And that got my mother upset with Winston.'

'Because she didn't want Ned to be upset with her?' Caroline asked.

Meg fidgeted with her hair. Then she began banging her head in a slow rhythm against the wall.

'They didn't talk for years, Mother and Grandy. It's just that he's dying now. Mother never would have married him anyway. She doesn't go for old men.'

'How about your mother and brother, Meg?' Caroline asked softly. 'Did they get along after she got out of the hospital?'

Meg gave a barely perceptible nod. Then she said in a low voice, 'They always got along.'

Caroline kept her professional stance. 'They were close.' Another tiny nod. 'Very, very close.'

'Was Ned with your mother that night, Meg?' Caroline paused, intently watching her patient. She had to be careful not to move too fast. 'The night your father was shot.'

Meg twined a strand of hair tightly round and round her

finger. Tears slipped down her cheeks. 'He was supposed to be sleeping over at Grandy's. Ned lied to me.'

'You saw Ned in the bedroom?'

'No.' Meg hesitated. 'He was running away.' She spoke so quietly Caroline and Ben had to lean forward to make out her words. 'Out the window. Into the darkness.'

'Did Ned know you saw him?' Caroline asked.

'I phoned Grandy. Ned came back with him. He took care of everything.'

'Your grandfather?'

'Ned.'

'What did he take care of?'

'Us. At first I was angry at him. But I was also scared. Ned was so comforting. So tender. So loving. And he took charge of everything.'

Meg slid down the wall until she was sitting on the floor. She bent her legs, pulled her nightgown and robe over her calves and wrapped her arms around her knees.

'You love Ned very much.'

Meg's lips quivered as she looked up at Caroline. 'He's always looked after me. Sometimes I've wanted to tell him that I've looked after him, too.'

'Maybe he already knows that,' Caroline said.

There were no candles. The lighting was bare neon strips. The plastic-covered menus were spotted with ketchup and grease stains. The only thing gold on them was a splatter here and there of golden mustard. Instead of harps or violins, some *Elvis Lives* fan had stuck a couple of bucks' worth of quarters in the jukebox and was covering the King's songs from A to Z.

As Ben and Caroline worked on their chicken burgers and fries, Elvis the Pelvis was growling out his yearning for some tender loving. All Caroline wanted at the moment was some reasonable concessions.

'Would you grant me fifty-fifty?' Caroline demanded.

'What? That there's a fifty per cent chance Ned's the killer, not Meg?' Ben wasn't buying those odds.

'Dan Spaulding had Ned and his mother pose for the painting, Ben. What was Ned? All of sixteen at the time? Who knows what other perverse . . .'

'You're putting a lot of trust in the ravings of a couple of seriously disturbed women. You don't know . . .'

'They may be disturbed, but I believe Faith and Meg were both telling the truth. I believe Ned and his mother did more than pose. I think they were having a sexual relationship. And that, when Dan Spaulding walked into the bedroom with that painting that fateful night, he saw his son in bed with Faith. I believe incest was the *real* catalyst for the tragedy that followed,' Caroline said. 'Meg saw her brother running away from the house right after her father was murdered. I think either Faith pulled the trigger to protect Ned, or Ned may have even been the one who urged his mother to shoot his father.'

'I gather, to stick with Greek metaphors, we're talking basic Oedipus here. Son metaphorically kills off Daddy and gets Mommy all to himself.' Ben took a bite of his burger and washed it down with a swallow of club soda. 'And that the way you'd have it, we should be calling our strangler the *Oedipal* killer.'

'It might be more accurate.'

'So why wasn't Ned off strangling his momma's *boy toys* as Marcia so colourfully referred to them? Why do in his sister's boyfriends?'

'Because I believe that Ned's transferred his incestuous feelings from his mother to his young sister – who's the spitting image of Faith as she was ten years ago. And he's moved from symbolically killing his real father to literally killing anyone he perceives as a threat to his sister.'

'And you think Meg knows Ned's the killer?'

'It could be.'

'So, I'm supposed to conclude that Meg loves her brother so much, she's willing to take the rap for him?' He looked up at the grimy tin ceiling and gave a weary sigh. 'Well, I, for one, have had enough of Greek tragedy for one day.' Ben eyed his half-eaten burger. Caroline hadn't taken more than a couple of nibbles of hers. 'Let's have this stuff wrapped to go.'

'You take care of that while I call in for messages.' Caroline slid out of her chair. She headed for the pay phone near the rest rooms.

Her voice mail was stuffed to the gills. Susan Steinberg had called her several times. A number of patient cancellations – all four members of her Wednesday evening group included. Disappointing, but no big surprise. On the positive side – then again, maybe not – Sylvia Fields had called in asking to see her on Wednesday at one instead of Thursday. Sylvia who drove a big, black Mercedes. The last message was from Greg Pomeroy. He sounded extremely agitated.

The call from Greg had come in a couple of hours ago. Caroline was angry at herself for not checking in sooner.

Ben sauntered over, carrying their oversized doggie bag. 'What's up?'

'I've got to reach a patient.'

'Why don't you call from my car? It'll be more private.'

Four rings and then the answering machine went on. *You've reached six two eight two . . .*

'Damn,' Caroline muttered. 'He's not home.'

The recording stopped abruptly and was followed by a sharp click.

A man's voice. 'Hello.'

'Greg?'

'Who's this?'

'Caroline Hoffman. I got your message.'

'It's about time.' He paused. 'Sorry. Didn't mean to jump on you. I'm upset. I'm *very* upset.'

'I can understand . . .'

Pomeroy cut her off. 'No, you can't. I got this extremely disturbing phone call yesterday. Some computer-generated voice that says to me, if I'm smart I won't go talking to the cops about any stuff Meg talked about in our therapy group.'

Caroline looked over at Ben behind the wheel. 'Greg, I'm speaking to you from Ben Tabor's car. He's my lawyer. And Meg Spaulding's lawyer, as well. I'd like him to hear about this call. Is it okay with you if I switch on the speaker?'

There was a long pause. 'Yeah. Okay.'

She flipped the switch. 'Have you reported this threatening call to the police, Greg?'

'Are you crazy?' Pomeroy sounded ready to explode. 'You think I want this loony coming after me? You think I want my name plastered all over the news? Have the whole world know I'm in your sex addicts' group? It's hard enough for an ex-classics professor who got dismissed for sexual harassment to find a job.'

'No. Of course you want to protect your privacy. And I don't blame you for feeling frightened.'

'We're all frightened.'

'All?' Caroline asked with concern.

'Yeah,' Pomeroy said. 'I took the chance of calling around to the rest of the group. They all got the same kind of weird warnings. Tina even got one in the hospital.'

Caroline's mind filled with bitter self-reproach. This was her fault. She'd put every one of her group therapy patients in danger. If she hadn't videotaped their sessions – if she hadn't stupidly brought that one tape home – if, if, if —

'You think Meg's got someone on the outside . . . you know . . . trying to keep us in line?'

'What makes you think Meg Spaulding's behind the calls?' Ben asked.

'Because I'm sure she's the Aphrodite killer.'

Ben switched off the speaker for a second. 'What's Pomeroy's address?' he asked Caroline. He switched on again as she dug into her bag for her appointment/address book.

'You still there?' Pomeroy asked nervously.

'We're here,' Ben said. Caroline pointed in her book to her patient's address. 425 Washington Street in Somerville. Ben headed for I-93 North.

'So tell me what makes you so positive Meg Spaulding's the killer, Pomeroy?' Ben asked.

There was a pause. 'Do either of you know that Aphrodite was given a number of different surnames? Among the people of Cyprus, she was known as *Aphrodite Eleemon* – The Merciful. Then there was the Spartans. They worshipped her as *Aphrodite Morpho* – Aphrodite Enchained.'

'That's very interesting, Greg,' Ben said.

'And among the ancient Erinyes, she was known as *Aphrodite Androphonos*. Can you translate that, Dr. Hoffman? How about you, Counsellor?'

'You're the expert,' Ben said. 'Translate it for us.'

'*Aphrodite Androphonos*. Goddess of Love. Killer of Men.'

'I still don't see why you wanted to drive all the way over here to Somerville. I told you everything there was to say on the phone.' Greg Pomeroy nervously rubbed his hands up and down his arms. Caroline and Ben, meanwhile, made special note of the large collection of beautiful lithographs – most with a strong ancient Graeco-Roman motif – hanging on the walls of the professor's otherwise modest living room.

'I'm feeling really agitated. I don't know, Dr. Hoffman. Maybe you could prescribe something . . .'

'Greg,' Ben cut him off abruptly. 'Why am I getting the feeling you're holding back on us? If you're involved . . .'

'Involved!' Pomeroy blanched. 'I've got nothing to do with this. Nothing.'

Shakily, Pomeroy made his way over to his Early
American-style plaid couch and sat down. On the pine
coffee-table in front of him was a bottle of bourbon and
a glass half full of the pale amber liquor. Pomeroy lifted
the glass and made short work of what was left of his
drink.

Caroline, not too happy with Ben's aggressive questioning technique or her patient's alcohol consumption, took a
seat beside the professor. 'Greg, if you know anything at all
about these murders . . .'

Pomeroy set his empty glass back on the table. 'I saw the
painting.'

Ben squinted at him. '*The Godless Aphrodite* painting?
You mean the print of it in the news?'

'No. I saw the original.' Pomeroy got up abruptly and
walked over to a grouping of three lithographs on the wall.
'The Rape of Persephone. I bought this trio at the
Spaulding Gallery four years ago. While this guy who sold
them to me was wrapping them up, he let me view some
unframed lithos stored in a back room. I'd mentioned I was
a classics professor, and he was extremely accommodating.
Spaulding's *Aphrodite* painting was tucked away in a corner.
I was very taken with it. Of course at the time, I knew
nothing about the artist or his family.'

Caroline lifted an eyebrow as she looked over at Ben. So
much for Meg's claim that Ned had destroyed the infa-
mous painting. Was Meg lying, or had her brother lied to
her? What else might their *Oedipus* have lied about?

'Did you ask about the painting?' Caroline asked Greg.
'Not that day. I was rushed for time. But I went back the

next afternoon to inquire about it. The guy I'd bought the lithos from wasn't there. I spoke to the owner.'

'Ned Spaulding?'

Pomeroy nodded at Ben. 'When I asked if the Aphrodite painting was for sale, he gave me this blank look. Denied having the painting. Or that it even existed. I thought maybe it was hot or something. I dropped the whole thing. Forgot all about it.'

'Until Meg Spaulding joined our group?'

'It's funny,' Pomeroy said. 'The connection didn't hit me until I heard about that first murder. When I read that the violinist had been strangled with a chain, it triggered an image of that painting in my mind. *The Godless Aphrodite*. The goddess's face came back so vividly.' Pomeroy exhaled. 'It was Meg Spaulding's face. And then I started putting other pieces together. It was all pure supposition, of course.'

'What pieces?'

Pomeroy frowned. After a moment's thought, he continued.

'After group a couple of weeks ago – that session when Meg opened up about her sexual addiction – she was very worked up. I don't blame her. It's a wrenching experience, facing your demons.'

'Absolutely.' Caroline could well commiserate.

'I gave her a lift home. While we were driving, she told me that this guy – the one from the toy store – somehow found out who she was and called her at home a few days after their encounter. He wanted to see her again.'

'Did she see him again?'

'No. She told me she got scared and threatened the guy. Told him that if he ever called again or if she ever saw him again, he'd be one very sorry man. And she sounded to me like she meant it,' Pomeroy added pointedly.

'She didn't tell you anything about him?' Ben asked.

'Only that she was freaked that he knew her name.'

Pomeroy's gaze moved bleakly from Caroline to Ben. 'What I've been thinking is, maybe that violinist – Korza – it could be he was the man from the toy store. That he was Meg's first victim—'

'. . . or *Ned's* first victim,' Caroline persisted, as she and Ben sat in an Irish pub next door to Greg's building. 'It doesn't alter my theory.'

'I'd say it puts a kink in it,' Ben said. 'Pomeroy provides us with a solid motive for Meg wanting to get rid of Korza.'

'And . . . Martin?'

Ben waited until the waitress set a Coke and a half-pint of tap beer on their table and left.

'Same argument.' Ben took a sip of the Coke. 'Couldn't Martin have recognized Meg from the Institute? Oh, not at first, but once they—' He let the rest of the sentence hang, knowing Caroline could all too easily fill in the blanks. 'Goes for Kramer, too,' Ben said, eager to pass over Caroline's murdered lover. 'All three men posed threats to Meg. All three could have *outed* her. She had plenty of motive to get rid of each of them.'

'So did Ned. To protect his sister. And because he's obsessed with her. It would be a motive for breaking into my apartment, stealing Meg's record and the videotape, then making those threatening calls. And he could easily have borrowed his grandfather's Mercedes . . .'

'Why run down one of the few people who are on his sister's side?' Ben countered.

'He doesn't want me digging up family secrets. And Meg reminded me of something else. When Faith's psychiatrist got on the stand during her trial, since it was an insanity defence he wasn't held to confidentiality restrictions and apparently he revealed a lot of emotion-laden information from his sessions with Faith.'

Caroline stared at her glass of beer. Another shifting of the puzzle pieces suddenly gave it a totally new shape and direction she hadn't fully considered until that moment. She swung her gaze back to Ben. 'What if it wasn't him?'

'You've lost me. I thought you were all but convinced it was Ned.'

'I didn't say I was convinced. And I'm not talking about Ned now. I meant that we don't know for certain Peter Korza and the man Meg seduced in the toy store are one and the same. The man may still be alive. Still obsessed with Meg. Out there—'

'Did anyone ever tell you that sometimes you're too damn smart for your own good?'

'My mother. But the way she said it, I always felt like it was something to be ashamed of.' Caroline smiled faintly. 'The way you say it, I feel this kind of warm glow of pride.'

'Remind me to say it more often, then.'

Her smile deepened.

36

'I'll grant you this. You've got nerve, Lieutenant Baush.'

Jesse grinned. 'And on Saturday night you said I had charm. That's two for two.'

'Sorry,' Susan Steinberg said coolly. 'You're still batting zero on my card. And since Caroline's been released and you've got your real killer under wraps, I can't imagine the reason for this visit. Or this . . .' She gestured to the items Jesse had brought along and spread out on her kitchen table – a half-dozen cartons of take-out Chinese food.

'I thought I owed you for ruining your dinner the other night.'

'It's literally impossible to ruin a frozen dinner, Lieutenant. It starts out that way.'

He laughed. 'How about calling me Jesse? I figure if two people break bread together – or fried rice – they should switch to a first name basis.'

'We aren't breaking bread or rice together, Lieutenant.'

'Why not? Because you hate my guts?'

'You're showing your talent for acuity again.'

'So how come you didn't just slam your front door in my face?'

'You took me by surprise.'

'I never meant to deceive you the other night, Susan. It was a misunderstanding.'

'Bullshit.'

'I bet you don't curse out your patients when they're trying to tell you how they're feeling,' Jesse said, teasing.

'First of all, you're not my patient,' Susan said curtly. 'And second of all, you're not saying a word about how you feel.'

'It's not easy for me to talk about my feelings.' Jesse's expression turned serious. 'Especially when they concern my stepsister. You see, the wrong woman's locked up in that psychiatric hospital . . .'

'I don't believe this. You've got a serious problem, Lieutenant Baush.'

'You're so right, Susan. It's more serious than you imagine.'

'I don't want to hear it.'

'Look, you're a psychiatrist. Sure, to the untrained eye, this case looks real nice and tidy. But that's the problem. It's too tidy. Too slick. What Meg Spaulding really is, besides being wigged out of her mind, is an easy mark for someone who really *is* slick. And that someone is . . .'

'Let me guess. Your stepsister. My friend and respected colleague. Lieutenant, you're the one who's wigged out.'

Jesse kept his cool. 'I can see how I sound to you, Susan. But, remember what you told me Saturday night? That you don't know Caroline very long or very well? That she's not much of a talker? Well, I've known her practically my whole life. We grew up together. Went to school together. Ended up living together as brother and sister for a time. I know Caroline very well. Too well.'

Folding her arms across her ample breasts, Susan eyed him defiantly. But she couldn't resist. 'Go ahead.'

Counting on that response, Jesse launched into his detailed theory of how Caroline had framed Meg. Only in presenting it to Susan Steinberg, he eliminated the accusatory tone he'd used with his stepsister.

'What concerns me,' Susan said, 'is you really believe every word you just said.'

Jesse stepped closer. Put his hand lightly on her shoulder just at the crook of her neck. Although Susan stiffened slightly, she made no protest.

'Uh, uh,' he said, his hand slipping along her shoulder. 'What's scary is, you don't think it's absolutely unbelievable.' He brushed his hand down her arm before drawing it away.

'Think about what I've said for a while, Susan. You call me if and when you want to talk.' He pulled out one of his cards from his wallet, took a pen from his pocket and wrote a number on the back. 'Here. You can reach me day or night.'

She took the card. Held it thoughtfully.

He started to zip up his jacket.

'Wait,' Susan blurted.

Jesse bit back a smile. The old charm was still working for him. Susan made it almost too easy.

'Don't get the wrong idea, Jesse. I still say the police have the right person in custody. But since you've brought all this stuff . . . and I am crazy about Chinese food . . .'

He let the smile out. 'I'm crazy about Chinese food, too, Susan.'

'It looks like you had company.' Caroline eyed the half-empty cartons of Chinese food on Susan Steinberg's kitchen table, the two dirty plates on the counter next to the sink. 'I hope you didn't chase your dinner guest out of here because of me.'

Susan flushed. 'No. Don't be silly. It was nobody. Nobody important.'

Caroline gave her friend a curious look. Not like Susan to be so circumspect. Or so testy.

'If you're having second thoughts about my staying over for the night . . .'

'No. No, absolutely not. You can't go back to your place. What if it's broken into again? It's not safe. I've got the spare room all set up.'

Caroline wanted to know more. 'You've got a secret boyfriend.'

'What? Don't be . . .'

'Silly? I'm not prone to silliness, Susan. Look, let's just drop it, okay? You have every right not to have your privacy invaded.'

'God, Caroline, you'd think I was a spy or something. Why are you making such a big deal over this?'

'I didn't think I was.'

Susan backed off. 'So, okay. A guy did drop by. We ate

some chicken fried rice and beef with broccoli. If you want to know, the food was lousy.'

'And the guy?'

'He could be a louse.'

'So, you're undecided.'

Susan shrugged. 'I don't even know if I like him. I certainly don't know if I trust him. Or if I believe a word he tells me.'

Caroline smiled. 'I'll tell you one thing. He's got you interested.'

'You're right about that.' Susan was dead serious. 'I'm interested.'

Caroline yawned into her fist. 'Right now, I've got to get some sleep. First thing tomorrow, Ben and I have to go over to Neponset and have another talk with Meg Spaulding. I think we may have a possible new lead.'

Susan's eyes widened. 'Who is it?'

'Remember that videotape I showed at the staff meeting last week. The one where Meg talked about picking up this man . . . ?'

Caroline woke, disorientated. It was pitch black. What time was it? How long had she been sleeping?

Thinking she was in her own room, she reached for where her bedside light would be. Her hand brushed across nothing but air.

What the—

And then Caroline remembered that she was in Susan's spare bedroom. She checked the illuminated dial on her sports watch. 11:47.

Her head was fuzzy. And she had to pee. As much as she wanted to roll over and go back to sleep, she decided to make a quick trip to the bathroom. Clad in an oversized nightshirt she'd borrowed from Susan, she felt her way across the room. When she opened the door, she heard her friend talking.

Had Susan's new mystery boyfriend returned?

But there was no male voice. No other voice at all. Susan was talking to someone on the phone. Right around the corner in the kitchen.

Caroline was about to shut the door and wait a while to go to the bathroom when she caught a snatch of conversation that made her stay put.

'. . . *could be this man Meg Spaulding had a quickie with a couple of weeks ago at some toy store. Although she's not even sure he's still alive. Her other theory is Ned Spaulding—*'

There was a brief pause.

'*No. You're not listening. What I'm saying, Jesse, is that they're all viable suspects—*'

Caroline turned away from the door.

'. . . I swear, I don't even know why I called you, Jesse.' Susan Steinberg kept her voice low as she spoke into the phone. She picked a piece of cold broccoli out of the take-out container and slipped it into her mouth. 'I feel like I'm getting in the middle of something I don't want to be in.'

'You're already *in*, Susan.' Jesse kept his voice low, too. 'And I'm glad you are. Otherwise, we might never have crossed paths . . .'

'I can't talk about this any more now. I've got to go to bed.'

Susan hung up, put her elbows on the kitchen counter, and pressed her face into her palms. *What am I doing? This is pathetic. Don't I have any self-respect at all?*

She heard footsteps. A moment later, she saw Caroline, dressed, donning her jacket, passing by the kitchen and heading for the front door.

'Caroline . . .?'

'I'm out of here.'

Susan's mouth gaped open. But, for a change the garrulous psychiatrist was speechless.

Jesse headed eagerly back to his bedroom where he'd left Amy naked and sound asleep. Their second shot at an all-nighter. He was juiced – already picturing himself slipping quietly back into bed, cupping Amy's tits in his big hands, burying his face in their softness—

Amy was sitting up in bed, the sheet pulled up to her neck. 'So who was on the phone?'

Jesse gave a little start. 'I thought you'd dozed off, babe.'

'I'm wide awake now.'

'It was nobody. Connors from Vice. Just checkin' something out. Blah, blah, blah.' He started to unzip his jeans. He was wearing nothing underneath.

'Connors change his first name? To Susan?'

Jesse's hard-on took an instant dive. He threw up his hands in disgust. 'You eavesdropping on me now, Amy? Shit, I don't need this.' He pulled up his half-undone zipper and redid the snap on his jeans.

'Who's Susan?'

'Nobody important.'

'Nobody important that you're fucking?'

He laughed. 'Yeah, right. I'm fucking her. I'm fuckin' them all.'

Amy got out of bed, pulling the sheet around her naked body, and stood right in front of Jesse. The top of her head barely cleared his chin, so she had to tilt her head up to look at him in the face. 'Including your sister? You fucking her, too?'

'I don't have a *sister*.'

'No, you don't *have* her. But you *want* her, don't you, Jesse? You want her so bad, I bet you have wet-dreams about her—'

Amy saw Jesse clench his fist, but she wasn't alarmed. He'd never laid a hand on her.

She didn't even flinch, much less duck away.

Bad call. Should have realized there was always a first time.

Caroline, wearing a pair of Ben's navy flannel pajamas, lay under a blanket on the sofa-bed in his den. It was almost three in the morning. She'd been trying to sleep for the past couple of hours. She turned onto her stomach. A few minutes later she was rolling onto her back. Trying to get comfortable. An impossibility. She could still hear Ben moving around in the living room. Obviously, he was having trouble sleeping, too.

She blamed herself for his restlessness. She should have gone to a hotel after taking off from Susan's apartment.

But after that jarring episode at the Regency, Caroline knew it would be a while before she'd feel comfortable venturing alone into another hotel. And she was uneasy about spending the night in her apartment until that new security system Ben made her order after the break-in was installed.

She got out of bed and walked into the living room.

Ben was sitting on his sofa, still wearing the khaki slacks and blue-and-white striped button-down shirt he'd worn the day before. He was thumbing through a *Sports Illustrated*.

'I can't sleep.'

Ben looked up from his magazine. 'Can I get you anything?'

'You have any peace of mind around the house?'

He smiled. 'Don't I wish.'

'You didn't ask me why I showed up here in the middle of the night.'

'You looked beyond exhausted. I thought it could wait till morning.'

'It is morning,' she pointed out.

Ben nodded.

'My stepbrother's done one of his inimitable numbers on Susan Steinberg. They've been seeing each other. I suppose I shouldn't be surprised. Certainly not as far as Jesse's concerned. He'd use anyone to get at me. But Susan—' Caroline faltered. 'I was really starting to see Susan as a friend. I don't make friends easily. I never have.'

'I'm your friend, Caroline,' Ben said softly. Said like a promise.

For some reason, Caroline found his pledge unnerving.

'I don't know if I'm more angry or more hurt. About . . . Susan. You'd think I'd have learned by now, but betrayal still has a way of blindsiding me.'

Ben got up from the sofa and walked towards her.

Caroline followed his progress silently.

When they were less than a foot apart, Caroline nervously placed her hand on his chest. Not sure if she wanted the physical contact or wanted to stop him from taking this a step further. One thing was certain. She knew she didn't want to break down in his arms again. She kept her hand where it was. Over his heart. Kept it there as he placed his hand over hers. As his mouth moved over her mouth.

'You need to get some sleep. This is a good-night kiss,' he murmured against her lips.

The contact was brief but tender. A profound contrast to Jesse's vengeful kiss yesterday morning.

When Ben released her, the irony of it struck Caroline powerfully. In the course of a couple of astonishing days she'd got herself kissed by two men who, at different times in her life, had been a focus of her secret, shame-filled fantasies.

Tuesday

37

'Ryan and I've been talking,' Sylvia Fields was telling Caroline at their ten a.m. session. 'We're both behind Meg one hundred percent. By which I mean, both of us believe absolutely in her innocence. Ryan was so sure it was Meg's mother who was doing the murders.' Sylvia frowned. 'But from what I heard on one of the tabloid news shows the police aren't even considering her as a possible suspect. They also said that you had an encounter with Faith Spaulding Sunday night at her house on the Vineyard, Caroline. Do *you* think she checks out?'

'Sylvia, this is your time to talk about your feelings, not find out what I think.'

'What you think has direct bearing on my feelings,' Sylvia countered. 'My *feeling* is that Meg is innocent . . .'

'No. That's a thought, not a feeling.'

'Oh, please don't be such a *shrink*, Caroline,' Sylvia said peevishly. But then her features seemed to collapse. 'I adore Meg. She means the world to me. Each time I walk past her empty office, my heart breaks a little more. Are those *feelings*?'

'Yes, those are all very much feelings, Sylvia,' Caroline said quietly, dividing her thoughts between the conversation with Sylvia and her nagging concern about her patient's black Mercedes parked out in the lot.

Meg was sitting up in bed. An *Architectural Digest* lay open on her lap. She kept her eyes on it as her door was unlocked and Ben stepped into the hospital room.

While the door locked behind him, Ben gave his client a quick but comprehensive once over. She was still wearing the blue-and-white seersucker robe over her nightgown. She looked surprisingly composed. Stunning. Riveting.

Meg gave him a glance, then returned to the magazine. 'Where's your sidekick? Sleeping in? You two an item, Counsellor?'

'Why do you ask?'

Meg smiled. 'A question with a question. You're even beginning to sound like her.'

'I thought we could talk a little bit about your brother today.'

Meg's smile vanished. 'I know what you're thinking, but you're wrong.'

'What am I thinking, Meg?'

'Ned is not the one who's been following me. My brother isn't a killer. I'd know if he was.' Her tone was emphatic.

Too emphatic? 'He'd tell you?'

'He wouldn't have to tell me. I would be able to see it in his eyes.'

'Is that right?' Ben wasn't all that keen on the seductive look he saw in hers.

'Don't waste your time on Ned. It's somebody else.'

'Who?'

'Would I be locked in this loony bin if I knew?'

'Maybe you need to think a little harder. Give me some kind of lead. Your forty-eight-hour observation time's almost up, Meg. Maybe Fuller'll extend it. Maybe he won't. You don't seem in acute psychological distress right now.'

'Do you always believe everything you see, Ben?'

'Why are you playing these games, Meg?'

'Which games are we talking about?'

Ben assessed her seriously. 'You're hours away from being formally charged with three counts of first-degree murder with special circumstances, Meg.'

His point hit home. Her seductive manner evaporated. 'I want you to believe I'm innocent. I was just trying, in the way I know best, to be . . . persuasive. To win your full support.'

'I'm not the one you have to persuade, Meg. I told you once before, if you have any concerns that I'm not going to give you the best representation . . .'

'I still want you—' she paused, her voice imploring, 'to believe.'

He sat down in the orange chair at the side of her bed. 'Okay, then let's talk about the guy you picked up at a toy store in Faneuil Hall.'

Meg's face registered confusion. 'Who?'

'I saw the videotape where you talked about him. I also know that he found out who you were. Where you lived. I know he called you. That he wanted to see you again.'

The magazine slid off Meg's lap. Off the bed. She watched it fall.

'Did you ever see him again, Meg?'

Ben thought she must have tuned him out. He was about to repeat the question, when he caught a subtle shake of her head.

'Then it wasn't Peter Korza?'

She looked back at him, her expression blank. 'Who? Oh, the man at the museum.' She bit down on her lip. 'No. I never saw . . . Peter . . . before that evening.'

Ben nodded. Chalk up another point for Caroline.

'Do you think this guy from the toy store ever saw *you* again?'

Meg's eyes widened with concern. 'You think he's the one that's been following me? Watching me? Killing those men?' She bit down harder on her lip, leaving little teeth marks. 'You could be right. There was something about him that was different from the others. Something in his eyes . . .'

'Let's slow down. First thing we need to do is find him, Meg. Do you know his name? Where he works? Lives?'

Meg shook her head in despair. 'If he's the killer, I'm done for. You'll never find him. I don't know anything about him.'

'You know what he looks like.'

'They all look the same.' There was nothing flirtatious in her behaviour now. 'They all look a little bit like you.'

'He was black?'

'That's not what I mean. Their race, their age, their general appearance – none of that means anything to me. Their faces are always a blur. Bodies, too. The words – just static. It's only the eyes that make any impact. The eyes tell it all, Ben.'

He was transfixed as Meg's hand moved with a fluid grace to his face, her fingertips touching the creases at the corners of his dark eyes.

There was an unfamiliar buzzing, broken abruptly by the cutting sound of a man's voice behind him.

'Wouldn't you call this burning your *candle* at both ends, Tabor?' Jesse Baush taunted, taking on a *Thinker*'s pose as he stood in the doorway of Meg's hospital room.

Ben discovered that there were a large number of shops that sold toys in Faneuil Hall Marketplace, the thriving, kitschy food and shopping extravaganza created out of a trio of block-long granite-faced historic buildings in the North End. Even at three o'clock on a Monday afternoon, crowds of locals and tourists meandered along the sunny cobbled pedestrian ways dotted with benches and push-carts selling everything from Guatemalan hand-knit sweaters to Italian ices.

A large cluster of onlookers were gathered outside the central building's West Portico, watching a mime artist get himself trapped in an ever-shrinking imaginary box. Ben paused for a minute to watch the show, empathizing with the predicament.

The routine finished and Ben continued his hunt, walking into a large bi-level toy store, located in the

Marketplace's North Building. He wandered around both floors, checking out the staff for several minutes. Most of them looked to be in their early or mid-twenties. As before, he started with the men, figuring they'd be more likely to have taken a note of the gorgeous *looker* coming on to some *lucky* male customer.

One of the salesmen had only started working there the week before. The others couldn't remember a thing. Ben went on to the saleswomen. All six of them. *Nada.*

Having hit a blank wall, he was heading out of the shop when he felt a tug on his jacket sleeve. He turned around to face a petite young woman with shoulder-length ash-blond hair held off her face by a pair of wire-rimmed glasses perched on top of her head. She wore a snappy taupe silk business-suit. 'I'm the manager. Kelly Dawber. I was in my office. One of my employees told me you were questioning everyone on my staff.'

Ben introduced himself and gave her his card.

Kelly Dawber slid her glasses down in place, then inspected both the card and its bearer intently before asking Ben to come back with her into her office.

The manager's office, in the rear of the store, was a shoe box holding little more than a basic desk, a couple of wooden chairs, and a long bank of file cabinets. An orchid was perched under a small grow-light on the edge of the nearest file cabinet.

'You want to tell me the real reason you're here?'

'What do you mean? I told you . . .'

'Are you really who this card says you are?' The manager waved it in the air.

'You want to see my driver's licence?' Ben offered, baffled by her attitude.

'He showed me his driver's licence, too. And his business card.'

'You know the man I'm looking for?'

'I came close to calling the cops on him.'

Ben stared at her incredulously.

'I caught him sneaking out of the storage area in the back here,' Kelly Dawber said. 'I thought he was a shoplifter, but I have to say he didn't look the type. He gave me this sob story about how he was shopping for his kid's birthday when he got nauseous and made a dash for the employees' rest room. He did look rather green and sweaty, not to say dishevelled. Plus he took off his suit jacket, pulled everything out of his pants pockets, to prove he hadn't taken anything.'

'You said he showed you his driver's licence,' Ben prompted.

'And his business card.'

'You remember his name?'

She shook her head slowly. 'But you'll figure it out easy enough.'

'Why do you say that?'

The toy store manager gave Ben another of those assessing studies. 'Because he's a lawyer, too. In fact, he works at the same law firm as you.'

'Where is he?' Ben tried to cover the quiver in his voice by clearing his throat.

'He's not in today.'

'Is he sick?' *Oh, he's sick all right. Goddamn sick.*

Phil Mason's secretary, Jenna Wallace, shrugged. She was a tawny skinned beauty with short curly black hair, a lithe body, and a very appealing Jamaican accent. 'I don't know. He hasn't called in. I tried him at home earlier, but no one answered. I left a message. The man's been under so much stress lately. I gather things are really getting rocky at home.' She put her hand up to her mouth. 'I shouldn't be gossiping.'

'Phil talked to you about him and Patty having marital problems?'

'Maybe they'll work it out,' Jenna said, idly turning her glistening diamond engagement ring around on her finger.

'Maybe,' Ben said dubiously.

'Do you want me to give him a message when I hear from him?'

Ben shook his head. 'I left some papers in his office.'

'Do you want me to get them for you?'

'Um, no,' Ben said. 'No, that's okay. I'll get them myself.'

'Fine.' She went back to her transcribing as Ben circled round her desk and, with both reluctance and misgiving, headed into the office of his colleague and best friend, Phil Mason.

Ben shut the door behind him. There had to be some mistake. There had to be.

He walked over to Phil's desk. Sat down in the cushy black leather desk chair, booted up his computer and opened his day calendar application. Clicked back to the last week of March. Checked each date. Until he got to Monday, March 29th.

He stared at the screen. 'Fuck.'

First item on Phil's To Do list for that day was – **Pick up toy for Joey!** Phil's nine-year-old son. Ben's other godson.

Ben dropped his head on the desk, pressed his fingers hard into his temples. It was as though a grenade had gone off in his skull.

The door opened. His head shot up. It was Phil's secretary. 'Is there anything . . .'

'Get out!' Ben screamed at her. 'Please!'

Jenna, stunned, quickly shut the door.

Ben took several shaky breaths. Opened his eyes again. Paged forward on the monitor, coming to a second breath-grabbing halt on an appointment entry for Wednesday, April 1st. **ISP-8pm. Dr. Steinberg**

ISP – Institute For Special Problems. On Wednesday night, 8 p.m. Phil had an appointment scheduled with psychiatrist Susan Steinberg.

Eight p.m. on Wednesday nights was also when Caroline held her sex addicts' group at the Institute.

At least Phil'd had the good sense to seek help for his problem.

Only to run smack dab into the *cause* of his problem right where he'd gone to get help.

There was a phone number in the same box. Not the number for the Institute, which Ben knew from having called Caroline there.

He dialled it.

He hung up right after the familiar voice on the answering machine said – *This is Meg Spaulding* —

Ben sat in Phil's chair for several more minutes, his head in his hands, his eyes shut. The pounding in his head was only half of it. It hurt to breathe. Instead of air in his lungs, they were filled with rage. He wanted to curse Phil out. *What the hell were you thinking, man? What the hell were you* doing?

Ben snatched up the phone again. This time punching in a Scituate number.

'Hello, Patty. This is Ben. How's Phil feeling?'

'Beats me,' Mason's wife responded coolly.

'He isn't home?'

'No, Ben. Phil isn't home. He hasn't been home since Friday night. I don't know where he's staying. And I'm not expecting him back any time soon. I have to pick up the kids from school. I've got to . . . go.'

Ben made one more call before leaving Phil's office.

When Caroline walked into Susan Steinberg's office at the Institute, Susan leaped expectantly to her feet.

'Caroline, I've been positively sick about all this. I should have told you straight out about Jesse. He came over last night. Uninvited. He brought the Chinese food. We ate and that was it. Nothing happened. Nothing, absolutely nothing's going on between us. See, he came over for the first time on Saturday night, after you were arrested and – it was purely routine . . .'

'That's not why I'm here, Susan,' Caroline said stiffly.

'You have to at least let me explain. I was trying to help you. I was trying to convince Jesse that you weren't—' Susan flushed. 'Friends should trust each other, Caroline. I thought we were friends. At least, I thought we were getting to be friends.'

'I thought so, too. You should have been honest with me, Susan. And you should know, as if you couldn't figure it out for yourself, that Jesse's compelled to twist the truth because he's never resolved his . . . feelings about me—'

Susan's expression was no longer contrite. 'It doesn't all revolve around you, Caroline. That's the only deduction you can make – that Jesse's only using me. That he has no personal interest in me. Obviously, he couldn't be attracted to me. I'm too loud, too heavy, too unattractive. Isn't that what you think? That I'm not someone Jesse would ever want. Okay, so it's crossed my mind, too. One thing I'm not, is stupid. But we could both be wrong.'

Caroline could hear the abject loneliness in Susan's voice. The desperation. The self-deprecation. Self-hatred. These were all feelings Caroline could keenly identify with.

She still felt betrayed, but she couldn't help feeling pity, even some sympathy. It tempered her response. 'You're far from stupid, Susan. Jesse's got the looks, the sex appeal, knows how to make all the right moves. He could talk the diamonds off the back of a rattlesnake. But neither of us is wrong. Jesse *is* using you. And it's got nothing to do with anything negative about your appearance or personality. He'd use you if you were a cross between Princess Di and Julia Roberts. Jesse uses all women . . .'

'You're working awfully hard to make your point, Caroline. I hear it,' Susan said, her voice hardening. 'I really do appreciate your concern about my personal life . . .'

'To be honest,' Caroline said, 'I'm more concerned about mine at the moment.'

'That was going to be my next line. I'm concerned about

you as well, even if you don't think so. So please take this in the way in which it's intended. I think you've got some unresolved issues you need to work through concerning your stepbrother. These things are never altogether one-sided.'

Caroline stared at the psychiatrist, in no way clear how that advice was *intended*.

Susan checked her watch. 'I've got a patient due in a few minutes. Is there anything else?' Her voice got a notch higher.

'Yes.' Caroline's voice dropped a notch. 'You saw a new patient a couple of weeks ago. A man by the name of Philip Mason.'

'Are you serious? You came here to ask me about a patient?'

'He's a lawyer. Late forties. Tall. Dark hair touched with grey. Very distinguished looking. He had an appointment with you on Wednesday night, April 1st. 8 p.m.'

Susan looked at her for a moment longer, then flipped open her appointment book. Tabbed back to the date in question. 'He was a no-show,' she said curtly. 'I never heard from him again. What's this about, Caroline? Who is this Mason? Why are you so interested in him? Does this have something to do . . .'

'You must have a number for the man. Possibly an address.' It was routine to get that information when a new patient made an appointment at the Institute.

Susan's gaze dropped again to her appointment book. 'Just a phone number.' She recited it brusquely.

*

Caroline jotted down the number as soon as she got back to her office. She was tempted to test it out, but she knew Ben was anxiously awaiting a call-back. She reached him on his car phone, a block from the Institute. He arrived five minutes later.

Ben stared at the number. 'It's not Phil's home or the office.' He spoke dully. His rage had been replaced with a numb emptiness.

'Do you want me to dial it, Ben?' Caroline asked gently.

'No.' He reached for the phone. Punched in the number – a Boston exchange. Let it ring a half-dozen times. No answer. No machine.

Ben called Marcia Kirshbaum.

'I've got a phone number, Marcia. I need an address to go with it.' He rattled off the number.

'You don't sound happy, Ben.'

'I'm not.'

'Whose number is it?' Marcia asked.

Ben hesitated. 'Phil Mason's.'

'What? What the hell's your buddy Mason got to do with this case?'

'It looks like Phil was one of Meg Spaulding's – conquests.'

'I can't believe it.' Marcia sounded equally unhappy about this new, alarming turn of events.

'There's nothing to believe yet. Let's not take any giant leaps here.'

'Absolutely. We're definitely going to take baby steps on this one, Ben.'

'Phil's always been one of the good guys.' Ben's voice was raspy.

'Yeah,' Marcia said. 'Only sometimes good guys do bad things.'

'Yeah,' Ben said.

The only question seemed to be – *how bad?*

Thanks to a very complete computerized phone book on CD ROM, Marcia Kirshbaum called back with the address they needed in less than fifteen minutes.

374 Commonwealth Avenue turned out to be a stone's throw from the Institute. Ben wanted to go over by himself, but Caroline, who had no further appointments scheduled for the day, insisted on coming along.

The white brick town-house where Phil Mason had apparently taken up residence had been converted to apartments like so many of the mansion-sized homes along the stately tree-lined boulevard. As Ben and Caroline approached the building, Ben scanned the street.

'Shit. I don't see his—' He came to a dead stop.

'What is it?'

Ben sounded desperate. 'He drives a Mercedes. Phil drives a black Mercedes sedan.'

They stared at each other.

'You okay?' he asked her.

Caroline nodded.

'That makes one of us,' Ben admitted as they climbed the steps to the front door that led into the building's lobby. Locked. He went down the name tags beside the buzzers for each apartment. No Mason.

'Here's one that's empty.' Caroline pointed to a slot missing a tag halfway down.

Ben nodded, but made no move to press the buzzer.

'If Phil's there, I could go up first, Ben. He might have an easier time opening up to me.'

Ben pressed the buzzer. There was no response. After several tries, he pressed the one at the bottom, marked MANAGER.

A scratchy woman's voice came out of the grilled speaker. 'Who is it?' she snapped.

'I'm looking for Phil Mason's apartment,' Ben said.

'He's in 2A.'

'It says here Kruger lives in 2A.'

'Kruger moved out last month.'

'Thanks. Sorry to bother you,' Ben said. Caroline was already trying the 2A buzzer. It was jammed.

Ben pressed the grouchy manager's buzzer again.

'Is this some sort of a prank? 'Cause I'll call the cops . . .'

'2A's buzzer's stuck.'

'What do you want from me? I got a rotten cold and you just woke me up from my nap.'

'Look, the guy in 2A, Phil Mason, is a friend of mine. And he hasn't been feeling well either. I really need to see if he's okay.'

A beleaguered sigh whispered from the speaker. A moment later, the woman buzzed them in.

Ben and Caroline took the stairs to the second floor. There were two apartments, one at either end of the narrow hall. 2A was to the left.

Ben tried the doorbell. There was no response.

He knocked several times. Still nothing.

'Either he's not there or he's not in the mood for

company.' Ben banged harder. Shouted Phil's name. A hefty woman who looked to be in her fifties clopped down the stairs.

'You wanna wake the whole building? Maybe your friend's not home.'

'I guess we won't be sure unless we check inside. He might have passed out,' Ben said, addressing the irate manager.

The woman looked even more put out, but she produced a large ring of keys from her pocket, sorted one out. 'I'm going to open the door for you, but if there's any funny business,' she warned Ben as she extracted a cellular phone from her pocket, 'I'll call 911 so fast even *your* hair will stand on end.'

As soon as she unlocked the door, Ben grabbed the knob. 'I better go in alone. See if he's decent.'

He edged open the door. 'Phil? Phil, are you in there? It's me. Ben. I just want to talk to you, Phil. See how you're doing.'

Only silence inside the dark apartment.

Ben flicked on the light switch in the hallway, but as he stepped over the threshold, Caroline caught his arm. 'You did this in Chicago,' she reminded him. 'And ended up regretting it.'

'Far as I can see, life turns out to be mainly about regrets,' Ben said soberly and walked inside.

'And I thought I was a pessimist,' the manager said.

Caroline watched Ben proceed cautiously down the carpeted hallway and then disappear around a corner. After a minute or so had passed, she glanced nervously over at the manager. 'I think I better . . .'

'I think we both better,' the manager said firmly.

They found Ben standing in the middle of the bedroom. Caroline gasped. Plastered on the walls all around the room were magazine and newspaper photos of Meg Spaulding. There were also several recent blow-up photographs of her. Close-up candid shots taken with a telephoto lens.

There was more. Hanging off a tie rack on the open closet door were several chains, each around a yard long. On the night stand next to the bed was Meg's stolen case file and the incriminating videotape.

Caroline was shocked. Phil Mason wasn't even a piece of the jigsaw puzzle. Now, it turned out Phil was her intruder. Phil had ransacked her apartment. Phil had pressed his fingers around her neck. Warned her to *keep quiet or else.* Phil had followed her to the airport and tried to run her down in his black Mercedes. Or, at least aimed to put the fear of God into her. To show her he would carry out his threats. To her. To her patients—

All because Phil Mason had become utterly obsessed with Meg Spaulding. A promising life ruined. How often had Caroline seen it happen? But this was far worse. Not only one man's life destroyed here. There were three men that had been savagely strangled—

Caroline tried to picture Phil Mason as a vicious killer, but it seemed unbelievable that he – a successful, dedicated lawyer, a man with a wife and two young children, and Ben's dear friend – was capable of such violence. As difficult as it was for her to imagine, Caroline not only knew but could see that it was far worse for Ben. His anguish was heartbreaking.

It didn't help matters when the manager, after taking one look inside that obscene bedroom completely lost it. 'The Aphrodite Killer. Mary, Mother of Jesus, right here in my building. I can't believe it. Oh my God, oh my God. I'm calling the police.' But the poor woman was shaking so badly, the phone fell from her hand.

It was Ben who stooped down and picked it up. He dialled Washburn's private line. Got him on the first ring.

'It's Ben Tabor. You better get your people over here to 374 Commonwealth Avenue . . .'

'You might want to get yourself over to Cambridge. We got a colleague of yours . . .'

'Phil Mason?' *Sometimes good people do bad things.*

'Yup. A student found Mason's Mercedes parked in front of the Harvard Law Library. Didn't see his body at first—'

Ben winced. 'He's . . . dead?'

'Suicide. It's a pretty ugly scene, Tabor. Practically swallowed the barrel of a .38.' There was a pause. 'He stripped down first. Clothes were in a pile in the back seat.' Another pause. 'A pile of chains in his trunk.'

Ben stared straight ahead of him. His gaze fell on the blow-ups of the enticing, exquisite Meg Spaulding. He felt a terrible hatred for her burn like a five-alarm fire in his blood.

'You still there, Tabor?'

He shut his eyes. 'Yeah. I'm here.'

'Mason left a note.'

Afraid his legs would give out, Ben went and sat down on the edge of the bed.

'What's it say?' Ben asked.

As Washburn read the note, it wasn't his low timbred voice Ben was hearing. It was Phil's.

'Dearest Patty. Forgive me. I'm so ashamed. Please believe that I love you, Joey and Allison with all my heart. I must have been out of my mind. What other explanation can there be? Eternally. Phil.'

38

Meg looked at the photograph of Phil Mason taken with his family that Christmas. Without any hesitation and with little emotion, Meg positively identified the lawyer as the man she'd seduced at the toy store. And confirmed that Mason had phoned her a few days later, asking her for a date.

'The police will insist on a full statement, Meg,' Caroline said. 'Do you feel up to it?'

Meg nodded, continuing to stare at the photograph. 'He doesn't look like a murderer, does he?'

'There's no physical evidence tying him directly to any of the murder scenes. The police are just beginning their investigation.' Ben spoke in his cool, clipped lawyer voice. He could have been talking about a stranger instead of the man who'd been his best friend for close to twenty years.

But Caroline wasn't fooled by Ben's self-possession. He had simply gone inside himself to disguise the pain.

'He had green eyes,' Meg said, studying the photo with an almost clinical interest. 'They look hazel here, but in real life they were quite green. I suppose that's his wife.'

'Yes,' Ben said impersonally. 'And his two children.'

'The boy's name is Joey, right?'

Caroline saw Ben flinch for an instant. She felt so sorry for him. Wished there was some way to ease his suffering. But there were no short-cuts around pain. He had to work through it the best way he could.

'Yeah. Kid's name's Joey,' Ben managed to choke out.

Meg seemed oblivious to his emotional battle. Her gaze remained on the photo. 'When I first walked over to him at that toy store, he was examining these action figures. Mentioned he was looking for a birthday present for his son. If it hadn't been for his boy's birthday, we would probably never have met. And none of this would ever have happened. That whole family's really in for it. I hope the little boy doesn't end up blaming himself,' Meg said wistfully. 'Kids usually do feel that they're to blame.'

Detectives Green and DeSanto concluded taping Meg Spaulding's detailed statement at 8:45 p.m. and added it to the cassettes they'd already made since late that afternoon – including a garbled, intermittently hysterical statement from the manager at 374 Commonwealth Avenue, a lengthy interview with Caroline Hoffman and Ben Tabor, and a briefer one with Phil Mason's wife in Scituate. Also in police possession was Phil Mason's .38 with his prints on it, his signed suicide note, the collection of chains and Meg memorabilia, the incriminating videotape, Caroline's case file on Meg Spaulding, and copies of the two postings off the lawyer's computer.

'So, what do you think?' Green asked DeSanto as they headed across the lobby of Neponset Hospital towards the exit.

'Too damn tidy is what I think.' She also thought she sounded just like Jesse. 'I hate having to let Spaulding walk just yet.'

'Hey, why do all murder solutions have to be sloppy?'

'Nature of the beast, Alfonse.'

They stepped outside. Boston looked bleak. Overcast grey sky, grey concrete pavement, rows and rows of dark cars in the parking lot. Even the two detectives were grey – Green with his charcoal jacket, DeSanto's pant suit the colour of gunmetal. DeSanto was also sporting a pair of sunglasses. Had been wearing them all day, inside and out. *Eye strain*, she'd told her partner. When he'd plucked off the glasses before she could stop him and he saw her black eye, she'd switched her story. *Walked into a door*. Green had let it drop.

'Look, with the suicide note and all the stuff we found, it adds up that he's our doer,' Green argued as they headed for his Taurus. 'Spaulding seduced Mason, they have a quickie, she disappears. He tracks her down. Gets insanely jealous when she won't see him and stalks her, killing the guys she screws after she saunters off all satisfied.'

'So, where does Kramer fit in? Spaulding admits she had sex with the other two guys, but she swears she didn't fuck Kramer. And I believe her,' DeSanto said. 'He doesn't fit her pattern. She knew Kramer from her group. Her thing is doing it with strangers.'

'We got a different motive here, is all. Kramer sees the first killing at the museum and tries his popular blackmail scheme on Mason. Bad move on the peeper's part. Mason's already done two guys. What's one more? Especially one that could rat him out?'

DeSanto remained dubious. 'Yeah, but I don't see this hot-shot attorney throwing everything away . . .'

'Amy, Amy, Amy . . . we're talking *lawyers* here,' Green cut her off. 'You know the old joke about the Mafioso who calls a lawyer and says, the boss wants to give you a half million bucks, but we're gonna kill your wife, steal your children, and kidnap your parents. And the lawyer thinks for a moment and replies, "Okay, what's the catch?"'

Caroline cooked up scrambled eggs with diced tomatoes and shredded cheddar cheese. She set two plates on Ben's kitchen table and dished it out.

'It's ready, Ben.' After calling out to him a couple more times, Caroline went to find him.

He was sitting on the side of his bed, his eyes fixed on a pill in his hand.

Her eyes narrowed with concern. 'What's happening? Dinner's on the table. You'll feel better if you have a little something to eat.'

'Is that your prescription for my pain, Doc? Don't you think Percodan's a better bet?'

'It won't cut it for *psychic* pain,' she said.

'And eggs will?'

'No, Ben. There's nothing for it but time.'

'Really? Has that worked for you?' he asked sarcastically.

'Is it working now? Because,' he thumped his chest, 'these wounds in here just seem to build and build with every passing day.'

'I guess we've both been through the wars.'

'You don't know the half of it.'

'That half that has to do with your marriage, you mean?'

He darted a quick look in her direction. 'You're good.'

'Tell me.'

Ben squinted into the distance. But he was really gazing into his past. 'We grew up together in Chicago. The three of us. Me, my cousin Mitch, Kim. I don't remember a time when my cousin and I weren't nuts about her. Mitch took Kim to his senior prom. I took her to mine.' A bare hint of a smile. 'She took us both to hers.' He lost the smile. 'Couldn't marry us both, though. I was the lucky one. Only my luck ran out with Kim after Chicago.'

Caroline sat down beside Ben on his bed. 'What happened?' she asked gently.

He leaned forward, dug his elbows into his knees, rested his chin in his cupped hands. He was still staring into space as he spoke. 'After the shoot-out, Kim flew out and visited me every single day at the hospital. The dutiful wife. But she was hurting so bad, just looking at her increased my own pain. When I got home and her anger surfaced, things got worse. One day, we finally had it out. And she said what I feared most. That she could never forgive me. That it was all my fault Mitch and Jimmy were dead. And Kim was right.'

The past cracked and fragmented before Ben's eyes. 'So much for fifteen years of marriage. Not that what Kim and

I had was perfect. Far from it. We had more than our share of problems. I just never realized Kim never *did* make up her mind which of us she wanted. Until the bitter end.' He looked back at Caroline. 'Maybe part of the problem with us the whole time was that it was always this win-lose thing with me. Like she was some prize Mitch and I were always after. And I won. I've always had this thing about winning. These past few months . . . I've been putting in a lot of thinking time. There should be something more to life than a great win.'

'Where is Kim now?' Caroline asked.

'Last I heard, California. That was three months ago – when the divorce papers arrived. I'm not going to play it macho and say it doesn't still hurt. Or that there still aren't some days – and nights – when I miss her.'

Caroline put a comforting hand on Ben's shoulder. 'In a very short time, you've lost most everyone you loved. Kim. Mitch. Jimmy. Now Phil. Naturally, the hurt's just been growing and growing.'

Slowly, as if it took great effort to move a muscle, he looked over at her, searching her beautiful face, seeing her concern, her genuine compassion. He'd never felt so emotionally vulnerable.

Caroline took the pill out of his hand and set it on the bedside table.

'Now what?' he asked. Throwing back the line she'd tossed at him at that inn on Martha's Vineyard. It came out sounding more shaky on his lips.

She pressed her head against his. 'Do I really have to tell you, Ben?'

Her voice curled around him. Through him. Her touch seemed to fix him for the moment, miraculously stopping time with all its pain and sorrow. There was only Caroline. She was his for the taking. If he could be sure what she was offering.

'I don't want this to be about pity—'

Caroline pressed her fingertips to his mouth. Then slowly slid her thumb across his lower lip. 'Is that what you see, Ben? Look closer.'

They were naked, their clothes tangled up with the beige comforter in a pile at the foot of his bed. Caroline sat astride Ben. Her palms cruised over the smooth contours of his chest, slipped between their bodies, her fingers circling the head of his penis.

He groaned from deep in his belly.

Her hand moved lower, down the shaft, cupping his testicles. The hardness and softness incredibly arousing.

She began a slow slide down his body, her tongue marking a trail along the way. When her lips brushed the tip of his penis, her tongue flicked out to mark the tender spot.

As her mouth opened to engulf him, Ben's hands firmly gripped her shoulders, lifting her back up.

She panicked, flooded by rejection. 'What's wrong? Don't you want me to—?'

She looked up at his face. Solemn and intense. Shadowed under his sharply defined cheek-bones.

'Do you lead when you dance, too?' he whispered.

Caroline blanched. 'What? I'm . . . not . . . I'm . . . sorry—'

He drew her down to him, rolled over with her so that they lay side by side.

She started to say something, but he shook his head. 'Shh. Let it go, Caroline.' He stroked her cheek, smoothed back her hair, pressed his lips lightly to hers.

She felt poised between the pure sensual pleasure of his touch and the worry that she could never be good enough – please him enough. Her sense of security as well as all her hopes seemed tied into his satisfaction with her.

'We'll do this together, Caroline. Neither of us has to be in control. Why don't we see what happens?'

'I'm nervous.'

'Me, too,' Ben confessed.

They wrapped their arms tightly around each other so they were practically bonded together, her pale breasts cushioned flat against his dark, bony chest. Clinging to each other, they kissed, over-eager but intent.

Their lovemaking was fumbling, fevered, clumsy yet single-minded. If there was a line between longing and desperation, they discovered that it was a very thin line indeed.

Wednesday

39

The police weren't issuing any statements. But enough had been leaked for the media to run with the story of Phil Mason's suicide, and to jump the gun and headline him as the alleged Aphrodite Killer.

Jesse Baush slammed the newspaper down on the speckled grey and white Formica table. 'Talk about a rush to judgement,' he muttered as Amy DeSanto, still sporting sunglasses, slid into the wooden booth across from him at Checkers.

'Only reason I'm here is to give you a piece of my mind for that shiner you laid on me the other night,' she told him. 'And to give you back this.' Determinedly, she slid a house key across the table.

Jesse made no move to pick it up. Acted like it wasn't even there. 'Washburn satisfied? Vargas? They both satisfied it was Mason?'

'What about me? What about if I'm satisfied? You don't give a fuck . . .'

'And no one's dug up a single alibi for Mason for the times of any of the murders? Or haven't they even bothered looking?'

DeSanto snapped her fingers. 'Do I even exist here, Jesse?'

He completely threw her off by breaking into a wide grin. 'You take the key back and you exist, baby. We both more than exist.'

'What do ya want from me, Jesse? The case is still open, but it looks like we'll be closing it real soon.'

'You know what's really goin' on, Amy. Since Mason's conveniently dead, they can pin this mess on him and avoid having to bring someone to trial. No muss, no fuss. Nobody upstairs ends up doing a balancing act on a few wobbly toothpicks.'

'Oh, you're right, Jesse. The mayor, the D.A., Homicide – everyone's pleased to let a serial sex killer roam free while they pin the murders on a suicide victim with a lair full of choke chains, pictures of his goddess plastered all over the walls, the stolen tape and case record, and who writes a suicide note that reads like a confession . . .'

'Yeah, but Mason didn't really confess to anything, did he?'

'No, but no one can account for Mason's whereabouts when those guys bought it,' she countered. 'Mason's wife says he wasn't home Tuesday night. His secretary says he showed at the office at ten on Wednesday morning. That's particularly striking because most mornings, according to the office manager, Mason was a real early-bird. Often at his desk at the crack of dawn.' DeSanto paused while a waitress came over for her order.

'Just coffee.' The waitress filled Amy's empty mug, topped up Jesse's, and shuffled off.

'And you buy it?' Jesse demanded.

'I buy it,' Amy said. 'Unless another body shows up with Aphrodite's name on it.'

'So what you're really saying is you're caving under pressure,' he said sarcastically.

'Look babe. If anyone was likely to come to trial it would have been Meg Spaulding. Or, on a long shot, brother Ned. No way was it ever gonna be your stepsister. Please, Jesse, before we have to admit *you* to Neponset Hospital, forget about Linny already. It's about time, isn't it?' The bruise around her eye was beginning to fade, but DeSanto knew she was risking a fresh shiner.

Not only didn't Jesse take another swing at her, she actually saw him nod.

She was probably making her own foolish *rush to judgement*, but Amy lifted up Jesse's house key and stuck it back in her pocket.

Ben and Caroline had been talking about Phil Mason since they woke up that morning. And they both reached the same conclusion – each coming at it from different angles, each of them for different reasons. The Phil Mason they each knew could not have been a serial killer. The problem was proving it.

'It makes me sick.' Ben threw the morning paper in the trash can. He was dressed in a finely tailored three-button grey worsted suit, white shirt, paisley tie. Clothing-wise, he looked to Caroline like the Ben Tabor of old. His face, though, despite last night's loving respite, bore the telltale signs of grief, fury and exhaustion that had done nothing but intensify over this past nightmarish week.

Caroline, wearing Ben's robe, her drawn face as telling as his, poured them both coffee. She handed Ben a mug. 'What do we do now?'

'I'm going over to the firm to talk to Phil's secretary and the rest of the staff. I've got to find someone who can provide Phil with an alibi during one of those times . . .'

'Wouldn't they have come forward by now? The police have already questioned most of them, Ben.'

He leaned heavily against his butcher block counter. 'I don't know where else to start. If I run into a brick wall there, I'll go back to Commonwealth Ave. and knock on every door, talk to every tenant. I'll drive down to Scituate, poke around there. All I know is, I'm not going to rest until Phil's cleared and I force the police to resume their investigation.'

'You mean turn them back to Meg as their prime suspect.'

'She *is* their prime suspect, Caroline. But, believe me, I don't want to throw her to the wolves any more than you. Since we spoke to her yesterday, I'm more inclined to believe she really is innocent.'

Caroline brightened.

Ben set his mug on the counter. He cupped her face in his hands. His lips hovered over hers for a few seconds, then he tenderly kissed her. 'Some morning afterglow, huh?'

Caroline looked at Ben's haggard but loving face. Returning his kiss with a little extra intensity. Smiling at him as she lightly stroked his hair. 'Last night's glow will tide me over for quite a while.'

'We haven't even had a real date yet.'

'When this is over.'

Ben exhaled deeply. 'Yeah. When this is over.' He picked up his mug. Took a few sips. 'You make great coffee. I haven't had a woman puttering in my kitchen for a long time. It's nice.'

Caroline was looking contemplative. 'You know what this means, Ben.'

He looked nervous. Maybe she'd read more into his remark than he'd meant. Or maybe he'd meant more than he'd meant to mean. What the hell did that mean? He blamed his convoluted thinking on sleep deprivation.

Caroline was smiling. 'I'm not talking about us, Ben.'

He looked flustered. 'I wasn't . . . Did I say a word?'

'I'm talking about the killer. We eliminate Phil and Meg, that means we're back at square one. Now I can picture one or two people right in the centre of that square.'

Ben frowned. 'Don't even think about it.'

'Ben, the killer thinks he or she is in the clear. I'm not in danger unless . . .'

'Unless you go poking around.'

'Which is exactly what *you* plan to do.'

Ben pulled his suit jacket open. He had a gun tucked into his waistband near his left hip.

'You aren't going to . . . you wouldn't . . . use that thing.'

'I'm taking necessary precautions. One of them's this

Beretta. Another's making sure you stay put.'

'I know you like having a woman in your kitchen, darling, but I'm afraid I can't stick around here all day,' she
teased. 'I've got patients to see this morning. One, anyway.'
Appointment cancellations were still pouring in. All
Caroline could do was hope that some of her patients
would eventually return and new referrals would pick up.

'And after you see your patient?' Ben cross-examined.

'Maybe I'll go off and buy myself a gun.' She was only
half joking.

Ben clutched her waist, holding her as if she might actually take flight. 'Last night you listed all the people in my
life I've lost. All the agony I've gone through. I'm almost at
my limit, Caroline. If I lose you, too . . .' His voice was
filled with trepidation.

She cut him off with a fierce, passionate kiss. Then she
held him tight. 'You're not going to lose me, Ben. I don't
want to be lost any more.'

Ben was trying, with little success, to console Phil Mason's
secretary, Jenna Wallace, as they sat together in one of the
law firm's sleek, cherry-wood panelled conference rooms.
He'd issued orders that they weren't to be disturbed.

'I can't believe he killed anyone. Mr. Mason wouldn't
hurt a fly. It just tears me apart, the disgusting lies they're
saying about him.' Jenna's lips quivered and she pressed
her fingers to her mouth.

'Think about how his poor family feels. His wife. His
kids,' Ben said.

'He was the best boss,' Jenna lamented. 'Did you see the

police sealed his office? They said . . . I . . . I couldn't even go in there. They might as well hang signs up – guilty, guilty, guilty.'

'I don't believe Phil murdered anyone,' Ben said fervently. 'That means the real killer's still at large. The police aren't going to wake up until there's another murder—'

Jenna began crying in earnest again. 'He . . . didn't . . . do it. I know . . . he didn't . . . couldn't . . .'

Ben pulled his chair a little closer to hers. 'Jenna, you told the police that Phil left the office last Tuesday night at six. Is that right?'

'Yes. We . . . we left together.'

'You left together?'

'I mean – we left the building at the same time.'

'Where did Phil go? Did he go to his apartment?'

'How would I know?'

'Did you know he'd rented an apartment on Comm Ave a few weeks ago?'

Jenna looked despairing. 'He might have . . . mentioned it.'

'When he mentioned he and Patty were having marital problems?' Ben pressed.

'A lot of the lawyers who live out of town keep an apartment or a room . . .'

'Have you ever been there, Jenna?'

'Where?' she asked lamely.

'374 Commonwealth Avenue.' Ben deliberately eased the tone of his voice now. Shifting from prosecutor to defence counsellor. Phil would have been proud. Better late—

'I'm engaged to be married,' she retorted.

Ben had little trouble reading between those lines. He took her hand, gave her a reassuring nod. Spoke softly but intently. 'Jenna, listen to me. If the police can't account for Phil's whereabouts during the times of those murders – that means last Tuesday night between approximately nine and ten p.m., early Wednesday morning, Saturday around eleven o'clock . . .'

'He was here on Saturday,' Jenna said. 'He works every Saturday till noon at least. You know that.'

'But how do *you* know? You told the police you weren't here this past Saturday morning.'

Jenna ran her index finger along the edge of the burled wood conference table. 'No. I wasn't here, but—'

Ben decided to take a new tack. 'You knew Phil and Patty were having marital problems. He talked to you . . .'

'That's not a crime,' she said petulantly.

'No, it's not.'

Jenna clutched the shredded tissue as if her life depended on it. 'Anthony, my fiancé, is crazy jealous.'

'I know this is rough for you,' Ben said, resting a hand on her shoulder.

'It started with just a friendly dinner. Phil – Mr. Mason – seemed kind of blue. And Anthony was in Connecticut. He's on the road a lot. He's the New England rep for . . .'

'This was last Tuesday night?'

Jenna nodded.

'Where did you go eat?'

'We were going to go to a restaurant, but we ended up

getting some take-out from the deli down the street. Neither of us were all that hungry. We got sandwiches.'

'The Gardner Deli? At the end of State?'

Again, Jenna nodded.

'And you brought the sandwiches back to his place on Comm Ave?'

'Phil was so . . . lost. We ate a little and we were talking – mostly about his marriage falling apart – and suddenly he broke down.'

'What did he say?'

'He wasn't making any sense. I was really worried about him. He was clutching me for dear life, begging me not to leave.'

'You spent the evening with him.'

Jenna started to cry again. This time more out of shame than loss. 'I spent . . . the whole night. We slept in . . . Wednesday morning. I'll go to the police. I'll give them a statement. Only . . . I'm meeting Anthony for lunch. Please let me tell him first. Before he hears it . . . all over the news.'

Ben headed straight from the law firm to the Institute to give Caroline the good news. There was little question, however, that the cops would once again zero in on Meg Spaulding as their prime suspect. So he'd still have Meg for a client unless he could provide the police with a better suspect. He wasn't too optimistic of his chances.

He was furious to learn Caroline wasn't at work.

'Where is she?'

'She hasn't come in yet,' Renée explained.

'She told me she had appointments this morning.'

'She's got an eleven o'clock.'

Ben checked his watch. 10:35.

'Unless he's a no-show,' Renée was saying. 'She's had her fair share of those. I feel so bad for her. Caroline's a terrific therapist. It's vile how the media can destroy a perfectly innocent person's life and then go merrily on to destroying the next.'

'Tell me about it. Can I use your phone?'

Ben rang up Dr. Gilbert Fuller at Neponset Hospital.

Fuller was abrupt. 'I'm about to see a patient, Mr. Tabor.'

'Is Caroline over there? I thought she might be seeing Meg . . .'

'Caroline Hoffman's not here. And neither is Meg Spaulding. Ms. Spaulding was released from the hospital approximately fifteen minutes ago.'

'What? Did the cops . . . ?'

'The police already took Ms. Spaulding's statement. They have no reason to hold her at this juncture. I found no further clinical indicators that would require Ms. Spaulding to be hospitalized, involuntarily or otherwise. I recommended she continue her out-patient therapy. Actually Ms. Spaulding accepted my referral back to Dr. Hoffman.'

Lou Washburn snatched up the can of Dr. Pepper on his desk, flipped the tab, took a swig and grimaced as he swallowed. He held the can up for examination. 'Diet. Shit. Can't anybody get anything right around here?'

DeSanto and Green, standing on the other side of the homicide chief's desk, shared a quick glance. Neither said a word.

Washburn angrily flung the can into the trash. The soda splattered as the can clanked against the pile of empties inside. He squinted at the sandwich he'd pulled out of a small brown paper bag. 'This better be ham or heads'll roll.'

'Are you going to tell us what's up, Chief?'

'What's up is, this department is becoming a public laughing-stock, that's what's up! It's like we've got a fucking revolving door here. First you screw-ups pull Hoffman in and the media jumps all over it. Then comes Meg Spaulding. I'll grant you, she looked like a winner. I thought, hallelujah, we'll be able to wipe the egg off our faces. No sooner am I grabbing for a handi-wipe than we got ourselves a whole fucking new sweepstakes winner for Aphrodite Killer of the Day! We're setting a departmental record, boys and girls.'

Green nervously cleared his throat. 'I gather we've got a . . . problem with Mason?'

Washburn was as close to apoplexy as either detective had ever seen him. And they'd both seen him more than steamed. 'Yeah, Green. I'd say we had a *problem* with Mason. Tabor just called me. Seems our *latest* doer of the day's got a goddamn solid alibi for Tuesday night and Wednesday morning. Attorney Mason was *doing* his secretary. She's coming in to give a statement after lunch.'

DeSanto could imagine Jesse Baush whispering *I told ya so* in her ear. 'I say we get Meg Spaulding back . . .'

'I'm giving you both clear warning.' Washburn cut her off, biting out each word. 'Next damn Aphrodite Killer either of you drag in here better come attached to a signed confession. This one's gotta stick or I swear to God I'm gonna . . .'

'We get the picture, Chief.' Green was at his most earnest.

DeSanto backed her partner up on that with a little one finger salute.

'One more thing,' Washburn barked. 'Not only has Meg Spaulding been released from Neponset, but Hoffman's missing. At least Tabor can't seem to find her and he's worried she could be in trouble. One of you boneheads has to go dig her up. And somebody get me a goddamn real Dr. Pepper!'

40

A bell jingled as Caroline stepped inside the cool, spacious gallery.

A stylish young man in a taupe suede jacket and dark brown suede slacks popped out of a small office. His brow furrowed as he regarded Caroline cautiously.

'Mr. Cowen? I'm Caroline Hoffman. I'm the one you spoke to . . .'

'Where's Ben Tabor? I thought when I called Mr. Tabor's apartment, you said you'd get in touch with him and have him come.'

'I couldn't reach him . . .'

'Tabor should have told me who he was that first time he came in here. I think people should be straight with each other. That investigator of his, Marcia Kirshbaum, she apologized for him. I don't hold grudges. And I didn't want to call the cops. I suppose I could have called Mrs. Kirshbaum. She left her card and all. I just felt, with Tabor being Meg's lawyer—' He pulled out a wad of tissues from his trouser pocket, carefully peeled one off, using it to dab at his glistening face. He was working up a real sweat.

'Look, Mr. Cowen, you're obviously very agitated . . .'

'Agitated? I'm a complete wreck.' He shoved the hanky back in his pocket, then held out his hands to show her. The tremor was significant. 'If Ned knew . . . I feel like a turncoat.'

'You said Ned went to the Vineyard to be with his mother for a few days.'

'I'd really rather deal with Tabor. I'd just as soon wait for him . . .'

'Mr. Tabor may be tied up all day. What if Ned decides to come back early?'

'I'm going to be out of a job,' Cowen said mournfully. 'Either way—'

Caroline gave him a stern look. 'I think we both know there are more serious things at stake here than your job.'

He smoothed back a loose strand of dark brown hair that had escaped his ponytail.

'You said on the phone you found something *suspicious* in Ned's apartment. What exactly . . .'

'I wasn't spying . . .'

'I know. You explained. You were looking for some documentation papers on a painting for a customer.'

'Right. It wasn't in the file down here. Ned's got some other files upstairs. In his den. The customer was really pressing me. I have a key to Ned's apartment. He gave it to me. For just such times as this. Well, not like *this* I guess. I wish I hadn't gone up there now. The newspapers say the cops know who did it.'

Caroline maintained her uncompromising demeanour. 'You're nervous because you think the police and the media may be wrong. You have good reason to feel that way. I think they're wrong, too.'

The gallery employee's face was the colour of putty.

Caroline glanced at her watch. 'I have to see a patient in exactly forty-five minutes. Now, please tell me what you found, Sean.'

Cowen hesitated. 'Maybe I should . . . show you.'

Cowan stood beside the birch file cabinet in Ned Spaulding's combination den/home office adjoining his bedroom. The room was an almost perfect square with a high ceiling and caramel-painted walls. An Indian seagrass mat covered the centre of the oak floor which was stained a moss green. There was a large metal and chocolate brown laminate desk and chair set between two long windows that overlooked Beacon Street and the Public Gardens. Three filing cabinets fitted into a stretch of bookcases and birch-veneered cabinetry along the wall on the right side of the room. The drawer of the middle file cabinet was pulled halfway out.

'I didn't think I should touch it,' Cowen said, digging his hands deep into the pockets of his suede jacket. Sweat dripped from his face, leaving dark dots on the lapels. 'It's . . . in the back.'

Caroline pulled the drawer out further and looked into the well at the back. Behind a row of neatly ranked up folders was a lush black wig. She didn't think she should touch it, either.

'There's something else. In . . . Ned's bedroom.' Cowen

flushed. 'Okay, so I did snoop around a little. I just *had* to look in his closet to see if there was anything else. You know, high heels, a black dress – but it was locked. That made me more suspicious. I found the key in the downstairs office safe that . . . opened it.'

'Did you find the clothes?'

Cowen shivered. 'No . . . but there is something in there.' He pressed his palm against his forehead. 'Look, I really don't feel well. I'm going to close the shop for the day and go home. I think I'm running a fever. I'll leave you to . . . call the police. Whatever—'

With all Caroline's theorizing about Ned's sexual aberrations, she wouldn't have imagined his bedroom resembling this 1930s Rococoesque boudoir. The total effect was disturbing. More a lush stage set than a living space. Especially the king-sized four-poster bed directly across from the armoire. The bed, utterly feminine with snow-white linens, overflowed with puffy white pillows of assorted shapes and sizes, the frame between the ornately carved bedposts draped with a gauzy white cloth.

Two tall windows, flanking the white lacquered armoire, were curtained with matching filmy fabric, resembling white fire as the shimmering late morning sunlight streamed through.

Caroline went up to the huge Art Deco wardrobe – its interlocking silver diamonds forming a mosaic along the side panels. As she grasped the silver knobs and pulled open the doors it felt excitingly like opening the portals to a Greek temple.

The magnificent canvas was about three feet high by four feet wide. The background was a muted swirl of pearl grey and eggshell blue. The foreground, bathed in a shaft of shimmering cream-coloured light originating from the heavens above, was a tableau of two lovers embracing, their bodies bound together not only by lust, but by a long rope of chain. *The Godless Aphrodite* scrawled in red across the bottom of the canvas might have been painted in blood.

The power of the creation lay in how compellingly the artist captured the hapless couple's fate in Aphrodite's magnificent, anguished eyes. Caroline was riveted.

'What are you doing here?'

Caroline spun round at the sound of the voice, surprise and panic painted on her face. Ned Spaulding's face, however, depicted nothing but undisguised contempt.

Caroline edged away, stumbling over an ornate metal magazine rack, nearly falling. She quickly regained her balance, leaning for support on the window sill.

Ned walked straight to the painting. His contemptuous frown vanished as he stared directly into the goddess's mesmerizing green eyes, transfixed.

'Everybody knew it was my father's finest work. Even Grandy. And say whatever else you might about my grandfather, the man has incredibly high aesthetic standards. Mother begged me to destroy the painting, but I absolutely couldn't.' Ned paused, his gaze roaming the bound lovers. 'What do you think?'

'About the painting?'

'Very good. The perfect shrink remark. Are you perfect, Caroline? Far from it, from what I've heard.'

'You don't like therapists very much.'

'Therapist. Interesting word, therapist. Put a space after the *e* and what do you get? *The rapist.*'

'You feel that you've been raped? You feel like a victim?'

Ned paled. 'I *am* a victim. Look at that painting. The man in it is me. I posed for it. Nude. With my mother. The fucking lunatic made us do it.'

'I know,' Caroline said quietly.

A vein throbbed at Ned's temple. 'How did you know that? Meg didn't know anything about it . . . My mother . . . I should have known you'd worm it out of her. Too bad my father isn't still alive. I'd love to see you have a go at him. I wonder what you would make of him.'

'Ned, your father was a very sick man. He preyed on the three of you. Each of you has been paying an awful price for his sadistic perversions.'

Ned was looking at Caroline now. She saw something sorrowful flicker in his eyes. Then it was gone.

'It hasn't all been awful.' He smiled. Boyishly. Conspiratorially.

Caroline suddenly recalled Ned's mother's smile when she confided her secret up in the attic. Like mother, like son – Ned was clearly as deranged as Faith. And probably more dangerous.

Her heart pounding, Caroline debated making a run for it.

Ned's smile deepened. As if he were reading Caroline's thoughts he gestured for her to come and stand by him. When she made no move, he said, 'You don't want me to hurt you.'

The implicit threat was spoken in an incongruously sympathetic tone of voice that made Caroline all the more uneasy. She followed Ned's command and moved to his side, praying he wouldn't touch her. She knew she'd pull back if he did. And that might set him off.

'Look at her,' he crooned softly. 'Mother was so beautiful. Aphrodite personified.'

'Don't you mean the god*less* Aphrodite, Ned? That is your writing, isn't it?' Caroline challenged. It was a risky manoeuvre to gain the upper hand but hadn't she done it so successfully with his sister and his mother in the last few days? Besides, Caroline had to know the answer. It was the missing strand that wove all the threads together.

Ned gave her a deprecating sneer. 'You think you're so smart. But don't think because you know that much that you've got it all figured out.'

'You must have been so distressed and confused . . . when your father walked into your mother's bedroom and found you . . .'

'My mother didn't tell you that. Meg? My sister told you that? Meg told you I was with my mother that night?' His eyes glinted madly. He grabbed her arm, pinning it behind her. Caroline yelped in pain. And cursed herself for having given away what Meg told her.

'See how dumb you are. Screwing with my sister's head. Mother's. Mine. I've had it. We've all had it. You hear me.'

Caroline's heart nearly stopped when from his pocket he pulled a gleaming snub-nosed pistol. He pressed the cold metal barrel to her right temple.

Even though terrified, Caroline chided herself for her

hubris. She'd definitely over-stepped herself this time.

Her *last* time?

'You are trespassing, Caroline. I have a right to protect my property.'

Caroline's pulse was hammering in her ears. Suddenly, she heard a high keening cry. She was so scared it took her a split second to realize she wasn't the one who'd screamed. Ned, momentarily disoriented as well, loosened his grip on Caroline, letting the gun slip away from her head.

And then they both saw Meg.

Ned let go of Caroline's arm altogether and gaped at his sister. 'Meg . . . ?' Reflectively, he pointed the gun in her direction.

'Liar, liar!' Meg screamed at her brother. 'You swore you destroyed it. You swore!'

Oh God, the painting. Meg had walked into her brother's room and that was what she saw. All she saw—

Ned's face was the colour of chalk. 'I . . . I'm sorry, Meg. Please . . .'

Caroline was terrified that in his distraught state, he might shoot his sister. 'Ned, put down the gun,' she said sharply. 'You don't want to hurt Meg.'

Dazed, his gaze dropped to the weapon just when Meg came at him, slapping him, crying, screaming—

As Ned tried to fend off her stinging blows, Caroline's eyes stayed fixed on the gun still clutched in Ned's hand, praying that it wouldn't go off accidentally.

'Please don't . . . Meggie . . .' Ned was sobbing. 'I love you . . .'

Meg shoved him so hard, he slammed into Caroline.

The impact sent her flying against the foot of the bed, onto the mattress. Ned stumbled but remained on his feet. They both watched Meg turn to the open armoire. Seething with rage, she balled her hands into fists and punched viciously at the painting. 'I don't want to see you with Mother! I don't. I don't. I don't . . .'

'No . . . Meg . . . no,' Ned wailed, waving the gun wildly. 'Stop . . .'

But Meg was intent on her task. Over and over, she rammed her fists into the painting, puncturing the canvas, making huge holes, ripping, tearing, shredding at it. Destroying *The Godless Aphrodite*.

Caroline prepared to rush Ned from behind and try to wrestle the gun from him. But he abruptly clutched his hands together, the weapon sandwiched between them, and bent his head as if in supplication. 'I'm sorry, Meg. I'm . . . sorry for everything. Oh God, Meg . . . please . . . please . . .'

Meg struggled to catch her breath. There was nothing left of the canvas to attack. She stared at the ruined painting. The damage she'd wrought didn't seem to register at first. Then the tears spilled from her eyes.

Caroline watched Ned stumble over to his sister. Reach out to her. Cautiously touch her shoulder.

Slowly, Meg turned to him. Their eyes met. Tears streamed down both their faces. Then Meg lifted her hand. Ned flinched, as if she was going to strike him again. Instead, she caressed the side of his wet cheek, reddened from her slaps and scratches.

Ned choked up. 'I'm glad . . . you did it, Meg. I couldn't

. . I didn't have . . . the strength . . .' He cast his gaze on the painting. 'It wasn't my fault. It wasn't . . .'

'It's going to be all right, Ned,' Meg rasped.

'No,' he sobbed. 'It's never going to be all right.'

Caroline came over to them. Smiling weakly, she gave her patient a reassuring nod, then turned to Ned. 'Ned, give me the gun.'

Ned blinked to see clearly through the tears in his eyes.

For the first time, Meg seemed to notice the gun in her brother's hand. She looked aghast. 'What are you doing with that?'

At first Ned looked ashamed. But then he bridled, his hand still firmly on the pistol. 'You're supposed to be in hospital, Meg.'

'They released me. Aren't you glad?'

He gave her a wary look. 'Did you send your shrink here to spy on me?'

'Ned, you know I didn't . . .'

'And you came snooping, too, Meg.'

'Ned, I'm sure your sister came here because she wanted you to be the first to know she was free. Because you've been so worried about her. Meg didn't even know the painting still existed. She had nothing to do with my being here. What you need to do is take a few deep breaths, Ned, clear your mind, think it all through calmly, rationally.'

Meg held her hand out. It was remarkably steady. 'Give me the gun, Ned. I'll put it away. We've both gone a little haywire. But it's over now.'

Ned looked at Meg's outstretched hand. He seemed about to relent. But then his gaze shifted up to his sister's face.

'You shouldn't have told those lies about me, Meg. If I can't trust you, who can I trust?'

'You *can* trust me.'

'No. You're just like Momma. You even look just like she used to look. And you act the same.' His voice hardened. 'You take everything from me, but you never give me what I need.' His bitterness and anger frightened Caroline into realising the danger was far from over.

'What do you need, Ned? Tell me,' Meg pleaded.

Caroline watched in dread as Ned aimed the gun right at his sister's chest. Meg merely stared straight at her brother, nothing but tenderness and love in her eyes.

'Do it. Do us both a favour, Ned. Go ahead,' Meg goaded him. 'Pull it. Pull the trigger.'

'No, Ned.' Caroline spoke firmly though she was frantic. 'Meg doesn't mean it. And you need her. You love her.'

Agitation and confusion spread across Ned's face and body. The gun wavered between his sister and Caroline, his hand shaking badly.

Caroline forced her voice to remain steady. 'This isn't the way you want this to go, Ned.'

He looked at her. And then he became suddenly, eerily still. 'No. Not this way.'

Before Caroline could heave a sigh of relief she saw, with a horrible sense of déjà vu, Ned turn the weapon on himself, pressing the barrel of the gun to his own temple.

Meg dropped to her knees at her brother's feet, her hands clutching at his trouser legs. 'Don't do it, Ned. Please, please. I need you. I love you so much.'

He squeezed his eyes shut.

No one spoke. No one moved. No one breathed.

Until Ned exhaled loudly, his hand dropping to his side. An instant later, the gun clanked to the floor. Slowly, he folded over at the waist, until his forehead touched the top of Meg's head.

Caroline quickly grabbed the gun while Meg draped her arms around her brother's neck. Holding him. Rocking him. Stroking him. Like a baby. Like a lover.

At that moment Detective Amy DeSanto rushed into Ned's bedroom, whipping her gun out of her shoulder-holster.

'Drop it,' she barked.

Caroline didn't register the command immediately. Then she realized the detective was referring to her. She let go of the weapon as if it had suddenly ignited.

'Kick it over here.'

Caroline gladly obeyed.

Meg and Ned were both watching. The two of them, as much as Caroline, were stunned by DeSanto's surprise arrival on the scene.

Keeping her semi-automatic trained on the trio, DeSanto cautiously knelt down and took possession of Ned's gun. 'Suppose one of you tell me what's going on.'

Meg got to her feet, her arms remaining entwined around her brother's neck. 'Why are you here? You've got your killer now. You have no business . . .'

'Phil Mason's secretary gave her boss a posthumous alibi. It would've been nice if she'd provided it a little sooner,' DeSanto said sardonically. 'Like before we let you walk, Meg.'

'No,' Meg cried out, clutching her brother.

'You're not taking her in again,' he warned.

But DeSanto'd had it. 'I'm taking all three of you in . . .'

'No,' Ned said firmly. 'I'm the only one you want.'

Meg looked bewildered. 'What are you saying, Ned?'

He kept his gaze fixed on DeSanto. 'My sister's innocent. She didn't kill anyone.'

'Ned,' Caroline jumped in. 'Don't say anything more. We'll all go with the detective to police headquarters. I'll call Ben Tabor . . .'

'No. Meg's been through enough,' Ned said adamantly. 'I did it. I'm the one you want,' he told DeSanto. 'I killed those men.'

DeSanto was in a quandary. Her eyes narrowed. 'You saying you're ready to sign a confession to the murders of . . . ?'

'Yes.'

'All three men?'

'Yes.' No hesitation.

Meg was still clinging to Ned, crying into his shoulder. He was patting her back. 'It's okay, Meggie. You don't have to be afraid any more,' he soothed. 'I'm going to take care of everything. Just like always.'

'I hope you're fully aware,' Caroline told DeSanto, 'that a signed confession from Ned Spaulding in his current state of mental duress won't be worth the paper it's printed on.'

'You can argue that from the witness stand, Doc.' DeSanto trained her gun on Ned as she approached him. 'Step away,' she ordered Meg. Ned had to pry his sobbing sister off him. He placidly extended his hands as DeSanto slapped cuffs on his wrists and began reading him his rights.

Caroline watched the detective lead a grim, obedient Ned Spaulding out of his apartment, Meg at their heels. Whether or not his confession would ever hold up in a court of law, Ned had admitted to what Caroline had suspected for days now. That he was the one responsible for the murders.

So why didn't she feel vindicated?

Thursday

41

He leaned over, slipped his fingers through her hair, combing it away from the side of her face. He stroked her tear-stained cheek. 'It breaks my heart to see you hurting.'

'Ned did it for me, Ryan.'

'No, Meg. He did it because he couldn't help himself.'

'What's going to happen to him? He could be sent away to prison for life. What if he's . . . executed? I'll die if he dies.' Meg's voice broke. She turned her head into the pillow.

Ryan sat down on his bed and lifted Meg up into his arms. 'No. None of that's going to happen. Ned's insane, darling. They'll put him in a psychiatric facility. Just like your mother.'

'Yes. That's what they'll do. And once he's sane again, they'll have to let him go free. Meanwhile, I'll visit him. I'll go every single visiting day. Not like . . . before.'

'I'll take you there myself,' Ryan murmured.

Meg looked up at him and smiled tremulously. 'I still

didn't really thank you for coming to get me last night at the police station. For bringing me here to your apartment. For letting me sleep . . .'

'You don't have to thank me, Meg.'

'Yes, I do. I would never have slept a wink if you hadn't . . . been there for me. You know what I'm trying to say.'

Ryan was dressed and ready for work. He placed a light, comforting kiss on Meg's forehead, then gently laid her back down on the bed. 'Sleep some more. It'll be the best medicine.' He sighed. 'I hate having to leave you alone all day. But I should be able to get away early. Will you stay here? Will you wait for me?'

Meg nodded as the phone rang on the bedside table. Ryan sat down on the edge of his bed and lifted the receiver to his ear.

It was Sylvia Fields.

'Ryan, I'm worried sick about Meg. No sooner is the poor thing cleared by the police than her brother turns out to be the murderer. I called her place till very late last night and again this morning. I finally drove over to her apartment, but the doorman says she never even came home last night.'

'He's right. She didn't, Sylvia. Meg's right here.'

'Oh . . . I see.'

Ryan winked at Meg. She rolled her eyes, then took the phone from him.

'Hello, Sylvia. Listen, I'm okay. But I'm going to keep a low profile for a few days. I'll try to make it to the office by next Tuesday . . .'

'Take as long as you need. I'm so sorry about Ned.'

'Please, Sylvia. I don't want to . . .'

'I know. I understand completely. You must be so distraught. Are you going back to therapy? Will you still be seeing Caroline?'

'Actually, when I called in to my answering machine this morning, along with your messages was one from Caroline's secretary. Caroline's rescheduled our Wednesday group for this evening. Obviously, I haven't returned any of my messages yet, but I'm considering going to the group.'

'I think it would be good for you,' Sylvia said enthusiastically. 'I have an idea. Why don't I swing by the Institute when the session's over and pick you up? You can stay at my place for a few days . . .'

'Ryan's letting me stay here.'

There was a brief silence. 'Do you think what you're doing is smart, Meg? You've been through so much . . .'

'Ryan's helping me through it, Sylvia,' Meg said tartly.

'Is he?'

Meg smiled at Ryan, seeing the tenderness in his blue eyes. 'Yes, he is. In fact, I think I'm falling in love with him.'

Ryan took her hand and gently pressed it to his lips.

'Are you there, Sylvia?'

There was no reply.

'Sylvia?'

Dial tone.

'Thanks for nothing, Sylvia.' Meg dropped the receiver into the cradle.

'Is she angry?' Ryan asked.

'She'll get over it,' Meg said.

'I better get down there.' He started to rise, but Meg grabbed his arm.

She gave him an earnest look. 'I really am going to behave myself from now on, Ryan. You just watch.' She put her hand up to her mouth, realizing what she'd said. 'I take that back. I don't want anyone to ever watch me again.'

Antsy. At loose ends. Time stretching thin and taut. Like her nerves.

Be good. Behave. Do it for Ned. Do it for Ryan.

Meg made Ryan's bed. Took a shower. Put on Ryan's soft white terry robe that gave off a faint lemony smell. Mmm.

I love. I am loved. Love will save me.

She wandered around his living room, looking over her architectural sketches that Ryan had hung on his walls.

See how much he loves you. Respects you. Isn't that worth more than— ? No, don't even think about it.

She made herself lunch. Grilled cheese sandwich. Sliced tomato. Coffee. Felt very domestic puttering around Ryan's tiny galley kitchen. After she ate, she washed and dried the dishes. Wiped down all the counters. Swept up the narrow strip of Spanish tile floor.

Keep busy. Don't start those thoughts. Don't start wanting what you can't – shouldn't have.

She curled up on Ryan's sofa and turned on the TV. It was on the weather station. Nor'easter was due to roll in by evening.

Winds sweeping through her already.

She went back into Ryan's bedroom. Slipped off her clothes. Stood naked, staring at herself in the large mirror over his bureau.

Look but don't touch.

Her nipples immediately got hard.

Wrong thought.

She turned away from her reflection and walked, naked, to the window. As she parted the curtains she noticed two young men hurrying across busy Brookline Street. They were both wearing baseball caps. Maybe they were heading over to Fenway Park. The baseball field was just down the street. She pictured the guys, sitting up in the bleachers, watching a ball game. Rooting for the home team.

Getting all excited. All worked up.

She got dressed. A good, brisk walk. Maybe she'd take in a movie. Go to a museum. Shopping. Anything.

Anything but—

'"Do you do this often?" he asks. I smile seductively. "No," I tell him. "You're the very first."'

Natalie interrupts Meg. 'So he'll feel special?'

'More than that,' Greg says. 'So he'll feel *blessed by a goddess*. Right, Meg?'

'Screw you, Greg.'

Chris, always the one to try to defuse the tension in the group, jumps in. 'Tell us what happened, Meg. Did you stay right there in the parking garage?'

'He wanted to drive us somewhere more private . . .'

'But then it wouldn't be any good. No danger, no risk. No high.' Natalie makes these comments unjudgementally.

'I asked him what he was afraid of,' Meg says. "Same as you. Getting caught." I ask him if I looked afraid. He smiled.' Meg pauses, a glimmer of a smile on her face. 'He told me I didn't look one bit scared. That I looked like I could make all his dreams come true.'

'Did you?' Chris asks.

Before Meg can reply, Natalie breaks in. 'What about you, Meg? Did he do it for you? Did he help alleviate all the pain you must be going through, what with your brother . . .'

Meg glares at her.

'I'm sorry, Meg,' Natalie says. 'Really, go on with what happened.'

Too late. Meg vehemently shakes her head. 'No. No, no, no,' she cries, squeezing her hand into fists. 'I can't finish it. I don't want to relive that stupid scene. It makes me . . . sick. I tried so hard. Even when I saw him getting into his pickup truck – you don't know how desperately I tried to stop myself. How I kept pleading with myself to just turn around and walk away.'

'You're wrong that we don't understand what you're going through, Meg. We're all fighting the same battle the best we can,' Chris soothes. He's come to the session in drag. Lush shoulder-length brunette wig, cotton candy pink jersey minidress, black patent spiked heels – announcing at his arrival that he has to show this part of himself if he's ever going to feel fully accepted by the group.

'Meg, you did what you always do when you're under tremendous stress,' Caroline says gently. 'When so many painful events are . . .'

Meg springs up from her chair in the centre of the circle. 'I told you when I came in tonight that I don't want to talk about Ned,' she almost shouts.

'Ned's only part of that pain,' Caroline prods her gently. 'Why don't you talk about how you were feeling when you were with this man in his truck?'

Meg collapses back into her seat, covering her face with her hands. 'I was out of control. Again. Worse than ever. What is it going to take—?' Her voice is thick with frustration and despair.

It was pouring. Jesse Baush drummed his fingers on the steering wheel as he sat in his jeep in the parking lot, his eyes fixed on the rear door of the Institute. He had to keep wiping the fogged up window with his jacket sleeve. After a couple of minutes, he checked his watch again. 9:40.

He worried there was a chance she might come out of the front entrance instead of the rear. He decided to make a dash for it and wait for her in the lobby. That way, he couldn't miss her. Though he wasn't sure what he would say when he saw her.

As soon as Jesse stepped inside the Institute's empty lobby, he felt torn. Confused. Guilty, even. But he had sincerely believed in his carefully constructed theory. Only now that Ned Spaulding had confessed to the murders could he even begin to concede that his theory had been faulty.

He wiped the rain away from his face. Unzipped his bomber jacket. Paced the marble floor. The case was closed. He owed his stepsister – what? An apology? Was that why he'd driven all the way over here in the middle of a Nor'easter? What was the big hurry?

But that was him. He'd always been impulsive. Once he got something in his head, he couldn't hold off. He had to act. Besides, he figured Linny wouldn't be too thrilled if he showed up at her apartment after their last encounter.

He ran his tongue over his lips. As if he could still taste her. Her lips. Her tongue. That fumbled, dumb-ass kiss. And to think it was one of the most erotic moments of his entire goddamn life.

How was it possible to hate someone so much and at the same time want her so intensely?

Amy'd given him the answer to that one. There *was* a thin line between love and hate. Hard to even see the line sometimes. Hard to figure out which emotion – love or hate – was driving his engine, causing all that heat and steam inside him, firing up all those sordid but unrelenting fantasies—

The squeak of a hinge roused him from his twisted thoughts. Then a voice.

'You wouldn't be following me, now would you?'

Jesse Baush's startled eyes shot to the door of the ladies' room.

He's burning up, the fire raging inside him making him sweat, expunging the hurt, the pain, the frustration. Leaving only pure, unadulterated desire.

This isn't what he came here for.

But that was debatable. Not really a question of what but

who. No question at all that he's been a walking, breathing hard-on for a week. Insatiable. Unquenchable.

Maybe now. Maybe now at last—

A deep guttural groan of pleasure. With his eyes closed, Jesse can easily pretend it's Linny wreaking havoc on his body. Linny's soft, sensual lips and wily tongue moving over him, kissing, licking, sucking. Linny's long, slender fingers coiling so fiercely around him.

He'd pretended before, but never with a woman who so reminded him of the woman of his 'dreams'.

Her hands cruise down to his tight, firm balls. She squeezes hard as she murmurs delicious obscenities in his ear.

The cubicle in the women's bathroom is restricting their moves, but Jesse Baush isn't complaining—

42

'. . . using her addiction as her primary coping mechanism. Nor is it any coincidence that Meg Spaulding's latest sexual binge took place not an hour before the start of our session this evening. It was the patient's attempt to dare the group – dare me as her therapist – to help someone who'd sunk so low. Yesterday's episode that culminated in her brother Ned's confession to the murders coupled with his arrest, has left Meg reeling with feelings of devastation, betrayal, and shame. And she is finding it almost impossible to juxtapose her self-destructive sexual preoccupation with her budding conventional relationship with her boyfriend Ryan . . .'

Caroline's phone rang. Scowling, she paused the dictating machine and picked up.

'Are you sitting down?'

'Ben?'

'Just got a call on my car phone . . .'

'Where are you?'

'Heading back from Scituate. Phil's place. Listen. The call was from Marcia Kirshbaum. She just handed over a hundred bucks to the night manager at the MacKenzie Hotel for information.'

'What information?'

'Ned's got himself a solid alibi for Tuesday night.'

'Don't tell me. He was at the MacKenzie Hotel? With his mother?'

'Close. The night manager saw him lurking around the hotel lobby from eight until midnight. Apparently, keeping watch.'

'Oh God, Ben . . .'

'Yeah, I know. Group over?'

'Yes. Everyone's gone.'

'You leave, too. I should be at my place in about twenty minutes. I'll meet you there. We'll talk.'

'Okay,' she said distractedly.

'Caroline?'

'Yes?'

'What are you thinking?'

'I'll tell you when I see you.'

'Okay. See you real soon.'

'Ben, do the police know yet?'

'Marcia's probably breaking the news to them as we speak.'

The whole southeast quadrant of Level One of the underground garage on Lansdowne Street across from Fenway Park was roped off with yellow plastic crime-scene tape. A half-dozen squad cars, two unmarked black sedans and an

ME van were on site. Most of the activity was centred around the dead man splayed across the front seat of a white '89 Ford pickup. The corpse was naked. His navy blue jersey shirt was jammed down his throat. His hands were squeezed between his thighs. And he had a metal chain lashed around his neck. A positive ID hadn't yet been made, but the truck was registered to a James Gage of 310 Beale Street, Quincy.

Green and DeSanto, looking miserable, feeling worse, stood a short distance away with Ed Hurley, the man who'd made the 911 call. Hurley'd parked his Olds Cutlass next to the pickup at a little past nine that evening. He didn't pay much attention to the truck until he spotted the FOR SALE sign stuck onto the side window. His brother was on the look-out for a used pickup, so he'd stepped on the running board and peeked in to check the mileage.

'Christ, Christ, Christ,' Hurley kept repeating. 'I never seen nothing like it. I swear, I almost puked. Jeez, it coulda been me. If some hot chick had come on to me – it's that sex killer, right? Meg Spaulding? But I thought you guys nabbed her brother for the murders yesterday. I seen it on the TV. Wrong again, huh!'

Caroline was locking up her office files when her phone rang again.

This time it was Detective Amy DeSanto. Demanding to know if she'd seen Meg Spaulding any time that evening.

'And don't give me any of that patient-doctor confidentiality shit,' DeSanto snapped. 'We got ourselves another body.'

Caroline's throat went raw. 'In a . . . garage?'

'Where is she?'

'I don't know.' Caroline thought back, trying to remember if Meg had said where she was going. 'She was at group tonight, but it ended a half-hour ago. . .'

The Nor'easter's howling wind and rain assaulted Caroline as she crossed the Institute parking lot. Her hair whipped across her face. Leaning into the storm, she made her way to the far end of the crowded lot. On Friday nights, the place was leased to a nearby dinner theatre for patron parking.

Leaping over puddles, splash-landing in others, Caroline raced through the rain towards her car, rummaging in her purse for her keys. Soaked through and not even halfway there, she started past a familiar looking red Jeep Cherokee on her left. When she saw a Red Sox sticker on the right-hand corner of the front bumper, she came to an abrupt stop.

It was Jesse's car.

Caroline doubted her stepbrother had come to the Institute seeking psychiatric help. Not that he didn't need it. No, Caroline thought. He'd come here seeking a certain psychiatrist. Dr. Susan Steinberg. And not for therapy!

Caroline's eyes shot to the Institute. All the lights were off. Were Jesse and Susan up there in Susan's dark office?

She heard a car's engine somewhere in front of her. She saw a dark sedan pull out of a spot, heading in her direction towards the exit, wipers working furiously against the lashing rain.

Caroline was momentarily blinded by the car's head-lights as its high beams flashed on. Instinctively, she stepped back in the space alongside Jesse's Jeep. As the sedan passed, Caroline caught a glimpse of the passenger in the front seat. It was Jesse. But Susan Steinberg wasn't at the wheel. It was Meg Spaulding.

Caroline's heart sank. For all her jumbled emotions about her stepbrother, there was one thing about which Caroline was totally unconflicted. She didn't want to see him wind up with a chain strapped around his neck!

Caroline was pinned behind a white Honda, two cars behind Meg's, as they tore down rain-swept Storrow Drive, the winding parkway hugging the Charles River. Visibility was so poor, Caroline almost missed Meg hooking a sharp right at the exit just past the Longfellow Bridge. Flooring the accel-erator and quickly swerving around the Honda, she lost control of her car on the rain-slicked tarmac and skidded towards the median. Yanking the wheel to the right and gunning it, she brought her Saab under control. Grunting with frustration, she cut off the Honda and raced for the exit.

Without hesitation, she slammed on her brakes and downshifted. The driver of the Honda, lacking Caroline's driving skills, crashed into her left rear bumper in the mid-dle of her sharp turn onto the exit. The Saab lurched to the right, kissed the guardrail with a grinding screech, spring-boarded back across the exit lane, then whipped into a gut wrenching tailspin. By the time Caroline, shaking with ten-sion, was able to bring the car to a stop, it was turned backward halfway up the ramp.

By that time, the tail lights of Meg's car had long disappeared.

Once her tremors lessened, Caroline managed to manoeuvre the Saab around in the right direction. She drove to the end of the ramp and made a left turn – the only option – onto Embankment Road. The road ran along a grassy stretch of bike and walking paths bordering the fog-shrouded Charles River. At night, with the storm raging, the area was utterly desolate.

Meg's car was nowhere in sight. Nor were there any other cars on the road. Shaken and frustrated, Caroline knew she had no choice but to give up her mad folly, find a phone, put in a call to DeSanto. At least pinpoint for her the general area where Meg's car had been heading.

Caroline drove slowly and cautiously now, not only in the sobering wake of her terrifying skid, but because things didn't sound too good under the bonnet of the car. She could barely make out a group of mysterious looming structures ahead on the right. As she drove closer, her headlights brightening the area, Caroline saw that it was a riverside playground.

Thinking there was likely to be a public phone by the little brick outbuilding at the far end of the play space, she pulled up as close to it as she could get. Leaving her high beams on to provide her with some much needed visibility, she made a dash through the rain for the bunker-like structure.

Ben Tabor pulled into his assigned parking spot behind his building. He was disturbed to see that Caroline's Saab wasn't parked in the guest space beside it. He was even more disturbed when he saw Detective Amy DeSanto nose into the spot in an unmarked police car.

'What timing!' DeSanto said as she slipped into his front passenger seat. She was drenched.

Ben felt his whole body stiffen. He knew something was wrong.

'Have you heard from your client?'

Ben squinted at the detective. 'Which client?'

'Meg Spaulding, that's which client. She call you? She meeting you here? You got some idea where she might be?'

Ben had to fight his urge to grab DeSanto by the throat. 'Tell me what the fuck's going on.'

'We got ourselves a fresh Aphrodite victim . . .'

'Where's Caroline?' he barked.

'I don't know . . .'

DeSanto's pager went off. She used Ben's car phone.

Alfonse Green picked up. 'Amy? We just got a call . . .'

43

Caroline sloshed all around the little building. No phone. Chilled to the bone, exasperated, frightened, she trudged back to her car, scanning the misty darkness as best as she could. Halfway, she noticed two small circles of light flashing on and off in the distance. Down what seemed to be a bike path. It took Caroline a few seconds to realize that she was looking at either the fog lamps or tail lights of a vehicle.

It had to be Meg's car.

Caroline raced to her Saab, leaped behind the wheel and turned the key. Nothing.

Shit. She tried again.

Dead.

Shit. Now what?

A debilitating combination of exposure and her escalating fear was making her shake uncontrollably.

It was definitely not a good idea to continue the chase alone on foot in a deserted area during a torrential storm.

She leaned across her seat to the steamed-up passenger side window. Wiped the clouded glass off with her palm so she could peer out. The lights were no longer visible. Had they been extinguished? Or had the car driven off?

Despite her fears, Caroline had to go to see for herself. Punching her emergency flasher button on, she abandoned her car and cautiously made her way down the asphalt bike path.

The car was still there, about fifty yards ahead, maybe twenty feet from the riverbank. Crouching low, Caroline stealthily approached it. She gasped when she saw the chrome letters by the tail light, only now realizing that the dark sedan she'd been following this whole time was a 320SE. Sylvia's Fields's black Mercedes!

What the hell?

Terrified of what she might find inside the car, Caroline steeled herself and peered in through the back window. It looked empty. Her apprehensive inspection from the front passenger side confirmed it.

But there was a phone in the car. In the armrest.

She ran around the Mercedes, testing all the doors. Locked. Naturally.

She started searching the sides of the path for a rock to break a window. The tip of her foot slammed into some kind of sign post. If she could pry it out of the ground, she could use it to break the car window.

She was gradually beginning to loosen it when a flash of lightning hit almost overhead. Terrified of being struck, Caroline released her hold on the post and jumped back. As she did she caught a glimpse of the inscription – HISTORIC

TUGBOATS LUNA and . . . VENUS. Aphrodite's Roman name!

Caroline understood at last. This was no random destination. This was a carefully executed plan. The obsessive-compulsive mind in action. Perfect. Macabre but perfect.

Bracing herself, she edged closer down to the riverbank. Saw the dim light coming from the pilothouse of one of the old tug boats anchored at the water's edge.

A ghostly silhouette passed by one of the windows of the little cabin.

Common sense told her she should go back and yank that marker out of the ground, use it to break into the Mercedes, and call for help. But did she have the time? And if it set off the car alarm?

Soaked to the skin, she ducked down on the muddy embankment as a flash of lightning scissored through the sky, followed instantly by a bone-shattering clap of thunder. She kicked off her waterlogged heels, rolled up her drenched wool slacks, and removed her knee-high stockings so she'd have a firmer grip on the slippery ground. In the darkness, she slid her way down the sodden grassy slope to the tug.

She was grateful for the raging storm now. The wind and rain muted her footsteps and drowned out her strained breathing as she snuck up the cold metal gangplank and stepped onto the old boat's wooden deck.

Intent of keeping an eye on the pilothouse, she tripped over a thick coil of line and stumbled, banging into a giant metal hook dangling from the rail of the tug. Choking back a cry of pain, she straightened herself and limped her way forward to the looming pilothouse.

Crouching low, she ignored the torrent of freezing water splashing on her shoulders from the edge of the roof as she cautiously peered into the small cabin.

What she witnessed was a chilling tableau. On a Persian carpet runner in a corner of the little room, lit by a small hurricane lamp on a nearby table, a totally naked couple lay entwined in each other's arms. Caroline would have thought she'd caught the pair in the thrall of hot lust were it not for the shiny metal chain snaked around their bodies and wrapped around their necks. A grotesque re-enactment of Dan Spaulding's inflammatory painting. Only in this flesh and blood rendition, the lovers were Meg and Jesse.

Caroline was afraid the pair were dead, but she saw Jesse's head make a slight movement. Seconds later, she noticed Meg's eyes flicker open and then close again.

'What do you think, Caroline?' came a whisper.

Before she had the chance to respond, she felt something cold and hard loop around her neck. Her hands reached for the chain, but she couldn't budge it. She gave a strangled cry, gagging as the metal noose tightened and she was dragged inside the pilothouse.

'I'd say I've created a pretty decent replica of *The Godless Aphrodite*. With a slight variation. But then every artist has to add something unique. A special *twist* in this case.'

A tug on the chain dropped Caroline to her knees not two feet from the ill-fated lovers. She was close enough to see they both were gagged.

Ryan Gallagher smiled as he knelt down and, with his free hand, snatched up the end of a chain that led from

Jesse's neck to Meg's. 'Tell me the truth, Caroline. Did you ever suspect me?'

'It should have connected sooner,' she reproached herself, 'when Ben said to me a few days back that a jilted lover's always a prime candidate. And there you were, Ryan, so loving, so concerned, so *normal.* The consummate candidate. The true prime suspect.'

Ryan grinned, but his eyes glinted with hatred. 'It all started when I spotted Meg with that asshole lawyer in the toy store. But I didn't have my plan in place then. How was I going to stop Meg from ruining everything I knew we could have together – love, passion, true understanding. And then it came to me. Remind her of her mother's godless fate. Only the message just wouldn't penetrate. I kept trying and trying to get her to see the terrible error of her ways, but—' He shook his head sadly. 'I even gave the cops a killer so they'd let her go . . .'

'Phil Mason? You set him up?' Caroline was disbelieving.

'It was incredibly easy,' Ryan boasted. 'I phoned him, confessed I was the Aphrodite Killer, told him I would turn myself in if he'd represent me. I arranged the meet – I thought Harvard Law School was a nice touch – and the schmuck hustled his ass right over. Maybe he thought he could win redemption for his sins with Meg by bringing in the killer himself. He certainly wasn't going to win any prizes in that department with that pathetic apology note he wrote his wife. I guess I should have mailed it to her for him, but then that *suicide* note did come in handy.' Ryan loosened the chain around Caroline's neck and stuck his index finger in his mouth. 'Pow! Kaboom!'

He chuckled. 'After I finished Mason off, I zipped on over to his little hideaway and redecorated the place. Those photos I'd taken of Meg were terrific, if I do say so myself.'

Even though Caroline truly did shiver at Ryan's cold-blooded account she exaggerated her reaction, deliberately encouraging his deluded self-congratulation. With luck she would be able to capitalize on the opening he'd given her.

She grasped the chain at her neck. A quick yank freed it and she whipped it swiftly, fiercely at Ryan's face.

But in his hypervigilant state, he merely lifted his hand and caught the chain mid-flight. His face registered nothing but mild annoyance at the interruption. He wrenched it from her hand, speedily wrapping it back around her neck twice over. Caroline could barely breathe.

'I could kill you right now.' Ryan's remark was punctuated by another crash of thunder. He grinned. 'The gods of Mount Olympus must approve. Doctors think of themselves as gods, don't they, Caroline? And, as the myth goes, after Aphrodite's husband ensnared his wife and her lover in chains, he called in the gods to bear witness to his wife's unfaithfulness. So you provide the perfect finishing touch to this Greek tragedy.'

'In the myth,' Caroline tried once more to deflect his intentions, 'didn't Aphrodite's husband forgive her . . . ?'

'You think forgiveness is possible?'

'Yes, Ryan. I do.'

He scowled, glancing at Meg whose eyes remained closed. Caroline hoped that Meg had just passed out.

Ryan sighed. 'I don't know. I really don't know.

Sometimes we go beyond a certain point and then forgiveness is impossible.'

Caroline had to distract him. 'And Sylvia's Mercedes?' she asked hoarsely. 'How'd you manage that?'

Ryan offered up a twisted smile. 'The other day, I told Sylvia I was having car trouble. You really should learn to look both ways before you cross the street, Caroline. Especially at airports.'

'Is that what you told Sylvia tonight as well?'

'Funny thing is, tonight in this crazy storm my plugs must have got wet or something and I truly couldn't start my car. Sylvia was going to be working late. She knew I was planning to pick Meg up after group. So the dear heart was very happy to lend me her keys especially after I promised to swing by work with Meg afterwards. Guess old Sylvia will have to call a cab tonight—'

'. . . I got anxious when he didn't come back to pick me up. I don't know why, but I didn't have a good feeling about Ryan. He was suddenly becoming so possessive of Meg,' Sylvia Fields told Amy DeSanto, Alfonse Green and Ben Tabor in the homicide squad room. 'Something nagged at my brain. Then I remembered during Ryan's job interview a couple of years back, I saw on his résumé that he'd worked one summer during high school at a restaurant on Martha's Vineyard. The date listed on his résumé was for the summer after Meg's father was murdered. But I started thinking, he could have deliberately put down the wrong date . . .'

A detective rapped on the door and popped his head in.

'A trucker overheard the APB and called in. He spotted what he thinks is a white Saab parked with its flashers on at the side of Embankment Road—'

Rain pounded on the roof and pelted against the windows. But however fierce and powerful the raging storm outside, a storm far more dangerous had erupted within the pilot-house.

Ryan's attention was on Meg again. 'You didn't even know I existed that summer on the Vineyard. Your mother was the one that was hot for me. Took me to bed one night when your daddy was gone. When the door burst open Faith thought it was a burglar. She grabbed for the gun in her bedside drawer. The lights came on. It was your daddy, dragging in that painting. Your mother froze up like a statue. I don't think she even remembered I was there, much less that I was the one who squeezed her finger on the trigger.'

A stifled cry of anguish escaped from Meg's gagged mouth.

'I really went there to see you, Meg darling. I figured I'd screw your wacky mother and later in the night, sneak upstairs to your room just to watch you sleep. I loved you so much I wanted to get as close to you as I could. I knew you were the one. For life.'

Ryan glowered at Caroline. 'This is really all your fault. If you'd cured Meg of her sickness, none of this would have happened.'

'It's not too late, Ryan,' she entreated. 'Addiction cures take time. Like drugs or gambling. She can't help herself.'

'And what about your stepbrother? He a sex addict, too? Not that it matters much now. Too late for cures.'

Somehow Jesse managed to turn his head enough for Caroline to read such a tangled mix of emotions in his gaze. Shame. Guilt. Sorrow. Fear. And reflections of all the old wounds that now would go unhealed. She imagined her stepbrother could see much of the same mirrored in her eyes.

Ryan leered at her. 'I know what you're thinking, Caroline. That I'm just as sick as them. You're wrong. I'm a world apart from every last one of you. And you know why? You know what makes me better? I am blessed with the ability to feel and express the true power of love. This morning, I actually believed Meg had finally been blessed, too. She confessed she loved me. But it wasn't enough. It was never going to be enough.'

Maintaining the pressure of the one chain around Caroline's throat with his left hand, his right hand firmly clasping the chain entwining the ill-fated lovers, he looked sorrowfully down at Meg. 'My god*less* Aphrodite.' His eyes darkened with intensity as he twisted the chains. 'I will love you to your dying breath.'

As the chain tightened like a vice around her neck, Caroline kicked out sharply. Her bare foot landed nowhere near Ryan. He laughed at her useless effort and tugged a little harder on her chain.

But it hadn't been totally in vain. Her foot had made contact with the table leg, unsteadying the hurricane lamp.

Rocking, the lamp teetered and flipped on its side. And started rolling. To a dead stop inches from the table's edge.

An image of Ben rose in her mind. She clung to it for comfort, but the vision was blurring into hundreds of dots on a black screen as she struggled not to pass out.

An explosive bolt of thunder rocked the small cabin. Startled, Ryan's foot jerked to the side, his heel inadvertently nudging the leg of the table.

Caroline, barely conscious, watched in dazed anticipation as the hurricane lamp resumed its agonizingly slow roll to the edge of the table – and over. Crashing right at Ryan's feet. The glass funnel shattering. Releasing the kerosene-fuelled fire.

Ryan yelped in shock as flames from the lamp ignited the cuffs of his linen trousers. Violently pushing Caroline to one side, he frantically swatted at his legs, screaming as sparks leapt to his shirt sleeves.

Caroline collapsed on the floor against the wall. She saw, with horror, that the edges of the ancient rug beneath Meg and Jesse had ignited, too.

Jesse and Meg, helplessly bound, watched the smoking line of flames move closer. Panicked, Jesse tried to shift his weight to roll them away from the fire.

Caroline quickly loosened the chain round her neck, and rushed over to Jesse and Meg, ignoring Ryan's cries, ignoring the fire, smoke, heat, even the shards of the scattered broken glass slicing into the bottoms of her bare feet. She quickly yanked the gags out of their mouths. Meg began crying hoarsely. Jesse tried to speak, but he was overwhelmed by a coughing spasm.

Her eyes tearing from the smoke, Caroline worked furiously to uncoil the pair. She unwrapped the chain from their necks and managed to free one of Jesse's arms when Jesse suddenly yelled out, 'Caroline!' and pushed her aside. The smouldering table leg in Ryan's burned, bloodied hand slammed, instead, into Jesse's side. He gasped in agony.

Caroline frantically ripped the chain off her neck.

Ryan felt it cinch around his neck as he was about to land another blow on Jesse. He yelped in surprise, then gagged as Caroline, with resolute determination, tugged as tight as she could.

Powered by madness, Ryan managed to twist around and throw her off. She stumbled backwards, losing her grip on the chain. Ryan, coughing, gasping, lunged for her. Caroline tried to fend him off but his strength overpowered her. She felt his fingers wrap viciously around her neck, as strong as any chain.

'Ryan . . . please. Please . . . save me.' Meg's raw voice quivered.

Caroline felt the pressure of Ryan's fingers at her throat ease up ever so slightly. His head turned in Meg's direction.

'I do love you, Ryan . . .'

Less pressure still on her throat. Caroline sucked in waves of smoky air.

Ryan's face was a study in anguish and uncertainty. 'Meg . . . Meg. How can I ever forgive you . . . ?'

'Give me one more . . . chance,' Meg begged.

For an instant, Caroline thought he'd release his hold on her and rescue Meg from the fire. But Ryan's moment of indecision passed. Crying out, 'You will always betray me. I know,' his fingers tightened relentlessly around Caroline's throat.

Suddenly there was an ear-splitting crack of thunder—

As if he'd been struck by lightning, Ryan's whole body went rigid. Gasping in pain, his head shifted in Meg's direction as he dropped with a thud at Caroline's feet.

Dumbfounded, Caroline stared at the blood gushing from a wound in his side. She couldn't fathom what had happened until she looked up through the acrid smoke and flames and made out a phantom figure framed in the doorway.

Her vision cleared. She saw that it was Ben with a gun in his hand.

Others came rushing in behind him – Green, DeSanto, uniforms.

People shouting, sirens in the distance, lightning and thunder clashing in the black sky overhead. A maelstrom of commotion and activity took over as the rescue unfolded.

For a moment, all Caroline could think was – she'd made it. The hardest battle she'd ever fought – and she'd survived.

But as she gripped Ben's hand, Caroline knew she'd achieved more than survival.

Postscript

Several immortals are called to view Aphrodite and her lover chained together. Apollo, noting Aphrodite's stunning appeal, even under these humiliating circumstances, questions a young god, 'Is there any peril at all that could dampen one's desire for Aphrodite?'

The young god responds readily, 'My king, no matter how many chains would bind us, or how disapproving the immortals might be, I, too, would sleep with her if I could.'

The gods burst out laughing as they hear him, and have the cuckolded blacksmith, Hephaistos, reluctantly unchain his wife and her lover.

As soon as she is free, Aphrodite flies to her temple in Paphos. Here the Graces bathe the goddess of love, and anoint her anew with the oil of ambrosia, the irresistible fragrance that clings to the immortal gods . . .

from Homer's
THE ODYSSEY

Other bestselling Warner titles available by mail:

The prices shown above are correct at time of going to press. However, the publishers reserve the right to increase prices on covers from those previously advertised without prior notice.

Ⓦ

WARNER BOOKS

WARNER BOOKS
Cash Sales Department, P.O. Box 11, Falmouth, Cornwall, TR10 9EN
Tel: +44 (0) 1326 569777, Fax: +44 (0) 1326 569555
Email: books@barni.avel.co.uk.

POST AND PACKING:
Payments can be made as follows: cheque, postal order (payable to Warner Books) or by credit cards. Do not send cash or currency.

All U.K. Orders	**FREE OF CHARGE**
E.E.C. & Overseas	25% of order value

Name (Block Letters) _____

Address_____

_____

Post/zip code:_____

☐ Please keep me in touch with future Warner publications

☐ I enclose my remittance £_____

☐ I wish to pay by Visa/Access/Mastercard/Eurocard

Card Expiry Date

_____